They entered a spacious gallery, its walls dominated by several intimidating portraits of royalty and a striking image of a ship in peril on stormy seas.

"Okay," said Dave T. "I'm gonna stand guard here at the door. Here." He tossed a small object to Shane, who caught it in the air. It was an ivory handle, about five inches long. "Open it." Shane did so, revealing the blade of a straight razor. "Okay, see that painting there with the poor fuckers on the sailboat? Go over and slice it out of the frame. Carefully. There's a lot of money at stake for all of us."

Shane took the razor and carefully drew it around the perimeter of the canvas on his side of the painting, then passed the blade to Jake, who did the same.

"All right. Peel it out and roll it up. Slowly and carefully."

As delicately as possible, Jake used the razor blade to pry the canvas away from the edge of the frame at the top corner, then passed the razor back to Shane so he could do the same. Working in unison, each holding one top corner of the canvas, they slowly pulled it away from the frame, rolling it as they went. Flecks of paint and canvas wafted to the floor, each speck no doubt reducing the painting's value. When it was completely rolled up, Shane handed his end off to Jake, who awkwardly tucked the Rembrandt in the crook of his arm.

"All right," said Dave T. "Next up is The Concert by Vermeer…"

CHARLESGATE
Confidential

by **Scott Von Doviak**

A HARD CASE | HARD CASE CRIME | CRIME NOVEL

A HARD CASE CRIME BOOK
(HCC-135)
First Hard Case Crime edition: September 2018

Published by

Titan Books
A division of Titan Publishing Group Ltd
144 Southwark Street
London SE1 0UP

in collaboration with Winterfall LLC

Print edition ISBN 978-1-78565-719-1
E-book ISBN 978-1-78565-718-4

Design direction by Max Phillips
www.maxphillips.net

Typeset by Swordsmith Productions

The name "Hard Case Crime" and the Hard Case Crime logo are trademarks of Winterfall LLC. Hard Case Crime books are selected and edited by Charles Ardai.

Printed in the United States of America

Visit us on the web at www.HardCaseCrime.com

That time's long past, but what would I not give
To see that whorehouse where we used to live?

—Kurt Weill, The Threepenny Opera,
"The Ballad of Immoral Earnings"

It breaks your heart. It is designed to break your heart.

—A. Bartlett Giamatti,
The Green Fields of the Mind

JUNE 8, 1946

The eighth floor of the Charlesgate Hotel was invisible. The hotel's architect, J. Pickering Putnam, had designed it that way for reasons known only to him. It was hardly the only quirk of the Gothic Revival-style building, which opened for business in 1891, flourished in the early 20th century, and was now in steep decline. There were rumors, of course. Putnam belonged to a Satanic cult. The hotel was financed with Mafia money. The foundation was ingrained with rare metals specifically chosen to attract paranormal activity.

Dave T neither knew nor cared whether any of that was true. But he did know the eighth floor couldn't be seen from outside the building. And he knew that rooms were cheap now that the Charlesgate had fallen on hard times. Once it had been the jewel of the Back Bay, attracting Rockefellers and heads of state. Now Jimmy Dryden from Somerville ran whores out of the sixth floor, splitting the hourly rates with the house. The grapevine had it that the hotel was about to be sold to one of the local universities as residential space, but Dave T would worry about that when the time came. The only thing that mattered now was that the Charlesgate was the perfect place for his weekly poker game: secluded, private, overlooking Kenmore Square and Fenway Park beyond. The out-of-towners got a kick out of seeing the lights of Fenway during the summer months, and the Red Sox were having a good year. A pennant kind of year.

The poker game typically attracted a mix of regulars and out-of-towners, and that was the case tonight. Dave T would deal all night and take the house cut when they shut the lights, but he never gambled anymore. He sat at the head of an ornate oak banquet table dating back to the Charlesgate's glory days. Two guys from Marko's crew had muscled it up the back stairway, eight stories from the basement, a couple years back. It wouldn't fit in the elevator, so Dave T slipped them twenty bucks each and a standing invitation to sit in on the game if they'd hump it all the way to the top. The table could seat eight easily, ten in a pinch. Tonight it was ten. A radio perched on the kitchen counter crackled with the Sox broadcast, Jim Britt and Tom Hussey on the call.

"Stud," Dave T said, for no good reason. Five-card stud was the only game ever dealt on the eighth floor of the Charlesgate. It was the only game ten people could play at once. He sent the cards around and the bullshitting soon followed.

"Anyone heard from our friend down Middleboro?"

"I were you, I wouldn't be expecting no Christmas card."

"What I heard, he was messing around with one of the Casey girls. Way I hear it, Old Man Casey finds out, sends a couple of the cousins from Pawtucket up to Middleboro there. They find our friend in his garage, working on his Packard. One of the cousins kicks out the jack and down comes the Packard, two tons of steel. End of the line for our friend. Way I hear it, anyway."

"First of all, how is he *our* friend? He's our friend, he's not your friend."

"Ladies," said Dave T. "Cards are up. Jack high bets."

Men tossed chips into the center of the table. Quinlan's chair creaked as he shifted, his breathing labored as always. Quinlan owned a liquor store in South Boston—or rather, the store's liquor license was in his name. Everyone knew who really owned it. It was Quinlan who had first asked about the man from Middleboro, and it was clear he already regretted it. "I didn't mean it that way," he said. "Just asking."

"Knock it off, ladies," Dave T said. "You know the rules. Friendly game, no shop talk." That was the longstanding policy. In truth, Dave T didn't mind a little gossip. As long as he kept up the pretense that house rules forbade shop talk, the players felt more relaxed and, paradoxically, more willing to shoot the shit and let slip the occasional valuable nugget of information. Dave T dealt in information. Know everything, say nothing. Nobody at the table knew his last name. No one could say for sure whether he was Irish, Italian, or the King of Sweden. But they all trusted him. He was the dealer.

"Cards around and pair of nines bets."

"Check."

"Check? Check my pants, I got somethin' for ya there." Dryden tossed two white chips into the pot.

"Not what I heard," said Hugh Mullen, doubling Dryden's bet.

"Come on, are we playing cards or are we playing—"

A shotgun blast put an end to the talk. Men dropped their cards and reached for their guns.

"Hands on the fucking table!"

The first man through the door held a still-smoking shotgun. He'd blown out the lock and the whole knob assembly with it. Two men followed him into the room, one holding a .38 pistol in each hand, the other carrying a briefcase. All three faces were hidden by potato sacks with eyeholes cut into them.

"I want to count twenty hands on the table," said the man holding the two guns. "I count less than twenty hands, my friend here shoots someone in the head. We don't care who."

Dave T made a show of placing both palms flat on the table. "You jokers know whose game you're robbing?"

"That's why we're here. Now this can go real smooth. My

friend with the briefcase will just empty the bank, and then we'll hit the road."

"No bank here, fellas. This is just a friendly game. Sorry you wasted your time, but if you'll see yourselves out…"

The man with the briefcase headed straight for the liquor cabinet under the window facing Kenmore Square. "Except we already know where the fuckin' bank is. Just like we knew where to find this game. Food for thought, huh?"

He slid open the cabinet door, tossed aside a few bottles of scotch, and pulled out a cash register drawer. "Ain't this convenient. Divvied up by tens and twenties and everything."

He set down the briefcase, popped it open, and filled it with the contents of the cash drawer. The men with guns kept them trained on the poker players. The only sound now came from the radio: top of the ninth, two out.

"Good, you guys been listening to the game. So you know it was twelve nothin' in the third inning. Pesky got three hits, Teddy scored four runs, and this thing is just about over. When it ends, there's gonna be at least twenty thousand happy Red Sox fans pouring into Kenmore Square. Even figurin' some people left early, such a pounding they put on Detroit."

From the radio: "…and Bloodworth pops up to short, and this should do it. Pesky gloves it and the Red Sox win this one 15–4. Never in doubt."

"There ya go," the man with the briefcase said, making his way to the exit. "In about ninety seconds, my friends and I are gonna melt into that crowd and you ain't never gonna see us again. But just to make sure nobody gets any smart ideas…"

He gestured to his colleague who was holding the shotgun. The man took two steps toward Dave T and lowered his weapon six inches from the dealer's nose. "Get up."

"Fellas, you got your money."

"Get up!" He popped Dave T in the nose with the business end of his weapon, drawing blood. Dave T never flinched, but he stood as instructed.

"You fellas are writing a real bad ending for yourselves here. Should have just stayed home and enjoyed the ballgame."

"Tomorrow maybe. Come on, let's go." The man with the shotgun nudged Dave T toward the door. The one with the briefcase was already out in the hall. Once Dave T cleared the doorway, the third robber stayed a moment longer, watching men tense up, itching to take their hands off the table. "Do yourselves a favor," he said, keeping his pistols aimed squarely at the group. "Just stay here and listen to the postgame show. There's always another card game."

He backed out the door, kicking it shut behind him. It swung back open immediately, its broken knob assembly bouncing off the doorjamb. By then two of the Mullen boys were on their feet, guns drawn, making for the hallway. About ten paces away, the robber with the shotgun stood with his weapon at Dave T's head as his friends stepped into the elevator.

"Take a powder, fellas," Dave T said. "You can see this man is serious. What say we just let 'em be on their way."

"Well said." The robber pushed him to the floor and hopped aboard the elevator. Dave T could see the shotgun still trained on him until the door closed. A bell sounded and the elevator started down.

"Call Pete down at the front desk and tell him to shoot those sonsabitches before they make the exit!" Dave T scrambled to his feet and started down the stairs, taking them two at a time. Fast as he could go, it was still eight stories and he was no match for the elevator. By the time he got to the lobby, the front desk was deserted. Dave T pushed through the front door and into the mild June night.

Out on Charlesgate East, as predicted, happy Red Sox fans could be seen in every direction. Short of breath, Dave T took a seat on the front steps. A minute or two passed before Pete emerged from the darkness of the park across the street. He was short of breath, too.

"Lost 'em," he said. "By the time I got the call, they were already out the door. If they jumped on the train at Kenmore, they could be on their way to anywhere."

"That was their plan," said Dave T. "Don't sweat it."

"I never seen them come in. They couldn't have come in the front door. I never took my eyes off it, I swear!"

"I believe you. Check around the ground floor. I bet you find an open window. Those boys had help."

"You know who they were?"

"Not yet. This time tomorrow, next day at the latest, I'll know."

"How's that?"

"Because anyone dumb enough to take down my card game is dumb enough to yap about it. And they'll be yapping, tonight, tomorrow night. And then I'll know."

By now Dryden and the Mullens had joined them on the front steps of the Charlesgate. Dave T stood up and wiped his bloody nose on his sleeve.

"How 'bout them Sox?"

SEPTEMBER 27, 1986

Jackie St. John, wearing nothing but a number 56 Lawrence Taylor jersey over her cherry-red panties, opened the Parker Brothers box with a conspiratorial wink. I didn't care about the Ouija board, possession of which was (according to legend, at least) strictly forbidden in Charlesgate. I didn't care about the fat joint the Rev had rolled and was now passing around the room, or the suitcase of Old Milwaukee someone had paid Paul Seitz five bucks to fetch from Marlboro Market and smuggle back into the dorm. All I cared about was Jackie St. John and her smoky laugh and her pencil-eraser nipples pressing up against number 56.

Jackie wasn't just out of my league—we weren't even playing the same sport. She probably never would have acknowledged my existence, except somehow she'd found out I was really into the Who, and *she* was really into the Who, so she stopped by my room one night to tape some bootlegs and debate whether "Boris the Spider" or "My Wife" was the greatest John Entwistle song. That's one of the things the movies always get wrong. You see a movie set in the '80s and the kids are always listening to the B-52s or the fucking Cure or something. Well, I went to college in the '80s, and my dorm was full of Deadheads and Led Zeppelin freaks and even a few guys who listened to Yes all the time, although I never figured *that* one out. The day I got to Boston in the fall of '85, my first stop after dropping all my stuff off in my dorm room and meeting my freaky acidhead roommate was Nuggets, the used record store in Kenmore Square. A cramped, dusty cellar crammed stem to stern with vinyl, Nuggets was heaven on earth for a kid who'd grown up in the woods of Maine thirty miles from the nearest mall. I ended up buying a stack of Who bootlegs from an enormous, surly Samoan dude with a pink mohawk, using up all the "walking around" cash my Dad had pressed into my palm as I was leaving my childhood home that morning.

Anyway, Jackie St. John and her pale blue eyes and her cascade of candy-apple-red hair had the idea for Ouija night. Everyone knew Ouija boards were against the rules in Charlesgate, even though no one had ever seen this in writing. It's not like our acceptance letters read "Welcome to Emerson College. You'll be living in Charlesgate Hall, which is, as you know, haunted. Ouija boards are strictly forbidden." Besides, who in their right mind was going to check for Ouija boards when four hundred students were moving into the building on the same weekend? Refrigerators were illegal too, thanks to the ancient shitty wiring in the place, but I still managed to smuggle in a dorm fridge which, along with my VCR and movie collection (*Spinal Tap*, *Repo Man*, *The Road Warrior*, all the classics), had helped me make friends freshman year.

Jackie, though, had brought a Ouija board with her to college, so she must have known about Charlesgate's checkered past before she ever got here. Otherwise, who would bother? Six of us had gathered to drink some beer, smoke some weed, and summon the spirits of Charlesgate. Seeing as how we were all under twenty-one, we were breaking three Emerson rules all at once. If the RA stopped by, we'd be standing tall before the Man in the morning.

The Rev had volunteered our room for the occasion. We shared a triple in the southeast corner of the sixth floor with Murtaugh. It was a choice room assignment. Most of the triples in Charlesgate were really doubles with a set of bunk beds crammed into one corner. Once you added bureaus, desks, milk crates full of albums, and all the other crap students haul from home, there wasn't enough room left for a fly to fart. But room 629 was one of a kind on the sixth floor, because it was actually a suite. In the far right corner, by the foot of my bed, two steps led up to our secret lair, the Love Room, where we kept the stereo, a couple of comfy chairs, a life-sized cardboard Leatherface standee from *Texas Chainsaw Massacre 2*, and a futon that would fold out on those rare occasions when one of us (usually Murtaugh, truth be told) got lucky.

The Love Room had been built out on the roof decades after the original construction of Charlesgate. Its walls were concrete, so we could crank the stereo and the RA would never hear it. On this particular night, the Love Room was festooned with candles and burning incense, which was decidedly not our usual style. In addition to the three of us who shared the room, our Ouija group included Jackie, her roommate Dana Perry, and a watery-eyed waif from the all-female seventh floor ("the Nunnery"), whose name I didn't know.

"Someone stuff a towel under that door. There's one in the laundry basket."

I waved off the Rev's joint and went rooting through our filthy undergarments in search of a towel to block the pot smoke from seeping into the outer room, just in case an RA stopped by for a visit. In Charlesgate, we held the Resident Assistants in about the same esteem as the meter maids writing parking tickets down on Beacon Street.

"Use your boxers, Tommy. No pot smoke could penetrate that wall of stink."

"Blow me, Murtaugh." I found the towel and stuffed it in the crack between the door and the floor.

"We need some spooky tunes," said the Rev, stroking his yellow tangle of beard thoughtfully. "Maybe some Crimson?"

"I've got the *Halloween* soundtrack here somewhere," said

Murtagh with a devilish smirk. He was big on the devilish smirk. It worked for him.

"No way," said the waif I didn't know. "This is scary enough as it is."

" 'If desired, set the mood by dimming the lights or turning them off,' " Jackie read from the inside cover of the box. "Okay, we've got that covered. 'Set the planchette in the center of the Ouija board.' " She did so. "So who's going first? Besides me?"

I volunteered, of course, because if I was holding the planchette at the same time as Jackie, our fingers might brush against each other, and in my mind, that was the first step in an inevitable chain of events that would end with me waking up beside her in the Love Room wearing only a smile. Pathetic, I agree, but that's just how 19-year-old guys think. For all I know, it's how 89-year-old guys think too, but I'm not quite there yet.

"What are we gonna ask it?"

"First we have to ask if anyone's here." Jackie scrunched her eyes shut and cleared her throat. "Spirits of Charlesgate…are you with us?"

The planchette began to move under my fingertips. I was applying very little pressure, but I can't swear that I wasn't nudging it, ever so slightly, toward the upper left corner. Whether Jackie was helping it along, I could only guess. In any case, the answer was "YES."

"How many of you are with us?"

The planchette slid downward a few inches, settling on "1."

"Did you die in Charlesgate?"

"YES."

"When did you die?"

"1"…"9"…"4"…"6."

"1946. Um, let's see…ask a question, Tommy."

"Like what?"

"I don't know! Aren't you a journalism student?"

"Okay, um, spirit: How did you die?"

The planchette vibrated under my fingers but it didn't move.

"Maybe that's a sore subject," Jackie said.

"Yeah. Um…all right. Spirit: What was your name in life?"

The planchette moved. Jackie read the letters. "D…O…R…"

But before Jackie could finish, she was cut off by an ear-splitting squeal. Jackie screamed and jumped back from the board, knocking over one of the candles set up on an end table behind her. By the time it registered with me that the ongoing shrieking noise was the Charlesgate fire alarm, the candle—one of those fat scented deals encased in a glass holder—had shattered against the wall, and the window curtain was going up in flames.

In the moment, there wasn't much time to appreciate the irony of a fire that had essentially been caused by a fire alarm. We could laugh about that later, assuming we all got out alive. I grabbed the towel I'd just stuffed under the door and crossed the room in three long strides. Everything seemed to be happening in slow motion. Nobody else had moved except Jackie, who was still screaming, staring at the flaming curtain in horror. I smothered the curtain with the towel, ripped it down off the window, balled up the towel, and pounded it against the wall a half-dozen times for good measure. The alarm was still blaring.

"Okay, séance over," I said. "What do you say we get the fuck out of here?"

Fifteen or twenty minutes later, we were standing on the sidewalk across Charlesgate East, watching the red lights of the fire engine flash while the inspectors checked the building. When Jackie grabbed my hand and raised it above our heads, I thought

I might levitate off the sidewalk and float across the River Charles.

"Hey!" she shouted to no one in particular, her voice hoarse and sexy after all that screaming. "Hey, this is the guy! This is the guy who saved Charlesgate!"

A smattering of applause broke out—along with a few sarcastic whoops and whistles, but I didn't care at all.

"Where did you see our listing?"

Rachel O'Brien, assistant manager of Back Bay Modern Living, owners of seven condominium complexes throughout the Boston metro area, including the Charlesgate, led the client down the sixth floor hallway to Unit 67. The client had identified himself as Charles Finley, a lawyer with Goodwin Palmer downtown. Mr. Finley had explained that he was getting divorced and looking to move back to the city after years out in Medford.

"Actually, I didn't see a listing. It's just this building caught my eye. Kind of a…classic, right?"

Rachel smiled and began fumbling through her substantial keyring. "It's beautiful, isn't it? This is the only one-bedroom we have available with a view of Kenmore Square. I should tell you, since you didn't see it, that we have it listed at $349,000."

"You aren't scaring me off. I just happen to have 350K put away for a rainy day."

Rachel chuckled with no trace of humor. Finding the key she was looking for, she popped open the door to Unit 67 and led Finley inside.

"There's that view," she said, gesturing toward the bay windows in hopes that the sight of the Citgo sign would distract Finley from noticing he wouldn't be getting the roomiest living space $349,000 could buy. The unit was unfurnished; just an empty living room with hardwood floors, a tiny kitchen behind a bar to the left, and a short hallway leading to the bedroom and bathroom beyond.

"This was some kind of fancy hotel back in the day, right?"

"Oh yes. The Charlesgate was *the* destination on the eastern seaboard during the Gilded Age. Only the best people. We like to think that's still the case."

Finley walked to the bay windows and stared out at Kenmore Square below. It was just past 5:30 in the afternoon, and foot traffic was heavy trailing out of the T station and up Brookline Ave towards Lansdowne Street. The Yankees/Red Sox game would be getting underway in about an hour and a half.

"But it wasn't always the best people, am I right?" Finley turned around and flashed a tight grin at Rachel. "I mean, I've heard some stories. Didn't the guy who designed this place kill himself right in this building?"

Rachel cleared her throat. "My understanding is that Mr. Putnam did pass in the Charlesgate, but I can assure you, it was *not* suicide. Natural causes."

"My bad. Can we see the rest of the place?"

Rachel took a moment to consider it. Finley certainly wouldn't have been the first nutjob who wanted to tour "haunted Charlesgate" under the pretense of condo shopping. She'd been impressed with his Hugo Boss suit, but up close he looked rough, like a hardhat playing dress-up. Maybe he'd worked his way through law school on the docks or in a warehouse. But she decided to give him the benefit of the doubt. After all, her commission from the sale would pay for another vacation in Belize.

"Of course. Right this way." Rachel stepped to the kitchen entryway. "As you see, we have the granite countertops. Real ones, not that faux-granite you often find nowadays. These are all-new fixtures and cabinets, also a brand-new dishwasher and the stainless Bosch refrigerator with French door bottom freezer and ice dispenser."

Finley followed Rachel down the short hallway. "Bathroom on the left, with marble tub and glass shower door. Good water pressure, too. All this plumbing is new. And the bedroom is here on the right." She pushed the door open and stepped inside. "Again the bay windows, and you have a walk-in closet at the other end."

"I guess I must have got the story screwed up," Finley said. "The way I heard it, the architect...Putnam? Way I heard it, he was some kind of high priest of the Black Mass or something. Weird occult shit, human sacrifice, all of that."

Rachel sighed. So he was one of them after all. "Mr. Finley, I'm sure you can appreciate that any building with a history as long and colorful as the Charlesgate attracts its share of tall tales and ghost stories. It comes with the territory, but honestly, I am not an expert on the subject. Whatever happened here in the past, the Charlesgate is now one of the most appealing high-end residential communities in metropolitan Boston. If you're really interested in the building's past, I can recommend the Emerson College library, which I understand has an extensive file on the subject available for in-house study."

"Oh, that's all right. To tell you the truth, I'm really not all that interested in the building itself. Just what's inside it."

Finley closed the bedroom door behind him, blocking Rachel's only means of exit from the room. For the first time, she noticed that he'd put on a pair of gloves, and spotted a neck tattoo peeking above his collar. She stiffened and clutched the small canister of pepper spray in her pocket. She'd been through this before.

"Mr. Finley, our tour is over. Please step away from the door."

"No problem."

Rachel O'Brien had no time to scream as Finley lunged toward her, wrapping his left arm in a tight chokehold around her neck. With his free hand he took hold of her jaw and wrenched her head to the side until he heard her neck snap. He held his hand over her nose and mouth until he was sure her breathing had stopped.

After her body hit the floor, Finley went through her pockets, tossing the pepper spray aside and taking her oversized keyring. Then he left the bedroom, closing the door behind him.

Fat Dave was making Manhattans down at the Red Room Lounge. Fat Dave made the best Manhattans in town, but that's not why his customers did their drinking at the Red Room. It wasn't for the atmosphere, either; unless you liked chipped tile floors, hard wooden stools and ripped vinyl booth seats with the stuffing sticking out, the place had little to offer in that regard. Tucked away on quiet Lincoln Street, just a few blocks from South Station, the Red Room had the reputation of a safe, neutral watering hole for what was known in law enforcement circles as the criminal element. The reason for that reputation was Fat Dave, a six-foot-five, 350-pound slab of a man known for keeping the peace. There were no vendettas at the Red Room, no wars. No one ever started anything there. If anyone did, it didn't last long. For men who wanted a place to have a drink without worrying about taking a couple bullets to the back of the skull, it was the city's most reliable option.

As a result of his lounge's unique appeal to underworld clientele, Fat Dave heard everything. And because he knew Fat Dave heard everything, Dave T dropped by for a Manhattan two nights after his card game got hit.

"Other Dave!"

"Ho, Other Dave! What's the good word?"

"Drink, drank, drunk. These are good words."

"Getcha Manhattan?"

"I would love a fucking Manhattan. And gimme a Gansett while I'm waiting."

Fat Dave cracked open a Narragansett tall boy and set it in front of Dave T, who eagerly swigged from the can. He glanced around the Red Room, saw a handful of regulars and no one he didn't recognize. If you drank at the Red Room, chances were you'd sat in on Dave T's card game a time or two.

"Heard you had some trouble the other night," Fat Dave said, scooping ice into a mixing glass.

"I've had two straight days of trouble. You hear about that business over at Billy's Tap?"

"Think I heard something about that." Fat Dave poured a half-ounce of sweet vermouth into the glass. "This was last night?"

"Yeah. See, this is why it's a good thing you got no dartboards in here, no pool table, none of that crap. Anything that gets the competitive juices flowing is bad for business."

"Says the guy with the card game."

"Well, that's different. It's not physical. Besides, the guys who play my game, they know better. Cuz if they *don't* know better, they know they ain't never coming back. That's what makes it a friendly game. That's why I can get North End greaseballs and Southie micks and mutts from Somerville at the same table and there's never any beef. Same deal you got here. Only Billy, he don't really operate that way."

Fat Dave shrugged, stirring Mount Vernon rye whiskey into the vermouth. "Not my place to say."

"Well, you don't have to say it. Actions speak louder. It's like this: Do you know my last name?"

"It's…T-something."

"Yeah. T for what? Tarantula? Tipperary? See, you don't know. And I don't know yours either, because we're not in this thing. This Italian, Irish, whatever the fuck. Tribal shit. My grandparents had their name changed at Ellis Island anyway, so what does it matter? See, we stay out of all that, and it works for us, but guys like Billy…" Dave T shook his head.

"Anyway, it was darts?" Fat Dave drained the contents of the mixing glass minus the ice into a lowball glass, dropped in a maraschino cherry, and slid it across the bar.

"Yeah, darts." Dave T stirred his drink. "So there's two teams of two, right? And all four of these knuckleheads are Irish, but that don't even matter, because two of them are with the Killeens and two of them are with the Mullens. And they got beef going all the way back to County Cork or whatever the fuck. But fine, a game of darts, what's the worst that could happen?"

"You tell me."

Dave T sipped his drink. "That's a fucking good Manhattan."

"I've been told."

"Anyway. The game isn't even close. The Killeens are knocking 'em down left and right. Closing 'em out and hitting triples before the Mullens are even on the board. So they start rubbing it in a little bit. More than a little, as I understand it. Maybe getting a little personal. And these Mullen boys, they're not known for their good sportsmanship in the first place. So the Killeens are ribbin' them about their aim, you know, and Chris, the crazier one of the Mullen boys, he says: 'So you don't think much of my aim, huh?' 'No, I don't think much of your aim.' So Chris, he pulls his dart out of the board, he grabs the closest Killeen around the neck, and he jams the dart right in his eye."

"Oh boy."

"Yeah. So now the other Mullen has to jump the other Killeen, and all hell is breaking loose. Now let me ask you this: You don't know my last name, I don't know your last name, but what's Billy's last name?"

"Killeen."

"You bet your fuckin' ass it is. So Billy comes flying over the bar with that Bobby Doerr autographed Louisville Slugger of his, and he's all over those Mullens like they're batting-practice fastballs. Puts Chris in intensive care, but the other one don't have to worry about no hospital bills, because he's dead."

Fat Dave whistled. "Sounds like a mess."

"It's a mess all right. I mean, ordinary circumstances, Billy knows the right palms to grease. But this one's not gonna slide so easy."

"Tough break for him, but what I can't figure is why you give a shit. See, when you came in here tonight, I thought it was about something else entirely."

Dave T tossed back the rest of his Manhattan and glanced around, as if to be sure no one was sneaking up on him. Nothing was moving in the Red Room except a small electric fan on a shelf behind the bar. "Yeah. Well, ordinarily, you're right, I wouldn't give a shit. Except without getting into specifics here, those Mullen boys were supposed to help me out with something I got in the works. And now that ain't gonna happen. Which is maybe my good luck, because obviously these guys are a couple of fuckups. Well, one's a fuckup. One's a dead fuckup."

"Believe me, you're better off. What I heard, that whole bunch of Mullens is ready to go to war with Marko."

"That's the rumor. They're crazy enough to do it, too."

"Well, like you said. Probably the only thing stopping them is you and your game."

"How do you figure that?"

"No one wants to screw up a good thing. Tensions simmer always, but as long as everyone can sit down together once a week and blow off a little steam at the poker table, everything stays in balance."

"Yeah, it's a regular United Nations. But anyway, speaking of my game…"

"The other night? Think maybe I can help you out with that."

"I was hoping you'd say that. How about another Gansett?"

Fat Dave cracked another tall boy and slid it across the bar. "Well, you know me. I like to keep my mouth shut. But like I said, your game has always been a safe place. That's gotta be respected. This ain't the Wild West up here."

"I appreciate it."

"So last night, while all that was goin' on at Billy's, it was pretty quiet in here. Just like it's always pretty quiet in here. Except for these three guys. And these are three guys you'd know. They were drinking a lot, which is not unusual, but they were buying rounds for the house, which is pretty fucking unusual. And they're laughing it up, two of them especially. The third one, you can tell he's kind of trying to keep a lid on it. So the loudest one comes over to buy another round for every-body. I says to him, 'Another one? You sure about that?' So he laughs again, reaches in his pocket and pulls out a fat roll of bills. He peels a couple of twenties off the top and sets them on the bar, then peels off another one for good measure. And you know what he says? Thinking he's being all clever? 'I had a good run at the poker table last night.'"

Dave T took a long pull off his tall boy. "And what did you say to that?"

"I said 'Good for you.' And he and the other guy laugh it up again, but the third one, he ain't laughing at all. He's giving his friend Henny Youngman there the stink-eye, like he fucked up big time. Which he did. I mean, I understand this kid's thinking: What's the point of knocking over Dave T's game if nobody knows you did it? He's thinking he's just made his reputation, but what he doesn't understand is nobody's ever gonna work with someone who knocked over Dave T's game. Some things are sacred. So...lotta balls, this kid, but no brains."

"Got that right." Dave T ran his fingers over the cracks and crevices of the wooden bar top. Everyone who was anyone had carved their initials into the Red Room bar. He'd done it too, but he couldn't remember where. "So these three guys you say I would know. Where would I know them from?"

SEPTEMBER 29, 1986

By the morning after the fire alarm, Jackie St. John and I had gone on our first date, had our first kiss, our first fuck, and our first fight. She'd met my parents, I'd met hers, we'd gotten engaged, married, raised our kids, and been buried side-by-side after a long and happy life together. Either that or our first date had been a disaster, I'd fucked the whole thing up as usual and would spend the rest of my life alone and miserable. Or something in between. I'd run every possible scenario as I tossed and turned, unable to shut my brain down. Lust had solidified into deep infatuation overnight. I relived the moment when she raised my hand above her head over and over again. It meant nothing, but it meant everything. It was all like a movie—hell, it was a whole damn film festival. The problem is, you're always the leading man in your mind. In real life, you may wake up to find out you're just an extra.

"Wake up, chief! It's Monday morning. Professor Pussyhound awaits."

I peered through crusty eyelids. Murtaugh was hunched in front of his mirror on intensive nosehair patrol. Sunlight streamed in through the window overlooking the Pit.

Freshman year I'd lived on the second floor, which circum-navigated the building. You could keep walking in circles for-ever on the second floor. But above that, Charlesgate was horseshoe-shaped. We were at one end of the horseshoe: Looking straight across the Pit, we could see all the windows of the rooms on the other side. But if you looked straight down, you'd see the Pit, which may well have been a lovely courtyard back in Charlesgate's glory days, but was now the building's largest garbage receptacle. On a hot day, the smells wafting up from the Pit were unspeakable. Right outside our window was a sizable ledge that must have once been a posh hotel balcony. We managed to hang out there for all of five minutes one afternoon before an RA yelled at us to get the hell inside. There were no secrets on the Pit.

"Let's go, Donnelly!" Murtaugh kicked my bed, spraying his entire body with Right Guard all the while. I groaned and rolled to my feet.

"Jesus, you can't possibly be tired. You slept through Sunday altogether, for Chrissakes."

"Yeah," I said. "That's why I'm tired. Too much sleep makes you tired. Look it up."

"Well, you missed out. Sox clinched the division yesterday. It was crazy! Kenmore was rockin'. This is the year, man, I'm telling you."

I put on a reasonably clean shirt and ran my fingers through my hair. "All right. Let's face the music."

That would be Music Appreciation with Nathan Pierce, known to us as Professor Pussyhound. Pierce had a reputation for fucking his female students in bunches, and whether that was true or not, he looked the part. He was a dead ringer for Robert Urich, a TV actor who was shooting *Spenser for Hire* in Boston at the time, and although he couldn't have been more than a dozen years older than us, his attempts at seeming hip were invariably lame. He smoked clove cigarettes by the open classroom window in flagrant violation of school policy, and was given to strained comparisons like, "Stravinsky was the Clash of his day."

Murtaugh and I took the Emerson shuttle, which dropped us off at the Wall, a stoop in front of the library on Beacon Street where students smoked and shot the shit between classes. As we were walking to class, I spotted Jackie sitting with some friends, and felt the back of my neck heat up. I let loose with a way too enthusiastic, "Hey Jackie, how's it's going?" She didn't even glance up, and her barely audible "Hey" put the funk in perfunctory. As soon as we passed, she and her girlfriends burst into laughter, and while there was every chance that had something to do with whatever they were talking about and nothing to do with me, I could not have been more mortified. Somehow Jackie had seen inside my head. She knew I'd spent the whole weekend in bed fantasizing about our life together. Maybe the Ouija board had told her.

Professor Pussyhound introduced us to the wonders of early 20th-century Italian opera that morning, but it's safe to say *Madama Butterfly* flew in one ear and out the other. After class I was still in a daze as Murtaugh and I hiked back to our end of Beacon Street for lunch. After two or three attempts at engaging me in conversation, he punched me on the shoulder.

"Ow!"

"Oh, there he is! Sorry, I thought I was walking alone here. What's up your ass?"

"Nothing, just…thinking about opera."

"Yeah, right. You look like someone raped your dog. Is this about a chick? Yeah, this is definitely about a chick."

I shrugged. "It's nothing. Forget it."

"Just tell me who it is. I bet it's not as bad as you think."

"I told you it's nothing. I've got…I've got a little crush on Jackie St. John."

Murtaugh snorted. "Yeah. You and every other heterosexual male in Charlesgate. Which is only half the males in Charlesgate at best, but still…well, I think you're a little bit over your skis, chief."

"Yeah, I get that now."

"Look, I'm not trying to bust your balls. You could totally get laid tonight if you wanted, but you've got to stay in your lane, you know?"

"Okay, well, thanks for the pep talk. Let's fucking eat, all right?"

The Canteen, our school cafeteria, was on the first floor of the dorm across the street from Charlesgate. Known as Fensgate, it had none of the history, charm, or quirkiness of our dorm. I never heard any stories of Fensgate being haunted, although I did hear about a kid who did a shitload of acid and took a tumble out a fifth-floor window, his head exploding like a cantaloupe all over Beacon Street. Like sightings of Eugene O'Neill's ghost, however, that was probably bullshit.

We had a free-floating lunch group of about a dozen regulars, any six or eight of whom would put in an appearance on any given day. Once Murtaugh and I had filled our trays with the usual assortment of fried meat-like items and piles of starch, we made our way over to our table, where Rodney, Brooks, Jules, Purple Debbie, and the Rev were already chowing down. These were my people. This was my tribe. I'd never found them in high school, but I'd found them now. For that alone, my Emerson tuition was worth every penny I'd spend the next ten years paying off.

"Donnelly's in love with Jackie St. John," Murtaugh announced as we sat down.

"I hate you," I said. "Have I mentioned that I hate you?"

"Really?" said Jules, a wide-eyed freshman from Texas who had somehow instantly clicked with our group. "Isn't she kind of…?" She wrinkled her nose.

"Unattainable?" said Murtaugh. "Yes, which is why I advised our colleague here to get laid post-haste. Do I have any volunteers?

Jules, you're looking for your first college fling, aren't you?"

"She's twelve years old!" I protested.

"I am not! And I'm sitting right here! Don't talk about me like I'm not here!"

"No offense."

"Anyway, I'm not looking for a fling, thank you."

"Right," said Murtaugh. "You're looking for Prince Charming. And Purple Debbie, I suppose you still claim to be dating your imaginary high school sweetheart…"

"Chad is *not* imaginary! You met him!"

Purple Debbie was called Purple Debbie to distinguish her from some other Debbie she'd gone to high school with and none of us had ever met. In all ways mentally and emotionally, Purple Debbie was still in high school.

"Can we drop the subject please?" I said.

"Yes, we can," said Rodney, a preacher's kid from New Hampshire who took to his college experience like a sailor on shore leave. Compared to the rest of us, Rodney was Barry Goldwater, but his parents still thought he'd sold his soul to the devil. "Chest Guy is making fake IDs. Twenty bucks. I'm in. Who's with me?"

"Me," Murtaugh, the Rev and I chimed in simultaneously.

"You guys," said Jules, wrinkling her nose again. "That's illegal."

"Yes," said Rodney. "That's the whole point. If they were legal, we wouldn't need them. Look, we're all over eighteen here. Five, ten years ago, we'd all be able to drink legally anyway. So it's completely arbitrary. Typical big government."

"Think of the boost to the local economy," said the Rev. "All those shows at the Rat, Bunratty's, TT the Bear's…we can keep a half-dozen local bands afloat easily. We're supporting the arts."

Judging from her still-wrinkling nose, Jules wasn't buying it, but that ship had sailed. "So that's four of us?" said Rodney. "Brooks, you're not in?"

"I turn twenty-one in three weeks. I only look stupid." Brooks was a theater major and it didn't take anyone more than one guess to figure that out. Looking back now, he was the most stereotypically '80s member of our group, with sculptured Flock of Seagulls hair, an all-black wardrobe and a penchant for eyeliner. He'd taken a year off after high school to volunteer for MASSPIRG, saving the planet door-to-door.

"Okay, so four of us. I'll let him know. Stay tuned for further instructions."

These were the further instructions: We were to report to Chest Guy's room on the sixth floor of Charlesgate at fifteen-minute intervals. We were to bring twenty dollars in cash each, non-negotiable. My appointment was for 7:45 that night.

I showed up a couple minutes early. Chest Guy opened the door and waved me in. He was on the phone, and true to his reputation, he had his shirt unbuttoned to the waist, all the better to show off his glistening pecs. He raised a finger and continued his conversation.

"Yes, I'm six foot even, 185 pounds. Very muscular. My chest is 40 inches, waist 32, inseam 34. Six-pack abs. My hair is a little spiky in front, collar-length in back. A bit like Simon Le Bon in 'Wild Boys,' if you've seen that video. I can fax you a head shot in the morning if you've got a fax machine. Sure, that's no problem…10:30 tomorrow morning? I'll be there. No, thank *you*. See you then."

He hung up. "Modeling agency. You know the drill."

"Sure." I didn't know the drill, and he knew I didn't know the drill, but whatever. I wanted to get through this as quickly as possible. Chest Guy skeeved me out.

"So I'm sure Rodney told you it's twenty bucks."

I fished my last twenty out of my wallet. For the rest of the week, I'd have to hit the Shawmut Bank ATM. It was the only one in town that dispensed five dollar bills.

"Good deal," said Chest Guy. "So here's how it works. We use the Maine license, because it's the only one in New England that still has the photo in the lower right-hand corner. You'll see why that's important in a minute."

"Fine," I said. I already had a Maine driver's license, only because I happened to be from Maine. Chest Guy fetched a piece of cardboard, about 18 by 36 inches, and a black magic marker, and handed them to me.

"As you can see, I've already filled in all your pertinent information. I just need your signature." I examined the piece of cardboard. It was an exact replica of a Maine driver's license, with my name, a fake address and birth date, and blank spaces where the photo and signature should be. I took the magic marker and scrawled an oversized signature in the designated space.

"Beautiful," said Chest Guy. He slapped some double-sided tape on the back of the cardboard and pressed it against the wall in the spot where a Def Leppard poster had been hanging the week before. He turned on a 10K light borrowed from the film depot and picked up his Nikon Tele-Touch. "Okay, now I need you to stand about six inches in front of the license so your head is framed by the square where your photo should be."

I did what he asked. "Okay, let me just adjust the light so there's no telltale shadow…great. Now smile like you've spent three hours in line at the Registry."

I offered a shit-eating smirk as Chest Guy snapped a half-dozen photos.

"All righty," he said. "It'll be ready on Friday, just in time for you to try it out."

"Looking forward to it. You sure this thing is gonna work?"

"How could I be? All sales are final and you use it at your own risk. And if you do get caught, remember, you bought it in the Combat Zone from some guy you never met before and never seen since. You bring my name into it, I'll drop you in the Pit headfirst."

He winked. I showed myself out.

Detective Martin Coleman lifted the yellow crime scene tape and stepped under it, trying not to spill his large Dunkin' Donuts coffee as he entered Unit 67. The two uniforms were inside as expected, milling around the body and shooting the shit about Dustin Pedroia's three doubles the night before.

"Fackin' Laser Show went off last night. Vintage Pedey."

"Well, he had to. Friggin' bullpen can't hold a lead. Five ribbies he gets, and it still goes extras. Oh—hey, boss."

"Gentlemen. Sorry to interrupt the postgame show, but who's the vic?"

"Rachel O'Brien, twenty-nine years old, realtor from Back Bay Modern Living. Unmarried, but engaged. Fiancé was on a business trip to the West Coast. He's in biotech sales or some shit. Had late meetings last night, wasn't expecting to hear from her. Time difference. Anyway, we got ahold of him a few minutes ago, he's a fackin' mess as you might presume."

Coleman squatted beside the body and sipped his coffee. "Crime Scene has been here, looks like." Actually, he knew for a fact they'd been there. He and his partner had just finished chasing down a lead on another case in Dorchester when they caught the call on O'Brien. Baseball and murder were both back in season, and everyone in Homicide had a full scorecard. Carnahan had a scheduled court appearance, so Coleman made the trip to the Back Bay alone.

"Just left. They weren't buying my theory that she tripped on her shoelaces and broke her neck."

"First thing you want to look for in that case, shoelaces. Of which she has none. Hold this for me, will you?" Coleman raised his coffee cup and the nearest officer took it from him. "What did they find?"

"One canister of pepper spray, unused, next to the body. Prints everywhere, but this unit has been shown almost two dozen times since it went on the market ten days ago, so…good luck there. Usual hairs and fibers. No open wounds. Guy obviously didn't want to make any noise. No gunshots, no screaming, just a body hitting the ground, which might annoy the downstairs neighbors if they were home, which they were not. Aside from the neck, no other visible bruising. Far as they can tell, not a pube out of place."

"That's good," said Coleman, rummaging through Rachel's pockets. "Hopefully we don't have to call in those sick fucks from Sex Crimes. So it's looking like this happened yesterday, am I right?"

"Best they can say before the ME gets ahold of her, sometime between two and ten yesterday. But we can do a little better than that. Her people at the realty office started to miss her when she didn't show for work this morning. Made several calls to her cell. The receptionist over at Back Bay Modern Living was able to pull up her calendar. Her last appointment yesterday was right here, this unit, 5:30 P.M. yesterday. Client was a Charles Finley, a lawyer with Goodwin Palmer downtown. Your next question is whether I called Goodwin Palmer to verify they have a Charles Finley on the active roster."

"Why am I even here? So you did that and they said…?"

"They have no such Charles Finley. Never heard of him."

"One shocker after another."

"Right, but Sully and I have a theory. Maybe Charles Finley is Chuck Finley. Know who that is?"

"Former pitcher for the Angels," said Coleman. "Married the chick from the Whitesnake video. You figure him for this?"

"No, but you ever watch *Burn Notice*?"

"What the fuck is *Burn Notice*?"

"TV show. Spies and shit. Anyway, this one character, Sam Axe—"

"Bruce Campbell," said Sully. "The guy with the chin, he plays Sam Axe."

"Yeah, and whenever he's undercover, Sam Axe uses the same alias. Chuck Finley."

"So we figure this guy is a *Burn Notice* fan."

"Good work, guys," said Coleman. "I'd say this case is just about wrapped up thanks to your keen attention to detail."

"Yeah. Anyway, couple hours ago the realty office finally sent someone down here to make sure she didn't drop dead while showing this guy Finley around. Which, as we can see here, she did."

"Indeed. So presumably, since she was showing this non-existent lawyer this lovely overpriced condo, she must have had a key. Such key as I've failed to find on the vic's person."

"Such key as we didn't find either, nor did Crime Scene. According to the receptionist, she had the key to every unit in the building on her ring, along with keys to the administrative, storage, maintenance, and function rooms. This Back Bay Modern Living was handling every aspect of the Charlesgate on behalf of some mystery owner, of whom we know not thing one at this point. Now, it's always possible that some of the residents have changed their locks since they took occupancy, but you gotta assume the perp had access to the majority of the building and had many hours to find whatever it was he may have been looking for."

Coleman held Rachel's lifeless gaze as he fished two small pieces of folded cardboard from her inside jacket pocket and slipped them into his own. This was something different, for sure. It beat chasing down leads on dead drug dealers in the Dot projects anyway. "Officer…"

"Billings."

"Officer Billings. I assume you asked for a comprehensive list of this distinguished old building's occupants?"

"You'll have it in your email when you get back to the station tonight."

Coleman stood and cracked his knuckles. He walked to the window and took in the steady flow of pedestrian traffic out of Kenmore Station, past the ticket scalpers and program hawkers toward Brookline Ave. He knew he'd have a full report from Crime Scene waiting on his desk when he got back to the office. Any fibers, fingerprints, or fluids found on the premises or the vic would be accounted for. The ME would do a more thorough search of O'Brien's intimate areas, but Coleman was guessing that would turn up squadoosh. "Y'know, used to be a homicide detective actually had shit to do when he got to a crime scene. But I guess I'm pretty much obsolete at this point. Except one thing it seems like you geniuses missed."

Coleman produced the two small pieces of folded cardboard from his inside jacket pocket. "Two tickets to the game tonight. Pretty damn good seats along the first base line. Now, she obviously wasn't going with her fiancé, who's out of town. So the question is, who was she going with?"

"You think that's relevant, boss?"

"I'll tell you what's relevant: Two perfectly good tickets to tonight's Red Sox/Yankees game, which I am going to book into evidence around 10:30 tonight. Maybe 11:30, these Sox/Yanks games always run long. Now, if you gentlemen will excuse me, I need to call my wife and tell her to get a sitter. One thing you should know about my wife, she can't stand them fucking Yankees."

Jake Devlin, his younger brother Shane, and their cousin Pat were on the third night of a booze-soaked bender. There would not be a fourth. This night found them at the Crawford House in Scollay Square, ignoring a comedy duo performing a hackneyed routine on stage. As usual, Jake was the closest thing to a voice of reason among the three.

"Let's call it a night, whaddaya say?"

Pat never called it a night until well into the morning and wasn't about to start now. "Jaybird, we ain't leaving until the girls come on, you kiddin' me? I don't know about you, but I didn't come here to see no comedy show. Besides, I heard Albert and Costellich do this one on the radio. The guy playing first base, his name is Who. That's the whole gag."

"Yeah, lighten up, Jake," said Shane, taking a sip from his drink. "We're a long way from the Purple Shamrock, am I right?"

The Purple Shamrock was a now-defunct social club in the Winter Hill neighborhood of Somerville where the three had grown up together. As kids they'd earned candy and comic-book money running errands for the broken-nosed toughs who never left the Shamrock. They came to be known as the Little Rascals, and the crew had assigned them each a name straight out of Hal Roach's *Our Gang* comedies. Jake was Spanky, Pat was Alfalfa, and Shane, who'd been a chubby kid, was Porky.

Things had changed. If Jake was the brains and Pat was the mouth, Shane was definitely the balls. It had been Shane's idea to hit Dave T's poker game. Jake had put the plan together. And Pat had blabbed about it at the Red Room two nights earlier. Not in so many words, but close enough to mean big trouble was coming their way sooner than later.

Jake allowed the ghost of a smile. "Yeah. Long way from the Shamrock. But third night in a row on the town...kind of attracting attention, no?"

"We been careful," said Pat. "Moving around, different parts of town. Come on, who you know comes down to Scollay Square anymore? Especially this place? It's for sailors on shore leave, not guys like us."

The Crawford House was a popular burlesque theater attached to an upscale hotel at the corner of Court and Brattle. A bottle of beer cost about five times as much as it did at the joints the Little Rascals frequented, but then again, those places didn't offer the spectacle of Sally Keith twirling her tassels. After the fat guy and the slightly-less-fat guy onstage finally got to the part about the shortstop I Don't Give a Damn, the crowd went crazy in anticipation of the Tassel Queen's first show of the evening.

"Here we go," said Pat. "Pay attention, Jaybird, you might see something you never seen before."

"I seen shit you wouldn't believe."

"Yeah, yeah. I know."

Jake had been the only one of the three to serve his country during World War II. He'd concluded his stint in the Pacific theater by spending six months as a prisoner of war, including seventeen days packed into the suffocating hold of the *Arisan Maru*, a Japanese hell ship. On October 24, 1944, that ship was sunk by Allied forces who had no idea it held over 1,700 American POWs. All but nine of them died. Jake came home with a medal and a hollowed-out look in his eyes. Shane and Pat had both been classified 4-F, Pat because of a hole in his eardrum and Shane thanks to the impressive criminal record he'd amassed as a teenager.

A few weeks after his discharge, Jake paid his first visit to the sixth floor of the Charlesgate, where he met a jaded, sloe-eyed prostitute who called herself Violet and styled herself after Veronica Lake. Over the next few months, he would pay as many visits to Violet as his savings and occasional odd-job earnings would allow. She thought he was falling in love with her, but love wasn't really part of Jake's emotional palette anymore.

Violet liked to talk afterward, and one night she told Jake all about the poker game held once a week on the eighth floor. Jake happened to mention it to Shane over drinks one night and Shane's eyes lit up. He'd heard about Dave T's exclusive poker game before, but never knew any details about it until now. He wanted to take it down.

"You got a criminal mind, brother," Jake had told him.

"What do you want to do, mow these guys' lawns for the rest of your life? This is our chance to make a score *and* a name."

So Jake talked to Violet. He found out when the next poker game would be held. He found out where the players' cash was stashed during the game, something Violet had discovered while delivering drinks and sandwiches one night at her pimp Jimmy Dryden's behest. She agreed to leave a window cracked open on the first floor, on the Marlboro Street side of the building. They could go up the back stairway, avoiding the muscle stationed in the lobby. She agreed to do this in exchange for $300, which Jake now owed her.

"Can I get you gentlemen another round?"

Jake turned to the waiter standing patiently behind him and was about to decline when Pat spoke up, twirling his index finger. "Yeah, drinks all around." The waiter nodded and stepped away.

"Come on, Jake," said Pat. "Lighten up. The show's just starting. Look, here she comes." The band struck up a sleazy grind as Sally Keith took the stage to whoops and catcalls. She winked over her shoulder, shaking her ample ass to the beat.

"There ya go, Jaybird! You seen anything like that in the Philippines? I bet them mama-sans didn't shake it like *that*."

"Shut up, Pat," said Shane. "You know he doesn't like to talk about it."

"He don't like to talk about anything! It's over a year he's been back and he still don't remember how to have fun."

"I'm sitting right here," said Jake. "Don't talk about me like I'm not. Maybe I don't talk enough for your liking, but you talk way too much for mine."

"This again? Look, I'm telling you. There's no point in knocking over a game like that—"

"Keep it down."

"I mean, there's no point in doing what we did if no one knows we did it."

"There's the money. Which we're burning through in record time."

"But it's a means to an end."

"It's one thing if they *think* we did it. If there's strong suspicion but no proof. You going around blabbing it everywhere, it's like you're shoving it in their faces. Nobody likes that, these guys especially."

The waiter returned with their drinks. With great effort, Pat managed to hold his tongue until he'd set them down and walked away.

"No offense, Jake, but don't talk to me like you know this world better than I do. While you were over there, and God bless you for that, I was out on these streets and in these barrooms. I know these people and how they operate."

"And I know 'em better than either of you," said Shane. "So why don't you both shut the fuck up and enjoy the show."

The Little Rascals stayed for the second show and the third, but still couldn't figure out how Sally Keith got the right tassel spinning one way and the left one twirling in the completely opposite direction. "Muscle control," Pat theorized, but that seemed both self-evident and inadequate as an explanation. Shortly after one in the morning, they stumbled out to Brattle Street heading for Shane's car parked in Pi Alley. A light drizzle had begun to fall.

"Fun is fun, boys," said Jake as they rounded the corner into the alley. "But fun is done. It's time to lay low for a while."

"A little late for that, fellas."

The voice came from behind them. They spun around, unsteady, reaching for their pieces.

"Nuh-uh. Hands where I can see 'em. My friends here have a pretty good bead on your heads."

Dave T cocked the Colt .45 he held at eye level. He was flanked by two of the Casey cousins from Pawtucket, their weapons of choice already drawn and aimed. He could have called anyone. There was no one in town who wouldn't back his play against the guys who took down his game. But Dave T preferred to work with out-of-town talent in times like these, and the Caseys brought an extra charge with them thanks to their recent activities in Middleboro. Word got around. Dave T believed the odds should always be stacked in favor of the house.

"Set your guns down, real slow. My friends here are gonna collect 'em, and then we're all gonna take a ride," he said. "I think you'll recognize the place."

The place was the Charlesgate, specifically the eighth floor, invisible from the street, home of Dave T's weekly game. The Caseys marched the Little Rascals inside and invited them to be seated at the poker table.

"Okay, you guys can wait outside," said Dave T. "I can take it from here."

The Caseys did so, leaving Dave T and his Colt .45 alone with the Little Rascals.

"So. Spanky. Alfalfa. Porky. You comfortable?"

The Little Rascals kept their mouths shut, but Shane visibly reddened.

"Oh, you don't like those names? Especially you, *Porky*. You were a fat kid, but you ain't fat no more. And you, Spanky. Did your part against the Axis powers. Came home expecting a hero's welcome. Except on Winter Hill, you were still just a little rascal. Am I right?"

"Sigmund fuckin' Fraud over here," said Shane. Dave T whacked him across the mouth with the butt of his Colt.

"But you don't wanna be the Little Rascals no more. You want to make a big name for yourselves. So what better way than to knock over my card game? I mean, that *was* the idea, right?"

Shane said nothing. Jake said nothing. But that wasn't Pat's m.o. and Dave T knew it. "You gotta admit, we proved ourselves. Am I wrong? We stepped up like men."

"Yeah, you stepped up. And on some level, I do admire that. I could use some guys like you on a thing I got coming up. Only one problem. Actually two problems, but we can solve 'em both at the same time. The first problem is, you guys took down my game. And I can't let that slide. I can't be *seen* to let that slide."

Jake saw his moment. "We can make this work," he said. "We can make this work for all of us."

"How so?"

"We'll pay you back. We'll pay you back with interest. And this thing you got coming up, whatever it is, we'll help you out. Gratis."

Dave T scratched his nose with the barrel of the Colt. "That's a start. But like I said, I got two problems. And the second one is,

I only need two more guys on this job. See, I *had* two guys, but they fucked up. One's dead, the other's in the hospital. Now I could use the Casey cousins, you know, the two gentlemen standing outside this door. But I don't necessarily like them for this type of work. You guys, on the other hand, I've seen what you can do under pressure. I think you can handle it."

"You know it," said Pat. "Whatever it is, we can handle it. This could be the start of a beautiful thing, am I right?"

"Hold your horses. We've still got two problems to solve. One, people gotta see I took action against you guys. And two, there's one too many of you. So here's what's gonna happen. One of you is gonna die. Right now. I'm gonna shoot someone in the head and I don't care which one of you it is. So you decide amongst yourselves. I'll give you two minutes to talk it over. Then you give me a name, or else I shoot all three of you and take my chances with the Caseys. Your two minutes starts right now."

OCTOBER 3, 1986

The office of the Emerson College newspaper, the *Berkeley Beacon*, was not coincidentally located at the corner of Berkeley and Beacon streets. The newspaper shared the third floor with the alumni magazine, the poetry journal, and other publications that came and went (such as the short-lived humor monthly *Gizzard*). The editor's cramped office was tucked away in the southwest corner, with a window overlooking Beacon Street. The sounds of rush-hour traffic wafted up as I moved a stack of last week's issue from the chair in front of Mighty Rob McKim's desk and took a seat.

"What's up, boss?" Although a sophomore, I'd just joined the *Berkeley Beacon* staff at the beginning of the semester. I was on my third major at Emerson: I'd started in television, switched to radio in the second semester of my freshman year, and now I was pursuing a degree in print journalism. Essentially, I was moving backward in time. By next semester, I'd be majoring in cave painting.

Mighty Rob leaned back in his chair and put his feet up on the desk. I didn't know why everyone called him Mighty Rob, but I was the new guy and figured all would become clear eventually.

"I liked your piece on the volleyball player there, Carol Knickerbocker."

"Crystal Nicodemus." Nicodemus was the leading scorer on the Emerson women's volleyball team, as well as the team's emotional leader. She also happened to be deaf. The story practically wrote itself.

"Right. Good piece. Concise."

"That's what I was going for."

"And the game stories have all been fine. I mean, what the fuck, it's not like there's a whole lot of drama to be mined from a GNAC basketball game, am I right? Especially here."

Emerson had been soundly defeated in all four games to start the season, never by fewer than twenty-five points.

"They were pretty competitive in the first period on Wednesday," I said.

Mighty Rob lifted his left asscheek and offered a long, sonorous fart in response.

"Yeah," I said. "I can't argue with that."

Rob waved his hand in front of his nose, then straightened up in his chair and fixed me with an earnest gaze. "Look. The sports beat on this paper has always been the bottom of the totem pole. Now, I know why you volunteered for it, so we might as well get this out of the way right now. We're not getting a press credential for the Red Sox postseason. And even if we were, there's no way in hell you'd get it. I've been busting my hump here for three years, and you'd better believe I'd be all over that like stink on rice if I thought it was a possibility. So just take a minute, come to terms with that, and let's move on."

I shrugged. I figured a press pass for the playoffs was a long shot, but what the hell. It would have been worth sitting through all those volleyball games to be in Fenway Park when the Red Sox finally won the World Series for the first time in sixty-eight years. "Well, the Lions are playing Emmanuel on Sunday afternoon…"

"No, no, no. You're done with sports. You don't seriously want to keep writing up those terrible games, do you?"

"Not really, but…"

"Look, Tommy. You aren't the most ambitious guy who ever

walked through that door. Not the most motivated. Frankly, you don't really seem to know what you're doing here at all."

I stood. "Okay, well. Good talk."

"Sit down, will ya? Let me finish. I'm building to something here. It's the pyramid structure we talked about. I'm laying a base. Now I'm coming to the point."

I sat back down. "Which is?"

"Which is that you've got something a lot of much more motivated, focused, ambitious people in this office are sorely lacking. You can actually write. That piece on the volleyball player, I'm not lying, it was really good. Once I forced you to bear down on it, apply a little discipline. That first draft was a little lazy, wouldn't you agree?"

"Well…"

"Come on. You know what I'm saying. You can do better than these Lions game stories. You're capable of writing something that might really grab some eyeballs. Something you could put in your portfolio."

"Like what?" I envisioned a muckraking expose of the college administration, which was in the process of trying to move the Emerson campus out of Boston and into Lawrence, a depressed North Shore mill town. Was there corruption involved? Bribery? Could I topple the current regime and become a hero to my schoolmates, who had no interest in decamping for East Bumfuck?

"You live in Charlesgate, right? You were there for that false alarm the other night?"

I straightened up in my seat. "Well…yeah…"

"And you know a little something about the history of the place? I mean, you've heard stories. Ouija boards and all that shit."

"Sure, but—"

"So this is what I want. Something that's never been done in the *Berkeley Beacon*. A comprehensive history of the Charlesgate. All the true stories as well as the tall tales. I want you to follow up on all these urban legends. Did Eugene O'Neill really kill himself in there? Was the architect a Satan worshipper? Does that little girl's ghost really roam the halls in the dead of night? I want the ultimate Charlesgate story. A multi-parter. And quite frankly, you're the only guy who can write it. This is gonna make your name and mine, too, just by association. You up for it?"

"Yeah, absolutely."

"Call it something like *Mysteries of Charlesgate*. No… *Charlesgate Confidential*. That's it. Kind of that old-timey tabloid vibe, you know? I'm excited about this. I want you to get started right away."

As I walked out of the *Berkeley Beacon* office that afternoon, I was pretty sure I'd figured out why they called him Mighty Rob. He'd convinced me I was about to write the *In Cold Blood* of haunted dorm stories. I think I floated the eight blocks back to Charlesgate. I slowed as I crossed Mass Ave, passing BosDeli and the happy hour crowd streaming into Crossroads. Dusk was settling over the city, and a cacophony of honking horns drifted from Storrow Drive as anxious commuters tried to squeeze in one last weekend on the Cape before the frost settled in, to admire the foliage or whatever the beautiful people did. I passed my parking space, the broken meter on Beacon Street. No one ever fixed it and my Buick never got a ticket.

Charlesgate now loomed above me. I craned my neck, trying to take in the whole building at once. I counted up seven stories. That was the all-female floor we called the Nunnery. The eighth floor could not be seen from the outside. It was only a half-floor. Not even that, really, just a short hallway with a few rooms on either side. I rarely went up there. The eighth floor crowd was tight-knit and standoffish, and rumors about them abounded. We thought of them as the crazy relatives locked in the attic.

At street level, I stood directly in front of the Beacon Street entrance, which wasn't really an entrance because it was always locked. The doorway was surrounded by intricate carvings, whorls and patterns and cherubic faces. One night while really high on the Rev's weed I'd stared at the faces, imagining they were the lost souls of Charlesgate, trapped in their efforts to escape, now forever part of the building. Maybe that would be a good way to introduce my first article. Probably not.

I rounded the corner to Charlesgate East. The building's name was carved in marble over the front entrance. A half-dozen girls with big hair and small skirts were on their way out, no doubt headed to kick off the weekend at Narcissus or Lipstick or one of the other Kenmore Square dance clubs. I caught the door before it closed and went inside.

I nodded at the RA stationed at the front desk and walked past her into the lobby. The student mailboxes were on the right, directly behind the front desk area. I checked mine. Nothing but a flyer advertising a fraternity's upcoming charity casino night. I continued down the hall, admiring the ornate tile mosaics. The Charlesgate lobby still carried a hint of faded glamour. Upstairs it was all chipped drywall and stained carpeting, but haunting remnants of the Gilded Age survived down here.

The office of the Resident Director, Gerald Torres, was on the right just past the mailboxes. On the wall opposite his door hung a framed poster of Uncle Sam. This was not the traditional "I Want You" pose, but a scarier, more ragged Sam holding a rifle over the legend DON'T WAIT FOR THE DRAFT: VOLUNTEER. It seemed out of place, an artifact of a different era in Charlesgate history. The mounted troops behind him suggested World War I, toward the end of the hotel's status as an elite destination.

"Donnelly!"

I snapped out of my reverie and turned to see Murtaugh stomping down the hall toward me.

"Where the hell have you been? We're ready to go!" He pressed a small laminated card into my hand. My fake ID. It looked…not that great. I had a real Maine license and could readily compare the two, which I did. It was immediately clear that the fake would never work in Maine. Anyone familiar with the real thing would never buy it. And if you looked really closely under a good light, you could see the outlines where the name, address, and signature had been pasted on the back-drop.

"Is this really gonna work?" I asked.

"The Rev went to Crossroads for lunch. He had three beers. No question."

"We're not going to Crossroads."

"Why not?"

"Because everyone's gonna go to Crossroads. Suddenly thirty people, young people the bouncer has never seen before, all show up at the same time. And they all have Maine IDs. No fucking way."

"Okay, that makes sense. So where are we going?"

"The Fallout Shelter."

Murtaugh stared at me liked I'd sprouted two extra heads. "Okay, but where are we *really* going?"

"What's wrong with the Fallout Shelter?"

"Nothing, I guess, if our plan is to get stabbed and dumped in an alley tonight."

Crossroads and the Fallout Shelter were separated by maybe twenty feet. Crossroads was on Beacon and the Fallout Shelter was on Marlborough, and they both rear-ended on the same alley—the alley that dead-ended behind Charlesgate. But in every other way, they were worlds apart. Crossroads was a college pub that gained a little hipster cachet from the fact that the author Richard Yates made his office in a booth at the back. The Fallout Shelter was a dive, pure and simple. It featured dollar Knickerbockers at Happy Hour, which stretched from 3 to 7 P.M., and offered free chicken wings from God knows where every Friday.

"We'll be fine," I said. "Dollar Knicks and free wings. What could go wrong?"

"Fine. But I'm gonna remind you that you said that every day for the rest of your life. Assuming you have one."

We didn't get stabbed and dumped in an alley, but it would be a night to remember. If only I could remember it.

Martin Coleman was hunched over his desktop, wearing out his scroll button, when his partner Ed Carnahan peered over his cubicle wall.

"The fuck you doing, Coltrane? Playing Candy Crush again? Get the fuck off Facebook and let's hit the Tap."

"It's our vic's Facebook page. She has 367 friends. Every one a suspect. You know the odds of a murder victim being killed by one of her own Facebook friends?"

"I do not."

"I don't either, but in most cases, it's pretty fuckin' good. If it's personal. This case, though, I don't think it is."

"All the more reason to shut that shit down and join me at the Tap. Come on, Coltrane." Carnahan always called Coleman "Coltrane," or when he couldn't be bothered with two syllables, "Trane." It was part of their witty salt-and-pepper banter, as mandated in the Boston Detective's Handbook.

"Can't do it, Carny. The wife's making meatloaf."

"Oh, well. Wouldn't want to get between a man and his meat-loaf. So what's the story on the dead chick? Any hot pics?"

"A few. She and her fiancé spent a week in Belize last month. Some bikini shots. But like I said, I don't think this is personal, and it definitely wasn't sexual. The killer took the keys and I think that's all he wanted."

"To what end?"

Coleman leaned back in his chair and cracked his knuckles. "Fuck do I know? All I know is, he had up to fifteen hours in that building before anyone was looking for our vic, and he had all the keys. Still has them, in fact, and it's gonna take management a while to change all the locks. Not just to the condos, but all the offices, conference rooms, storage areas, whatever. So far, all the residents we've been able to contact, nothing is missing. Nothing reported stolen. But that's still in progress."

"A lot of these people must have been home last night. It's not like he would have just let himself in and said, 'Whoops, wrong apartment,' right?"

"Which makes me think he wasn't after anything in the residences. He was after something else."

"Something worth killing for."

"Indeed. So what would that be?"

"An excellent discussion topic for us and the boys down at the Tap."

"No, I'm chasing down some leads here." Coleman minimized his web browser. Facebook disappeared, replaced by a PDF of a typewritten document. Coleman tapped his monitor. "I found this online. It's a thesis paper by an architecture student. Written in 1985."

"Sounds fascinating, but my barstool's getting cold."

"It's a feasibility study. The question is whether the Charlesgate, which was then a college dorm, could be turned back into a luxury hotel, which is what it was a hundred years ago."

"And what's the feasibility?"

"None, according to this guy. And yet, the building has since been converted to upscale condominiums. So I hope this dumbass flunked."

"So this is a lead how?"

"Appendix A is a full set of blueprints for the building. Circa the mid-'80s, anyway. Could come in handy."

"Great. Print 'em out and bring 'em on down to the Tap."

"At that time, the building belonged to Emerson College. So

I called the Emerson library to see if they had anything on the Charlesgate, might give me some clue. Turns out they've got a whole fuckin' file on the place. They put it on hold for me."

"So while I'm at the Tap, you'll be at the library. Figures."

"No. I told you, Donna's making meatloaf. But first thing tomorrow morning, I'll be at the library."

True to his word, Detective Martin Coleman of the Boston homicide division skipped out on nightcaps at the Tap with his partner and the other cops who frequented the place. The Tap wasn't really his speed: white boys watching hockey or listening to headbanging music. He went once in a while, just to keep up appearances, but sometimes the white boys forgot there was a brother in the joint and things got a little uncomfortable. Boston had changed a lot since Coleman had grown up in the Dorchester projects, but a black man could still be made to feel unwelcome now and then, even if he was a homicide detective surrounded by his brothers in blue.

What wasn't true was that his wife Donna was making meat-loaf. Or rather, it *may* have been true. Coleman had no real way of knowing, since Donna had thrown him out of the house three weeks earlier. And while it was undeniably true that she hated the Yankees, Coleman had gone to the ballgame alone the night before, using the empty seat beside him for beer storage. The clerk at the evidence room had given him a ration of shit when he turned the two Red Sox tickets in twelve hours after the game had ended. An oversight, he'd said. Fuck you, the reply.

Now, instead of going home to Medford or to the Econo Lodge in Saugus where he'd been holed up while trying to work things out with the missus, Coleman was on his way to the Emerson College library. It was a straight shot down Tremont Street from BPD headquarters to the library on Boylston Street.

The temperature had dropped some twenty degrees since Coleman arrived at his office three hours earlier. As far as Coleman was concerned, once baseball season started, there was no excuse for the weather ever to dip below forty degrees, but for some reason, New England rarely cooperated with his philosophy. But whenever he was on a case, a big case like this one, long walks were essential to his process.

After forty-five minutes, he arrived at the Emerson library, flashed his badge at the entrance, and got directions to the research desk on the third floor. By the time he reached the third floor Coleman had completely forgotten the directions and ended up wandering aimlessly through the stacks for five minutes before finally spotting a likely candidate for his destination.

"Is this the research desk?"

The librarian smiled. "You must be Detective Coleman."

"That's right, Ms...."

"I'm Sheila. We spoke earlier."

"Right. Sheila. Sorry, I was picturing more of a librarian."

"I am a librarian."

"I know, but...you look like a Hollywood librarian. You know, a hot redhead in nerd glasses. Only in the movies."

"Apparently not. Do you want to see my library sciences degree?"

"Uh...naw, naw. I'll just take the Charlesgate file if you've got it handy."

Sheila smiled tightly, reached under the counter and brought up a thick file jammed with newspaper clippings. "As I explained, this file can't leave the premises. Unless you have a warrant."

"No, I don't have a warrant. And that's fine. I've got all night. And look, I'm sorry if I offended you. I guess I'm a little old school. I haven't been to the library in a long time, and Mrs.

Anderson, my high school librarian, well, she looked like Shrek with a bad weave."

Sheila laughed. "Well, my high school librarian was Mr. Linscott and he looked like Beetlejuice. So this works both ways, you know."

Coleman picked up the file and winked. Then he winced. "I just winked, didn't I?"

Sheila laughed again. "You did. But it wasn't *that* creepy."

"Well, I'm…I was about to say I'm a happily married man, but I think my wife would disagree with that."

"Your wife, huh? Well, you know, if you were single…"

Sheila had Coleman's full attention.

"…I'd still have a boyfriend. So sucks to be you."

Coleman laughed, tucked the file under his arm, and set off to find a quiet place to read. He found a couch on the second floor near the film studies section and settled in with the folder. It was arranged roughly chronologically, from most recent to oldest. The newer articles were fluff pieces from the real estate section about the rebirth of the Back Bay as a high-end residential community. Any references to the history of the Charlesgate were brief and unenlightening. Coleman flipped back through the stack, pausing on a yellowing article from the Emerson newspaper, the *Berkeley Beacon*, dated October 10, 1986.

The headline read: *Charlesgate Confidential, Part I: Myth vs. Reality*.

The byline read: *Tommy Donnelly*.

The Berkeley Beacon

October 10, 1986

Charlesgate Confidential, Part I: Myth vs. Reality

By Tommy Donnelly, *Beacon* Staff

Even if you don't live there, you've probably heard the stories about Charlesgate, the Emerson dormitory that houses nearly 400 students at the corner of Charlesgate East and Beacon Street. The architect who designed the building practiced black magic and committed suicide in the building. The famous playwright Eugene O'Neill also died within its walls. A little girl fell down an elevator shaft and her ghost still haunts the sixth floor. Ouija boards are strictly forbidden by the Emerson administration.

Welcome to *Charlesgate Confidential*, a multi-part series that will attempt to unravel fact from fiction and set the record straight about the history of this notorious building. This first installment deals with some of the best-known urban legends from Charlesgate's nearly 100-year history.

MYTH: The Charlesgate's architect killed himself in the building he'd designed.

REALITY: J. Pickering Putnam did die in the Charlesgate Hotel, but it was not by his own hand. Born in Boston in 1847, Putnam studied at the École des Beaux-Arts in Paris and the Royal Academy of

Architecture in Berlin before returning to the United States in 1872. Putnam designed a number of buildings in the Back Bay, including several brownstones on Marlborough Street, but the Charlesgate Hotel was his crowning achievement. Built in 1891 at a cost of $170,000, the Charlesgate was described as Boston's crown jewel upon opening, catering to the most exclusive clientele on the Eastern seaboard. Putnam himself was one of its permanent residents, living in the building until his death in 1917. There is no indication that Putnam died by other than natural causes. Nor is there any reason to believe Putnam's design for the Charlesgate incorporated building materials specifically chosen to attract or entrap paranormal entities, like something out of *Ghostbusters*. Putnam died before he could see his dream project lose its luster with the onset of the Great Depression. One thing seems certain: If Putnam could see what was going on in the Charlesgate today, he'd never stop rolling in his grave.

MYTH: Eugene O'Neill died in the Charlesgate.

REALITY: This one is easily disproved, although the confusion is understandable. O'Neill did die in a Back Bay hotel that is now a "haunted" dormitory, but it wasn't Charlesgate. Boston University owned the Charlesgate in 1953, so it's unlikely O'Neill would have died there unless he happened to be dating a young coed. It did not yet own the Shelton Hotel, however, which is where the author of *The Iceman Cometh* and *Long Day's Journey into Night* spent his final days. He died in Room 401 on November 27, 1953, and rumors persist to this day that his ghost haunts the fourth floor of Shelton Hall. It's easy to see how one ghost-infested dorm might be mistaken for another.

MYTH: The sixth floor is haunted by the ghost of a little girl who fell down an elevator shaft to her death.

REALITY: This story has surfaced in several articles about Charlesgate's alleged paranormal history, but at press time, the ghost had yet to respond to the *Beacon*'s interview requests. One version of the rumor states that it was Putnam's daughter Elsa who fell to her death and now haunts the Charlesgate. We know this to be false: Elsa lived in Boston until 1979 and had four children of her own. Most versions of the story entail the little girl looking for her ball, or the ball rolling out of nowhere down a long hallway, followed by the ghost child. "It was two little girls," sixth-floor resident and confirmed believer Jules Van Cleve insisted during a recent interview. "I came around the corner and saw two little girls standing at the end of the hall, staring at me." When reminded that this happened in the 1980 Stanley Kubrick film *The Shining*, Van Cleve said, "Oh, that's right. That movie scared the [expletive] out of me."

MYTH: Ouija boards are banned in Charlesgate by the Emerson administration.

REALITY: No Emerson administrator contacted by the *Beacon* was willing to admit this on the record. "Are you kidding?" said Charlesgate resident director Gerald Torres. "Like we don't have enough to worry about with you scofflaws smuggling refrigerators and beer and illegal narcotics into the building? I'm going to confiscate a board game by Parker Brothers? Get out of my office." However, one RA speaking on condition of anonymity insisted that Ouija boards were singled out as contraband during an orientation meeting. Clearly some mysteries of Charlesgate were meant to remain unsolved.

JUNE 11, 1946

"Your two minutes are up."

The Little Rascals had said nothing since Dave T presented his ultimatum. They'd exchanged a number of meaningful looks, but the meaning remained unstated. If Dave T had to guess, though, he'd peg the meaning as something along the lines of, "What the fuck are we gonna do? Besides shit our pants?"

Finally Jake spoke up. "Come on, pal. You're not just gonna shoot one of us in the head."

"Oh, I assure you, I am. I'm either gonna shoot one of you in the head or, if you don't give me a name, I'm gonna shoot alla ya in the head. And it's gonna happen right now, so give me a fucking name."

Dave T aimed directly at Jake's nose. Jake swallowed hard. "Pat," he said.

Shane didn't hesitate. "Yeah, Pat."

Every vein in Pat's neck popped. "What? Fuck you guys! I vote Shane!"

"Doesn't matter," said Dave T. "You could vote for the Pope of Rome, but you'll still be outnumbered two to one."

"Oh, Jesus!" Pat clutched his head, leaned forward, and ejected the contents of his stomach. Jake and Shane looked away. The choice was really no choice at all. Jake and Shane were brothers. Pat was a cousin—a cousin they'd grown up with, as close as a brother—but a cousin nonetheless. And it was his big mouth that had gotten them into this mess.

"One thing, though." Dave T stood and walked to the door, keeping the gun trained on Pat all the while. "Your friend here was right. I'm not just gonna shoot you in the head." Dave T rapped his knuckles on the door. It opened and the Casey cousins stepped inside. "You're gonna take a ride with my associates here. So say your goodbyes, because there's no coming back from this one."

Pat sat up, wiped his mouth on his sleeve, and stared down Jake, then Shane. Neither would meet his gaze. "No need for goodbyes. I got no family here."

Dave T gestured for Pat to stand, which he did on unsteady legs. A Casey grabbed him by each arm and escorted him from the room. Dave T closed the door behind them.

"What are they gonna do with him? Where are they taking him?" Shane asked.

"What do you care?" said Dave T. "You were ready to see his brains splattered all over the wall a minute ago. It's like I said, the cousins are taking him for a ride. All you need to know is, you're never gonna see him again. He's part of your old life. Your new life starts right now. It's gonna be better than the old one, I guarantee you."

Jake and Shane both stared at the floor, saying nothing.

"I'm gonna assume your silence infers I have your full attention, so here's how this is gonna go. You boys are going home. You're gonna collect all the money you stole from me and my friends, minus whatever you've already spent on whores and booze. We'll figure out how much that was, and you'll pay me that amount out of your share of the job we're gonna do together. Plus interest. Let's call it twenty percent. At some point tomorrow afternoon you're gonna get a phone call. I'm gonna call the pay phone at the Rosebud Diner, so you be there with the money all afternoon tomorrow. I'll call with a time and a place for us to meet. You're gonna meet me there, just you two. You try anything funny, you say anything to anyone else about this, and you won't see me at this meeting place. You won't see anything. You might hear a couple of gunshots right before a bullet passes through each one of your tiny brains, courtesy of the cousins. You got all that?"

Jake and Shane both nodded.

"All right. You follow these instructions to the letter and we'll talk about that job I mentioned. You boys stand to make a lot of money. More than you ever dreamed or, quite frankly, deserve. So don't fuck this up. All right?"

They nodded again.

"All right. You can go now."

The remaining Little Rascals opted to walk the two miles back to Pi Alley. The first mile passed in silence. Finally Shane spoke up.

"What do you think they did with Pat?"

"I doubt they sent him on an all-expenses-paid trip to Havana."

"So what are we gonna do about it?"

"What do you *want* to do about it?"

"I dunno...I mean, Pat's family. We've been tight since we were kids, but...on the other hand, Dave T would have been well within his rights to kill all three of us. Maybe we should consider ourselves lucky to be alive."

"Right."

"And not only that...you heard what he said. We stand to make a lot of money. I mean, I feel terrible for Pat, wherever he is, but this thing may work out for us after all."

"Uh-huh."

"I mean, if I'm wrong, tell me I'm wrong."

"You're wrong. You may not have noticed, but that man back there? He pulled the trigger on all three of us in that room. You and I, we just haven't hit the floor yet."

"You're not making any sense."

"Look. Why do you think he doesn't want to do this job, whatever it is, why do you think he doesn't want the cousins for this job?"

"Like he said. This type of work, whatever it is, he prefers us."

"That's right. He prefers us because he can't just kill the Casey cousins after the job. Some very dangerous people down Providence might take that the wrong way. But us? He sure as shit can kill us when it's over, and nobody says boo. They might even applaud."

Shane processed this piece of intelligence the rest of the way back to the car. He kept his mouth shut for most of the drive, but finally spoke up once they were safely inside the Somerville city limits.

"So what are we gonna do?"

"We're gonna do just what he says. We're gonna follow his instructions. We're gonna play along, and somehow, somewhere along the way, we're gonna figure out how to kill him first."

OCTOBER 4, 1986

Things were moving. Things that shouldn't have been moving. I was perfectly still. I was clutching my pillow to my head, holding on for dear life. Images from the night before came into my brain unbidden. I clenched my eyelids tight, trying to ward them off. No good could come of remembering.

I detected movement in the room. Clanking noises. A light. I weighed my options. If I held the pillow tightly against my face, could I smother myself to death? Probably not, but I would eventually pass out and that wouldn't be so bad.

But…things were moving, as I mentioned. Any second I might have to pray to the porcelain god. Yorking all over my bed would do me no good. So, with great care and no sudden movements, I peeled the pillow from my face. The light hit me like a prison shiv to each eyeball. I made out a shadowy figure looming over me. It could only be Murtaugh.

"On second thought," I said, "let's not go out last night."

Murtaugh shook his head. "Too late for that, chief. Do you remember anything about last night?"

"Trying not to."

"I bet."

"We went to the Fallout Shelter. We had…a few beers. There may have been some shots."

"Oh yeah. Shots of Jack. You bought the first round. And the fourth."

I sat up. Very, very slowly. "Decent jukebox. They had…Prince."

"You reenacted the entire 'Kiss' video. Solo."

"How did that go over?"

"You got a standing O."

"So far, so good. And stop shaking your head at me. You were drinking, too."

"Yeah. The difference is, I've been drinking since I was a sophomore in high school. Whereas you were a good boy."

"Jail."

"What?"

"The Charles Street Jail. I'm seeing the Charles Street Jail in my mental slideshow from last night."

"Yeah. We went to Buzzy's." Buzzy's was a sandwich stand right outside the walls of the Charles Street Jail. They were famous for their roast beef sandwiches, which were inedible any other time of day but really hit the spot at two in the morning after a long night at the Fallout Shelter.

"Oh yeah. Buzzy's."

"Ask me how my sandwich was."

"How was your sandwich?"

"I don't know. Because you yuked all over our table, then you grabbed my Fabulous Roast Beef out of my hands, wiped your mouth on it, and tried to hand it back to me."

That did sound vaguely familiar. "Oh. How did you not punch me in the nose?"

"It's not too late."

The room had gradually come into focus around me. One problem: It wasn't our bedroom. It was the back room. The study room. The TV room. Or...the Love Room.

"So...why am I not in my bed?" I had my blanket and pillow, but I was lying on the futon we kept in the back room.

"Cast your mind back through the hours. Is there a particular face you remember? A face...really close to your face?"

"No, I..." But wait. There was such a face. "Oh no. Purple Debbie?"

"Purple Debbie."

I weighed my options. There was a slight chance the five-story drop into the Pit wouldn't kill me, so I decided to press on. "Details. I need details."

"Well…we got back here around quarter to three in the morning and you thought it would be a good time to go ghost-hunting. Research for your great investigation. You dragged me down to the basement and started banging on this locked door, because you were sure that's where they were hiding. When I finally convinced you to give it up and come upstairs, you decided that would be a good time to run through the halls banging on everyone's door and inviting them to a party in our room. You also stopped at all the bathrooms and turned on all the showers, which was just *so* hilarious."

"Oh my goodness."

"So about eight or ten people decided to take you up on your offer. It was as if I had brought home an exotic animal specimen and everyone wanted to get a look before the zookeeper showed up to take you home. Any of this ringing a bell?"

"Um…did I flip somebody off?"

"Oh, you flipped *everybody* off. That was your big move. And the more people laughed, the angrier you got. Finally you told everyone to get the fuck out, which they did. All except Purple Debbie. She was concerned. She thought she should tuck you in and stay by your side to make sure you didn't choke to death on your own vomit."

"That sounds like her."

"Yeah, I thought so. And after all, what could happen? She has that legendary boyfriend from high school she'd never, ever cheat on. Her future husband, you know."

"Brad. No—Chad."

"Chet, I think. Anyway, it doesn't matter, because Brad or Chad or Chet, whatever, he called Purple Debbie the other night to let her know he met someone else."

"He's fucking another girl?"

"No. He's smoking some dude's dick up there in Haverhill. Which I think comes as no big surprise to the rest of us, but Purple Debbie…well, you can imagine."

"Oh, Jesus. This is turning into the worst John Hughes movie ever."

"No shit. So anyway, Purple Debbie tucks you in. She kisses you on the cheek. You seem like you're completely passed out. She kisses you on the forehead. Still nothing. She kisses you on the lips. Now, all of a sudden, you're making out with Purple Debbie."

"Oh no."

"Oh yeah. And it's like really loud and slurpy. So finally the Rev, who's been trying to sleep this whole time, he yells, 'Get a room!' So Purple Debbie takes your hand and helps you up, grabs your pillow and blanket, leads you in here, and locks the door behind you. None of this sounds familiar?"

It did, very, very vaguely. "So then what?"

"How the fuck should I know? If you want the details, you're gonna have to get 'em from Purple Debbie. If you've got the balls."

"Well, what time did she leave?"

"No idea. She was gone when I woke up, which was about five minutes before you woke up."

"Ugh. Jackie wasn't around for any of this, was she?"

"No. But she's gonna hear about it. You know how it goes around here. Besides, I keep telling you to forget about her and get laid. Looks like you did. Maybe."

Once again I pondered my options. "It's not too late for me to transfer to another school. The University of Maine would still take me."

"But you can't use your fake ID up there."

"That doesn't matter, because I'm never drinking again."

Murtaugh was unconvinced.

APRIL 25, 2014

Coleman woke up slumped in a chair, the contents of the Charlesgate file spilled all over his lap. Still groggy, he collected himself, stuffing the various articles back into the folder. He checked his phone. It was 4:30 in the morning.

He wandered through the stacks until he found the research desk. Sheila was still there.

"Good morning, Detective Coleman."

"Are you closed? Why didn't you wake me up?"

"We're open 24/7 for the two weeks before finals. And I didn't wake you because you looked like you needed the rest. We do have a policy against overnight napping, but what was I gonna do, call the cops on you?"

"I guess not."

"Find anything interesting in that file?"

"Umm...maybe." In fact, Coleman had found something very interesting. So interesting it just might be a valuable lead, if only he could believe a word of it. "Do you have a copier I could use? Or a scanner?"

"Sure. Can I see your student ID?"

"Uh...what?"

"You need a student, faculty, or staff ID to operate the scanner. So we can charge your account."

"Well, Sheila, seeing as how I'm not a student or faculty or staff, do you think I could talk you into scanning some documents for me?"

"Maybe. Of course, you understand if I do that for you, my account will be charged."

"Right. Well, let me ask you this: What time does your shift here end?"

"Six in the morning."

"Okay, so how about this: You do this for me, and I'll buy you breakfast. How does that sound?"

"Breakfast where?"

"Breakfast wherever. I usually do Dunkin', but…"

"Oh, no. No Dunkin'. The Bristol Lounge."

"Never heard of it."

"It's in the Four Seasons. It's got four and a half stars on Yelp."

"Fine. But I'm gonna need one more favor from you."

"What's that?"

"These articles I want you to scan for me, they're from the Emerson newspaper. I'd like to get in touch with the guy who wrote them, name of Tommy Donnelly. Have you got access to some kind of database of former students, you could look this guy up for me?"

"I do. It's called Google."

"Excuse me?"

"Or you could contact his agent. We've got a few of his books here, you could look up the name."

"I don't follow…wait a minute. *Thomas* Donnelly? *Zuma Nine* Thomas Donnelly?"

"One and the same."

Thomas Donnelly was a famous true-crime writer, Coleman knew, because his wife was addicted to Donnelly's books. His best-sellers included *Zuma Nine*, the story of a gang of surfers who, inspired by the movie *Point Break*, began robbing banks up and down the California coast, and *Army of Angels*, an exposé of a white supremacist group operating a Christian summer camp in the Texas hill country.

"I didn't make the connection. Well, now I really want to talk to him."

"Take a number. The alumni office has been trying to reel him in for years. They'd love him to come back and speak at graduation, and they'd *really* love him to open his wallet and put a new wing on the journalism building, but no such luck."

"Why is that?"

"Dunno. Maybe he had a bad experience here. He lived in that haunted dorm you've been reading about, right?"

"Yeah, but after reading his articles, I get the impression he didn't exactly believe the place was haunted. So where is he now?"

"As far as I know, he lives in Australia. About as far away as you can get."

"Australia, huh?"

"Yeah, he went down there to research that book on the Outback Ripper. *Deadsville*? And I guess he never came back. Why do you want to talk to him anyway?"

"Something he wrote in one of these articles. It's probably nothing. Definitely far-fetched. Anyway, you can read all about it while you're making those scans. I'll be back at my comfy chair, grabbing a few more winks."

An hour later, Sheila woke Coleman by tossing a stapled twenty-page document into his lap. "I scanned 'em *and* copied 'em for you. You'll have to give me your email address to get the PDFs."

"Oh, I get it. This was all a scam to get my digits."

"Your 'digits'? 1992 is calling, detective. It wants your high-top fade back."

"Were you even born in 1992?"

"Sure wasn't."

Coleman winced. "Well, as a matter of fact, I did have a

high-top fade in 1992. But in my defense, I was a junior in high school."

Sheila did some mental calculations. "So you're old enough to be my perverted uncle."

"If you're into that."

"That's for me to know and you to find out."

"Let's get some pancakes."

After pancakes, and after an animated discussion of Tommy Donnelly's Charlesgate articles, and after Coleman had determined that Sheila was not, in fact, into the whole perverted uncle thing (but was *really* into the whole free breakfast thing), and after convincing himself this was just as well, because he still had hopes of saving his marriage, Coleman headed back to BPD headquarters. True to Sheila's word, the scans of Donnelly's Charlesgate articles were waiting in his inbox when he got back to his desk. A Google search later, he had confirmed that Donnelly's agent was one Dana Knowles at Levine Greenberg in New York City.

"So how was the meatloaf?"

The sound of his partner's voice derailed Coleman's train of thought.

"Huh? Oh…great. Great as always."

Carnahan cracked his knuckles. "Really? Because it looks to me like you're wearing the same clothes you had on when I left here last night."

"Nah. All my suits look like this."

"Don't bullshit me, Coltrane. I am a trained Boston po-lice detective. You ain't been home. Let me sniff your crotch."

"Excuse me?"

"What? You afraid I'll smell the scent of a woman on you? The sweet, sweet smell of puss-ay?"

"No, I just don't want your nose anywhere near my junk. I ain't been with no other woman, Carny."

"That don't mean you haven't tried."

"I ended up spending the night at the Emerson College library, if you must know. I might have an interesting lead on our Charlesgate vic. A long shot, but interesting."

"Well, put a pin in it. I have a *real* lead on our vic. We heard back from one of the Charlesgate residents, a Mrs. Osborne. She was out of town for a week. Got home last night, found her front door was unlocked. And she'd been robbed."

"No shit."

"No shit. We're seeing her at noon. Maybe you should take a fuckin' shower."

JUNE 12, 1946

The Rosebud Diner in Somerville was a refurbished trolley car that smelled of strong coffee and burnt toast and employed only geriatric women with foul tempers. Jake and Shane Devlin sat in a corner booth, picking at a plate of bacon and eggs. Jake had his Navy-issued duffel bag at his feet. The bag was stuffed with twenties and fifties and hundreds—all the money they'd jacked from Dave T's card game, minus what they'd spent on their three-day debauch.

"I could really use a drink," said Shane.

"No way. We need to be stone-cold sober. All our senses sharp. Our lives are on the line here."

"A condemned man is entitled to a last drink."

"That's a last cigarette he's entitled to. Smoke up. All you want. But no booze. Take this fucking seriously."

"I am, but—"

"You aren't. You weren't over there, living every day with death staring you in the face."

"Hey, it's not like I didn't *want* to go."

The pay phone rang and a hunched, grim-faced waitress answered it. A few seconds later, she gestured to Jake.

"This is it," said Jake, standing. Shane watched him walk to the phone, take the receiver from the waitress, listen without saying much, then hang up and return to the booth.

"So?"

"So there's a taxi waiting for us outside. Pre-paid. Destination unknown. We get in and it takes us there."

"Or…"

"Or what?"

"Or we take that satchel full of cash, get a different taxi, take it to the airport, and buy two tickets to…wherever the fuck. Havana, like you said."

"And then what?"

"And then we live. And then this cocksucker doesn't get to shoot us in the head. Who cares 'and then what'?"

"This guy, his connections, you think he can't find us in Havana?"

"Then fucking Brazil. Australia."

"You got a passport?"

"No."

Jake picked up the duffel bag. "So let's go."

"Mexico, then. Canada."

"Shane, look around you. These guys sitting at the counter. The booth by the door. These people are not our friends. I guarantee you, we walk out of here and don't get in that taxi, we won't get half a block before one of 'em spatters our brains all over the pavement. Now get the fuck up and let's go. We're gonna see this through and we're gonna wait for our moment and when it comes, we're not gonna miss it."

With the eagerness of a death row prisoner rising to walk his last mile, Shane followed Jake out of the Rosebud. The noonday sun was jarring after the dank of the diner, and the air was heavy, the first really humid day of the year. The taxi idled in front of the newsstand across the street. Before climbing into the back seat, Shane caught a glimpse of the *Boston Daily Record*, its sports page headline trumpeting the Red Sox victory over Cleveland the day before.

"If I die today," he said to Jake, once he'd settled in his seat, "I've lived my whole life without ever seeing the Red Sox win the World Series."

"Settle down," said Jake.

"This is the year. Teddy back from the war, knocking the cover off the ball. I really wanted to see it."

"You'll see it. Just get a grip." Jake was trying to concentrate on the taxi's route, in hopes of gaining whatever slight advantage such knowledge might yield. At Porter Square, the cabbie turned left onto Massachusetts Avenue.

"So where are we going today?" Shane asked, taking the direct approach.

"I don't talk to you," the driver responded.

"Well, I hate to tell ya, pal, but you just did."

The driver had no response to that.

"You Greek?" Shane asked. "I used to work with a Greek guy, looked a lot like you. You got a brother?"

Nothing. Jake continued to track the route, not that there was much to it. The driver stuck to Mass Ave through Harvard and Central Squares.

"You follow baseball at all? The Sox laid a whipping on Cleveland last night. I know it's only June, but they're looking pretty good."

Greek or not, baseball fan or not, the driver had nothing to add. The cab was crossing the bridge over the Charles River from Cambridge to Boston. At Beacon Street, the cabbie turned right. Jake realized they were now a block from the Charlesgate, where he and Shane—and Pat, can't forget Pat, God rest his soul, probably—had robbed Dave T's card game, only four days earlier. It had seemed like a good idea at the time.

"So we're going to the Charlesgate, huh?" Shane had picked up on it, too. But the driver blew through the intersection of Beacon and Charlesgate East. At Kenmore Square he made a left onto Brookline Ave. He pulled to a stop in front of Lefty's Tavern at the corner of Brookline and Lansdowne.

"You get out here."

"Yeah," said Shane. "I hope they fuckin' tipped ya, 'cause you ain't gettin' jack from us."

Jake grabbed his duffel and he and Shane stepped out of the cab. In a mirror image of their getaway from the poker game a few nights earlier, the sidewalks were now crowded with pedestrians streaming into Fenway Park. Across the street, the famous left-field wall loomed.

"This is good," said Jake.

"How do you figure?"

"Public place. Day game. This guy's connected, but no one's connected enough to waste us in Lefty's on game day. Let's just play it cool."

Dave T was sitting at the bar with someone Jake didn't recognize. He looked like George Raft in *They Drive by Night*. The Casey cousins were nowhere to be seen. On the bar next to Dave T's drink was a tin canister of some sort, about the size of a coffee can. Jake dropped his duffel at Dave T's feet and sat on the stool beside him. Shane took the stool to his left.

"How much is in there?" Dave T asked.

"You don't want to count it?" Jake replied.

"Why should I count it? Are you planning to lie to me?"

"Of course not. No point. There's $12,736."

"All right. Well, I happen to know there was fifteen large in the drawer that night. Ten players, $1,500 buy-in. So right off the bat, we know you spent $2,264 on your three-day bender. Impressive."

"We spent $1,264," said Jake. "I put a grand in an envelope for Pat's mother this morning."

"Least you could do," said Dave T. "But not my problem. Comes out of your end just the same. So: twenty percent equals three large, plus $2,264 equals $5,264 out of your take of this job. How you split that up, I could give a shit."

The George Raft lookalike hadn't moved, not even to give

Jake and Shane the once-over or acknowledge their existence in any way.

"Who's your friend?" Shane asked.

"This is Mr. Cahill. He's my driver when I need one. If you're waiting for Mr. Cahill to shake your hand or say howdy-doody, you'll be waiting until doomsday."

"That's fine," said Shane. "What I'd really like is a drink."

"You don't need a drink," said Jake.

"No, that's fine. We should all have a drink. Dickie! Three cold beers over here and another ice water for Mr. Cahill."

The bartender, Dickie, popped open three Narragansetts and set them on the bar, then refilled Mr. Cahill's glass from the fountain.

"Fifteen grand," said Dave T. "You jamokes risked your lives for fifteen grand, and you didn't know what to do with it when you got it. If I hadn't caught up with you, you'da blown it all on whores and booze. And now one of you is…"

"What?" said Shane. "One of us is what? Where's Pat? What did those animals do to him?"

"You gotta let that go, Porky."

"Don't you fuckin' call me—"

"*Shane*." Jake flashed him the devil eyes. "Let it go."

"Listen to your friend…Shane. We're on to new business now. And business is good. It's gonna make that fifteen grand look like a drop in the bucket. I'm talking about millions. The biggest heist this city has ever seen. And it's gonna be like taking candles from a baby."

"Candy," said Shane.

"What?"

"Candy. The saying is 'like taking candy from a baby.' What would a baby be doing with candles?"

"What the fuck do I care? Point is, we got no worries at all.

Now finish your beers. Mr. Cahill and I have tickets to the game today, and your taxi is waiting for you outside. The trunk is gonna be open. There's something in there for you. Take it out, get in the back seat, and take a look at it. The driver will take you back to the Rosebud."

"And then what?"

"I'll be in touch, next day or two. Oh, one more thing." Dave T slid the tin canister across the bar to Shane.

"What the hell is this?"

"Take a peek."

Shane pried the lid loose and popped it off. He peered into the canister.

"It's your cousin Pat," said Dave T. "I don't want there to be no confusion. You don't need to know the specifics. I sympathize with your loss, but we all know it had to be done. Out of respect, as a gesture of good faith, I'm giving you the remains to dispose of as you see fit. Me, I'd want to be scattered on the warning track across the street. Forever Fenway. Now enjoy the rest of your day. Go Sox."

Dave T raised his beer. Mr. Cahill sipped his water. Shane closed the lid and tucked the canister under his arm. He and Jake got up and exited the tavern to find their taxi waiting right where they'd left it. The only difference, as promised, was that the trunk was now open. Jake and Shane approached it and looked inside.

"What the fuck? We're doing his dry cleaning now?"

Sure enough, the only thing in the trunk was a dry cleaning bag. Jake reached in and lifted it out, tossing it over his shoulder. He and Shane got in the back seat of the cab. Shane held up the canister.

"Can you believe this guy? The balls on him."

Jake shot a glance at the cabbie. "Save it, Shane. Let's see what we got here."

As the driver U-turned and retraced his route back through Kenmore Square, Jake unzipped the garment bag. Catching a glimpse of its contents, he furrowed his brow. He unzipped it further and showed it to Shane.

"Fucking cop uniforms?" said Shane. "What the hell is this guy getting us into?"

OCTOBER 6, 1986

Two days later, Operation Avoid Purple Debbie was still in full effect. I'd steered clear of the Canteen, even though my financial situation didn't exactly lend itself to paying for meals. Fortunately I'd been able to scrounge enough Wild Pizza coupons to keep myself alive on under five dollars a day. After wasting all of Saturday holed up in the Love Room with a pillow over my head, I'd spent Sunday at the public library on Boylston trying to research my Charlesgate series. One small problem: I had no idea what I was doing. I found a book on historic buildings of Boston, but it had been published in 1923, when Charlesgate was hardly historic. Boston was brimming with *real* history, after all, and my dorm didn't quite hold the cultural significance of Faneuil Hall or the Old North Church.

I sifted through volumes of *Boston Globe* indexes, but found only a few scattered references to Charlesgate. Using those references, I was able to retrieve the corresponding rolls of microfilm, but most of the articles made only fleeting references to the hotel, usually in society page columns about the well-to-do types who happened to be staying there on a given weekend.

Finally I admitted defeat and made my way to the research desk. An Ichabod Crane lookalike regarded my approach like that of a flea-bitten stray.

"Um…hi. I'm researching an article on a particular building here in town, and I'm not having much luck."

"That is a shame."

"Yeeeah, so that's why I was wondering if you could help me.

It's the Charlesgate? At 4 Charlesgate East between Beacon and Marlborough?"

"I am familiar with the Charlesgate."

"Oh, great! So…where should I start?"

"You should not. You should stop."

"Excuse me?"

"You should not write the article at all."

I took a step back and surveyed my surroundings. "What is this, a prank? Is there a hidden camera in here?"

"I should hope not."

"Well, maybe I'm missing something here, but I thought you were the research librarian. I'm doing research. It's really not your business why, or whether it's worth doing."

"It is not worth doing."

"Hey, listen—"

"In fact, you should forget all about that building. Pick another. There are many wonderfully historic buildings here in Boston."

"Look, I don't know what your problem…oh. Wait. I get it. You…you actually believe the place is haunted, don't you? Oh, you have got to be kidding me. What, you think if I write this article, demonic spirits will devour my soul?"

"Of course not. Sir, I could easily point you to volumes with titles like *Haunted Hub* and *Real Boston Ghost Stories*. You will find many fanciful tales of the Charlesgate within their covers. They are rubbish. The last thing this world needs is another article spewing the same old nonsense."

"Well, that's not your problem."

The research librarian let out a heavy theatrical sigh. "Indeed. You will find the books I mentioned, and others like them, in the Occult section." He began to write some numbers down on a notepad. "But I must tell you, the history of the Charlesgate is rich enough without having to resort to this spookshow poppy-cock."

"So lay it on me, Jeeves. I don't know why you assume I'm only interested in the occult aspect."

He peered over his Nathaniel Hawthorne spectacles, as if seeing me for the first time. "Very well. If you can come back in a few days, I should be able to pull some material for you. In the meantime, you may want to check the *Architectural Digest* indices for articles about J. Pickering Putnam. He is the architect who designed the Charlesgate. I would also suggest any number of Houdini biographies you'll find on the second floor."

"Houdini? Did he live in the Charlesgate?"

"No, but he did attend a séance there in 1924. A séance he thoroughly debunked, I might add."

"Cool. I'll check it out."

"And of course…" The librarian handed me the notepaper with the Dewey decimals he'd jotted down.

"Thanks," I said. "I'll check in with you in a few days."

"Fair enough."

I found the books he'd mentioned and several others of similar ilk. The same stories—half-assed anecdotes, really—were repeated in each of them with little variation, but of the bunch, *Haunted Hub* was the most promising. It was more detailed, it debunked several urban myths reported as fact in the other books, and best of all, the author lived in Boston and he'd thanked his agent in the acknowledgments. Tracking him down shouldn't be difficult.

Another idea had occurred to me as well. When Emerson took over the Charlesgate in 1981, the building came with several rent-controlled tenants the college had been powerless to evict. At least one of them still lived in the building, and she was a legendary presence on the third floor, regarded by some as yet another supernatural manifestation. New residents were inevitably shaken to encounter what appeared to be a sixty-something bag lady, often smoking a cigar and muttering to herself as she made her way between the elevator and her apartment. No one knew her name and everyone was convinced she hated the students who surrounded her with a white-hot fury. Yet she was the only link between Charlesgate's current incarnation and its murky past. I would have to talk to her, or at least try.

I figured the odds of reaching a literary agent at his office on Sunday afternoon were long, but it was still too early to head back to the dorm if Operation Avoid Purple Debbie was going to be a success. I took a leisurely stroll to the Nickelodeon and saw *Blue Velvet* for the third time. Even with my student discount it was a costly avoidance strategy, but I figured I was safer with Frank Booth than with Purple Debbie at this point.

The movie ended at quarter to six and I was still in no hurry to get back home, so I headed over to Pizza Pad for a slice. After a moment's hesitation, I ordered a beer with it. So much for never drinking again. They didn't even check my ID.

I took a seat in a booth near a television broadcasting the six o'clock news on WBZ. The sportscaster was previewing the American League Championship Series between the Red Sox and the California Angels, set to get underway the following night at Fenway Park, just two blocks from where I sat. Several members of the team, including first baseman Bill Buckner, commented on the team's postseason hopes.

"The dreams are that you're gonna have a good series and win," said Buckner. "The nightmares are that you're gonna let the winning run score on a ground ball through your legs. Those things happen, you know. I think a lot of it is just fate."

I wish I could tell you this struck me as either a profoundly sane admission from a professional athlete or a jinx for the ages, but the fact is, it hardly made an impression at the time. I was too wrapped in my own problems to give much thought to the baseball playoffs I'd been hyped up for just a few days earlier. Truthfully, I wasn't quite sure why I was so intent on avoiding Purple Debbie. I'd never thought of her in any kind of romantic context, both because of her incessant yammering about her boyfriend and my own unrealistic feelings for Jackie St. John. And it's not that Purple Debbie wasn't cute, but...she just seemed too high school to seriously consider as a romantic prospect, even though she was actually a few weeks older than me.

Still, I wasn't particularly proud of my chosen course of avoidance. She was a friend, after all, and a floormate I'd have to see on a nearly daily basis no matter what happened. Who knows, maybe we'd both laugh it off and everything would go back to normal.

I trudged back to Charlesgate with two equally disquieting goals: to clear the air with Purple Debbie and to interview the residential tenant on the third floor. As Bill Buckner had predicted, it all came down to fate. When the elevator opened in the Charlesgate lobby, I nearly ran straight into Purple Debbie.

"Oh...hey," I managed.

"Where the hell have you been?"

"Uh, well...I'm working on this piece for the *Beacon*. A series, actually. I've been mostly holed up at the public library, but I was looking for you earlier."

"Uh-huh."

I glanced over at the RA on duty at the front desk. It was the pompous dude from the second floor who made a point of letting everyone know he was a direct descendant of Patrick Henry.

"Hey, can we talk somewhere a little more private?"

"Actually, I have a date," she said.

"Oh. Wow. Back on the horse, huh?"

"A date with *Chad*. My boyfriend."

"Uhhh…okaaay."

"What is *that* supposed to mean?"

"It's just…I thought I heard you two broke up?"

"Who told you *that*?"

"Uh…nobody. Just…that's the word on the street."

"The word on the street? What are you even talking about?"

"I…must be confused, I guess. Look, I've got to work on this article. If you want to talk later—"

"Whatever." She pushed past me and headed out the front door. For a minute I didn't know how to feel. After a bit more consideration, I decided I'd gotten off easy. One daunting task down, one to go. I jogged up the two flights of stairs to the third floor and knocked on the door to #311.

The door opened a crack, revealing a pair of wide-open eyes above a chain lock. "There you are! What took you so long?"

The door closed, I heard the chain being removed, and it opened again. I stepped inside. Walls of cardboard boxes on either side of me formed a narrow hallway leading into the room, which smelled of cabbage and stale cigar smoke. A brownish haze hung in the air. In front of the window overlooking the Pit stood a Christmas tree, fully decorated and lit.

"I filed my report three days ago," the resident was saying from somewhere behind the wall of boxes. "What took you so long?"

"Your report, ma'am?" I found a small opening in the wall and squeezed through. The room beyond was piled high with newspapers. Hidden among the stacks were a few antique pieces of furniture that looked like broken-down remnants of the building's golden age. A tiny kitchenette was squeezed into one corner, and something green bubbled in a frying pan on the stove. Charlesgate already had the reputation of a fire trap, but the tenant's room looked like it was ready to go up in flames any minute.

"Sit down, will you?"

I took a seat on a dull orange couch. Heavy springs dug into my hindquarters. The resident sat across from me in a rocking chair, lighting a cigar. I cleared my throat.

"Ma'am, I think there may be some kind of misunder-standing—"

"They followed me home again, you know."

"Pardon me?"

"The Soviet agents. They followed me all the way back here again tonight in their helicopter, just like I said in my report."

"Ma'am—"

"You know my damn name! Stop calling me 'ma'am'!"

"But…I'm afraid I don't, uh, remember—"

"Mrs. Coolidge! I am Mrs. Coolidge, and you know that because it's in all of my reports. You know they land that heli-copter right on the roof. I hear it at night and I can see the lights. It's all because of what my husband knows, but he's been dead since 1968. Assassinated! It was covered up, you know. He had the secret plan to end the Vietnam War, but they didn't want it! It was the Soviets who put the second Richard Nixon in office. If you look at the footage you can tell the difference. The color Nixon don't look nothing like the black-and-white Nixon, but everyone just pretends they don't even notice! Well, I put the photos in my report, you've seen them."

Granted, I was not a particularly seasoned journalist at this point, but I was starting to get the feeling that interviewing Mrs. Coolidge might not be the most fruitful course of action.

Still, I didn't want to give up too easily. "Mrs. Coolidge, my name is Tommy Donnelly. I live here in the building, I'm one of the Emerson students? And I actually wanted to talk to you for a story I'm writing for our student newspaper. If this is a bad time, I can come back later."

She puffed her cigar, eyeing me through narrow slits. "You ain't from the Public Safety office?"

"No. I'm sorry, but I don't know anything about these reports of yours. They sound fascinating, but—"

"And you ain't a Soviet agent, right?"

"Definitely not. I'm a journalism student and I'm writing an article about the Charlesgate. And I thought I should talk to you, because you've lived here since…how long have you lived here?"

She leaned forward and pointed her cigar at me. "You trying to get me evicted, ain't you? Well, let me tell you, it's been tried by men a whole lot better-dressed than you!"

"I'm not trying to get you evicted. I'm just trying to get a sense of what life in the building was like before we students arrived. I understand Boston University owned it until 1972, and when they sold it, it became kind of a…well, there are all kinds of rumors about junkies, criminals, Satanic cults. But obviously if *you* lived here…well, then it couldn't have been that bad, right?"

"Student newspaper, huh?"

"Uh, yes. *The Berkeley Beacon*?"

"I like newspapers. Not for the articles, though. They're all lies. I like the classified ads in the back. That's where you find the real information. The truth gets out, but they have to sneak it out, you know? You have to know the codes, and they change them every day. My husband used to get them delivered every morning, but…" She shook her head sadly.

"Well…I'd like to write the truth, Mrs. Coolidge. With your help."

"Not tonight," she said. "I need to check on you first. I still have contacts, you know. We don't meet face-to-face because it's not safe. Anyway, it's time for me to read. I read three hours every night. Never had a television. All these boxes you see are filled with books I've read. That's why they want this." She tapped the side of her head. "All the information."

I stood up, mainly because I couldn't take the springs digging into my ass for one more second. "All right, Mrs. Coolidge, sorry to disturb you. If there's a better time…?"

"I'll find you. After I check with my contacts."

"Uh…fine." I started back toward the narrow entryway into the hall of boxes, figuring that was the last I'd see of her.

"Wait." She stood, slowly shuffled toward me, and took me by the arm. "There are secrets in these walls," she whispered. "Men have killed for these secrets. And they will again. You can believe that."

Strangely enough, I did.

APRIL 25, 2014

"April showers, bitch!"

A cloudy morning had given way to a sudden downpour as Detectives Coleman and Carnahan sprinted across Beacon Street and took cover under the alcove at 4 Charlesgate East. Coleman tipped rivulets of rain water from his porkpie hat while Carnahan ran a handkerchief over his chrome dome.

"What's the number again?"

"Unit 61."

Carnahan punched in the number on the building's keypad. After a moment, a female voice crackled through the speaker. "Yes?"

"Boston police."

The door buzzed open and Coleman and Carnahan entered the ornate lobby. Gold-speckled mosaic tile gleamed beneath intricately carved columns. Carnahan stepped over to one of them and used it to scrape the mud off his shoes.

"Classy," said Coleman.

"How much you think these cocksuckers paid to live here?"

"Depends on the unit, I guess."

"A one-bedroom, say."

"Maybe three, four hundred grand?"

"Jesus. And I bet they don't even allow pets. No thanks. I'll take a house in Waltham with a yard and a dog to shit in it any day of the week."

The elevator dinged and a uniformed officer stepped out. Red hair, full in the face. Coleman recognized him from another case a few months earlier, but couldn't place the name.

"Detectives."

"Hopper, right?" said Carnahan. He always knew their names. They probably all hung out at the Tap together, shooting pool and pushing the boundaries of sexual harassment while Coleman was pretending to go home to meatloaf.

"That's right."

"What's the situation up there?"

"No forced entry. No prints. Woman says she's sure it was locked when she left on her business trip, and she's sure some things are missing."

"Like what? Her panties? Maybe Coltrane took 'em when he was here the other day."

"Only because I know you're always running low on clean undies. Let's get this over with."

The detectives and the patrolman rode up to the sixth floor. As the doors opened, Coleman gestured to the room across the hallway.

"That's where our vic was found, which you would know if you'd bothered to join me."

"You know I had to be in court on the Hernandez thing."

Coleman considered mentioning the Red Sox tickets he'd scavenged from the corpse, but thought better of doing so in front of the uni. Hopper led them down the hallway to the left, then another left to a dead end, where he knocked on the door to Unit 61.

"Mrs. Osborne? It's Officer Hopper. I have the detectives with me." The door opened, revealing a striking woman in her mid-forties. Dark hair with white Bride-of-Frankenstein streaks cascaded down to her shoulders. Coleman felt his pulse quicken. She must have been a knockout when she was younger, but she was still a beauty as far as he was concerned. He stuck out his hand.

"Mrs. Osborne, I'm Detective Coleman. This is Detective Carnahan. Homicide Division." She shook their hands without enthusiasm.

"Nice to meet you, but I still don't understand why you're here. This is a simple robbery."

Coleman and Carnahan exchanged glances with Hopper, who shrugged. "I thought you guys should tell her."

"Tell me what?'

"Mrs. Osborne, while you were out of town, there was a murder just a few doors down the hall from you."

"Oh my God! Who was it?"

"It wasn't a resident, ma'am. It was a woman who worked for the company that handles your property, a Ms. Rachel O'Brien. None of your neighbors mentioned this to you?"

"I just got back this morning and honestly, I don't really know any of my neighbors."

"Did you know Ms. O'Brien?"

"Not well. She showed this unit to me and my husband, but that was four years ago. Recently we exchanged some emails regarding an event I'm organizing in the building, but other than that, I've only seen her to nod hello a handful of times over the years."

"And your husband? Was he out of town as well?"

"He no longer lives here. He's my *ex*-husband, or he will be as soon as the paperwork is finalized, which should be any day now."

"I see." Coleman struggled to contain his glee. Carnahan noticed. "Well, the reason we're here is that Ms. O'Brien's keys were not on her person when her body was discovered. It's a strong possibility that whoever killed her took them, and that, in fact, may have been his motive."

"What? You think he killed this woman just to rob my apartment?"

"Well, not necessarily *your* apartment, no. Not specifically."

"Has anyone else in the building been robbed?"

"Not that we know of, but—"

"So why wouldn't he just break down my door? This isn't Fort Knox. He really had to kill someone for the keys?"

"That's all speculation, Mrs. Osborne. There may be no connection at all. In fact…are you absolutely certain you locked the door before you left on your business trip?"

"I can't swear to it in court, but I always lock it. I can't imagine that I would just forget. Either way, someone was definitely in here. I had a framed poster on the wall over the couch there. When I got home the frame was on the floor, the glass shattered, and the poster was ripped in several pieces scattered around."

"What kind of poster?"

"A movie poster. *Annie Hall*."

"Woody Allen, huh?" said Carnahan. "He's been in the news lately. Pretty creepy guy, you ask me."

"What does that have to do with anything? You think Mia Farrow did this?"

"I'm not ruling it out. Officer Hopper tells us you found some items missing?"

"Yes. Most importantly, my laptop."

"Your laptop. You went on a business trip and didn't take your laptop?"

"I took my work laptop."

"And where do you work?"

"Hill-Robenalt. It's a PR firm. I do publicity for three of the major film studios. Setting up screenings, interviews, set visits, things like that."

"Oh yeah?" Carnahan perked up. "Can you get us into the new Godzilla movie early?"

"I don't work for Warners."

"Damn."

Coleman shot him the stinkeye. "Tell us about the laptop."

"It's a MacBook Air. Less than a year old. A sticker on the back, so it looks like the apple is the hood ornament of like a '70s van."

"Anything on the computer a thief might be interested in? Something specific, worth breaking into your unit in particular? Proprietary information?"

"Like I said, it's my personal computer. I use it for email, browsing the web, social networking. Skype, Netflix, iTunes… I just downloaded the new Beck album. Think they were interested in that?"

"Another possibility. Where was the laptop?"

"It was on the desk over by the window when I left last week. I was in the middle of a big project, and now…" She shook her head.

"A big project? Not work-related?"

"No. I'm on the alumni committee for my alma mater. I've been working to set up my class reunion in a few weeks."

"What school?" Coleman asked.

"Is that relevant?"

He shrugged. "At this point, we have very little to go on. Anything could be relevant."

"Emerson College."

Coleman's eyebrows shot up. "Emerson? Really?"

"Yeah, why?"

"This building used to be an Emerson dorm. Did you know that?"

She laughed. "Did I know that? Yeah, I lived here for three years when it was a dorm."

This got Carnahan's attention. "Seriously? When was this?"

"Is that your way of asking how old I am?"

"Nah, nah, I'm just—"

"It's okay. It was '85 to '88. I lived on this floor, in fact."

"It's a little nicer now, I bet."

"Nicer looking, yes. Friendlier, not so much."

"How did you end up living here again?"

"My husband and I were looking for a place after we got married. He was my second husband and I was his third wife."

Carnahan whistled.

"Yeah," she continued. "So he wanted to live in the Back Bay, and I knew this place had recently been converted to condos. I set up a viewing, mostly because I just wanted to see what they'd done with the place. I mean, when I lived here the first time you could never imagine it looking like this. Bugs, rats, ceilings caving in, fire alarms at three in the morning…"

"Sounds awful."

"I loved every minute. And when we looked at this unit, my husband fell in love with it. I never thought in a million years I'd end up back here, but here I am."

"Minus the husband," said Carnahan.

"Right. Thanks for the reminder, detective. Is there anything else?"

"Mrs. Osborne," said Coleman. "You said you lived here from '85 to '88?"

"That's right."

"This might sound a little out of left field…"

"But why stop now?"

"Right. So back then, did you by any chance know a Thomas Donnelly?"

Mrs. Osborne smirked. "Yes. I know Tommy."

"Are you still in touch?"

"Once in a blue moon. I think I got a Christmas card from

him six or seven years ago. He's not on Facebook if that's what you're asking."

"It's just that I was reading some articles Mr. Donnelly wrote for the Emerson paper back in the '80s."

"Oh, the Charlesgate articles? Exciting stuff, right? Wait, do you think this murder has anything to do with all that?"

"It's a long shot for sure. You said you're planning your class reunion. Do you expect Mr. Donnelly to attend?"

"Not a chance. He moved about as far away from here as he could get and still be on the same planet."

"Australia, right? But he's doing well for himself. He can certainly afford it."

"It has nothing to do with money. I just don't think he'd ever come back to this building."

"This…wait a minute. The reunion is being held here? In the Charlesgate?"

"In the big ballroom downstairs, the Gold Room. That's why I was emailing with Ms. O'Brien a few weeks back. Taking care of the logistics."

"I see. One more question, Mrs. Osborne, if you don't mind my asking. What was your name when you lived here the first time? Back in college, I mean?"

"St. John. My maiden name is Jackie St. John."

JUNE 12, 1946

It was a slow night at the Red Room lounge. A thunderstorm had rolled in around sunset, and most of the regulars had evidently decided to do their drinking at home. Fat Dave was contemplating closing up early when Jimmy Dryden burst through the front door, holding a soaking wet *Boston Globe* over his head.

"Holy shit, it's raining pitchforks and assholes out there."

"So I hear," said Fat Dave as Dryden took a seat at the bar, dumping his wet newspaper on the stool beside him. "Getcha Manhattan?"

"That's just what the doctor ordered. Well, not my doctor, he's a prick. Says I should quit drinking, like I got so much joy in my life I can just start giving up the few things that make it bearable."

"I hear you." Fat Dave got to work. "So what's new?"

"I came into some unexpected money."

"That's always a good thing."

"Well, in this case, it was already my money to begin with. It went away, but then it came back around."

"I don't foller ya."

"Well, you may have heard about Dave T's card game the other night."

"Oh yeah. You were there?"

"In the flesh. Cocksuckers with fuckin' shotguns and potato sacks over their heads bust in and clean us out. And I was on a hot streak, too. Just my luck."

Fat Dave set a fresh Manhattan on the bar. "Figures."

Dryden shrugged. "Hey, it happens. We all know the risks.

At least with Dave T, you know you got robbed honestly. Some guys out there ain't above taking down their own games, and you know who I'm talking about."

"Oh yeah."

"So anyways, I'm back there at the Charlesgate tonight doing some business on the sixth floor and that guy Cahill, works for Dave T sometimes, he stops by. Only he don't want no tail. He's just there to give me an envelope. Inside the envelope, fifteen Ben Franklins. My buy-in from the game."

"Huh. Nice of Dave T, reimbursing you like that."

"Nice, hell. Don't get me wrong, Dave T is a standup guy, but he's no sucker. His game wouldn't last a minute if word got out he was paying guys out of his own pocket after getting hit. Nah, he caught up with those potato sack motherfuckers somehow."

"Huh. And you got no idea who those guys were?"

Dryden shrugged. "Fuck would I know? Did you miss the part where I said they had fuckin' potato sacks on their heads?"

"I heard you, but…you didn't recognize their voices? Their builds? Nothing like that?"

Dryden drained his Manhattan and slammed the glass on the bar. "No. What? I'm Charlie Chan now? You trying to tell me something, just come out and fuckin' say it!"

Fat Dave took the empty glass and started building another Manhattan. "I'm just saying, I'd have thought you mighta recognized those cocksuckers, potato sacks or no. They grew up about a pussy hair from your house, after all."

"Oh, so you're in the know? This is your way of saying you weren't even there, yet you know who took down the game."

Fat Dave plucked a maraschino cherry from its jar and plopped it into Dryden's drink. "You know me, I hear things. That's what I do."

"And what did you hear?"

Fat Dave whistled the *Our Gang* theme.

"Whaddaya...*oh*. The Little fuckin' Rascals? Those little shits? You gotta be kiddin' me. These were *men*."

"Jimmy, kids grow up. You must have heard about this. I know you don't have any yourself, but you do understand that little boys grow up to be men if they live long enough."

"Ungrateful little shits. I used to let them play ball in my yard. One time the fat one hit a line drive through my kitchen window, I said, 'Forget it, kid. It happens.' I should kick his fuckin' ass."

"My guess, it's a little late for that."

"Oh, you think Dave T...well, I guess he'd have to, right? You can't disrespect the game and get away with it."

"Damn straight."

"Still...kinda harsh for a first offense, no? You don't think he could have just, I dunno, given them a warning?"

"Jimmy, these guys ripped you off. You just called them ungrateful little shits."

"Yeah, I know. But you know me, I'm a soft-hearted guy. And it really wasn't that much money. I mean, I'm happy to have it back, don't get me wrong. But Jesus, kids make mistakes. I made more than a few."

"It's business, Jimmy, and like I said, they ain't kids no more. They knew the rules."

"Yeah, the rules. Well, I never cared much for rules myself." Dryden tossed back the rest of his Manhattan. He reached into his envelope for a bill and slid it under his empty glass.

"Jesus, Jimmy, that's a hundred bucks."

"I know. Just want to, you know, settle my tab."

"Well, I don't know off the top of my head what your tab is, but I know it ain't no hundred smackers."

"Hey, like I said, Dave, it's found money to me. I never expected to see it again. You been good to me over the years. Maybe next time I'm in here, I'm a little light, you'll remember this."

"You bet, Jimmy. Hell, I was thinking of closing early tonight anyway. This makes it easier."

"Good. We're all in this together, right?"

"Yeah. Tell that to Marko and the Mullens. Things are heating up there and it's gonna be bad for business for all of us if they go to war."

"Marko's been layin' low, huh?"

"He's locked down tight there on Prince Street. Gotta be planning something."

"Well, let's hope cooler heads prevail. Take care of yourself, Dave."

Dryden gave a quick salute, gathered his soggy newspaper, and headed out the door. Fat Dave washed his glass and took a quick lap around the bar. He had the place to himself. But just as he was on his way to latch the front door, it swung open and another customer stepped inside.

"Closing early, pal. Game called on account of weather."

The customer lowered the hood of his rain slicker. Fat Dave knew him.

"This won't take long," Jake said.

"Oh…how ya doin', kid?"

"Didn't expect to see me tonight, didja?"

Fat Dave gestured around. "Like you see, the place is dead. But I guess if you want one quick drink, I could set you up."

"No, that's all right. I'd prefer it if you didn't go back behind that bar. I know you've got a shotgun back there. I saw you bust it out one night when things got out of hand."

Fat Dave shrugged. "Yeah, me and every other barkeep in Boston. What's it to you?"

"What's it to me is I don't want to get my face blown off tonight. It may happen tomorrow or the next day, but tonight I'd really rather avoid it."

"Why would you think I'd blow your face off, kid? Doesn't sound real good for business."

"I get the feeling you weren't counting on much more of my business anyway."

"Kid, I'm not following you at all. I don't know what's got you all twisted up, but I am closing early tonight, so if you don't want a drink, what do you say we talk about this some other time."

The bar light caught a flash of metal as Jake pulled something from his raincoat pocket.

"I brought a souvenir home from the war," Jake said. "This is a Browning HP. Funny thing is, it wasn't mine. It was presented to me in the hospital in Manila. I was dehydrated, half-starved, suffered near-failure of every organ. I don't even know who gave it to me. Nurse said it was a gift from an admirer. What's to admire? I spent months as a prisoner of the Japs, asshole to elbow with men dropping dead in every direction. Better believe I woke up ready to die every morning. But I also woke up ready to do whatever I had to do to stay alive. None of that has changed."

Fat Dave raised his hands and slowly lowered himself onto a barstool. It groaned beneath his weight. "I appreciate what you did for this country, kid. But I got no idea what that has to do with me."

"Four nights ago, my brother Shane, my cousin Pat and I robbed Dave T's card game. I think you know that."

"How would I know that?"

"Because we were in here the next night. And my cousin Pat, who never could keep his mouth shut, I think he gave you a pretty good idea what we did."

"Kid, this is all news to me."

"I don't think so. See, I spent this afternoon wondering exactly how Dave T figured out it was us. And then I remembered hearing about how you guys go way back."

"Kid, you're making a big mistake."

"Well, that's possible. I mean, I'm not one hundred percent sure about this. I might be making a mistake, it's true. But then I ask myself: At this point, what fuckin' difference does it make?"

"Kid, you pull that trigger, you are gonna bring a shitstorm down on your head like you never dreamed."

"And if I don't, same thing. All things being equal, I'd rather pull the trigger."

He did, three times. The bottles in the racks behind the bar jumped when Fat Dave's body hit the floor.

OCTOBER 8, 1986

Two days of relative normalcy passed. I went to class. I showed up for my work-study job in the development office. (My job consisted mainly of filing news clippings about prominent Emerson alumni. Norman Lear, Henry Winkler and Jay Leno were the names I most frequently encountered.) On Tuesday night, Murtaugh, the Rev and I hosted a viewing of Game 1 of the ALCS, in which the Red Sox suffered an 8–1 ass-whupping at the hands of the Angels.

I'd also managed to get in touch with Timothy Sprague, the author of *Haunted Hub*. He'd agreed to meet with me for an interview, on the condition that said meeting take place at his apartment in the Bay Village. I wasn't crazy about the idea of meeting an occult expert alone in his home, so I decided to solicit some backup.

"Hey, Rev, what are you doing tonight?"

My roommate was idly plucking his bass guitar while watching the end of a *M*A*S*H* rerun. "Oh, I dunno, man. Probably jamming with the boys in the back stairwell. Some weed might be smoked."

"Wednesday night, in other words."

*M*A*S*H* ended and a *Barney Miller* rerun began. The Rev played along with the opening bass riff of the theme song. *Bum. Ba da dum. Ba da dum. Ba da da da da da da da...* "Why do you ask?"

"I was hoping I could talk you into coming with me on an interview tonight."

"You have a job interview tonight? What, you want me as a reference?"

The Rev was wearing a tie-dye t-shirt. He had a beard down to his midsection and a tangle of dreadlocks. I definitely did not want him as a reference.

"Not a job interview. An interview for an article I'm writing for the *Beacon*."

"Why do you want me to come with you?"

"Because I feel like this guy might be a freak."

"And you want to have a freak on your side?"

"Exactly."

"Cool, man. Sounds like a blast."

So the Rev rode with me on the T down to Arlington Street. From there we walked south to Cortes Street in the Bay Village.

"The Gay Village," said the Rev.

"What?"

"They call this the Gay Village. Like, this is a highly gay part of Boston."

"Is that a problem?"

"Hey, I go to Emerson, don't I? I don't give a shit."

I rang the buzzer for apartment 3A at 23 Cortes Street.

"Who goes there?"

"Uh…it's Tommy Donnelly? I talked to you earlier about the Charlesgate?"

"Entrez vous!"

The door buzzed open.

"I hope this guy has roof access," said the Rev.

"Why is that?"

"So we can go up to the roof and smoke a bowl."

"That's what I thought you were gonna say."

We walked up the three flights of stairs and knocked on the door to 3A. The door swung open, revealing a curtain of beads and the glow of a blue light beyond. I pushed my way through, followed by the Rev.

"Hello?"

"In the back!"

I was tempted to turn and run. The far wall was covered with a mural replicating the cover of the Yes album *Tales from Topographic Oceans*. The furniture consisted entirely of bean-bag chairs. The other walls were plastered with black-light posters for Led Zeppelin and the Grateful Dead. Lava lamps burbled on the fireplace mantle. The sound of a Theremin filled the air.

"Chief," said the Rev. "I've died and gone to heaven."

"That's why I brought you, Rev."

"I'm back in the workshop!" the voice called again.

"The workshop," I muttered. "Sounds unpromising."

"Nah," said the Rev. "It's cool. Santa has a workshop, right?"

We passed through a second set of beads and entered the workshop. It wasn't noticeably different from the rest of the apartment: lava lamps, beanbag chairs, stoner posters. It did feature a small desk topped by an ancient typewriter, as well as an end table crammed with all manner of occult bric-a-brac: Magic 8-balls, Tarot cards, books of magick, and what appeared to be a human skull. Our host stood in the corner, waving his hands as if conducting an orchestra. It took me a minute to realize he was playing the Theremin.

"Welcome to my inner sanctum! Which one of you is Tommy?"

I raised my hand. "That's me. I hope you don't mind I brought my roommate along. He's…into this kind of stuff."

"Everyone calls me the Rev," my roommate said, extending his hand.

"The Rev! *Powerful*. I like that." Sprague shook his hand enthusiastically. The abandoned Theremin whistled mournfully before fading to silence. "Well, gentlemen, pull up a beanbag. I was just about to bust out some mind-roasting hash my girl-friend brought back from Istanbul. I'm happy to share."

"Oh, I don't know if that—"

"Absolutely, man," said the Rev, shutting me down. "Your girlfriend sounds cool, taking a chance like that. I've seen *Midnight Express*."

"Yeah, right? Yeah, she brought this stuff back in her poop chute. But don't worry, she's got a *real* nice poop chute."

Sprague broke up a few chunks of hash on a *Their Satanic Majesties Request* album and began rolling a joint. "So you're interested in the Charlesgate, right?"

"Uh, yeah. I'm doing an article, actually a series of articles, for our school paper. The Rev and I live in Charlesgate, as a matter of fact."

Sprague's eyes widened. "No shit? Aw man, I wish you'd told me, I would have met you guys there. We could get up to some *real* freaky shit in that building. Here, spark this baby up."

He passed a fat joint to the Rev, who was only too happy to oblige. After taking a few hits, he passed it to me. I tried to pass it right over to Sprague, but he held up a palm in refusal.

"Man, you gotta hit that. It will open you up to this world you're gonna be writing about. You don't want to approach this thing from a closed-off place, man. You want all those doors of perception wide open."

"Yeah, that's not really my process…"

"That's my whole point, man. This isn't about the same old process. You left that behind when you walked through those curtains, man. Here in the workshop, we are outside of time and space. I need to know you're with me, man."

"Yeah, but I…all right. Fine." I took a token drag off the joint and immediately launched into a coughing fit. When I finally got myself together, I could see that the Rev was enjoying this all too much. I passed him the joint. "So can we get started here?"

"Sure," said Sprague. "I assume you read what I wrote about the Charlesgate in *Haunted Hub*."

"Yeah, that's why I'm here. I read a few of those books, but yours was the best of the bunch. You actually bothered to check your facts, rather than just regurgitate all the same urban legends. For instance, some of the other books said Eugene O'Neill died in the Charlesgate, but that's not the case."

"Right. That happened in a different building. Easy to debunk. That's my business, you know? You get caught passing off some old bullshit as the truth, your reputation is shot. And reputation is all I have. The thing is, I try to visit all the places I write about personally, but the Charlesgate is one nut I never could crack. Your college already owned it by the time I was researching *Haunted Hub*, and they wanted nothing to do with me. I tried to sneak in, I tried to get some students to sneak me in, but no dice. I think I creeped 'em out."

"Imagine that."

"But you guys, you must have had some experiences there. Rev, don't tell me nothing freaky ever happened to you in the Charlesgate."

"Well...yeah, there was something. Really freaky. One night freshman year I woke up at about 4 A.M. I sensed this...presence in our room. There was a sound like some kind of, I dunno, *gateway* opening up. And a smell that hit me like a freight train. I was afraid to get out of bed, but...then I heard this noise. Like a chainsaw starting up. I was scared shitless, but I figured this is a matter of life and death, I gotta move."

The Rev paused as the joint reached him again on its third pass around the room. After a long drag, he continued. "So I gather all the courage I can muster and I jump out of my bed and turn on the light. And there, in the corner by the door, is my roommate Mark Fuller. He's snoring like a chainsaw, he's got his pants around his ankles, and he's taken this huge, steaming dump right there in the corner. Now, you may say this was not a supernatural event. But I would disagree."

The three of us laughed so hard, I wouldn't have been surprised if we all crapped our pants simultaneously. By the time I got myself under control, we were no longer in Sprague's inner sanctum. We were on the roof deck. I had no memory of getting there. The Hancock tower loomed like an interplanetary spacecraft coming in for a landing.

"We should be there now," Sprague was saying. "In the Charlesgate. All the answers are there. You're part of the cycle. You've been there before, you will be there again. All that ever happened. All that ever will happen. Separated by a thin membrane we call time. It's meaningless. It doesn't exist."

"You have always been the caretaker," I said. The Rev choked on a lungful of Turkish hash smoke.

"What is that?" said Sprague. "I don't understand."

"*The Shining*? Oh, never mind. Hey, what about Houdini? You know he debunked a séance there, right?"

"He had to do that. See, Houdini was a real magician. I mean the authentic black magick. All the tricks he did for audiences, they were all bullshit, of course. But that was his cover. You can bet he knew the truth about the Charlesgate, and he tapped into that hidden world. The idea of phonies in there, pretending to summon spirits, it really pissed him off."

"Wait, let me write this…oh, shit."

Sprague's head elongated and split into two identical faces, one good and one evil. Out of the corner of my eye, the Rev had turned into a skeleton.

I squeezed my eyes shut, concentrating on the cool evening breeze, pretending the roof deck wasn't spinning around me. "Anyway, so I was wondering if maybe there was something you found out while researching the Charlesgate that didn't make it into your book. Like, something non-supernatural but still pretty freaky, you know?"

I fumbled my notepad and pen out of my pocket. Both of Sprague's faces mocked me. They knew. They knew what had happened between me and Purple Debbie, and I still didn't know. I wanted to ask him, but...didn't I just ask him a question? Why wasn't he answering?

A thousand years later, he did. "Yeah, as a matter of fact, I found out something that was too hot to print, man. My publisher wouldn't touch it. The Boston Mob would have burned their office to the ground."

And he told me. He told me the story and I took careful notes. It was great. It would make my whole Charlesgate series. Mighty Rob McKim would lose his mind. I'd take over as the editor of the *Berkeley Beacon* next semester. I'd have a bright career in journalism stretching out ahead of me.

It had something to do with the Boston Mob back in the 1940s. A heist gone awry. A gangland execution in the alley behind Charlesgate. Murdered prostitutes. Bodies stashed inside the walls. Hidden treasure in secret rooms. I wrote it down. I got it all.

I was walking down Newbury Street. The Rev was beside me humming "Sugar Magnolia."

"Hey." My tongue was thick and heavy in my mouth.

"Hey hey," said the Rev.

"Did we leave?"

The Rev laughed. "No, man, we're still there."

"Good. I have some follow-up questions."

Newbury Street melted into the sixth floor of Charlesgate. I sensed the presence of Purple Debbie. I sprinted to our room. Slammed the door behind me.

"There you are! I been lookin' for you!"

"Chief," said Murtaugh. "Is this your girlfriend?"

I managed to focus. It wasn't Purple Debbie. It was Mrs. Coolidge, the mystery tenant from the third floor.

"This isn't a good time," I said.

"I checked with my contacts, like I said. They never heard of you."

"Okay."

"That means one of two things. Either you're deep cover, a Soviet sleeper agent they don't have on their radar."

"Seems unlikely."

"Or you are who you say you are."

"Let's go with that."

"All right, then. You want to hear my story? Because I have a story that will make all the little hairs on your dick stand on end."

"This…this might not be the best time for that."

Mrs. Coolidge shrugged. "That's your business, but I might be busy later. I don't operate on your schedule."

"I understand, but…it's really important that I lie down right now."

She leaned in close, squinting. "Somebody drug you, boy?"

"As a matter of fact, yes. Somebody drugged me."

She pointed at Murtaugh. "You. Get him some oranges. And two quarts of purified water, not the stuff out of the taps here. You may have to induce vomiting."

"Yeah, I…I'm not going to be doing that."

"Don't sass your elders, young man. I know people. *He* can tell you that. If he ever recovers. Oranges. Not tangerines.

Those come from China and you don't know what they're putting in them."

If Murtaugh and Mrs. Coolidge continued their conversation after that, I didn't hear it. I retreated to the Love Room, locked the door behind me, and collapsed onto the futon. The room spun around me for a few seconds, but I closed my eyes and took a few deep breaths and everything settled back into place. Sprague's Turkish hash packed a wallop, but it probably wasn't laced with angel dust as I'd first suspected. Normality was, if not restored, at least in sight.

I pulled my notepad out of my pocket. I feared my notes would be at least partly illegible, given my state of mind earlier, so it was important that I transcribe them right away. In the morning, I might not remember anything at all.

I flipped open to the first page, the only one with any writing on it. Not so much writing, actually, as drawing. Where I thought I'd been taking notes on Sprague's story, I'd actually drawn a sketch of the Rev as a skeleton. It wasn't bad: a skull with dreads smoking a blunt. If I gave it to the Rev, he might get it tattooed on his shoulder. But it was no help to me at all. The night was a complete loss.

Then I noticed that I'd signed my artwork. But I hadn't signed it with my own name. There was only one word written on my notepad.

That word was "Vermeer."

APRIL 26–29, 2014

9:47 P.M.
JackieO@hill-robenalt.com
To: tdonnelly@qmail.com

Hey, Tommy—

It's been a while and I have no idea if you'll get this. This is the only email address I have for you, so I'm giving it a shot. I know it's a long shot, but our 25th class reunion is coming up next month, and I know everyone would love to see you there. I sent you an invitation c/o your agent, so who knows if you ever received it. You're the biggest success story of our graduating class, unless you count Chest Guy for the year he spent as an MTV VJ, which I do not. I know you're a LITTLE far away (lol), but I suspect you can spring for a plane ticket if you want to! Maybe even first class. :) And the Sox will be in town that weekend and I KNOW you'd love to catch a game at Fenway.

Your name came up yesterday, actually. A BPD detective came by asking about you. Not that you're in any trouble! But there was a murder here in the building last week, and I guess you're still the expert on all things Weird Charlesgate. (Or should I say Cheesegate? God, I almost forgot we used to call it that.) I was out of town when it happened, but whoever did it might have broken into my condo. My personal laptop was stolen (I'm using my work one right now) and a few other personal items as well, including a photo album from our Emerson days. I'm kind of weirded out, but the detective was cool…actually kind of hot in an Idris Elba kind of way. (Stringer Bell 4-eva!)

Anyway, thought that might pique your interest. God, I don't even know if I ever told you I was living in C-Gate again. There's a story there, as you can imagine. Get back to me if you receive this. And again, we'd love to see you at the reunion. I've attached the Evite.

Best,
Jackie

✳ ✳ ✳ ✳

Conversation started Monday

Jackie St. John Osborne, David Murtaugh and 3 others

Jackie St. John Osborne
Hey all! Just checking in to make sure you're all set for Reunion Weekend. (Woot!) Hopefully you've all got your flights and accommodations arranged, but if you need help with anything, let me know. In case you're wondering, C-Gate is as f✳✳ked up as ever! I'll tell you all about in person. Oh! And if ANYONE has heard from Tommy D, PLEASE let me know. Would love to drag him back here for this festive occasion. I tried emailing him, but I got a "mailbox full" reply. If anyone has a current email address for him, shoot it my way.

Deborah Tocci has left the conversation

Jackie St. John Osborne
Whoa! I guess Purple Debbie's still a little bitter! LOL!

Michael the Rev Wellman

Hey, Jackie! Good news: I'll definitely be there, and I'm bringing the beer with me. Just like Smokey and the Bandit, I'll be driving halfway across the country with a truck full of suds, but it won't be that Coors pisswater like in the movie. I've got one keg of each of my specialty brews: Waterloo Pale, Armadillo Amber, Bombshell Blonde, and of course, Charlesgate IPA. I'll be hitting the road in my refrigerated truck on the 16th. It's been about three years since my last vacation, so I'll be taking my sweet time. I'm finally going to see Graceland, dammit! Anyway, can't wait to see you all and really curious to see what they've done with Cheesegate. Oh, and I wish I could tell you I've heard from Tommy, but no such luck. He sent me his last book, autographed and everything, but that was almost two years ago. Hard to believe he'd show up for this, but it would be cool, right?

David Murtaugh

Hey, guys. Sorry I didn't see this earlier, but I don't check Facebook that often. I'm keeping pretty busy—12-hour shifts at NFL Films and squeezing in as much time for my kids as I can. I know: Murtaugh the Family Man. Who would have guessed? I haven't heard from Tommy either—bastard didn't send me an autographed book, but then, we didn't part on the greatest of terms. (I seem to recall someone pouring a beer on someone's head, but time plays tricks with my memory.) At this point, it's no more than a 50/50 chance I'll be able to make the reunion, but knowing you're all going to be there makes it hard to resist. I'll do my best.

PS: Sorry to see Purple Debbie's still holding a grudge. Did I ever tell you she gave me a blowjob in the Fallout Shelter men's room about a year after we graduated? Now THAT I remember.

Jackie St. John Osborne
OMG. TMI. And other acronyms.

Michael the Rev Wellman
High five, Murtaugh!

Brooks Cohen
Proust's madeleine, Murtaugh's blowjob, same difference. Greetings, dear old gang of mine. It's been too long. Sorry none of you have heard from me in over 20 years, but I'm a douchebag L.A. entertainment lawyer now and I have a reputation to protect. And Murtaugh, you were right: I was a homo all along. My husband Greg and I will be at the reunion. Murtaugh, if you don't show up and say something hideously inappropriate to him, I'm going to be sorely disappointed.

Brooks Cohen is now friends with David Murtaugh and Michael the Rev Wellman

David Murtaugh
Brooksy! Still saving the planet?

Brooks Cohen
Didn't I mention I'm a douchebag entertainment lawyer now? No, I had an epiphany. George Carlin said it best: the planet will be fine. We're all fucked, of course. I donate to environmental groups, but I think we're past the point of no return. We've got maybe 25 years before we're living in the world of Mad Max, so we might as well enjoy it while we can.

David Murtaugh
So glad I asked! What do you hear from Rodney these days?

Brooks Cohen

As far as I know, he's still up in his Unabomber cabin in New Hampshire, wearing his tinfoil helmet and shooting squirrels for his supper. No chance he'll ever join Facebook. The NSA is watching!

Michael the Rev Wellman

Don't tell me he's a 9/11 truther.

Brooks Cohen

Oh, that's only the beginning. He stopped talking to me when he figured out I was part of the Bilderberg conspiracy.

David Murtaugh

He seemed like such a harmless kook in college. I guess we shouldn't expect to see him.

Brooks Cohen

Not if he sees us first. Oh, Jackie—try this email for Tommy: TD1@thomasdonnelly.com. That was good as of 2010 or so— a client of mine was trying to secure the movie rights to DEADSVILLE, but it never got off the ground. AMC eventually made a terrible miniseries out of it and I seriously hope to get the chance to give him shit about it someday.

※ ※ ※

11:13 P.M.
JackieO@hill-robenalt.com
To: TD1@thomasdonnelly.com

Hello again. I thought I'd give this one more try (although you probably never saw my last email and there's no guarantee this will get to you either). The latest reunion update: The Rev is in! I don't know if you know this, but he's the brewmaster at some hip, famous award-winning brewpub down in Austin (because of course he is). He's driving up here with samples of his wares. He is exactly the same as you remember him, except now his dreads have gray streaks and dip down below his waist. Murtaugh is a maybe. Brooks will be there with his husband(!). Rodney is probably a no-show—he's some kind of black helicopter nutjob now apparently. Purple Debbie is probably a no-show, too (and you WOULD NOT BELIEVE something Murtaugh told me about her—you better show up just to hear that).

That detective stopped by again today. I started to worry I was somehow a suspect, but it turns out he was off-duty. He just wanted to ask me out to dinner. Well, like I told you, he's my type, so I agreed. But I'm a little jealous—he seems almost more interested in YOU than in me. I guess he thinks this murder ties in with the stuff you were researching about Charlesgate back in the day. Anyway, I'll try to pump a little more info out of him tomorrow night. (And that's not all I'll try to pump—lol.)

Let me just tell you, I feel like I'm sending these emails into outer space. I know we were never really all that close, but we shared an experience I'll never forget that night back in October of '86—the night the Red Sox blew the World Series. (Yeah, I was a Mets fan back then, but I've lived here long enough that I've come around. Those three world championships don't hurt. This will make you jealous: I was at Game 6 last year in our company seats on the Monster. How's that for symmetry? I came THIS CLOSE to catching Shane Victorino's homerun ball.) It may not have been "the Curse of the Bambino," but supernatural forces were definitely at work that night. Every time I see that stupid Bill Buckner clip, I can't help but think about it. Anyway, Red Sox fans eventually forgave Buckner—not that there was really anything to forgive. He was a scapegoat that night, and so were you. Yeah, I was mad for a while—furious is more like it—and you can't blame me for that. But all is forgiven. Come back if you can.

Evite attachment:

❋ ❋ ❋ ❋

4:03 A.M.
Thomas Donnelly <TD1@thomasdonnelly.com>
To: JackieO@hill-robenalt.com

Hi, Jackie! Great to hear from you. You're right, I never got your earlier emails (so I have no idea who "that detective" is—intriguing). In fact, it's a miracle I got this one. I've been on assignment…well, you wouldn't believe where I've been. The ends of the earth, let's put it that way. And there's no internet there. I'm at the airport in Sydney right now. Home for about 24 hours and then I'm heading out again for the next couple weeks.

Bill fucking Buckner! I saw a clip of him throwing out the first pitch in '08 and it damn near brought a tear to my eye. Every Sox fan remembers that night in '86 as a nightmare, but they have no fucking idea how bad it really was. Only you know and I know, as the song goes. I wouldn't blame you for hating me, but I'm relieved to hear you don't.

I feel like I'd be tempting fate to ever set foot in Charlesgate again, but as it turns out, I have to be in the States next month anyway. A little legal loose end I have to take care of, but no need to go into that. If I can get that straightened out, I may be able to make the reunion, but PLEASE don't tell a soul you heard from me. Let's keep it our little secret for now. I'd definitely love to see you again, and if I get drunk enough, maybe I'll tell you all about the huge crush I had on you back then. (Remember the night with the Ouija board and the fire alarm? It comes back on me just about every time I hear an alarm going off.) And if I get REALLY drunk, maybe I'll tell you the whole truth about what happened that night in '86. And I don't mean Mookie Wilson's ground ball rolling through Buckner's legs.

Dave T sat at his desk on the eighth floor of Charlesgate, the telephone receiver pressed to his ear. To Joey Cahill's trained eye, he didn't look happy.

"Uh-huh…right…Jesus, I can't believe it. I just fuckin' saw him a couple nights ago. It ain't gonna be the same without him. No one could make a Manhattan like Fat Dave…Yeah… Well, you hear anything, you let me know. Whoever did this, they're not getting away with it. All right. Take care, Jimmy."

Dave T hung up. Cahill raised his eyebrows.

"Fat Dave. Shot dead in his own bar. When he didn't open up this afternoon, a couple of his rummy regulars jimmied his office window and found him there on the floor, half his fuckin' head blown off."

"Shame," said Cahill.

"You're goddam right it is. And I got a pretty good idea what happened. One of those two knuckleheads knocked him off. Probably the older one."

"How do you figure?"

"The kid's not as dumb as he looks. He knows his loudmouth friend was shooting his mouth off in the Red Room. He puts two and two together, he figures Fat Dave's the reason his cousin ain't around no more. Figures he's got nothing to lose at this point, so blammo! Revenge, pure and simple."

"And so?"

" 'And so' what?"

"The job. Maybe we go with the Casey boys after all."

"Can't do it," said Dave T. "We do that, we've gotta cut in

our Providence friends, and that creates problems with our friends in the North End. Especially now, all that's going on with Marko, that's no good. Right now only you and I know exactly what we're doing, and I want to keep it that way. The other two guys have to be expendable. And they're more expendable now than ever. Nothing changes."

"What about the fence?"

"What about him? Right now, he only knows the general picture. The type of merchandise. Yeah, once it hits the news, he'll know it was us, but he's getting a solid cut anyway, right off the top. And he's down in Florida. No connections up here aside from me. He moves the stuff overseas, we get our share and split it with no one else. No one ever knows we did this, and if they figure it out, who cares? We're long gone. Look, you know I don't believe in the perfect crime, but this is as close as we're gonna get in this world. And once it's done, we're gonna be set for life. A thousand lifetimes. But you got anyone you need to tell goodbye, better do it tonight. After tomorrow, you'll never see them again."

"I got no one to tell goodbye. You know that."

"And that's why I picked you."

"But these kids. They're onto you. You don't think they'll take a whack at us?"

"I think they very well might do that. In a way, Fat Dave, God rest his soul, that might have been a good thing for us."

"How's that?"

"Now we know not to underestimate these little shits. Everything's in place, but now I've got one thing left to do. An insurance policy. These guys aren't gonna get the drop on us, but if somehow they do, I'm gonna make sure they never make it out of Boston alive."

"Comforting."

"Don't worry about it. I just gotta make a run down to that garage I got in Quincy and pick up a couple items I put in cold storage. All you have to worry about is whether we're absolutely set for tomorrow night. Our guy is on duty? Not the other guy, the big guy who might actually put up a fight?"

"I've checked every night for the past three weeks. Our guy is on tomorrow for sure. And if somehow he's sick or gets fired, we just say, 'Thank you for your assistance,' and walk away and come up with some other crime of a lifetime."

"Yeah, right. We'll just wait for the World Series and rob all the beer stands at Fenway Park."

Cahill didn't smile often, but he did now. "World Series. You really think it's gonna happen?"

"It's early yet. Don't buy no tickets, because we're gonna be halfway around the world by then. Maybe we'll read about it in the *Sydney Daily Telegraph* a couple weeks later."

"Figures. They'll finally win the Series and I'll miss it."

"Hey, if you want, you'll be able to buy the team. Make Tom Yawkey an offer he can't resist."

Cahill smiled again. "I just might."

Dave T reached into his bottom desk drawer and pulled out a pint of Jameson. He tossed it to Cahill, then pulled out a matching bottle, popped the cap off, and raised it.

"To Fat Dave, God rest his soul. He made one hell of a fucking Manhattan."

"Slainte."

They drank.

OCTOBER 9, 1986

In the morning I asked the Rev if he remembered anything about our visit with master of the occult Timothy Sprague.

"Yeah, man. I remember some mind-roasting Turkish hash."

"Besides that. There was an untold tale of Charlesgate past, right?"

"Uh…yeah. That's right. Some kind of Mob hit or heist gone wrong, I believe."

"Do you remember any details? My notes from last night are kind of illegible."

"Let's see. I think…there were six guys. An ex-con, a bartender, a sniper, a couple others. They took down a racetrack. And all of them got killed except for the ex-con who organized it all. But when he got to the airport, his suitcase broke open and all the cash scattered to the wind."

"Chief. That's the plot of *The Killing*. The Kubrick movie? It was on *The Movie Loft* the other night."

"Oh yeah. I guess I confused Timothy Sprague with Dana Hersey. That was some primo fucking hash, man."

"Great. I guess I'll call the guy and see if I can set up another meeting, sans hash this time."

"Include me out."

I found Sprague's number and dialed. There was a click followed by a recording telling me the number I had dialed was not in service.

"Weird. His phone's disconnected. I just called him yesterday, same number."

The Rev whistled in approximation of the Theremin that Sprague had been playing the night before.

"Hardy fuckin' har. Shit, I owe my editor the next part of my Charlesgate series and I've got nothing but the same old second-hand stories."

"I got something for you. The other day I went down to do my laundry and this dead chick was in there folding her undies."

"What makes you think she was dead?"

"She was all pale and shit, like a corpse. And she didn't even look at me. It's like I wasn't even there."

"Okay, so you got ignored by a Goth chick. I'll tell my editor to hold the presses."

"I'm telling you, it was spooky as hell."

"Why would a dead girl need clean underwear?"

"Well…maybe she died with dirty skivvies on. And now her personal hell is to wash her underpants over and over for all eternity."

"Anyway, I've got to get to class."

"All right, man. Sorry I couldn't be more help."

I did go to class, though it would be a stretch to say I was in attendance. It was Music Appreciation with Professor Pussy-hound, who spent most of the class engaged in an intense argument with Jackie St. John's roommate about whether or not John Cage's *4'33"* constituted a piece of music. (The subtext of this debate, obvious to one and all, was "Let's fuck each other's brains out after class.") I tuned out and tried to work on my next article. Unfortunately, I'd already used up my supply of tried-and-true Charlesgate legends. I'd have to sit down with Mrs. Coolidge and hope she actually had something to say. I was essentially punting to Future Tommy, which, come to think of it, was a pretty good summation of my entire life strategy to that point.

After class I milled around by the Wall for a few minutes, shooting the shit with classmates who were just as sick of

Professor Pussyhound as I was. I decided to hoof it back to Charlesgate in hopes some burst of inspiration would strike. I'd made it half a block when I heard a female voice behind me.

"My hero!"

I stopped in my tracks. Jackie St. John caught up to me.

"Oh. Hey, Jackie."

"Hey yourself…"

"Tommy."

"I *know* that. You think I'd forget the name of the third greatest album ever recorded?"

"Third? Oh, that's right. We had this conversation. You have *Who's Next* first, right?"

"Damn right."

"And…wait, don't tell me…second place is *Quadrophenia*?"

"Bzzt. *Quadrophenia* is top five, no doubt, but I've got *The Who Sell Out* at number two. I lent you that bootleg of the outtakes, right?"

"Yeah. 'Sunday Morning, Cold Taxi.' Good stuff."

"Hell yeah. You think they'll ever get back together?"

"The Who? Oh, I doubt it. They all hate each other, and Keith Moon's always gonna be dead. Kenny Jones just doesn't do it for me."

"True. But that last album still had some good stuff on it. 'Eminence Front.' 'Cry If You Want.'"

"Yeah, that's true." As our conversation hit a lull, I realized I was walking Jackie St. John back to Charlesgate. This was a good thing. I hoped everyone I knew would come walking the other way and see us.

"So you're from around here, right?" she asked.

"Well, sort of. Maine."

"That's close, though."

"Yeah, southern Maine is close. But my folks live way up the coast. Downeast, they call it. About five hours from here."

"Acadia National Park, right? I hear it's beautiful up there."

"Yeah, I guess. But when you grow up there, you don't really think about it that way. I couldn't wait to get to civilization."

"No indoor plumbing, huh?"

"Worse. No cable." She laughed. My heart cranked like a jackhammer. "You're from New Jersey, right?"

"Yup. Whippany, NJ. No reason you ever would have heard of it."

"Ah, but I have heard of it. Guy's Pizza, right?"

"Holy shit! How do you know about Guy's?"

"We stopped there for dinner on a family road trip to Florida a few years ago. Totally random. Great fucking pizza."

"Bet your ass."

"I mean, Pizza Pad isn't bad either."

"True."

"Are you hungry? Because I was thinking of maybe heading over there for a slice."

"Oh, that would be cool, but…I better not. My boyfriend is taking me to dinner in the North End later, and we'll probably end up getting pizza."

I'm sure she said some things after that, but I didn't hear them. Pretty much everything after "boyfriend" was white noise to me. In fact, I don't even remember the rest of the walk back to Charlesgate. The next thing I remember is standing in front of Mrs. Coolidge's room on the third floor, knocking on the door.

The door opened a crack. I could see the glow of her cigar.

"It's me," I said. "If you're ready to tell your story now, I'm ready to hear it."

The Berkeley Beacon

OCTOBER 17, 1986

Charlesgate Confidential, Part II: The Lost Years

TOMMY DONNELLY, BERKELEY BEACON STAFF

If you live in Charlesgate or visit it frequently, you've probably seen Mrs. Selma Coolidge, even if you don't know her name. If so, you've no doubt wondered why this cigar-chomping woman in her sixties is sharing living space with 400 college students, especially if she's yelled at you to keep it down. If you ever stopped to talk to her—and if you could manage to sift through her highly imaginative worldview—you'd know Mrs. Coolidge represents one of the few links to the darkest, most mysterious period in Charlesgate's history.

In 1972, Boston University sold the Charlesgate to a private owner with little regard for Boston's rental codes. As the building rapidly deteriorated, it became a rooming house for anyone willing to pay and even some who were not. By the mid-1970s, the Charlesgate was populated by the fringes of society: artists, junkies, criminals, prostitutes, cultists and anyone else looking to maintain a low profile and low rent, and willing to overlook issues of appearance and safety.

Mrs. Coolidge lost her husband, Raymond Coolidge, in early 1973 and was left homeless and nearly destitute.

Scraping together what was left of her savings after paying off her husband's creditors, Mrs. Coolidge moved into a room on the third floor of the Charlesgate—the same room she occupies to this day. She made her way as a collector and seller of rare books. She had a knack for finding undervalued items at estate sales and secondhand shops and reselling them to collectors and rare-book purveyors at many times her original purchase price. Then as now she was a loner, avoiding most of her neighbors whenever possible, with one notable exception.

What follows is Mrs. Coolidge's story in her own words. Again it should be noted for the record that Mrs. Coolidge is subject to extreme flights of fancy during conversation, and I have edited what follows in the interest of eliminating extraneous tangents. She is a conspiracy theorist of the first order, and much of her story is all but impossible to confirm. Even so, it has the ring of emotional truth, and given the sketchy information available about this building in the 1970s, I felt it was worth reproducing her words here as one possible history of Charlesgate's lost years.

*

"In those days, my apartment was number 33. Across the hall was 34, and that's where Johnny lived. Johnny Seven. I know that wasn't his real name, but that's what he called himself. He was a musician. He had a band in the '60s called the Meat City Beatniks. They had a hit called 'A Month of Mondays.' It was a regional hit, only in New England, but I remembered it. He was shy, Johnny, and I didn't talk much either, but we seemed to hit it off. Not in any kind of sex way or anything like that. I was at least twenty years older than him, and after Raymond died, I had no interest anyway. But we had some other interests in common, mainly the Kennedy assassination and the Manson family, and we would talk about those things into the wee hours.

"Johnny liked to drink. I did too, but not like him. He'd do odd jobs, mostly working for moving companies, but he could never do it more than a couple weeks at a time. He'd stay home and work on his music. I could hear it drifting across the hall. He'd come knocking on my door about two or three in the afternoon and ask if I wanted to go to the Fallout Shelter. This bar on the corner, it really had been a fallout shelter in the '50s and '60s, but now it was just a bar with that name. I'd go with him just to talk, but he would get so drunk I'd have to half-carry him home at the end of the night and put him to bed. One time he was drunk enough to try to kiss me but I put an end to that in a big hurry. He was embarrassed the next day, but I told him it wasn't any big deal, just don't do it again.

"Around about 1975, things got real bad here at the Charlesgate. You'd hear screams in the middle of the night. I don't mean ghosts or any of that crap, I never did believe in that nonsense. But this doomsday cult had taken over the whole sixth floor. The End Times Church of the Final Retribution or Revelation or something like that. Who knew what was going on up there? You'd hear chanting come drifting down the elevator shaft at all hours. You'd see bloodstains on the stairs, men in black robes leading girls up the back staircase, young girls, 15 or 16 years old. Well, there was so much shit going on here in those days, it just seemed like part of the Charlesgate experience. But then Johnny started spending time up there on the sixth floor. When we'd go down to the Fallout Shelter, he'd tell me about how they weren't so bad and they helped him through some hard times. And he was drinking less, so that was a good thing. But I'd see less and less of him as time went on.

"It was the 4th of July, 1976. I'll never forget because that was the Bicentennial. It was a big deal. The Boston Pops played on the Esplanade, they had the Tall Ships in Boston Harbor, all of that. I came back here that night and I saw Johnny's door was wide open. I went in and saw the place had been totally ransacked. I knew he didn't trust banks and he kept all his money in cash in a guitar case in his closet. But now that guitar case was wide open in the middle of the floor and it was empty. Well, my first thought was those freaks on the sixth floor, so I went right up there. I heard the chanting. I followed the sound.

"It was coming from the room in the far southeast corner. The door was open a crack. I leaned in close and peered inside. I saw them gathered there, all in their black robes, a circle of candles in the middle. And blood dripping down. I looked up and saw my friend Johnny hanging there, his wrists bound to two ropes heading in opposite directions, both ending at upside-down crosses nailed to the ceiling. He was naked and he'd been slit from throat to belly. His guts hung from his body like he was a deer they'd slaughtered.

"I was scared for my life, but I called the police. They tried to tell me I was imagining things, because I'd called them a few times before on other matters and you know they had a special file on me. I finally talked them into sending an officer down, but it was almost two hours before he arrived. He checked the room out and found those people in their robes eating take-out pizza. Not a trace of Johnny Seven, but I know what I saw.

"The Church stayed another year and every few weeks they would approach me to come to one of their meetings. Of course, I never did. By 1978, the cult had either dissolved or moved on. The next year, Emerson College bought the building. They fought like hell to get me and the other tenants out of here. Most of them just went, but a social worker helped me and a few others pursue the matter in court. Under the rent control laws, they had no choice but to let me stay. And no one has ever asked me about it until just now."

*

I can confirm the last part of Mrs. Coolidge's claim. Emerson has no right to evict her, which is why she and several other non-student residents still remain. I can also confirm the existence of a doomsday cult called the End Times Church of the Final Revelation, and news articles dating back to the mid-'70s support the claim that they operated out of the Charlesgate for at least part of that time. "A Month of Mondays" was a regional hit for the Meat City Beatniks in 1966. Several articles in local papers name Johnny Seven as the songwriter and lead singer of the band. There is no evidence that Johnny Seven ever lived in the Charlesgate. His real name remains unknown, so there is no record of his death. No report was ever filed with the Boston police regarding a ritual sacrifice murder on July 4, 1976. If an officer did respond to Mrs. Coolidge's call, he never saw anything he considered worth reporting.

As a student journalist, I have no reason to believe Mrs. Coolidge's story. As a friend—and whether she would agree or not, I now consider her a friend—I couldn't help but believe her story. If you live in Charlesgate, and you see Mrs.Coolidge in the hall, chomping on her ever-present cigar, I urge you to say hello and strike up a conversation. I don't think you'll regret it.

APRIL 30, 2014

"We could go somewhere else if you want," said Coleman. "It's just, I've been wanting to check this place out and this is the first…well…"

"First date you've been on since the Clinton administration?" Jackie St. John Osborne inched closer to him as the rain started to pick up. He angled the umbrella to shield her from the onslaught. They were standing in line outside the Bleacher Bar on Lansdowne Street. What had begun as an overcast day with intermittent showers was turning into a rainy night in Boston town.

"Well, yeah. With someone besides…"

"Besides your wife. Do I have to finish all your sentences?"

"Ex-wife. Well, soon to be ex. I'm pretty sure, anyway."

"Keep digging, detective." The line started to move as people ahead of them bailed in anticipation of the Red Sox/Rays game being rained out.

"All I'm saying is, we don't have to eat here. There's a dozen places within two blocks. No reason we should stand in the rain."

Another group ahead of them departed, and suddenly they were inside.

"See?" Jackie said. "We're dry now. And I told you, I like this place. The Dersh reminds me of the hot pastrami sandwiches back home."

"New Jersey, right?"

"Yep."

"So you're a Yankee fan?"

"I grew up a Mets fan. And I was in college here in '86, as

you know. It was a little awkward, that World Series. I was one of the few people in my dorm happy with how it turned out."

"I was in fifth grade. I couldn't sleep for a week. Stayed up all night crying after the Buckner bobble."

"Yeah, me too. But not because of that. Anyway, fifth grade? Are you insinuating that I'm a cradle-robber?"

"Shit, you don't look a day over thirty."

"Okay, you're doing a little better now. Finishing sentences and everything."

They reached the hostess station. "Table for two?"

"Yes," said Coleman.

"It's your lucky day. We just had one open up in front."

The Bleacher Bar was both a part of Fenway Park and outside of it. It was a former garage converted into a restaurant. The entrance was separate from the park; you didn't need a ticket to the game, but you could still watch it from an unusual vantage point. The garage door was in center field. Watch a game on TV and you'd never know there was anything behind it, but from inside the Bleacher Bar, you had a clear view from directly behind the center fielder, through one-way glass.

The prospect of a game didn't look promising as Coleman and Jackie took their seats, however. The tarp was on the field and the game was officially in a delay. "April at Fenway," said Coleman. "You pays your money and you takes your chances. So are you still a Mets fan?"

"Are you kidding? I've lived in Boston for almost thirty years now. My resistance got worn down. I enjoyed 2004 as much as any townie, believe me."

"Pink hat."

"Oh, fuck you."

"I'm just messing with you! Man, and I was doing so well. Let's change the subject."

"You pick."

"Okay. So…heard from your friend Tommy Donnelly lately?"

Jackie bristled, pushing back in her chair. "What is this? Is this a date or something else?"

"Did I say something wrong?"

"Yeah, you asked me about Tommy. When you called me, you specifically said this had nothing to do with official business."

"It doesn't. It *is* a date. I just…I'm sorry. It's hard to take off my badge at the end of the day."

"So what? What's the fascination with Tommy Donnelly? What does he have to do with a murder that happened more than two decades after he blew town for good?"

"Probably nothing. But my leads at this point are fucking invisible. And some of the stuff your friend Tommy wrote about… well, it all sounds far-fetched. It might well be fiction…"

"It *was* fiction. Isn't that what he said at the time? That this stuff was all urban legends? Debunking the myths. That was the whole point."

"Yeah, but the Boston police took it seriously. Seriously enough to question him, right?"

Jackie shrugged. "When you're dealing with the biggest unsolved crime in the history of Boston, I guess any lead is worth pursuing. Right? I mean, you're the cop here."

"That's why I'm pursuing it. But that's not why I'm pursuing you."

"Oh hey, that was almost not completely lame! Good job."

Coleman laughed. "Blow me."

Jackie smiled. "Don't get ahead of yourself."

Coleman followed Jackie's lead and ordered the Dersh, a hot pastrami sandwich named after famed Harvard Law professor Alan Dershowitz. They split an order of bacon cheesy fries and drank two Sam Adams drafts each. The tarp never left the field and no players materialized. At 8:15, the game was officially called due to inclement weather.

"Bummer," said Coleman.

"Hey, we had a front-row seat to the grounds crew doing their thing. Those guys are amazing. Well worth the price of admission."

"Nice save," said Coleman. "But fortunately for you, I have a Plan B."

Jackie eyed him skeptically. "And what does Plan B involve?"

"Well, for one thing, it involves the wearing of ugly shoes."

"I don't own any ugly shoes."

"You don't have to. The ugly shoes will be provided. Jillian's is practically right across the street. We can run between the drops, as my Daddy used to say."

"Bowling? Wow, I haven't been bowling since…maybe since college."

"Excellent. Then there's a good chance you'll be impressed by my mediocre tenpin skills. Up to you, though. If you want to call it a night…"

"No. By all means, let's bowl."

Coleman paid the check and they dashed across Lansdowne and half a block down to Ipswich, where they entered Jillian's, an upscale fun emporium housing the Lucky Strike Lanes. The bowling alley was on the third floor, above a Spring Break-themed dance club and a sports bar/billiards room. Coleman paid for an hour in advance, and the attendant supplied them with shoes and a lane. While Jackie ordered a couple more Sams from the bartender, Coleman made a big show of selecting just the right ball. He promptly rolled a gutter on his first try.

"That's my rope-a-dope technique," he said. "Lulling you into complacency."

Jackie made a spare on her first frame.

"Not since college," said Coleman. "Right."

"I swear, detective."

"Ma'am, I've been doing this a long time. I know a lie when I hear one."

"So what's the deal? You always wanted to be a cop?"

"Ever since third grade, when my friend Dennis and I snuck into the theater showing *Beverly Hills Cop*."

"Good thing you didn't decide to see *Ghostbusters* instead."

Coleman laughed. "What about you? Working in PR, was that a lifelong dream?"

"Not really. It's what I studied at Emerson. I thought about broadcast journalism, but I was never good at the happy talk. I couldn't help rolling my eyes."

"I can see that."

"It pays well, my job. Sometimes it hurts my soul. Or it used to, before I was dead inside."

"Oh please."

"What I really wanted to do was illustrate children's books. I used to love to draw. I took a crack at it once. My friend wrote this book about a pig trying to escape a slaughterhouse. In retrospect, it was probably a little dark for the preschool audience, and my drawings didn't help. Petey the Pig looked like something out of a David Lynch movie. Anyway, I didn't stick with it. I sold out, and I can live with that."

"You can live very well, from what I've seen."

"You a gold digger, detective? I hate to burst your bubble, but there's no way I could live in the Charlesgate if my condo weren't already paid for. I do all right, but my ex did very well for himself."

"And you let him get away?"

"More like he traded me in for a younger model. Fifty-three years old, he suddenly decides he wants to be a father. I tell him that ship has sailed and well…"

"He found a new ship."

"Well, I should have known. He was married twice before me, like I told you and your partner the other day. And the last time, I was the younger woman."

"The circle of life. And you said this was your second husband?"

"Yeah, although the first one hardly counts. He was my college boyfriend and we hitched up way too young. Married at twenty-one, divorced at twenty-two."

"So no kids, huh? No interest?"

"I could never picture it. There's always pressure, of course, but I never felt that hole in my life. And like I said, my husband—second husband—wasn't interested either. Until he was. What about you?"

"Little girl. Eight years old. Alicia." Coleman took out his phone, selected a picture and showed it to Jackie.

"Cute as a bug."

"Daddy's little girl, except she's not too happy with Daddy these days. Won't even come to the phone when I call."

"So what happened there, with your wife? You screw around on her? No wait, let me guess: You were married to the job."

"That's right," said Coleman, picking up a spare. "Well, and I screwed around on her. Only once, and I would have got away with it, but…I had to tell her."

"Cracked under questioning, huh?"

"Guilty conscience. I'd make a terrible criminal. Anyway, my honesty allowed Donna to unburden herself. She'd been fucking my cousin Raymond for a year and a half. Shit, I should have started screwing around years ago. Best part is, she throws *me* out of the house. For all I know Raymond has moved his ass into my bedroom."

"You've got a gun, right? We could go down there, take care of this right now."

"Nah. They deserve each other. And maybe I deserve a little happiness now myself."

"Well, it's not gonna happen in this game." Jackie rolled her last ball, picking up eight more pins to add to her spare in the tenth frame. "That's me by…thirty-two? No, thirty-six!"

"Best two out of three," said Coleman. "And maybe we should put some money on it, make things a little interesting."

"How much?"

"Oh, I was thinking…maybe five million dollars?"

Jackie laughed. "And where, pray tell, did you come up with that figure?"

"That's the amount of the reward, right? Five million dollars. All these years later and nobody's claimed it."

Jackie set her ball down on the rack and folded her arms. "So that's your interest in Tommy? You think he can lead you to that reward?"

Coleman shrugged. "Why not us?"

JUNE 14, 1946

As they'd been instructed, as they'd been doing all week, Jake and Shane were seated in the booth nearest the pay phone at the Rosebud Diner in Somerville. Either the phone would ring or it wouldn't ring. If it didn't ring by four o'clock, they could leave. Come back the next day and do it all over again.

"We should just go," said Shane. "Just get out of town. Right now."

"We've been over this a hundred times. We're not going anywhere. You know how many times over there I heard we're going on a mission, we're probably not coming back? I went every time, I came back every time. I never said, 'No, guys, this time I'm not gonna go fight the Japs. I'll just stay here, read my Archie comics.' I did what I had to do."

"Well, thanks for the history lesson, but we're not exactly fighting for our country here. No one is gonna try us for desertion if we don't show up for this thing."

"Oh yeah? You really think we aren't under 24-hour surveillance? If this job is as big as Dave says, you think he's leaving anything to chance?"

"You went out the other night. Did that thing. Got away with it."

"Got away with it, but you think he hasn't figured out by now it was me wasted the fat man? I'm telling you, this guy is two steps ahead of us, and even if he ain't, we gotta assume he is. We gotta assume Dave T is expecting us to make a move sometime during this job. We gotta assume he has contingencies in place. This is a chess match now."

"Shit. I don't even know the last time I won at checkers."

Jake laughed despite himself. He couldn't remember the last time he'd done that. Shane noticed.

"You're in a good mood. You're enjoying this shit."

"It's different for me. I'm already on borrowed time. I should've died over there half a dozen times. Maybe my luck holds out. I'm gonna give it my best shot. I'm gonna get us out of this thing alive. Maybe even rich beyond our wildest dreams."

"You got no idea what Dave has planned."

"Nope. But I'm a pretty good improviser. Keep the faith, Shane. We ain't dead yet."

As if on cue, the phone rang. Jake raised a hand, stood up and answered it.

"Yeah."

"You're gonna take those dry cleaning bags to South Station tonight. You got wheels, right?"

"Yeah."

"Okay. Park in the overnight lot. Watch the signs. If you park in the one-hour lot, you maybe get towed, and if that happens, you'll never see your car again. Those bastards in the parking department are corrupt as the day is long."

"Good tip. Thanks."

"Once you're parked, you're gonna take those dry cleaning bags into the men's room, you're gonna change into the clothes inside 'em, you're gonna dump your old clothes in the garbage. You're gonna be outside on the corner of Summer and Atlantic at exactly 10 P.M. Any questions? No? Goodbye."

Jake hung up the phone and took his seat. "Well, it's a go for tonight. Whatever it is."

"What's the deal?"

"At ten o'clock tonight we're gonna be standing in front of South Station dressed like Boston's finest. That's all I know."

"You're packing your piece."

"Can't do it. They'll search us."

"So what exactly is your plan?"

"I told you. I'm good at improvising. Now let's just enjoy the afternoon. We've got a few hours. Let's go bowling or something."

"Bowling? Are you crazy?"

"We gotta do something. How about a last meal? The condemned man always gets one. If you could eat anywhere tonight, where would it be?"

They ate dinner at the Union Oyster House. Shane had the broiled fillet of sole, Jake enjoyed the Lobster Newburg, and they split a dozen cherrystones. At nine o'clock they hopped into Jake's Crown Imperial, dry cleaning in tow. At 9:25 they parked at South Station, in the overnight lot as instructed. By 9:45 they had changed into their BPD patrolman's uniforms. By 10 P.M. on the dot, they were standing on the corner of Summer and Atlantic.

Not thirty seconds had passed before a tan DeSoto sedan pulled up to the curb in front of them. Dave T stepped out of the passenger door, opened the back door and gestured inside. Shane and Jake exchanged a wary glance, then climbed into the back seat. Dave T slammed the door behind them and reclaimed his spot in the front.

"Got one more thing for you baby-faced boys," said Dave T. He held his hand out over the back of his seat. Jake reached out and took what he offered.

"What are these?"

"Mustaches. Here, this is spirit gum." He handed Shane a small bottle. "Smear it all over your upper lip and press those mustaches on."

"Is this a costume party?"

"It's a disguise, not a costume. You boys ain't gonna look like real cops without 'em."

Reluctantly, Shane and Jake applied the spirit gum and pressed on the mustaches.

"Looks good," said Dave T. "Who knows, someday you might be able to grow your own."

"That's funny," said Jake. "I'm gonna start laughing any minute now."

"Woke up on the wrong side of the bed this morning, huh? Well, you'll be laughing all the way to the bank once we finish up here tonight."

"Where are we going?"

"You'll see."

Joey Cahill was behind the wheel. He cut through Chinatown and picked up Boylston Street westbound.

"So in your mind," said Jake, "we do this job tonight and then all part as friends. No hard feelings."

"Sure, why not? We go our separate ways. If you're smart, you'll leave town right away. I'm gonna give you a phone number. Two weeks from now, you call the operator and ask for that number in Florida. When the operator connects you, you ask for Captain Spaulding."

"The African explorer."

"You got it. He'll have your cut, he'll wire it to wherever the fuck you are, Timbuk One or wherever."

Cahill cut down to Commonwealth Avenue at Arlington, continuing west.

"So Shane and me, we shouldn't have any concerns at all tonight?"

"Well, it's a job. There's always a risk. Otherwise, everyone would do it. Ted Williams would tell old man Yawkey to shove that baseball bat sideways and start making some real jack."

"Right, but from you. We have no concerns on that front?"

"I could ask you the same."

"You got the advantage on us. We don't know where we're going, what we're doing, nothing."

"You'll know soon enough. But as long as we're playing *Truth or Consequences*, I got a question for you. That night you boys took down my game. How did you get in the building? I gotta figure you had an inside man. Not that it matters so much now, what with us all about to be rich and blowing town and all. But I'm curious. You guys got one over on me and that doesn't happen too often."

"You got a point there," said Jake. "It doesn't matter much now. But what the hell, now we're partners and all, might as well tell you. It was Dryden, that whoremaster on the sixth floor. Matter of fact, I still owe him three large for the tip."

"Dryden, huh? Sounds like bullshit to me."

"Well, like you said. Doesn't matter much now, one way or the other."

Cahill drove through the intersection of Commonwealth and Charlesgate East into Kenmore Square. He hung a left on Brookline Ave.

"Holy shit," said Shane. "Fenway Park? We're knocking over Fenway fucking Park?"

Dave T laughed. "I thought of that. But no. That's small potatoes."

"Jesus. This I gotta see."

Cahill drove several blocks past the ballpark, then hooked a left on Fenway. A few hundred yards later, he turned left on Palace and killed the engine.

"There it is," said Dave T, pointing to a three-story building across the street. The building was designed to resemble a 15th-century Venetian palazzo, not that anyone in the DeSoto would have recognized such a thing.

Jake leaned forward, squinting. "What the hell is it?"

"That is the Isabella Stewart Gardner Museum."

"A museum? Are you shitting me? You think a fuckin' museum has more cash on hand than Fenway fuckin' Park?"

"No. But we're not taking the money. We're taking the art."

"Art? We're boosting, what, a bunch of pictures?"

"Don't know much about fine art, do you?"

"No, I never finished high school. I was over—"

"Yeah, I know. You were overseas fighting for our beloved country. Duly noted. Truth is, I don't know much about it either. But I got a guy, and he's got connections, and they will pay millions, maybe tens of millions, for the right paintings."

"And you know the right paintings?"

"I got a list."

"And what are we up against?"

"One pimply faced security guard. A fuckin' fortune in there and that's how they protect it. The fuckin' underwear department at Filene's is better guarded. I guess that's artsy people for ya."

"There's no way this is going to be that easy."

"I already told ya, kid. It's gonna be like—"

"Yeah, yeah. Like taking candles from a baby."

OCTOBER 10, 1986

Mrs. Coolidge's story was pretty good. I had no way to verify most of it, but as long as I made it clear this was a "lost legend of the Charlesgate," that shouldn't be a problem. Her story might even make for a good screenplay someday.

I wrote it up as the second part of my Charlesgate series for the *Berkeley Beacon*. I had a feeling Mighty Rob would really get a kick out of it, but at the same time, it would be hard to follow up. Little did I realize that the best Charlesgate story of all was about to fall right in my lap…or at least, that's how it seemed at the time.

The rest of my week was uneventful. The Red Sox had a travel day Thursday, with the ALCS set to resume in Anaheim on Friday, tied at a game apiece. Purple Debbie continued to avoid me, or we continued to avoid each other, depending on how you looked at it. On Friday I had no classes, so after making a token attempt at doing some homework, I decided to call it a weekend and head over to the Fallout Shelter. Enough time had passed since my last fateful stop at the watering hole that I figured no one would remember me. There had probably been three or four stabbings since then.

I took a seat at the bar. I didn't recognize the bartender, but then, why would I? He and I had the place to ourselves at 3:30 in the afternoon.

"What can I getcha?"

"I'll have a Knick."

"Sure thing. I see some ID?"

I passed him my fake. He looked at it without really looking at it and passed it back. He popped open a bottle of Knickerbocker and handed it to me. "Dollar twenty-five."

I paid him, including a generous twenty-five cent tip.

"So whaddaya think? Sox gonna bring this thing back to Boston?"

"Wouldn't it be pretty to think so?"

"Seems kinda like the Angels' year, right? The singin' cowboy and all that shit."

The front door swung open and I winced against the daylight. An older gentleman, maybe in his mid-6os, entered the bar. He took a seat two stools down from me.

"Getcha, my friend?"

"Do they still make Narragansett?"

"Sure, I can getcha a Gansett."

"That will be fine."

The old-timer paid for his Narragansett and took a long sip. "Ahhh. I haven't had a cold one in…a really long time."

"Been on the wagon?" I asked.

"Not on purpose. Last drink I had was a nasty cup of toilet wine."

"Toilet wine. I'm not familiar with that vintage. Where did you get that?"

"MCI Walpole. Well, it was Walpole when I went in, back in '56 after they shut down Charlestown. It was MCI Cedar Junction when I got out, ten o'clock this morning. But it was the same fuckin' place by any name, believe me."

"Wait, you got out of prison this morning?"

"Ten o'clock this morning. My obligation to the great state of Massachusetts has been discharged, and I think that calls for another beer." The old man drained his Gansett and set the bottle on the table. The bartender obliged him.

"You've been in prison since 1956?"

"No. I've been in since 1946. Ten years in Charlestown, thirty years in Walpole. Or Cedar Junction, whatever they want to call it."

"Forty years. What did you do?"

"Not a damn thing. Well, look, I was no angel. I did a few things. But what they accused me of? That I didn't do."

The bartender offered a shit-eating grin. "Only innocent men in prison, huh?"

"No innocent men. I never claimed to be innocent. Not guilty of this particular crime? Yes. I was set up. After that, it's up to the lawyers, and mine did me no good at all. Lucky I didn't get the chair. They still had it in this state back then, you know. The death penalty. And that's what they gave me at first. I spent a year on death row, but one thing and another, it got commuted to a life sentence. No chance of parole for forty years. Well, my forty years is up and I guess the parole board decided I'm not much of a menace to society no more. So here I am. How about another Gansett?"

The bartender opened another bottle. I raised my empty Knick and he opened one for me, too.

"So are you?" I asked. "A menace to society, I mean?"

"Do I look like a fuckin' menace? I'm a menace to myself. An old man with thirty bucks to his name, no living relatives, not a friend in the world. I'll be dead by Christmas."

"That's the spirit."

"Hey, if these fuckin' Red Sox can win the World Series, I'll die in peace. I've been waiting my whole fuckin' life. I was on trial in '46 when they lost to the Cardinals. Pesky held the ball, they said on the radio. In '67, it was the Cards again. The Impossible Dream, they called it. And impossible it was. In '75, that's the first one I saw on TV. Fisk hits the homer in Game 6, waves it fair, place goes nuts. Another Game 7 loser. And then the playoff in '78 with the Yankees. Bucky fuckin' Dent. They owe me, these cocksuckers. If they don't do it this year, I'll never live to see it."

"So what are you going to do? For…work or whatever? Don't you have a parole officer?"

"Oh yeah. He's already set me up with an interview at McDonald's. I've only ever seen it on TV. You deserve a break today, right? Minimum wage to clean the toilets at a burger joint. And that's if I get the job, which there are no guarantees. But whaddaya gonna do? Too late for me to go to computer school."

"Well, what did you do before? Prison, I mean?"

The old man laughed. "Kid, ain't you paying attention? I was a criminal! Small-time, sure. Matter of fact, one time my brother and I knocked over a poker game right around the corner here. That's why I came down this way, I guess. Nostalgia. Thought I could get a look at the ol' Charlesgate, but they turned me away."

I straightened up. "Charlesgate? Right here at the end of the block?"

"Yeah. What about it?"

"I live there."

Now the old man seemed to take a renewed interest in me. "What'd you say your name is, kid?"

"I didn't, but it's Tommy Donnelly."

"And you live in the Charlesgate. The crazy building with the towers and the devil faces and all that?"

"Yeah. It's an Emerson College dorm now. I'm a journalism student and I'm writing a…sort of a history of the building. If you've got some stories…"

"Oh, I've got stories."

"Well, maybe we could work something out. I don't have a

lot of money, but I could get you some food out of the Canteen, maybe—"

"Can you get me in that building?"

"Uh…well, sure. I guess I could tell them you're my grand-father or something and sign you in."

The old man leaned across the bar and extended his hand to me. "Pleased to meetcha, Tommy Donnelly. My name is Shane Devlin. And I got a story that'll win you the Wurlitzer Prize."

MAY 1, 2014

Coleman sat at his desk, which was covered with the photo-copied blueprints of the Charlesgate from the architectural study he'd downloaded. The floor plans dated back to the 1980s, and everything about the building's layout was completely crazy. What was now Jackie's condo had then been three separate dorm rooms and a common bathroom. The place had been gutted after Emerson sold off the building, and there was no telling what it had looked like in the years before the college took it over. *Architectural Digest* hadn't sent any photographers over in the '70s, the Charlesgate's dark ages.

"Heads up, Coltrane. We caught a call."

Startled, Coleman spilled his coffee all over the blueprints. "Goddammit, Carny!"

"Jesus, Coltrane. You are one jumpy-ass homicide detective. I might need to request a new partner. I don't exactly feel secure with your skittish ass backing me up."

Coleman mopped up his coffee with the blueprints. At least they were copies, although his notes were now illegible. "What do you want, Carny?"

"I just told you, we caught a call. Damn, Trane, your mind is not on the job."

"The fuck it's not. I was just working on our Charlesgate whodunit."

"By looking at blueprints? Trane, that case is colder than your wife's…meatloaf."

"Don't ever mention my wife's meatloaf again."

"Sensitive! I think it's your meat that's been loafing. You see what I did there?"

Coleman trashed the coffee-soaked blueprints and got up in Carnahan's face. "Yeah. I see. Let's go if we're going."

Carnahan drove. Coleman fiddled with his wedding ring.

"Where are we going, anyway?" Coleman asked.

"Southie. Excuse me, 'SoBo.' That's what they call it now the yuppies have taken over. Once again, the hard-working Irishman gets the squeeze."

"Carny, you're from fucking Vermont. Don't make like you're the last Mick standing in Southie."

"It's in the blood, Coltrane. If you can be an African-American even though you've never set foot in Africa, then I can claim solidarity with Southie."

"When have you ever heard me call myself an African-American?"

"Quit changing the subject. We were talking about Donna's meatloaf."

"I told you never to—"

"Never to mention it again. Which I wouldn't, except you bailed on me the other night because you were going home for said meatloaf. Which you always say. Which you never do."

"Jesus, Carny, I already told you I went to the Emerson library that night."

"What about every other night? Donna called the office looking for you yesterday. Apparently you weren't answering your cell. I'm making small talk with her, say I'm sorry I missed meatloaf night. She doesn't know what the fuck I'm talking about. Tells me she threw you out on your ass three weeks ago."

"So why did she call the office?"

"Just making sure you hadn't done anything stupid."

"Yeah, like I'd kill myself over that bitch."

"Don't try and come off all hard, Trane. I don't blame her for wondering."

"You don't know shit. I have moved on already, okay? I am out there…moving on."

"Yeah, right. You wouldn't even come out to the Tap the other night."

"Why would I come out to the Tap with a bunch of dudes when I could be out with a fine-ass…forget it."

"Forget it my ass. You went on a date? Bullshit."

"I said forget it."

"Oh, shit," said Carnahan. "That broad from the Charlesgate."

"I'm not saying it again."

"No, man. I caught that look on your face when she said she was getting divorced."

"What look?"

"That 'I want to get in this bitch's panties' look."

"Come on, man."

"You come on. This bitch is a person of interest in a fucking homicide we're investigating. And what, you fucked her?"

"We had dinner. We went bowling. I didn't fuck her."

"But you're planning to fuck her. You didn't ask her out to brush up on your bowling."

"She's a surprisingly good bowler."

"I'm serious, Coltrane. This is not good."

"It's all good if you keep it to your fuckin' self, like a real partner would."

"Don't put this on me, man. This is all on you."

"You said yourself, the case is cold. The trail is a dead-end. Jackie had nothing to do with this."

"If the killer broke into her place and stole her laptop, I don't see how you can say that."

"If ifs and buts were candy and nuts, we'd all have a merry Christmas."

"I have no idea what that means."

"It means we're here. Rotary Liquors, right? Pull over and let's get to work."

"To be fuckin' continued, Trane." Carnahan pulled into the tiny Rotary Liquors parking lot next to the responding officers' cruiser. He and Coleman ducked under the crime scene tape and entered the liquor store. What appeared to be a teenage boy with half his face missing was sprawled in a pool of blood in front of the counter. One of the officers was questioning a man Carnahan took to be the store's proprietor. He approached the other officer.

"What do we have here?"

"Pretty much what it looks like. This kid comes in, asks for a fifth of Johnny Walker. The owner there asks for his ID. The kid pulls out a Glock Nine. Without breaking a sweat, I'm assuming, the owner pulls his shotgun from under the counter and takes half the kid's head off before he can even think about pulling the trigger."

"The owner doesn't deny it?"

"Nah, he's pretty damn proud of it, tell you the truth. And the eye in the sky should confirm the obvious." The officer indicated a security camera monitor mounted overhead.

"Good. It's nice to have an easy one for a change."

Coleman was kneeling beside the body when his cell phone started to buzz. He checked the number. It was headquarters.

"Coleman," he answered.

"Coleman, it's Gomez. I just caught a call for you."

"I'm already on a call."

"Yeah, but this guy specifically asked for the detective in charge of the Charlesgate murder."

"Who is he?"

"Name's Woodward. Nicholas Woodward. Says he's an art detective."

"Art detective? That's a thing?"

"Apparently."

"Well, what's he want with me?"

"He says he might have a pretty good idea who popped your Charlesgate vic. You want his number?"

"Fuck do you think?"

JUNE 15, 1946

Officers Pinkham and McCullough sat in their squad car at the corner of Ipswich and Lansdowne as the clock struck midnight.

"I can't do these overnight shifts much longer," said Pinkham. "I got a very particular metabolism. I can't eat after midnight."

"So don't eat," said McCullough. "You could lose a few pounds."

"I can't go all night without eating. I don't eat, I get light in the head. You don't want a dizzy cop backing you up."

"I'd say that ship has sailed."

"Wise guy. But the problem is, there's no schedule to it. I mean, you work a regular day shift, it's easy. Breakfast is breakfast. You eat it in the morning. Lunch at noon. Dinner after work. Simple. But you work overnight, all that's out the fuckin' window. You don't know when to eat."

"I know when to eat. My wife packs me a sandwich, I eat it when I get hungry enough to eat it. What could be more fuckin' simple than that?"

"Well, you got a wife. It's different."

"You can make your own sandwich. It don't exactly require a college degree."

"I could really go for a ham and cheese. Charlie's is open until one. Swing over there and I'll get a ham and cheese."

"Here's what you do. You go to the deli. You ask 'em to slice you off a pound of ham, a half pound of cheese. I like cheddar, but you get what you want. You buy a loaf of bread, a jar of mustard, presto. Ham and cheese sandwiches for a week. You can even pick up some fresh tomatoes and lettuce at the Haymarket."

"I like a hot sandwich. Charlie's makes a hot ham and cheese. Fresh. Not sitting in a bag all night."

"Oh, well, excuse me, Chef. I didn't realize you were such a fussy eater."

"It's two blocks away, just swing over there. This town is dead tonight. There's not a peep on the radio. I'm starving."

McCullough sighed and started the car. "Fine. But I'm tellin' ya, we're gonna catch a call tonight. There's something in the air here lately. You heard about the fat man the other night?"

"Of course. Why, you know something?"

"I hear things."

"Things?"

"Things. I dunno. Guy had a reputation. Lotta lowlifes would like to take credit for that one."

"He had a lotta friends, too. Whoever did it, I wouldn't expect 'em to grow old."

"Probably not. But I dunno why we can't ever catch a call like that. Would make the long nights pass a little faster, that's for sure." McCullough pulled up in front of Charlie's Kitchen in Kenmore Square. "Here ya go, your highness."

"I'll be out quick." Pinkham popped out of the passenger side door and headed into Charlie's. McCullough kept his eye on the sidewalk traffic, hoping for something, anything to happen.

After five minutes, the car radio crackled. "All units. Reports of shots fired in the Fenway, near the Gardner Museum."

McCullough almost gave himself a hernia reaching for the radio mike. "Car 27 here. We're in the immediate vicinity. On our way."

McCullough leaned on the horn. Through the storefront window of Charlie's, he could see Pinkham at the counter, holding up his index finger. McCullough leaned on the horn again, then triggered the siren. Pinkham threw up his arms, then came running out and climbed back in the car.

"What the fuck, my sandwich isn't ready yet!"

"Fuck your sandwich. We got a call. Shots fired." McCullough squealed away from the curb and made a U-turn. He leaned on the pedal all the way down Brookline Ave before taking a hard left onto Fenway. No more than two minutes after pulling away from Charlie's, he stomped on the brakes in front of the Gardner Museum, shut down the engine and jumped out of the car. Pinkham followed.

McCullough drew his gun as he approached the Gardner entrance. The front door was wedged open. As he closed in, McCullough could see that it was wedged open by an adult human body. Judging by the red pool surrounding it, a dead adult human body. But McCullough wasn't taking any chances.

"This is the Boston police!" he shouted. "If you can hear me, raise your hands above your head!"

McCullough didn't expect a response and didn't get one. He took the last few steps forward, then kneeled beside the body.

The departed was a male in his late thirties. His shirt was soaked in blood. The ivory handle of a straight razor lay against the center of his chest, almost spotless, but the blade was thickly coated with blood.

"Holy shit," said McCullough. "What did I tell you? What did I just fucking tell you? We finally caught a good call."

"A good call? Is he dead?"

"Oh, he's very fucking dead. And I know who he is. Well, I don't know his real name, but I know his street name. This is a big one."

"Well, spill! Who the fuck is it?"

"You ever heard of Dave T?"

Whatever "Wurlitzer" Prize-winning story the old man who'd introduced himself as Shane Devlin had in mind, he was in no mood to share it with me at the moment. He didn't know if he could trust me, he said, and just like Mrs. Coolidge, he had to ask around about me first. I had no idea who he was planning to ask or what sort of information he was after, but I wrote down my name and phone number on a napkin so he could get in touch with me if I passed muster. In retrospect, maybe I should have given a little more thought to turning my contact info over to a man who'd just spent forty years in prison, but since he already knew where I lived, why not go all in? At that point, I figured there was at least an eighty percent chance the guy was a complete crackpot.

I'd filled up on free Buffalo wings at the Fallout Shelter, but decided to swing by the Canteen anyway just to see if I could catch the dinner crew. Sure enough, Murtaugh, Brooks, Rodney, Jules, and the Rev were at our usual table. And so was Purple Debbie. I decided to play it cool, taking the open seat directly across from her.

"Happy Friday, folks!" That didn't come out quite as nonchalantly as I'd hoped, thanks in part to the four Knickerbockers I'd guzzled while chatting with Devlin.

"Are you drunk?" Murtaugh asked.

"I'm not drunk. I had a couple Knicks at the Fallout Shelter."

"They let you back in that place?"

"Of course. What, you're surprised they have no standards? Anyway, I got talking to this guy who just got out of prison, and he might have some good shit on the old days of Charlesgate for me. It was a career day all around."

"Sounds like you've got a lot to be proud of," said Brooks.

"Yeah, well, I'm sure you've got something much more important going on."

"As a matter of fact, I do."

Rodney rolled his eyes, spearing his Salisbury steak. "Brooks has been hanging out with the no-nukes kooks."

"They're not kooks. We're organizing a protest against the Seabrook nuclear power plant next week."

"Which is in the sovereign state of New Hampshire and thus none of your goddam business. And you can tell Generalissimo Dukakis I said so."

"It's on the border. There are four Massachusetts towns within ten miles of the plant, which means they're in the evacuation zone, which means Governor Dukakis has to approve the evacuation plan before Seabrook can open. Radiation doesn't recognize state borders, Rodney."

"Hey, good for you, Brooks," I said. "I'd join you except, you know, this very important article I've gotta work on."

All this time, I could sense Purple Debbie staring a hole in the side of my head, but I hadn't been able to bring myself to meet her gaze. With great effort, I now did so.

"What's up, Deb?"

"Oh, look! I exist!"

I tried to laugh it off. "Of course you exist. What, you think I've been avoiding you or something?"

"Maybe I've been avoiding *you*."

"Well, that's kind of the impression I got."

"Sure you did. Because it's all about *you*, right?"

I glanced around the table. We had everyone's undivided attention. "Do you really want to do this now?" I asked.

"Do what? You started it."

"I said 'what's up.' That's all I said."

"Oh right, *you're* the bigger person. You know they're all on your side no matter what," she said, gesturing dismissively to the rest of the group.

"I have no idea what's going on right now," said Jules.

"In fairness to the senator from Maine," said Murtaugh, "I was in the room the other night, and—"

"Hey, hey, hey, we're not in court here," I said. "I don't need any expert testimony. Debbie, why don't we just talk about this privately—"

"I keep telling you, there's nothing to talk about! I'm back with Chad, case closed."

"You're back with your gay boyfriend?" Murtaugh asked.

"He's not gay! He was *confused*."

"Brooks," said Murtaugh. "You ever get confused and think maybe you like dick?"

"Umm…"

"Wait, why am I asking you? Rodney! You ever get confused and think maybe you prefer cock to the sweet, sweet poontang?"

"There's absolutely no confusion," said Rodney. "I am no man's butt-boy."

"What about you, Rev? Any confusion?"

"No, man. I got no problem with gay people, but dick is not on my menu."

"How about you, Tommy? Is cock—"

"Fuck you guys!" The Canteen seemed to go completely silent as Purple Debbie shrieked. "Fuck you all! Chad is NOT a homo. And you don't even have to ask Tommy! Because he ate my pussy like it was his last fucking meal!"

I don't think I actually slid under the table, but every instinct in me was crying out to do so. I didn't have to look up to know that every eye within a five table radius was on me. Purple Debbie stormed out of the Canteen to a wild round of applause —catcalls, whistles, the works. An eternity seemed to pass while I searched for something to say.

"So…you guys wanna go watch the game?"

The Red Sox lost Game 3 and the next day they lost Game 4. It didn't look good. A season that had begun with so much promise, with Dwight Evans hitting the first pitch he saw out of Fenway for a leadoff homer, was about to go down the toilet like so many others. But I had other plans for my Saturday. I went back to the Boston Public Library to search the daily papers from 1946 in hopes of finding out why Shane Devlin had received a life sentence. I started with the December 31 issue and worked my way backwards from there. Two hours later, I reached the October 16 issue. At the top of the front page, I saw this headline:

COP KILLER DEVLIN SENTENCED TO
DEATH FOR DOUBLE SLAYING

My new pal from the Fallout Shelter had been convicted for killing two men, one of them a police officer, on June 14, 1946. So that was reassuring.

MAY 1, 2014

Coleman pressed "End Call" and pocketed his phone. He had set up a meet with "art detective" Nicholas Woodward in an hour at Grendel's in Harvard Square. Now he just had to clear it with his partner.

"Hey, Carny. You got this under control?"

Carnahan shrugged. "Perp's on his way downtown with our guys. I'm guessing he's connected in such a way as to make bail almost immediately, and I will be shocked shitless if he doesn't plead self-defense. Ain't nothing left for us to do here. Why?"

"I mighta caught a break on our Charlesgate case."

"No shit?"

"Well...might be bullshit, but like you said, we got nothing going on this one."

"Hey, knock yourself out. I'll finish up the fine print here. Give me a call later. But Trane?"

"Yeah?"

"I ain't forgotten our earlier conversation. You wrap this up, great. Our girl's not involved, you have my permission to bring the ruckus to her fine-ass tuchus. Otherwise we've got more words ahead."

"Fine. Jesus, Carny."

Coleman jumped on the Red Line at Broadway and rode it all the way to Harvard Square. He walked the block from Out of Town News to Grendel's Den and took at a seat at the bar with five minutes to spare. He ordered a shot of Jameson and a Miller High Life and checked his text messages. A new one popped up while he was looking: "Walking in now." He turned to face the door. A white-haired man in a Louis Vuitton suit stepped in and carefully made his way down the steps to the bar area. Coleman raised a hand and the man joined him at the bar.

"You're Woodward?"

"I am. And you are Detective Coleman." His accent was posh London. Coleman shook his hand.

"Want a drink? It's on me, assuming you aren't full of shit."

"I am not. And I'll have a glass of Cabernet."

Coleman made the order, then set his phone on the bar, dictation app on. "You don't mind if I record this?"

"Not at all."

"You are Nicholas Woodward and you're an…art detective?"

"Yes. My official job title for many years was Fine Arts Claims Adjuster, but I've been retired for some time. Well, semi-retired. I still take on the occasional freelance assignment."

Woodward's piercing gaze and easy smirk reminded Coleman of the British actor Malcolm McDowell. "Is that why you're here?"

"Indeed. I've retired to St. John's Wood, but quite recently I received an offer I found difficult to refuse. You see, I spent several years here back in the late '70s to early '80s. In fact, I lived very near here and frequented this pub, which I why I chose it today. I was working for Lloyd's of London, and my primary assignment in those days was the Gardner Museum robbery. I assume you're familiar?"

"I grew up here. I am very familiar."

"Well, you see, it was my job to exhaust all possible avenues of recovering the stolen art. And I did that. I had no shortage of leads. It was the IRA, it was Whitey Bulger, it was the Kennedys. Every con artist in the Western Hemisphere was lined up to assist my investigation. Your familiarity with the case extends to the reward?"

"Five million, isn't it?"

"It is now. After the robbery, back in the '40s, it started at $500,000. It's gone up ever since. And in all that time there has not been one legitimate claim on the reward. One man was found dead at the scene of the robbery. A man with many known criminal associates who would kill for far less money. And yet none of them ever came forward."

"At some point this will all lead to a reason you called me here when I was in the middle of another murder investigation. I am not the art police, Mr. Woodward."

"I understand that. And this does concern a murder. Or at least, I believe it does. And as I mentioned, I've been an investigator for many, many years."

"My Charlesgate vic. You see a connection."

"As I said, I was employed by Lloyd's of London at the time of my original investigation. In 1981, I grew homesick and the company reassigned me to England. I was disappointed I'd never cracked the Gardner case, but eager for new challenges. The Gardner case never left my mind, but it…receded. Until two weeks ago. A documentary filmmaker contacted me. She's making a film about the robbery, and she offered to fly me back here for some interviews and possibly to follow up a few leads. This filmmaker, a Ms. Cindy Klein, is a graduate of Emerson College, and an admirer of another Emerson graduate, a true-crime writer named Thomas Donnelly. She'd wanted to adapt one of his books into a film, but was never able to get in touch with him. She'd also obtained a file of Mr. Donnelly's clippings from the Emerson newspaper, the *Berkeley Beacon*, including an article that referenced the Gardner heist. That's what sparked her interest. I had never seen this article—it was published years after I left the country, and in any case, I'm not in the habit of reading college newspapers. It was a fascinating read."

"Yeah, I've read it."

Woodward raised an eyebrow. "Have you? May I ask why?"

"Later. Cut to the chase, Mr. Woodward."

"Of course. The article postulates an interesting theory about the Gardner robbery, as you know. After reading it, I was very interested in speaking to Mr. Donnelly."

"You think this Donnelly knows where these paintings are? And for some reason he never came forward to claim the five million dollars?"

Woodward smiled. "Are you an art lover, Detective Coleman?"

"Not really."

"Neither am I, to tell you the truth. But I do love a mystery. Solving a mystery, that is. I think that's something you and I have in common?"

"That's the job. That's why I'm still listening."

"My point is this. I had no way of knowing whether Mr. Donnelly knew anything about the art or its whereabouts. But it was a lead, however tenuous. Had it ever been followed up? That I didn't know. So I wanted to speak with him."

"Something of a recluse, isn't he?"

"So I came to understand. Ms. Klein hadn't been able to get in touch with him, and my usual methods came up dry. His publisher was of no help. Apparently he contacts them when he finishes a book. They never even know what he's working on until he delivers it. But it occurred to me that the Emerson alumni office might have his contact information. Colleges generally keep close track of their big fish, so to speak."

"And you think they'd share that information with you?"

"Not officially, of course. Not as an institution. But institutions are made up of individuals. Individuals who might become helpful after hearing about a five-million-dollar reward. So I made an appointment with one such individual: Charles White, the direc-tor of alumni research and records at Emerson

College. As it turns out, Mr. White did not have the information I sought. But he thought he knew someone who might."

"Who's that?"

"A Mrs. Jackie Osborne. Formerly Jackie St. John."

Coleman motioned to the bartender, trying to maintain a poker face. "And who is she?"

"She was a classmate of Mr. Donnelly's at Emerson. Mr. White has been assisting her in setting up a class reunion at the Charlesgate, which I believe is the site of the murder you're investigating, as well as the building Mr. Donnelly wrote about in his article."

"So...your theory is that this Charles White is my Charlesgate perp? That seems like quite a leap."

"Maybe. But surely, Detective Coleman, you've encountered people who would kill for far less than five million dollars."

"So spell it out for me. You think this White made an appointment with the Charlesgate realtor and killed her for the keys to this...Mrs. Osborne's condo, so he could search it for Donnelly's contact info?"

"Hmm. No, actually, that had never occurred to me. Why, was Mrs. Osborne's condo searched?"

"Never mind that. What *did* you think?"

"That Mr. White believed the stolen art from the Gardner Museum might be hidden somewhere in the Charlesgate."

"Are you serious? For what, almost seventy years now? That place has been through three or four owners. As far as I know, it was stripped to the bone and completely remodeled when the current outfit bought it. That seems like an awful fucking long shot to kill someone over."

"Perhaps. But Mr. White grew very, very interested when I mentioned the reward. And even more interested when I estimated the current value of the stolen art."

"Which is what?"

"North of two hundred million dollars. At a rough estimate, of course."

"Jesus."

"But still a long shot, I understand. Except that I went back to meet with Mr. White on April 24, the day after the murder was reported. I had seen it on the news and my suspicions immediately turned to him. But when I got to his office, his assistant, a Ms. Tucker, informed me that White had called her that morning to say he wouldn't be coming in to work. That, in fact, something had come up and he was leaving his job. When she asked for an explanation, he simply hung up on her. I called again two days later to see if he'd had a change of heart, and once again this morning. Ms. Tucker assures me he hasn't returned, nor has she heard from him at all since his initial call. I suspect if you were to investigate further, you would find his place of residence abandoned."

"Even assuming all this is true, it's still thin from an evidentiary standpoint. But I don't think you called me here to help me solve a murder. I think you were hoping I'd let something slip about my investigation. Something that might help you locate those paintings."

Woodward smirked. "Why not both? I see no reason we can't help each other."

"So in this scenario, White disappearing without a trace, do you think there's a chance he found what he was looking for?"

Woodward raised an eyebrow and raised his glass. "That, detective, is the mystery."

JUNE 16, 1946

"After calling in the 10-54, you returned to the premises and you and Officer Pinkham entered the museum?"

"That's right. We entered with our weapons drawn and began our search. After approximately twenty minutes, we found the security guard in the basement. Tied up, with a gag in his mouth."

"You untied him and removed the gag?"

"Yes. He explained that he had opened the door to two uniformed policemen shortly after midnight. The officers claimed they were responding to a disturbance call, but after gaining admittance to the building, they quickly overpowered the guard and dragged him down to the basement, where they tied him up and gagged him. He heard a lot of commotion from the floor above, and estimated that he'd been in the basement for forty-five minutes when he heard gunshots."

Sergeant Higgins scribbled a few notes in his pad. He and his partner Sergeant Leonard had arrived on the scene ten minutes earlier, while Pinkham and McCullough were still searching the building. There was no missing the dead body, still wedged in the half-opened front entrance. Higgins and Leonard both recognized the departed immediately. Higgins inspected the body, fishing through its pockets and coming up with a wallet. He pulled out the driver's license and laughed.

"The legendary Dave T. You want to know his real name? Maurice Levine. Guy was a fuckin' hebe, no wonder he called himself Dave T. Better get on the horn to headquarters. We need all his known associates rousted and questioned. I know that's a long fuckin' list, so let's get started. And someone better wake up whoever's in charge of this place, break the bad news to 'em."

As Leonard headed back to the squad car, McCullough and Pinkham emerged from the basement with the security guard in tow. Pinkham waited with the guard, watching as Higgins questioned McCullough. His stomach was growling. He'd never gotten his ham and cheese from Charlie's.

Higgins finished up with McCullough and headed Pinkham's way. "Officer Pinkham?"

"Yes, Sergeant."

"Your partner says you found this gentleman bound and gagged in the basement? And no one else on the premises?"

"That's right. Excepting the dead fella in the doorway."

"Okay." Higgins nodded to the security guard. "I've got a few questions for you, young man. Officer, you and your partner can be on your way."

"Thank you." Pinkham nodded and headed for the exit, easing his way past the crime scene technician who was now examining the body.

"What's your name, kid?"

"George Holloway, sir."

"Sergeant is fine. How old are you, George?"

"Nineteen, sir…Sergeant."

"How long have you been working here?"

"Since September. I'm a student at Boston College. I work here overnight three times a week."

"And you're the only one here? You work alone?"

"Yes. I work eleven o'clock to eight in the morning."

"Has anything like this ever happened before?"

"No, it's usually pretty quiet. I study, I patrol the grounds once an hour, make sure everything's in its place. Easy money."

"So this museum full of priceless art is protected by you and you alone."

"Three nights a week. The rest of the week there's another guard, Richie Sutherland."

"I see. Why don't we take a little walk around here, see what's what?"

The museum's interior was built around a large central courtyard, rising four stories to a skylight ceiling that bathed the room in moonlight. Lush plants—palm trees, colorful orchids, and other tropical flowers—provided a serene, contemplative setting for a variety of sculptures surrounding an ancient Roman mosaic. A fountain burbled at the far end of the room, flanked by staircases. "Nice," said Higgins. "I've never been in here."

"It's beautiful. And quiet, like I said."

"So what exactly happened tonight to disturb the quiet? From the beginning."

"Like I told the officers, I was reading in the atrium when I heard a knock at the front entrance. That was unusual. We have a gate, as you know, and I'm sure it was locked. There's a window there next to the entrance, and when I looked out, I could see two police officers standing outside the door."

"And you let them in?"

"They said they were responding to a disturbance call, which didn't make any sense, because I hadn't heard a thing. I told them that, but they said they had to check it out anyway. So I let them in. And no sooner were they in the door than the two of them grabbed me, one by each arm. Then a third guy pops up, he must have been crouched out of sight. Not dressed as a cop. He told them to take me to the basement and tie me up. One of the guys holding me asks where the fuck the basement is…excuse my language, but that's an exact quote."

"It's okay, George. I want you to be exact."

"Right. So the third guy tells them how to get to the basement. He definitely seemed to be in charge, and evidently knew his way around."

"And this third guy. Is he the dead body back there in the entryway?"

"That's him."

"And you'd never seen him before. Never met him."

"Of course not! I'm a college student, like I said. I don't run around with criminals."

"Take it easy, kid."

"Sorry, I'm just a little…oh, no. No!" Before Higgins could register what was happening, George broke into a sprint, heading for the right-hand staircase leading to the second floor.

"Kid!" Higgins took off after him, reaching for his weapon. When George reached the staircase, he knelt on the first step and swept up what appeared to be sawdust from another stair. He turned to face Higgins and held out the handful of dust, a stricken look on his face. Higgins caught up to him.

"Kid, it's a very bad idea to run when a law enforcement officer is questioning you."

"I'm sorry, it's just…look at this." George rubbed his fingers together and tiny flecks of canvas and paint fluttered from his hand and drifted to the floor. "Do you see? Do you know what this means?"

"Fill me in."

"A painting has been damaged. At least one. Do you know how amateur art thieves operate? They cut the paintings right out of their frames. Sergeant, we have to check the rest of these galleries. Who knows how many priceless artworks those animals have defaced?"

"Who cares? Kid, I'm investigating a murder here. When

Robbery gets here, you can answer all their questions about what painting is missing from where. That's none of my concern."

George stared at him, slack-jawed. "Sergeant, these artworks are irreplaceable."

"So is that mug lying dead in the doorway. I personally wouldn't *want* to replace him, but it is my sworn duty to investigate the circumstances of his sudden demise. And you're my only witness."

"Sergeant, I told you, I was tied up in the basement."

"Two men wearing BPD uniforms took you down to the basement. And tied you up with what?"

"They had rope with them. And a rag they stuffed into my mouth, and electrical tape they used to hold it in place. They were prepared."

"Sure. But devil's advocate, if you were working with them, it would be in your best interest to be discovered bound and gagged in the basement, right?"

"I don't know. I don't think that way. I'm a college student. I'm studying business and finance, for Christ's sake. I grew up in a fishing village on the North Shore. I don't know any criminals! But I think *you* think I'm some kind of accomplice. So I think I better not answer any more questions without a lawyer."

Higgins laughed. "You're paranoid, kid. Like I said, I was just playing devil's advocate. I gotta exhaust all the possibilities. You want a lawyer, that's your business. But in my experience, which is quite extensive, innocent people don't ask for lawyers. Guilty people do."

George swallowed hard. "I know what you're trying to do. And I've told you everything I know. I'd like to search the rest of the building and see what else is missing."

"Knock yourself out. Robbery should be here any minute. One more question, though. You told Officer Pinkham you heard a commotion, followed by some gunshots. Tell me exactly what you heard. I mean, assuming you can answer that without your attorney present."

"I heard shouts. I couldn't make out what they were saying. I heard something heavy crash to the floor. Then gunshots—three, I think. Then a scream."

"You heard the gunshots before the scream?"

"Yes."

"It's interesting. Our dead friend there wasn't shot. And there was no gun found on or around his person."

"What can I tell you? I heard what I heard."

A distant voice called. "Higgins! Where are you?"

"Over here!"

A moment later, Sergeant Leonard jogged into the courtyard, out of breath. "Some fuckin' night. We caught another body, over Beacon and Charlesgate East. And we got an APB on a cop killer. Anonymous tip came in and it checked out. Uniforms found two bodies in the trunk of a Crown Imperial parked at South Station. One of 'em not yet identified, but the other is an MTA cop."

"Jesus. Must be a full moon. What about the APB?"

"Car is registered to a Jacob Devlin, Somerville. War hero, it turns out. Couple minor beefs as a juvie."

"South Station, huh? So this guy's probably long gone."

"Probably. But if somehow he's still in town, he's never getting out alive."

OCTOBER 12, 1986

When I got back to Charlesgate on Saturday night, I had a message waiting for me.

"Some dude called for you," said the Rev. "Said his name is Shane Devlin, and you should meet him at noon tomorrow at this address: 25 Evans Way."

"Thanks."

"Who is this guy?"

"I told you about the guy who just got out of jail I met at the Fallout Shelter, right? That's him."

"Right on. Why was he in jail?"

"He killed two people, including a cop."

"Oh…that's cool."

"Really? So you'd have no qualms about going to meet this guy at some random address?"

"Uh…not me, man. But you're the aspiring journalist. I mean, you gotta figure Deep Throat was a pretty shady dude, but Woodman and Epstein still met up with him in some creepy parking garage."

"Excellent point as usual."

"You gotta look at the big picture. You want Dustin Hoffman to play you in a movie someday, these are the chances you have to take."

"I feel a lot better about this now. Good talk."

And so at noon sharp the next day I found myself standing in front of a boxy four-story building with an entryway flanked by two lion sculptures. Shane Devlin was already there waiting for me.

"So did I check out?" I asked.

"Huh? Oh, yeah. You checked out fine."

"Mind if I ask exactly what you checked out? And with whom?"

"Look, your name's Donnelly, right? Well, I had some problems with a couple guys named Donnelly in Walpole back in the '60s. I just needed to make sure you weren't related to those Donnellys."

"You could have asked. I'm from Maine. My father's a lobster fisherman, so are my uncles. So was my grandfather after he got out of the Navy. We've got no relatives down here, and certainly no one you would have met in Walpole."

"Yeah, I know that now. No need to be so sensitive about it."

"You know, I checked you out, too."

"Is that right?"

"That's right. I looked you up in the Boston papers from 1946. So I know why you were in jail all that time. I just don't know why you didn't get the chair."

"Okay, so you know what I was convicted of doing. But that don't mean you know what I really done."

"I'm all ears."

"It's a long story, kid. I'll get to it. But right now, we're going in here." Shane gestured to the building behind us.

"What is this place, anyway?"

"Kid, I thought you were a college student. Don't they teach you any culture? This is the Isabella Stewart Gardner Museum."

"All right. So…we're going to look at art?"

"For starters. And I'm gonna need you to pay my way in."

"Awesome."

"It'll be worth it, kid. Trust me."

Between my student fee and my new friend's senior discount, admission to the museum set me back twelve dollars I'd earmarked for a suitcase of Milwaukee's Best. "This better be a great museum," I said.

"Kid, I got no idea whether it's a great museum or not. You're paying for a great story, remember?"

"So what's the story?"

"Patience. I never had any myself when I was your age, but forty years in the can did wonders for mine."

We stepped inside and entered a vast courtyard flooded with sunlight from a full-ceiling skylight above. About a dozen other visitors wandered the grounds or stared intently at the statuary.

"Looks about how I remember it," said Shane. "Different plants, probably."

"That would be my guess."

"Come on. We're going upstairs."

I followed him to the second floor and into a gallery labeled the Dutch Room. A handful of patrons were gathered inside, all staring at the same thing. It took me a minute to realize what held their attention.

"Is this supposed to be some postmodern art piece?" I asked. "It looks like an empty frame."

"It is an empty frame."

I squinted at it, sure I was missing something. "You're serious. All these people are here to look at an empty frame?"

"It wasn't always empty. Haven't you ever heard of the Gardner Museum heist?"

"Maybe." I vaguely recalled hearing something about it in the Introduction to Art History class I'd taken my freshman year, but as was my policy at the time, I hadn't paid much attention.

"That frame used to hold a painting called *The Concert* by an artist named Vermeer. Supposedly, it's the most valuable stolen painting in the world."

"Vermeer." Now that sounded familiar. It was the only word I'd written down when I thought I was taking notes on my interview with the occult expert, Timothy Sprague.

"Yeah, Johannes Vermeer. Seventeenth-century Dutch painter. Probably best known for *Girl with a Pearl Earring*."

"Listen to you. I wouldn't have taken you for an art expert."

"Heh. Well, I'm not an expert. But I've had a lot of time to brush up on the subject."

"Forty years. You said."

"Yeah, and I did a lot of reading in those forty years. Not much fiction. I don't really care for mysteries, stuff like that. But history, yeah. And art history…I had a special interest. And newspapers. I followed this case, the Gardner heist, very carefully."

"Why?"

"That night I supposedly plugged that cop, like you read about? Well, that was the same night this place was robbed."

"That's a hell of a coincidence."

"It's no coincidence. You know where this is going, don't ya? The night they found those people in the trunk of that car, I was right here. Robbing this place."

I laughed, only because I didn't know what else to do. "That's some alibi."

"Obviously, I never shared that piece of information with my court-appointed counsel. Which didn't help my case any."

"So this is your great story? I mean, I'd love to hear it, I really would, but…I don't see what this has to do with *my* story. Charlesgate."

"We'll get to that. First you're gonna buy me lunch. Then we're gonna go back to that bar from the other day, the Fallout Shelter, and we're gonna watch the Sox game and you're gonna buy the beer. And I'll tell you everything I know."

"Okay, first of all, the Sox are finished. Did you see the game last night? The way the Angels came back? It's over. Clemens can't go again in the series. The bullpen is toast. You can stick a fork in 'em."

"Let me tell you something, kid. There is a baseball game this afternoon and the Red Sox are playing in it. It may be the last game they play this year. It may be the last game I ever see. I got some health issues, I don't want to get into it. Point is, I ain't dead yet and neither are the Red Sox. So I'm watching that game this afternoon, win or lose. I've been waiting my whole life to see these sonsabitches win the World Series. So as long as they still have a chance, I'll be cheering 'em on."

"Fair enough. But I'm telling you. They're done."

Shane Devlin wanted a steak, but I talked him down to splitting a pepperoni pie at Pizza Pad. I tried to get him talking, but he put me off while he enjoyed his slices. The most I could get out of him was that the pizza was better than the variety served in the prison cafeteria.

At four o'clock we were seated at the bar in the Fallout Shelter in time for the first pitch of ALCS Game 5. On my way in the door, I'd caught a glimpse of Murtaugh and Rodney sharing a booth. They spotted me too, and Murtaugh started to wave me over, but I drew a line across my throat. I had a lot invested now, and the last thing I wanted to do was spook my new friend.

I ordered a couple of Knickerbockers. Shane took a long swig, emptying half his bottle in one go. "Ahhh. This is the life. Sitting in a bar watching the game. I missed this so much, I forgot I missed it. If I could do it all over again…well, that's a given, right? I would have done almost everything different."

"No doubt."

"Well, go ahead, kid. You're a reporter, right? Start asking me questions."

"Okay. I guess my first question is, why the hell are they still hanging those empty frames in the museum? Why don't they just get some new paintings? Or, you know, some new *old* paintings. Replacements."

He laughed. "They can't do it. The old lady, Isabella Stewart Gardner, she had it all in writing that nothing could ever be changed. Her collection was her collection and nobody could add to it. So really, they had no choice. Better to hang the empty frames than nothing at all."

"I guess. People seem to like 'em."

Cheers went up in the bar. Boston had taken an early lead in the top of the second.

"See, kid? Not dead yet. Next question."

"Did you really rob that museum?"

"Are you a cop?"

"You know I'm not. You checked me out."

"I'm just joking, kid. Yeah, I did. Wasn't my idea, the robbery. My brother Jake and I, we had to do it. We got into some trouble with this connected guy. Dave T he was called, but that wasn't his real name. Anyway, he had us over a barrel and he had this big score planned. He needed two guys, expendable guys. Guys nobody would miss."

"And that was you and Jake?"

"Yeah. See, this guy Dave T, he was…unaffiliated. He could work with the Italians, he could work with the Irish. Turned out he was really a Jew. Who knew? Anyway, he planned this job so no one would know about it. He knew certain people would be very pissed off if they didn't get their cut, and if they found out he did this thing, they'd cut his fuckin' head off. In particular this guy Marko who ran the whole North End back then. Everyone was terrified of him. So Dave T had it all planned so me and Jake would be found dead on the scene, he and his wheelman would blow town, and no one would ever see him again."

"But you're sitting here, so I'm guessing it didn't go down that way."

"It did not. I can give you all the details later, how the heist went down, how we got the drop on him, all that. Suffice it to say, Jake and I left Dave T dead on the scene. But what we didn't know is that he'd already made a contingency plan. He was a smart guy, he probably thought there was about a one in a hundred chance we were gonna get the better of him. But on that off chance, he was gonna make shit-sure we didn't get away with it. He was gonna have his revenge, even from beyond the grave."

The Angels got a run back in the third on a solo homer by Bob Boone. I ordered a couple more Knicks.

"So this brings us to the bodies in the trunk?"

"Right. We should have seen it coming. They had us park in a very specific place. South Station, overnight lot. They must have been watching when we parked, watched us walk away. The wheelman, Cahill, he was a whiz with cars. He popped the trunk and they planted the evidence. A frame job."

"And they just happened to have a couple dead bodies on hand?"

"They had one. My cousin Pat. He robbed the poker game with me and Jake, and he was the scapegoat. They killed him and stashed the body somewhere. Meanwhile this guy Dave T gives us a canister of ashes, says 'here's your cousin out of respect.' Knowing all the time he was gonna fuck us. Those ashes probably came straight out of his fireplace."

"What about the cop?"

"Transit cop patrolling South Station, probably in the wrong place at the wrong time. Or maybe they knew he'd be there. Just to double fuck us. Someone finds my cousin in a trunk, hey, he's just some lowlife. No need to call in the cavalry. Dead cop, though, even if he's just an MTA cop…anyway, they plant the murder weapon in the glove compartment, call in an anonymous tip, then pick us up in front of the train station as planned. This way Dave T knows even if things go bad for him, they'll go bad for us, too. And they did go bad for him."

"And for you."

"Yeah. They caught up to me the next morning. I was home, I was trying to figure out what to do next, and the cops show up. My fingerprints were all over Jake's car and I had a pretty extensive record. We'd dumped some clothes in the garbage at South Station when we changed into those cop uniforms. Dave T told us to do that, so he'd know where to find those clothes. Eyewitnesses put me and Jake on the scene in those clothes earlier that night. When the cops found the clothes, they were soaked in blood, matched the dead cop's. That's all they needed."

"You had no alibi."

"What was I gonna say? No, officer, you've got the wrong guy. See, I was robbing the Gardner that night."

"But at least robbery is a lighter charge than cop-killing."

"Well, remember, they had a murder at the scene of the robbery. Dave T. Not that any cop would miss him, but murder is murder. More importantly, I figured if I kept my mouth shut about the paintings, they might be waiting for me if I ever got out."

"They gave you the death penalty. How did you last forty years?"

Shane stared at his beer bottle for a long moment, picking at the label. "Extenuating circumstances. I don't really want to talk about it. Let's just say, the authorities were given good reason to show me a little leniency."

In the bottom of the sixth, Bobby Grich gave the Halos a 3–2 lead with a two-run shot that bounced off Dave Henderson's glove and over the fence.

"There it is," I said. "That's how we lose this one. Hendu gets to the ball and somehow knocks it into the stands. Perfect. This is how the season ends."

"Lotta baseball left, kid. You gotta keep the faith."

"You just spent forty years in jail, you're telling me to keep the faith?"

"Who would know better?"

"So you went to trial, you went to jail…what happened to your brother Jake?"

The old man took a long pull off his Knick. "Well…he wasn't around for the trial. We had split up that night, and…tell you the truth, I don't know all the facts. He disappeared. Cops beat the shit out of me trying to get his location. They really wanted him. The bodies were found in his car and the murder weapon was registered in his name. See, Dave T had confiscated our guns when he caught up to us after the poker game. Fuckin' guy thought of everything. But I couldn't tell the cops shit about Jake's whereabouts. It was a mystery to me."

"And you don't like mysteries."

"Like I said."

The Angels tacked on two runs in the bottom of the seventh. I spared a glance at Murtaugh and Rodney. Murtaugh mimed pointing a gun to his head and pulling the trigger. I nodded in agreement.

"So," I said. "Let me guess. You have reason to believe those paintings are somewhere in my dorm. That's why you want me to get you in there."

"Hey, you might make a good reporter after all."

"And these paintings are worth some money."

"Kid, there's a standard reward out there for information leading to the recovery of those paintings. It's five million dollars."

The contents of my Knick bottle ended up in my lap. The bartender was kind enough to lend me a rag.

"You okay, kid?"

"Yeah, sure. So…five million dollars."

"That's right. Now, I can't just waltz into the Gardner with the paintings and say, 'Here they are. Give me my five million dollars.' They don't give rewards to thieves, otherwise there wouldn't be a painting left in any gallery in the world. But you, a reporter, you could do it. You could come up with some story about your research, how you figured it all out, and lead 'em right to the goods. And then after it's all worked out, you and I split the money. I'd say eighty-twenty."

The eighth inning came to an end with the Red Sox trailing 5-2. They had three outs left in their season.

"Meaning eighty for me," I said.

"Fuck you. I mean eighty for me."

"Why you?"

"Because without me, you don't have shit."

"But you're old! You could never spend four million bucks. I'm young! Look, you get a million, I get four, I mean, that sounds reasonable, right?"

"Shut up, kid. This game is getting good."

"You're crazy. This game is fucking *over*."

There was one out in the top of the ninth. Buckner had singled, followed by a Jim Rice strikeout. A pinch runner, Dave Stapleton, stood at first. Don Baylor was at the plate. With the count full, Baylor lifted an outside fastball into the left-field bleachers. The score was 5-4.

"Here it comes, kid. The comeback of a lifetime."

"Uh-huh."

Dwight Evans was retired on a pop fly. There were now two out in the top of the ninth. Angels manager Gene Mauch pulled the starting pitcher Witt and brought in Gary Lucas to face Rich Gedman. On the first pitch, Lucas hit Gedman in the right arm, putting the tying run on first. Mauch brought in his closer, Donnie Moore.

"I'll make you a deal, kid. If the Red Sox lose this game, you get eighty percent. If they win, I get eighty percent."

Let's be perfectly clear. At this point, I was almost positive Shane Devlin was completely full of shit. I certainly had no illusions that I'd be finding a cache of priceless artwork somewhere in my residence hall. And I sure as shit didn't think the Red Sox were going to win the game with one out remaining in the ninth. Judge me if you must. I took the deal.

And:

Donnie Moore got two strikes on Dave Henderson. The Angels were one strike away from the pennant. Security workers lined the stands, bracing for the impending celebration, and the Halos' lockers were lined with plastic in anticipation of the champagne showers to come.

Henderson fouled off a pitch. The catcher, Boone, walked to the mound to have a word with Moore. Henderson fouled back the next pitch, prolonging the agony. Moore threw a split-fingered fastball and Henderson didn't miss it. "To left field and deep and Downing goes back," said announcer Al Michaels. "And it's gone! Unbelievable! You're looking at one for the ages here." The Red Sox had the lead and the Fallout Shelter went apeshit. Murtaugh came flying out of nowhere to tackle me off my barstool and knock me to the floor. But the game wasn't over yet.

The Angels tied the score in the bottom of the ninth and

had the winning run on third base with one out, but Red Sox reliever Steve Crawford induced a shallow flyout and caught a liner to end the threat. The game went to extra innings. The Red Sox got the tying run to third in the top of the tenth, but a double-play got the Angels out of trouble. The bottom of the tenth was uneventful. In the top of the eleventh, the Red Sox loaded the bases and Hendu came through again with a sacrifice fly to give Boston a 7–6 lead.

Schiraldi set down the Angels in order in the bottom of the inning, and the Red Sox were still alive, coming home to Fenway for Game 6. The Fallout Shelter was a madhouse. I was drunk. At some point, I looked up to see Shane Devlin winking at me.

"Hey kid," he said. "A million bucks is still nothing to sneeze at."

MAY 2, 2014

Jackie woke from a nap clinging to the ragged edge of a dream. As usual, she'd found a hidden passageway in her bedroom, a looping corridor that wound its way through Charlesgate past. She recognized no one. They were young, she was not, and they stared as she walked past, averting her eyes and murmuring apologetically. Now she was in the back staircase, guitar music echoing up from below. She pushed through a doorway, hoping to find herself out on the street, but instead she was in the ballroom. A shadow moved across the far wall and the fear was back, as if it had never left, as if that night had never ended...

But now she was on the couch and light was streaming in the windows and the intercom was buzzing. She shook off the dream and answered it.

"Hello?"

"It's Detective Coleman. Mind if I come up?"

She buzzed him in through the front entrance and waited at her open door for him to arrive.

"I wasn't expecting you," she said. "I would have taken a shower."

"This ain't a booty call," he said. "Official business."

She led him inside and he once again marveled at the spare, modern elegance of her condo. Gleaming hardwood floors and granite countertops, a spacious living room with cozy furniture tucked into its corners, a TV the size of a highway billboard, and probably a golden shitter for all he knew.

"Butler have the night off?"

"I told you I never could have afforded this place on my own. My husband wanted it."

"And you didn't object."

"Would you?"

"Hell, naw." He took the two steps up to the glass doors leading to the rooftop patio.

"Should we sit outside? It's finally May. Summer is almost here."

"That'll work."

"I'll get a couple of beers."

"Official business, I told you."

"So that's a yes?"

"Absolutely."

Coleman slid open the door and stepped out into the early evening air. It still had the crispness of spring, without the bite. He pulled up a chair at the patio table and took in the view of the setting sun reflected in the Prudential building. He was a long way from the Dorchester projects. Hell, he was a long way from the cookie-cutter suburbia of Medford.

Jackie brought out two ice cold bottles of Harpoon Ale and joined him at the table. They clinked bottles.

"I wonder what the poor people are doing tonight?" Coleman said.

"So what's the official business?"

"Got a lead on our murder here. And I need to ask you a couple questions."

"Should I call my lawyer?"

"I don't think so. But then, I would say that, wouldn't I?"

"I'll take my chances."

"Do you know a Charles White?"

"Sure. He works in the Emerson alumni office. He was helping me set up this reunion."

"Was?"

"Well, he hasn't returned my calls in a few days."

"That's probably because he's no longer with the Emerson alumni office."

"Huh. And…how do you know this?"

"I had a meeting yesterday with an art detective. Digging into the Gardner robbery again. And he met with this White about it, trying to get in touch with your friend Donnelly."

"What? Why does this Gardner thing keep coming up all of a sudden?"

"Well, the way this art detective Woodward, tells it, a documentary filmmaker got in touch with him about the Gardner heist. She's an Emerson grad herself, and her idol is your pal Tommy."

"Really?"

"Yeah, so it's like a chain reaction. She contacts this Woodward and in the course of trying to track down Donnelly, he meets with White. White can't help him, but he's really intrigued by the five-million-dollar reward."

"Who isn't?"

"Exactly. So since White knows you're trying to lure Donnelly back for your reunion, he figures you've got his contact information."

"And?"

"And you tell me."

"Wait. You don't seriously think Charles White killed that realtor…what? To get the keys to my apartment? Just to find Tommy's email address?"

"Well, let's break it down. You live alone."

"You know I do."

"So most people who live alone, in my experience, do not bother to password protect their personal computers."

"Okay."

"So the laptop that was stolen…was it password protected?"

"It was not."

"So if someone else, say this guy White, was to open your browser, he'd have access to your email. And he'd be able to email other people *as* you."

"Oh my God."

"Yeah. He could have emailed your friend pretending to be you."

"It wouldn't have done him any good. I didn't have a working email address for Tommy until recently. The one that would have been in my contacts, he doesn't use anymore."

"But this guy wouldn't have known that."

"Anyway, I changed all my passwords as soon as I noticed the laptop was gone. So he would have had a short window to work with. Also, wouldn't I have those emails in my Sent box?"

"He probably deleted them immediately."

"But they exist somewhere, right? On some server? You could subpoena them?"

"If I can put together a convincing probable cause, yes."

"And what are the chances of that?"

"Not great at the moment. All I have are the suspicions of a retired art detective. Yeah, White quits his job and disappears, but so what? That's not a crime."

"So what do you need from me?"

"Well, I was hoping you could get the emails, if they existed, from your friend Tommy. But it sounds like that's not the case."

"Nope."

"Have you heard from him at all?"

"Briefly. Between assignments. He's out of pocket now." Tommy had asked her not to tell anyone he might show up at the reunion, and Jackie planned to keep that confidence.

"What else can you tell me about Charlie White?"

"Like what?"

"Anything. Any dealings you had with this guy, anything weird you noticed."

"Honestly, he seemed like a normal enough guy. Maybe a little creepy."

"How so? Describe him."

"Well, he's a skinny little guy. He has a mustache, glasses, he was always wearing a bowtie. I think he said he was from Rhode Island. And a little...handsy?"

Coleman raised an eyebrow. "Handsy?"

"Yeah. Touchy-feely. I met with him, I think, three times, and each time he asked me out for a drink."

"And you said?"

"I politely refused. Maybe next time, I'm in a hurry, that sort of thing. But while we were talking, he'd touch me on the shoulder, leave his hand there a little too long. The third time he tried to go in for a kiss on the cheek, but I kind of pretended I didn't notice and pulled away before he could stick the landing."

"Anything else? Out of the ordinary?"

"Really nothing. He just helped me out with the mailing list, setting up hotel rooms, you know, with the Emerson group discount. Dug some mementos and videos out of the archives, stuff like that. Have you looked into this guy? Does he have a record or anything?"

"Not in this state. I'm waiting to hear back from Rhode Island, but I don't think I'm a priority with them. I really have nothing on this guy."

"Well, in that case...is this the end of our official business? Do you want another beer?"

"Sure."

The sun had set. Coleman drank in the lights of Boston spread out before him. He could get used to this. Jackie returned with two more frosties.

"There is something else we should talk about," said Coleman.

"And what's that?"

"My partner, Carnahan…he's kind of on to us."

"Kind of on to us? What does that mean?'

"He….thinks we're…seeing each other."

She smiled. "And are we? Seeing each other?"

"That's…the point is, you're a person of interest."

"I should hope so."

"You know what I mean. Technically…I mean, it doesn't look good if I'm seeing a…"

"Suspect?"

"No! I mean, of course you're not a suspect. But you are part of this investigation, and I'm the investigator, and…"

"Are you in trouble?"

"Not yet. But I'll tell you, I didn't exactly take the direct route here. I drove out Memorial Drive to the Fresh Pond Parkway, parked out at Alewife, took the Red Line to Park, Green Line to Hynes. Stopped at three stores along the way."

"Why did you bother doing all that if this is official business?"

"I guess…just in case, at some point it became unofficial business."

"And has that point arrived?"

"Well…that's kind of up to you."

Jackie eased her chair closer to his, set down her beer, and leaned in until her lips met Coleman's. He responded with no hesitation. Hungry tigers released from their cages into a field of deer show more restraint. After a long minute, they both came up for air.

"So," Jackie said. "What about what we discussed last time I saw you?"

"What do you mean?"

"Well, you seemed to be saying that we should do what you think Charlie White did, minus the murder. Go after Tommy and go after the paintings. And the reward."

"And are you up for that?"

"Isn't that going to cause more problems for you? Career-wise?"

"I don't think so. I'm murder police, not art police. Looking into this Gardner case, as far as I'm concerned, it's moonlighting. Maybe I'm not eligible for the reward, but you definitely are."

"You know I think this is all bullshit, right? Tommy looked for those paintings back in the day and it didn't end well."

"And yet they're still missing. And people are still looking for them."

"They could be anywhere."

"What about Shane Devlin? You ever meet him?"

"I sure did. And I don't want to talk about it."

"Fair enough. No hurry, right? Those paintings have been missing almost seventy years. We don't need to find them tonight."

"Did you have something else in mind?"

"Didn't you say something earlier about taking a shower?"

"I might have mentioned something like that. Care to join me?"

"I could probably use one, yeah."

"Right this way, detective."

JUNE 16, 1946

By 3:30 A.M., two robbery detectives and the museum director had arrived at the Gardner, the medical examiner had completed his investigation of the murder scene, and the victim's body was on its way to the coroner's office. Over the next five hours, a methodical search of the museum from top to bottom would confirm the theft of thirteen works of art, including five Degas drawings, two Rembrandt paintings, and *The Concert* by Vermeer.

For Sergeants Higgins and Leonard, their work in the museum was done, but their night was far from over. Police canvassing of the immediate vicinity had uncovered a second victim in the front seat of a tan DeSoto, parked approximately sixty yards from the museum entrance. This man, identified as Joseph Cahill, had been shot twice in the head. Since yet a third murder, just a few blocks away, had also been reported, Sergeant Leonard stayed with the Cahill scene while Sergeant Higgins responded to the disturbance at 4 Charlesgate East.

It was not the first time Higgins had been called to that particular address, as he informed the uniform who greeted him at the entrance.

"This place gives me the fucking creeps," Higgins said. "When I was a kid, this was the swankiest hotel in town. My mother took me here one day after shopping, just to walk around the lobby and look at all the fucking rich people. But the Depression came, and this place just went to hell. Couple years back, I got called here on a double. Guy had beat a whore damn near to death, but not quite. As he's walking out of the room, she pulls a snub-nosed Smith & Wesson from the night table drawer, plugs him six times in the back. That's about all she had left. By the time the ambulance got here, she'd died of her injuries. You never saw a case closed faster. They killed each other and they were both dead. But on my way out of here, I got stuck in the elevator. And I hear these...*sounds* coming down the elevator shaft, like a coyote or something. Then the lights go out. For maybe three or four minutes I'm crouched in the corner of the elevator with my gun drawn, listening to these howls in the dark. Then just like that, it's all over. Lights come on, the howling stops, elevator brings me back down to the lobby, and I got the fuck out of here in a hurry."

The uniform didn't seem to know what to say to this, so Higgins asked his name.

"Lehane, sir."

"All right, Officer Lehane, where are we going?"

"Back staircase. This way."

Higgins followed him down a hallway lined with decorative tile, through a long-defunct, cobwebbed ballroom crammed with old furniture, to a staircase landing where another uniform was chatting with a tearful young woman wearing a skimpy black negligee. A few feet away, the body of a man lay motionless in a pool of blood.

"What's the story, Officer...?"

"Cullen," said the second uniform. "Well, our victim here is Mr. James Dryden of Somerville. Ms. Gale here is one of his employees."

Higgins smirked. "Oh yeah? Let me guess, this is an accounting firm? You're Mr. Dryden's secretary?"

"What do you think?" said the teary-eyed woman in her underwear.

"I think this is Jimmy Dryden, who, when he was alive, performed a valuable public service right here in this building. And he greased the right palms to make sure his business ran smoothly. Although this turn of events may throw a monkey wrench into the works. So what happened?"

"Ms. Gale here was entertaining a client," said Cullen, "so she didn't see nothing. But she heard shouting from the hallway on the sixth floor, and then she heard a scream. And when she ran out to see what was happening, she found that Mr. Dryden, who last she knew was up there on that same sixth floor, was now on the ground floor. And it looked like he got there in a hurry."

"And Ms. Gale's client? Where's he?"

"Apparently he remembered another very important appointment. Gone before we got here."

"So nobody actually saw what happened? Maybe this guy suddenly felt guilty about the illicit way he was making his living and decided to end it all."

"I heard *two* voices," said Ms. Gale.

"But you couldn't tell what they were saying."

"No."

"So this other person just…disappeared? You didn't see anyone going down the stairs?"

"No, I didn't. For all I know, he could still be in the building. There's a lot of rooms, a lot of floors…he could be anywhere."

Higgins leaned on the staircase bannister and rubbed his eyes. "Okay. Thanks for your time, Ms. Gale. Why don't you find somewhere else to be?"

She didn't wait around to be asked twice. Her grief over Dryden's untimely demise had its limits.

"You're just letting her go?" Cullen asked.

"Do I look like a vice cop to you? I've got more important things to do than bust some two-dollar whore."

"So what should we do? Seal off all the exits, conduct a door-to-door search?"

Higgins shook his head. "No thanks. Who knows how many more bodies we'd find if we start down that road. We might never get out of here. No, more I look at this, I'm pretty sure we've got an accident on our hands here."

Cullen's confusion was transparent. "Are you serious, Sergeant?"

"No, I'm fucking Jack Benny. Cullen, I don't know if you've been on the horn tonight, but I've got two dead bodies back at the Gardner, and both of them are definite homicides. So I don't have time to dick around here with some guy, probably drunk, I bet the blood tests will confirm that, takes a header off a staircase. Either he tried to kill himself and succeeded, or he slipped and fell and it just isn't his day. Either way, it's a waste of my valuable time."

"But the girl—"

"Yeah, the girl heard voices while some john was pumping her against the bedpost. Look, if another witness turns up, that's great. Otherwise, I'm not seeing it."

"You don't think this might be connected with the Gardner thing?"

"I don't see how. Sure, these guys all know each other, but unless someone's going around town knocking off wiseguys one by one...you think that's what's happening here, Cullen? You think maybe the Shadow moved to Boston, didn't tell nobody? Maybe he's a Sox fan, am I right?"

"Well..."

"Only the Shadow knows, huh?"

Sergeant Higgins gave a dismissive wave and left the Charlesgate—along with any chance he had of solving the Gardner case, catching the killer, and recovering the artwork—without looking back.

OCTOBER 16, 1986

The Angels went down without a fight in the last two games of the series. Oil Can Boyd started on Tuesday in a game the Red Sox blew open with five runs in the third inning. About a half-dozen of us watched Game 7 in the Love Room, and after the bottom of the eighth, with the Sox comfortably ahead 8–1, Murtaugh and I ventured down to Kenmore Square to take in the celebration.

It was a harrowing victory party indeed. Bodies crowded shoulder to shoulder and back to belly, spilling off the sidewalks and deep into Commonwealth Avenue, which was closed to vehicular traffic. The heavy police presence didn't stop the drunken revelers from dancing on top of parked cars, spraying each other with foaming beers and chanting "Yankees suck!" for no really good reason. But who needed a reason?

"This is crazy," I said.

"Yeah, it's awesome," said Murtaugh.

It wasn't awesome for some poor bastard who had parked his Toyota Corolla in front of the Pizza Pad. Three townies were doing a jig on its roof and hood, pounding deep dents into its frame. Their dancing intensified and the roof began to cave in. The windows shattered, bringing screams from those closest to the car. Then the townies started chanting "Tip it! Tip it! Tip it!" A half-dozen BU frat rats took them up on the offer, piling along the curb side of the car and rocking it back and forth. The townies stage-dived into the crowd and the frat rats managed to rock the Corolla completely off its driver's side tires and flip it towards Comm Ave. More screams as the crowd backed away and the car's roof came crashing to the ground.

"Chief, I dunno about you, but I've had enough celebrating," I said. "I'm getting the fuck out of here."

"Pussy!"

"Yep. Smell ya later."

I made it home without incident. The next day, I met Shane Devlin at the McDonald's at Downtown Crossing. He was wearing the uniform with golden arches over his heart and pushing a mop across the floor. "I'll be done in five," he told me. "Why'ncha order a Filet-O-Fish or something?"

I ordered some fries and a small Coke and waited for him to finish. A few minutes later he joined me at the table, now dressed in civilian clothes.

"We gotta find these paintings, kid," he said. "This is the job my parole officer got me. When I went in the joint in '46, they didn't even have McDonald's. I'd see the commercials when I was locked up, always made me hungry. Must be good if so many people love it. Turns out it's crap."

I shrugged. "The fries are pretty good."

"If you say so. But listen, I did my share of mopping up in Walpole. I don't intend to make a living at it out here."

"I guess we better get started then." I tossed my half-eaten fries and we headed out to the Park Street T station.

"Food ain't the only thing that's changed," he told me. "I felt like going to a movie yesterday. I picked one that got a good notice in the paper. Craziest fuckin' thing I've ever seen. This guy is watering his lawn, he has a heart attack or a stroke or something. Hose goes shooting up in the air. His kid comes home from college, he's walking around in a field, he finds a fuckin' ear lying there. A human ear. It only gets weirder from there."

"*Blue Velvet*," I said. "Great flick, I've seen it three times."

"I walked out halfway through. You're a sick fuck, kid."

I laughed. We got on the Green Line and rode out to Kenmore Square. I took a glance toward Pizza Pad on our way out of the station. The trashed Toyota Corolla was gone. In fact, there was hardly a trace of the previous evening's craziness.

"Some guys completely destroyed a car over there after the Sox won last night. It was a madhouse here."

"I don't doubt it. Shit, they'll probably knock that Hancock Building over when we win the championship."

"Still feeling confident, huh?"

"Why the hell not? They rolled over the Angels. They're on a hot streak. And the Mets? That wasn't even a team when I went in."

We approached the Charlesgate entrance. "Just let me do the talking," I said. "But if anyone asks, you're my grandpa, you're from Maine, you're a retired lobster fisherman, and you're very proud of me."

"Sure, kid. Why wouldn't I be?"

I punched in the code and the front door lock clicked. I opened it and led Shane Devlin inside. The RA on duty behind the front desk was Missy from the Nunnery. Fortunately, we were on pretty good terms.

"Hey, Missy. Uh, this is my grandfather, Art Donnelly. He's in town for a few days, so he'll be visiting me now and then."

"Nice to meet you, Mr. Donnelly!"

Shane leaned onto the front counter. "Hello, young lady! I'm a retired lobster fisherman from Maine. We're very proud of Tommy."

I nudged him in the ribs. "Anyway, I'll sign him in."

Missy smiled at Shane and pushed the guest book forward. I signed in my "grandpa" and led him through the inner doors to the elevator lobby. I hit the button.

"I told you to let me do the talking."

"I was just practicing, kid. Getting our story straight."

The elevator door slowly creaked open and Jackie St. John stepped out.

"Hey, Tommy."

"Uh…hey, Jackie. This is…uh…"

Shane took her hand and planted a kiss on it. "Art Donnelly, my dear. I'm Tommy's grandfather. We're all very proud of him."

"I bet! Tommy, your grandpa's quite a charmer. I guess you must favor the other side of the family tree."

I made an awkward sound, somewhere between a laugh and a dog choking on a chicken bone. Shane didn't miss a beat.

"Our Tommy's always been a little shy," he said. "But give him a chance and I know the Donnelly charm will come out."

"Okay, gramps," I managed. "I think it's time to let Jackie be on her way." I pulled Shane into the elevator and pounded on the button for the eighth floor.

"Bye, Mr. Donnelly!" Jackie waved as the door slowly shuddered closed.

"Art, my dear! Art!"

The door closed and the elevator began its spastic journey skyward.

"What the hell was that?"

"Charm. Like she said. Jesus, this elevator is disgusting."

He was right. The floor was stained with moldy remnants of a thousand drunken nights. The walls were carved from floor to ceiling with graffiti ranging from "Keep cool, Diamond Dogs rule" to "Dyslexics Untie!"

"It wasn't disgusting in your day?"

"It was a different kind of disgusting. Last time I was in this elevator, someone was trying to kill me."

"Well, if it would make you feel at home…"

The elevator squeaked to a halt and the door opened. A couple of stoners were waiting to board.

"Holy shit," said the scruffier one. "It's JFK. I told you he was alive."

"Dude, are you JFK?"

"Kennedy?" said Shane. "No. But I was there on the grassy knoll. You know, the puff of smoke? That was me."

"Whoa. That's fucked up, dude."

I pushed Shane out of the elevator and the stoners boarded. The door closed behind us.

"I see you've kept up with the Kennedy assassination theories."

"I told you I had a lot of time to read. Tell you the truth, I knew a few people who might have taken a shot at him."

"Let's put that on the back burner. You said you wanted to start on the eighth floor, here we are."

"This is where it all started for me. The road to hell. I told you about Dave T's poker game. It used to be right here, every week. Right down the hall there. All kinds of wiseguys would meet here, Irish, Italian, Polack, whatever. It was a neutral place guys could play cards and leave their worries behind. Well, my brother and I, and our cousin Pat, young and dumb, we thought we could make a name for ourselves ripping it off. I think I saw it in a movie or something. Didn't really work out that way, though."

Shane started walking toward a half-opened door just down the hall on the right.

"Where are you going?"

"Just give me a second."

"Hey, don't go in there! Come on!" But it was too late. He was halfway through the door before I caught up to him.

"The stone giant stands between you and the goblin king's

treasure," someone inside the room was saying. "Roll for initiative...oh. Hello there."

"How are you fellas doing? You playing craps?"

I squeezed into the doorway beside him. Five nerds were sitting on the floor, all staring up at Shane, a handful of multi-sided dice in the middle of their circle.

"Uh, no," said a tall, pale fellow in a Dracula cape, shuffling through a stack of graph paper. "D&D."

"D and D? That's some kind of sex thing, right?"

"It's Dungeons and Dragons, grandpa," I said. "Sorry about this, guys. I was just giving my grandfather here the guided tour and he wandered off." I made an apologetic gesture I hoped conveyed the message, "Old people, right?"

"Dungeons and Dragons? You sure this isn't a sex thing?"

"It's a fantasy role-playing game, sir," said the Dungeon Master.

"Isn't that what I said?"

"*Come on*, grandpa. Sorry, guys. Enjoy your game." I pulled Shane away from the door and back toward the elevator. "What the hell is wrong with you?"

"Relax, kid. I just wanted to get a look at the room. That's where we robbed the poker game, except it's a lot smaller now. There's a wall right where the middle of the table used to be."

"Yeah, because when they turned this place into a dorm, they subdivided all these rooms. I mean, they obviously gutted the whole place. I don't know what you think you're looking for."

"There's plenty of hiding places in this building, kid."

"So you know where they are, the paintings? You hid them somewhere?"

"Not exactly."

"I see. So what are you envisioning here, exactly? I mean, let's assume for the sake of argument these paintings were hidden in here somewhere back in 1946. Wouldn't someone have found them when they were renovating the place? Like some contractors came in here to strip the building bare and they find some Rembrandt tucked behind a couch, you don't think they would have turned it in for the reward?"

"The kind of people who would have been hired to clean this place out wouldn't know a Rembrandt from a finger painting. They sure as shit wouldn't know anything about a reward some museum was offering. Look, maybe they threw it away. Maybe they took it home and hung it over the fireplace. But I'm betting there's a pretty good chance that kind of shit went into storage somewhere, and it might well be right here in the building. Maybe they're planning to auction it all off someday, but obviously that hasn't happened or the paintings would have been discovered by now."

"I'm sorry, but it just sounds really sketchy to me." I hit the button for the elevator. "Look, we made a deal. I would sign you into the building and you'd give me a story I could use. I fulfilled my end of the bargain. Now why don't you tell me your whole story so I can write my article?"

The elevator arrived. Shane glanced left, then right, then grabbed me by the throat and shoved me into the elevator cab. It was embarrassingly easy for him to overpower me. He was in his sixties, but he'd spent four decades pumping iron in Walpole and I was a soft college boy. The door closed behind him and he held me pinned against the back wall.

"Let me explain something to you, kid. I can play the sweet ol' grandpa if I have to, but I am *not* your grandpa. I didn't kill my cousin or that cop like they said, but that doesn't mean I never killed nobody. This may be a joke to you. You're a young college boy, probably never wanted for much, and you think the world is just waiting to reward you for your genius. Maybe it is. But I had more than half my life taken away from me. I got no time left to fuck around. You think I ran into you by chance at the bar? No, I was watching this place. I saw you come out and I followed you there. If it wasn't you, it'd be someone else. But you're in this with me now to the end. One way or another."

I'm pretty sure that's what he said. I was losing consciousness toward the end. He finally released me and I slumped to the floor. Someone had summoned the elevator and it cranked back to life.

"We square?" he said.

I coughed for maybe fifteen seconds and finally managed a nod. He extended his hand. I took it and he hauled me back to my feet. I was still catching my breath when the elevator opened into the lobby. The Rev was waiting there.

"Hey, man," he said.

Shane Devlin grinned. "How are you? I'm Tommy's grandfather. I'm a lobster fisherman from Maine. We're all very proud of him."

MAY 5, 2014

Coleman was a half-hour late meeting Nicholas Woodward at Grendel's. His day job had kept him in court longer than expected testifying about a triple murder he'd handled eighteen months earlier and for which he'd stayed up all night giving himself a crash refresher course. By the time he arrived, Woodward was already seated at the bar with his customary glass of Cabernet.

"Sorry I'm late."

"Not a problem. I know you're a busy man."

"I was a little surprised to hear from you again." Coleman shrugged off his coat and hung it on the back of the barstool, then took a seat.

"Yes, I can imagine. Last time we met, I told you I was here to participate in a documentary on the Gardner robbery. As it turns out, the funding has fallen apart and Ms. Klein will not be continuing with the project. Fortunately, my air travel has already been paid for, as has another week of lodging at the Charles Hotel. I don't intend to let this opportunity slip away. This will be my last chance at cracking the Gardner case and I could use all the help I can get. I thought we might come to an agreement."

"What kind of agreement? Miller High Life, please."

"It's not about the money for me, not anymore. This is my white whale, so to speak. Solving the Gardner heist would be the capper on my career. If you would be willing to work with me over the next week, and if we were able to crack the case, I'd be willing to split the money on terms favorable to you."

"Like…?"

"What if we split it sixty-forty in your favor?"

"Three million for me? I could live with that. But I need to know: How serious are we? Is it really worth our time?"

"There is no guarantee, of course. But if we pool our resources, I believe we have a shot. I've solved a few seemingly insoluble cases in my day."

"So tell me about that. I mean, how do you catch these guys? Is there a black market for stolen art or something?"

"No, that's a popular misconception. People assume there are wealthy Arabian sheiks with palaces festooned with the great stolen art pieces they've purchased on the sly. It's the *Dr. No* fallacy. The truth is, most art collectors won't touch a work they know to be stolen. What's the point? You can't display it for your friends if it's known to be hot merchandise. Occasionally lesser-known pieces slip through the cracks and are resold to museums, but that's becoming a rarity in our modern age. However, this case, as we know, dates back to the 1940s. It's possible the art has changed hands many times since then."

"But you don't think so."

"No. Because the more people who know the whereabouts of the art, the greater the odds someone will talk. Especially with such a large reward at stake."

"So why do you think these paintings were stolen in the first place? I mean, if it's such a hassle to unload them?"

"Despite what I just told you, I believe this to be a rare case in which the thieves had a buyer lined up to purchase the works, probably through a third party. And the reason I think so is because a list of the stolen artworks was found on the body discovered on the scene. The list doesn't match up exactly with the missing items, but it's close enough to signal that those thieves knew what they were looking for."

"So there really might be some wealthy sheik or James Bond supervillain with a lair full of stolen art?"

"Possibly. But as you already know, I believe there to be a much stronger possibility that the art never left Boston. That it may still be here to this day."

"I think so, too. As you probably know from your favorite prime-time cop shows, unsolved homicide cases are never closed. They just go cold. And as a Boston homicide detective, I have access to the files on those cases, including the file on one Maurice Levine, street name Dave T."

"The man found dead at the Gardner that night."

"Exactamundo. Now, the file is thin. The murder weapon was a straight-edged razor, no fingerprints. No witnesses, obviously, aside from a security guard tied up in the basement who heard screams and gunshots. This guy Levine had a clean record, but was evidently known to associate with the criminal element. The file contained a few interview transcripts with wiseguys of the time, none of whom offered up any helpful information. Another man found dead in a car across the street, a Joseph Cahill, he did have a rap sheet. Presumably he was the wheelman. The security guard gave a description of two other men dressed in Boston police uniforms, such descriptions ultimately proving unhelpful. I could try to re-interview him, except he passed away five years ago. That's the big problem we're up against here. Odds are everyone involved with this nearly seventy-year-old crime is dead or close enough."

"So we have nothing to go on. Nothing we didn't already know."

"Well...not so fast. See, these cold-case files are cross-referenced chronologically. Sometimes the passage of time allows us to look back and see patterns that weren't necessarily apparent back in the day."

"You have my attention."

"Turns out June 15, 1946 was a busy night in Boston town. Three other homicides were reported within an hour of the Gardner job. Two men were found in the trunk of a Crown Imperial at South Station, one of them a transit cop. And a pimp named Dryden was found dead. In the Charlesgate."

Woodward's eyebrows shot up. "What?"

"Yep. It was initially reported as a homicide by the responding officer. Within twenty-four hours the investigating homicide detective had cleaned the case off his desk by determining the death was accidental. The coroner backed him up."

"How did Dryden die?"

"He fell from the sixth-floor stairwell. Or maybe he was pushed. A witness questioned on the scene reported hearing an argument between Dryden and another individual immediately before this 'accident.' But no second person was ever found or even looked for, and the witness disappeared. Best I can tell from the file, she was a hooker working out of the Charlesgate under an assumed name, Dorothy Gale. That would be the girl from *The Wizard of Oz* lands her house on the witch."

"Quite. So no connection between these cases was ever made?"

"Well, look at it from the homicide cop's point of view. He's got this major shitstorm going down at the Gardner, he gets called over to the Charlesgate. Some piece-of-shit pimp took a header off the stairs and the only one saying it wasn't an accident is one of his whores. I'm thinking they didn't take the word of a working girl too seriously back in '46. No, all this guy is thinking is, how can I get this case off my desk as quick as possible so I can get back to the real business at hand. Really, he'd have no reason to believe there's any connection to the Gardner thing. If anything, this was some altercation between a john and the pimp, and why bother devoting significant resources and time to something like that?"

"I suppose that makes sense. But what about the bodies discovered at South Station?"

"What about them?"

"Was anyone ever charged with that crime?"

Coleman flipped through his pocket notebook. "Yeah. A Shane Devlin of Somerville. Served forty years for the deuce, released in '86. Maybe you recognize the name."

"From Donnelly's *Berkeley Beacon* article."

"One and the same."

"So one of these dead men in the trunk was…"

"His cousin, Patrick Egan. Donnelly wrote in his article that Devlin told him Egan had been killed by this Dave T after the two of them plus Devlin's brother robbed T's poker game."

"And the transit policeman?"

"Who knows? Wrong place, wrong time, probably. But Devlin told Donnelly he didn't do these murders, but did rob the Gardner."

"Information he shared with no one at the time."

"Right. Devlin never breathed a word about the Gardner heist. All we have is hearsay from Donnelly's article. And my brothers in blue never took it seriously at the time."

"They must have looked into Donnelly's allegations, no?"

"Just to cover their asses, sure. But clearly they never found any evidence."

"If they questioned Donnelly at the time, would there be a transcript?"

"There should be. I'll have to come up with some kind of plausible reason to have it pulled. Let me think on that."

Woodward slapped the bar three times, smiling. "This is exciting. We may actually have a lead after all this time. So what's next?"

"I've got a call in to the Charlesgate's management company. On the pretext of looking into the Rachel O'Brien murder, I've asked them to put me in touch with the contractor that gutted the place and converted it into condos. On the off-chance these paintings were stashed away in some hidden passage or storage room, maybe these guys moved them without knowing what they were."

"Excellent."

The opening riff of the Standells' "Dirty Water" cranked to life. It was the Red Sox victory song and it was Coleman's ringtone. He reached for his phone and saw his partner's picture on the screen. "Excuse me, I've got to take this."

"Of course."

Coleman walked away from the bar and answered the call. "Hey, Carny. Whassup?"

"I dunno, Coltrane. Maybe you can tell me why I'm getting follow-up calls from the Rhode Island staties?"

"Uh…well, that's gotta be about a lead I'm following up on our Charlesgate whodunit."

"Yeah. Thanks for keeping me in the loop."

"Carny, I figured it was bullshit."

"Apparently not."

"What do you mean?"

"You requested any info they had on a Charles White of Middletown?"

"Right, the guy from the Emerson alumni office who suddenly quit his job."

"Well, they have some information. Pretty fresh, too. They've identified a John Doe they found dead behind a Dunkin Donuts, just off 95 in Pawtucket almost two weeks ago. He'd been burned to a crisp in a dumpster fire. Staties just got the DNA test results back this morning, and lo and behold, it's this very same Charles White."

JUNE 16, 1946

The world faded in and out for Jake Devlin. One moment he was back in the hold of the *Arisan Maru*, gasping for air through unbearable heat and stink while men dropped dead around him. The next he was back on the docks of Boston, waiting for dawn to come. His fingers were sticky with blood from pressing against the wound in his left arm. Dark and fog enveloped him. He took a deep breath, hoping the salty smell of Boston Harbor would keep his senses alert, keep him from slipping into unconsciousness. He heard a police siren in the distance. It got closer until it got farther away.

He guessed it was 4:30 in the morning. A little over four hours earlier, he'd been sitting in a car with Shane and Dave T and the driver, Cahill. They were parked across the street from a museum he'd never visited. He and Shane were dressed as cops. Dave T explained the plan.

"You two are going to knock on the front door. When the security guard answers, you're going to tell him you're responding to a disturbance call. I'll be crouching out of sight until he lets you in. As soon as he does, I come up behind you with this gun. And I'll be holding this rope in the other hand. You two will take the guard down to the basement, tie him up and shove a rag in his mouth. You won't try anything funny. Why would you? We're going to make a lot of money together. But if for some reason you don't want to do that, remember that I have this gun. The guard won't have one. He's a kid. They don't take security serious here. After tonight, they will. We all understand each other?"

"I think so," said Jake. "This guy is gonna see us. He's not gonna see you. Is that about the size of it?"

"You're a naturally suspicious fella, aren't you?"

"Put yourself in my shoes."

"Sure. I understand. But just to review the lesson so far: I'll have this gun. You'll have jack shit. So it's in your best interest to lose your skepticism and trust me. Am I right?"

"Sure," said Shane. "Trust you."

"Okay then. So once the guard is secure in the basement, you'll join me in the courtyard, where I'll already be at work securing the items on our list. I estimate it will take no more than thirty minutes to acquire them all. Then we get the fuck out of here, Mr. Cahill drives you back to South Station, and I contact my fence down in Florida to let him know the job is done. Within forty-eight hours, I'll exchange the art for the promised payoff. You call the number I gave you and give my friend the account number for the wire transfer. Then you get your cut, and at that point, our partnership is concluded."

"We'd be legends," said Shane. "Except no one will ever know it was us."

"Yeah, well, why do you think I killed the Little Rascal who couldn't keep his mouth shut? I know you both threw his name out, but the truth? It was always gonna be him. Hope that helps you sleep at night."

It went according to plan at first. Jake and Shane rang the doorbell. The security guard answered. Jake explained that they were responding to a disturbance. The guard opened the door to let them in. Dave T jumped out of the bushes with his gun and ordered the guard inside. He directed Jake and Shane to the basement. They each took the guard by an arm and led him downstairs.

"Come on, fellas," the guard pleaded. "Don't do this. I'm just a college student. I'm gonna lose this job!"

After tying the guard up and gagging him, Jake led Shane to a dark corner of the basement.

"We're going to have to make our move soon," Jake said.

"Great. How?"

"We gotta get him to shoot at us."

"I don't think I heard you."

"We get Dave T to shoot at us."

"This is your plan? I think we can pull it off, but I don't exactly see how that benefits us."

"Maybe it won't. But we know for sure he's going to put bullets in our brains at close range if we don't do anything. If we can get him to expend his bullets shooting at us from a distance, our odds are better. Maybe we get shot anyway, but better to be a moving target than a sitting duck."

"I guess so. It ain't like I've got a better idea."

"All right. Let's just play along with him until he's ready to leave."

Jake and Shane headed back up the stairs, leaving the security guard straining against his bonds in the basement. When they reached the courtyard, Dave T was waiting there with a rolled-up canvas tucked under his arm and his revolver still at hand.

"Took you long enough," he said. "I was about to get worried."

"He fought us," said Jake. "He's stronger than he looks."

"I doubt that. Come on, we've got to move fast. We're going to the Dutch Room next."

"Fine. Lead on."

"No, after you. It's up those stairs, just past the statue of the Greek broad with no arms."

Jake nodded to Shane and they made their way across the courtyard to the staircase at the far end.

"Kind of beautiful in here, huh, guys? Smells good, too, all this greenery."

Jake didn't have much interest in admiring the aesthetics nor the aromas of Isabella Stewart Gardner's life's work, but he had to grudgingly agree. The inverted walls of a Venetian-style palazzo rose to meet a full-ceiling skylight that flooded the courtyard with silver light from the nearly full moon. Plants and sculptures lined the walkways on either side of the massive mosaic floor. Water flowed serenely through an ivy-covered stone fountain. It wouldn't be the worst place to die if it came to that.

At the top of the stairs on the second floor, Dave T told them to turn right. They entered a spacious gallery, its walls dominated by several intimidating portraits of royalty and a striking image of a ship in peril on stormy seas.

"Okay," said Dave T. "I'm gonna stand guard here at the door. Here." He tossed a small object to Shane, who caught it in the air. It was an ivory handle, about five inches long. "Open it." Shane did so, revealing the blade of a straight razor. "Okay, see that painting there with the poor fuckers on the sailboat? Go over and slice it out of the frame. *Carefully*. There's a lot of money at stake for all of us."

Jake and Shane approached the painting, which measured roughly five feet high by four feet wide and was mounted in a gilded frame. This was *Christ in the Storm on the Sea of Galilee*, painted by Rembrandt in 1633, not that Jake and Shane gave a shit. They each grabbed one of the ornate Italian chairs lined up against the wall and turned them to face either side of the painting, then stepped up onto them. Shane took the razor and carefully drew it around the perimeter of the canvas on his side of the painting, then passed the blade to Jake, who did the same.

"All right. Peel it out and roll it up. Slowly and carefully."

As delicately as possible, Jake used the razor blade to pry the canvas away from the edge of the frame at the top corner, then passed the razor back to Shane so he could do the same. Working in unison, each holding one top corner of the canvas, they slowly pulled it away from the frame, rolling it as they went. Flecks of paint and canvas wafted to the floor, each speck no doubt reducing the painting's value. When it was completely rolled up, Shane handed his end off to Jake, who awkwardly tucked the Rembrandt in the crook of his arm.

"All right," said Dave T. "Next up is *The Concert* by Vermeer. It's got a guy sitting at a piano with his back to us and two broads standing next to him."

"I see it," said Shane. He pointed to the Vermeer and he and Jake repeated the slicing and rolling process with this smaller work. The trio worked their way through the museum, accumulating a total of thirteen works of art. At Dave T's direction, Jake and Shane distributed the artworks between them, each holding several rolled canvasses and smaller drawings under their arms; another smart move on Dave T's part, as the added bulk would make it even more obvious if they were to try making a move on him.

"All right, that's it," said Dave T. "Let's get the fuck out of here. You first." By now he was holding nothing but his gun. The time had clearly come. Jake and Shane slowly picked up their pace as they reached the top of the staircase. The courtyard was to their left, about a twenty-five foot drop from the top step. Jake and Shane started down the stars, accelerating as they went. They were ten feet ahead of Dave T. Then fifteen. Then...

"Now," Jake whispered, about halfway down the stairs. They both tossed their priceless artworks behind them, directly in Dave T's path, and vaulted over the side of the staircase. They hit the floor and rolled to their feet, sprinting back the way they'd come in.

"Hey! Drop or I fucking drop you!" Dave T hustled down the stairs two at a time.

"Fuck you!"

The small entryway was thirty yards away when Jake heard the gunshots. He kept running, counting the shots in his head. He'd heard three when his left bicep exploded. The next sound he heard was his own screaming. He'd survived six months as a Japanese prisoner of war, but now some fucking card dealer for the Mob had drawn blood. He kept running. He heard one more shot, followed by a click. His vision blurred and he pitched forward. He hit the floor, looking up in time to see Dave T frantically trying to reload his gun while Shane charged him with the straight razor. When he saw what was happening, Dave T threw the gun at Shane and broke for the exit.

"What the fuck are you idiots doing? We're about to be rich!"

"No," said Shane. "*We're* about to be rich." He caught up to Dave T just as he reached the door, grabbed him with his left arm, and drew the straight razor raggedly across his throat. Dave T howled—actually it was more of a gurgle—and swatted helplessly at the air as his blood shot out in front of him. Shane swung out his right foot and kicked Dave T's legs out from under him. He crumpled to the courtyard floor. The hideous gurgling noises continued, but not for very long. His scrabbling hands fell limp. Shane dropped the bloody blade onto his chest.

Jake tried to pull himself to his feet using only his right arm, but kept slipping back down. The pain in his left arm was unimaginable. Shane finally noticed his plight and came running.

"No!" said Jake. "Get those paintings. We're not leaving here with nothing."

"But Jake—"

"Do it!"

While Shane collected the drawings and rolled canvasses, Jake finally managed to get to his feet. He spotted Dave T's revolver near the statue of the Greek broad with no arms, staggered over and picked it up. Dave T had managed to load two bullets before Shane caught up to him.

"Jesus," said Shane. "You're bleeding like a sonofabitch."

"Never mind. Slide one of those paintings around my arm so the gun is hidden." Shane did so and Jake pressed his good arm to his chest. From a distance it would look like he was carrying his share of the load. "Now let's fucking go. We've got one more loose end to tie up."

Across the street, Joey Cahill sat behind the wheel, checking his watch. It was past time to go. Just then he saw Shane and Jake breaking from the museum entrance, each carrying rolled up paintings. As they sprinted toward him, he leaned across the passenger seat and pushed open the door.

"Where's Dave T?" he asked.

"You'll see him in just a minute." Jake raised his good arm and shot Cahill twice in the head. Smoke wafted from the open end of the canvas wrapped around his arm. Cahill slumped to the steering wheel and Jake slammed the door shut.

"Okay, let's get the fuck out of here."

"Jake, you're bleeding like crazy—"

"What do you want to do, go to Brigham and Women's down the street and ask them to take out the bullet? The cops are gonna be all over this place in about five minutes. We gotta go!"

"Where are we going on foot?"

"Somewhere close. Somewhere we can stash these goddam paintings and figure out our next move."

"Just point me in the right direction."

"Where it all began. We're going to the fuckin' Charlesgate."

OCTOBER 18, 1986

We all gathered in the Love Room to watch the Red Sox eke out a 1–0 win over the Mets in the first game of the World Series, but my heart wasn't in it. A crazy old man who'd spent the past few decades behind bars had almost choked the life out of me and I had no one to blame but myself. He'd seemed like a harmless old coot until suddenly he hadn't.

I kept this turn of events to myself. When Murtaugh asked how my day with grandpa had gone, I just shrugged it off. I thought about going to the police. Maybe Shane Devlin had done something to violate his parole, maybe just being in the Fallout Shelter drinking a beer was enough to put him back behind bars.

But I didn't do it. Why? Did some part of me think I could still get a good story out of this, a gem that would make my portfolio shine when it came time to look for a real job after graduation? Or was I just greedy, wanting to believe there was some chance those paintings were still in Charlesgate, and if we found them I'd be set for life? Famous, even. Jackie St. John couldn't ignore me then, and hell, I could even ignore *her* if I felt like it.

On some level I knew this all sounded crazy, and if I'd talked it over with a sane person or two, they would have set me straight. But I didn't do that. I didn't want to drag my friends into this. Instead I pursued the story. I set up an appointment with the head of Emerson's physical plant. I told him I wanted to interview him about the Charlesgate for a *Berkeley Beacon* article. That was true as far as it went.

His office was in the basement of 100 Beacon Street. It

smelled like stale cigarette smoke, and a radiator banged incessantly throughout our interview. Mr. Horn was a short, chubby man with pasty skin and a greasy combover. He shook my hand and I resisted the urge to immediately wipe it on my pant leg.

"So what's this about?"

"You mentioned on the phone that you were working here when Emerson took over the Charlesgate?"

"That's right. They bought it in '79. Fall of 1980, we had it ready for students to move in."

"And what was involved in that process?"

"What wasn't? That place was not fit for man nor beast. The police had to clear it out first. Squatters, junkies, whores, Satan worshippers…a couple dead bodies, decomposing on the eighth floor from what I heard. And a couple legitimate residents, rent-controlled. They're still living there, far as I know."

"Oh yeah," I said. "At least one of them is."

"Oh, you've met Mrs. Coolidge?" He laughed, I think. He may also have been choking on a cigar butt. "She's a pistol."

"She sure is. So once the police had everyone moved out, I'm assuming there was a lot of junk that had to be cleared from the building?"

"You ain't kidding. Geraldo should have skipped Al Capone's vault and come here instead."

"So you were overseeing the whole cleanup?"

"Yeah, I was in there every day. We contracted it out, but I had to be on the premises to make sure no one made off with any hidden treasures. Once Emerson bought the building, they owned everything inside it. If we found a chest of gold doubloons or any other fuckin' thing, it belonged to the college."

"And did you find anything like that? Anything interesting?"

"No pirate treasure, but there was some strange stuff. One room was like the fuckin' Pit and the Pendulum. All kinda weird homemade torture implements. Thumbscrews, an Iron Maiden, something called a Scavenger's Daughter, you don't even want to know. Emerson didn't keep that shit, they had us get rid of it right away."

"But anything valuable?"

"Some stuff from way back when that place was a luxury hotel. Chandeliers, fine crystal, shit like that."

"And what happened to that stuff? Did it get auctioned off?"

"Not yet. We boxed it all up and stowed it in the stables."

"The stables?"

"Yeah, you know, down in the basement there in the Charlesgate. In its heyday, there were actual stables down there where the rich people parked their horses, with tunnels leading up to the surface. It's all blocked off now, so that's where we stashed all that shit. Someday they'll get around to auctioning it all off. Shit, if they did that, maybe they could afford to stay in Boston instead of moving out to fuckin' Lawrence."

"Wouldn't that be nice? So chandeliers, crystal…any paintings that you recall?"

"Sure, there were paintings. Sculptures. All kindsa knick-knacks."

"And as far as you know, these paintings would be stored down in those stables?"

"Sure, I don't see why not."

I remembered Murtaugh telling me about a locked door I'd tried to open on a drunken ghost hunt. "Huh. You know, it would really help my article if I could get a look down there. You know, get a sense of what it looks like, what's down there."

"I just told you."

"I know, but I want to be able to, y'know, paint a mental picture for the readers. Maybe even take a couple pictures."

"Look, it ain't up to me. I mean, I don't think it's any big deal, but there's liability issues, shit like that."

"Right. So basically you're the only one with access."

"Well, the resident director's got a key, too, just in case…
well, I don't know in case of what, but he's got one."

"Makes sense. Well, I appreciate your time. I'll get out of
your hair."

"Sure, sure. Hey, when's the article coming out?"

"Oh, it will probably be another week or two. I'll let you
know."

"Yeah, do that. The only time I ever been in the newspaper
before was in the police blotter when I got a DUI back in '81.
Not the best way to make the news."

"Sure thing. I'll let you know."

I shook his clammy hand again and headed out. Fall had
arrived in earnest, as the temperature had dropped at least ten
degrees since I'd entered 100 Beacon. I had no jacket, so I
caught a ride on the shuttle bus. I had a lot to think about.
Charlesgate's resident director was Gerald Torres. I'd been
summoned to his office once when my RA caught me with
a beer in my hand in the hallway. (The Fallout Shelter might
believe I was twenty-one, but Emerson had records indicating
otherwise.) If he had the keys to the stables, it might be possible to get my hands on them for a brief period of time without
him noticing. *If* I could sneak into the stables and *if* the stolen
Gardner paintings were actually there…well, it would probably
be too good to be true. But I had to give it a shot. The only
question was: Should I let Shane Devlin in on my discovery?
Or should I try to cut him out of the loop by arranging to have
his parole revoked?

The shuttle pulled to a stop in front of Fensgate. I stepped
off the bus and took a deep breath of crisp fall air. Something
had changed. I was thinking like a criminal. And I didn't feel
bad about it at all.

Coleman knew he was in trouble. The text from HQ said Lt. Weir wanted to see him right away. He doubted he was going to be offered a promotion and the Medal of Valor.

"Sit down, Coleman."

Coleman sat. "What's up, LT?"

"I'm guessing you already know what's up. I'm taking you off the Charlesgate case. You're going to be riding a desk for the foreseeable future."

"I'm gonna plead ignorance and ask you to explain why."

"Because you've been fucking a key witness in the case and because you've withheld evidence from this department."

"Whoa, slow down. I've been fucking who?"

"Can it, Coltrane. One of our only leads in this Charlesgate matter is the fact that this Jackie Osborne got her condo broken into and her laptop stolen, and you've been treating *Mrs.* Osborne to the black snake moan on the regular ever since you and Carnahan questioned her on the matter."

"Oh, so Carny ratted me out."

"Is that a confession?"

"Fuck this. Jackie is not a witness. She's barely a person of interest."

"Evidently she's of interest to you."

"We went on a date, that's it. And she's divorced, by the way."

"I'm sure your wife will be thrilled to hear it."

"That's a whole other story. And what's this evidence I've withheld from the department?"

"This cocksucker from the Emerson alumni office turned up dead in the Bucket. You didn't think that was worth sharing with your partner?"

"Hey, I didn't know the guy turned up dead until Carny told me. I just put in a call to the Rhode Island staties to run a routine check on the guy."

"And why is this the first I'm hearing about it? Why would you think this Charles White had anything to do with the Charlesgate murder?"

"Well, Jackie...*Mrs. Osborne* had been working on a project with him. Planning a class reunion."

"And? So?"

Coleman hesitated. He couldn't see any way that mentioning the Gardner paintings would help his current situation and lots of ways it might hurt. So he didn't mention them. "There's a possibility he would have wanted to get his hands on her laptop. She has some contacts in the alumni community he didn't have."

"What, so you think he slashed this O'Brien girl's throat just to get a few contact numbers for his day job? That is one dedicated motherfucking employee. I could use a few guys like that. Except alive instead of dead."

"This is why I didn't bring it to you, LT. Of course it's a long fucking shot, but we've got jack and shit otherwise. I was just covering the bases. Didn't think it was even worth mentioning."

"Except now the guy is dead. Coincidentally."

"I don't know any more about that than you do."

"And you won't until you read it in the *Herald*. You're off the case, like I said. And I don't want to see your face around here for a week. Administrative leave."

"Come on, LT."

"Should I make it ten days? Look at the bright side. You're

free to date whoever you please. You want my advice, though, you should patch things up with Donna. Be a steady presence in your daughter's life. A stable home life, Coltrane, makes for stable police."

"Thanks, Confucius. You mind if I get a few things from my desk before I go?"

"Be my guest. See you in a week. I'll have some pretty exciting paperwork waiting for you when you get back."

Coleman made a beeline for Carnahan's cube and caught him heading for the exit.

"There he is! My own personal Judas."

"Misquote Depeche Mode at me all you want, Coltrane, but I'm not gonna have my partner making a chump out of me. I warned you one time and you chose to ignore it. First rule of this job is CYA and that don't stand for Christian Youth Association."

"Blow me, Carny."

"No, I think you've got that department covered. And I don't have those pillowy lips like Mrs. Osborne. Now if you'll excuse me, I have some police work to do."

Coleman watched him go. Once he'd stepped onto the elevator, Coleman took a seat at Carnahan's desk. As he'd expected, there were several yellow Post-its surrounding the phone, including one that said SGT. HAYDEN CHILDS - RISP above a 401 phone number. Coleman picked up the desk phone and punched in the number.

"Childs."

"Sergeant Childs, this is Martin Coleman from Boston PD homicide. I wasn't sure if my partner had called you back yet."

"No, I haven't heard from anyone. You called about Charles White, right?"

"Yes, he's a person of interest in an ongoing investigation up here. But I gather I'm not going to get a chance to interview him."

"Not without Miss Cleo's help. We found him stuffed in a dumpster behind a Dunkins, burned beyond recognition, two slugs in the back of his melon."

"Sounds like someone didn't like him much. Any suspects?"

"Not yet. No match on the slugs. Now that we've identified him, we've subpoenaed his phone data, Internet, all that. May know more in a day or two, but right now it's a mystery."

"Any priors? That's what I was calling about before all this happened."

"No convictions. He was in trouble, though, back in '06. He was tried on a rape charge. But like I said, not convicted. Physical evidence wasn't there, but the accuser had earlier filed a stalking complaint and gotten a restraining order against him."

"Oh yeah?"

"Yeah, she was a RISD student. He was working there in some administrative capacity and apparently pursued her quite aggressively. Says in the complaint that she came home to her dorm and he was sitting outside her door. Followed her into her room and she had to get campus security to remove him. He left peacefully that time but according to the student, he later attacked her off-campus. He'd followed her to a bar, waited her out, then dragged her into his car and had his way."

"No physical evidence in his car?"

"He reported it stolen the next morning and we were never able to recover it."

"So the fucker did it and got off anyway."

"Our old friend reasonable doubt."

"Yeah."

"Anyway, that was about the end of his time at RISD. They didn't fire him—they couldn't, legally—but they made it clear that his work life would be very unpleasant if he stayed. I ended up having a beer with someone close to the situation and I was told that he was given a, quote, neutral letter of recommendation, unquote, if he'd agree to leave the institution of his own volition."

"What the hell is a neutral recommendation?"

"I'm guessing they said the bare minimum to allow him to find a new job without being too enthusiastic about it."

"So he becomes someone else's problem."

"Yours, it sounds like."

"Maybe. Hey, Sergeant Childs, you mind keeping me up to speed with anything else you might find out about this case? I'll text you my cell number."

"Sure thing, Detective Coleman. Just remember my name if I ever need a solid from the Boston PD."

"You got it."

Coleman hung up. He peeled the Post-it with Childs' number on it off the desk and stuffed it in his pocket. If he knew Carnahan, he'd never miss it.

JUNE 16, 1946

The first hint of daylight appeared over Boston Harbor as Jake approached the Rusty Anchor social hall. His wounded left arm was screaming and as far as he knew he was the most wanted man in Boston. Four hours earlier, he and Shane had made their way to the Charlesgate, leaving two dead men behind them at the Gardner Museum. Neither of them had thought to kill the security guard they'd tied up in the basement. By the time they were half a dozen blocks away, the cops had probably arrived on the scene and by the time they were closing in on Comm Ave the security guard had probably told the cops everything he knew. He had seen them both. His descriptions probably wouldn't add up to much, aside from the fact that they had mustaches and dressed as cops, but that would be enough to put the real cops on their trail. They'd already peeled off the fake facial hair, but they hadn't ditched the uniforms yet. They also had to stash the paintings, at least temporarily, until the heat died down—they couldn't exactly lie low while each holding an armful of the hottest merchandise in town. That's why Jake suggested the Charlesgate. It was nearby and his special friend Violet kept late-night hours there. Shane wasn't convinced this was the best idea.

"We're gonna leave this priceless shit with a whore? We'll never see it again."

"I'm ready to hear your better idea anytime."

"I don't even know this broad."

"But I do. She tipped us off to the poker game."

"And that worked out like gangbusters."

"Not her fault. Our cousin Pat and his big mouth are to blame there."

"Don't speak ill of the dead."

"My point is our options are limited. Violet is right here. Do I trust her one hundred percent? Of course not. But I'm about thirty seconds from passing out and…"

The sound of a distant siren, becoming less distant by the second, completed Jake's thought better than any words could.

"Okay," said Shane. "I guess we got no choice."

There was still one potential obstacle in their way if the hotel had someone on duty in the lobby. During poker games and other important occasions, a low-level goon was usually tasked to ride the front desk. The night they'd robbed Dave T's game, Violet had left a window ajar on the Marlboro Street side of the Charlesgate, a favor for which Jake still owed her $300. But there had been no time to place a similar request tonight, so they'd have to take their chances with the front entrance. Fortunately, as Jake and Shane were well aware, Dave T wasn't hosting a poker game this night and happily the front desk was unmanned.

The lobby was swimming around Jake as they crossed to the elevator and he nearly lost his footing when it began to crank upward. Either Violet would be out on the streets scaring up some business or she'd be in Room 601, getting down to business with a customer. Jake was betting on the latter. When they arrived on the sixth floor, he took a deep breath and gathered his strength.

"All right. There's no delicate way to do this." Jake set his armload of paintings down outside the door of 601, then tested the knob. It was unlocked. He pushed open the door and Shane, his arms still full of paintings, followed him through.

"Hey!" A pasty whale of a man rolled off Violet, his erection bouncing against his jiggling belly fat. Jake pulled the now-empty revolver from his belt.

"Boston Police. This is a raid."

Violet was staring at him, an uncomprehending look on her face. Jake didn't make eye contact. He kept the revolver trained on the john. "This would be a good time to put your pants on. Leave her money on the dresser with an extra ten for us."

"You corrupt sonsabitches."

"Hey, it's either that or we run you downtown and the missus can make your bail."

The whale fumbled in his pants for his money clip, peeled off a few bills, and dropped them on the night table next to the bed. He zipped his fly and began buttoning his shirt.

"You can finish getting dressed outside. Leave your jacket here. Now get lost."

The whale shot a nasty look at Violet, who offered only a sheepish shrug. Then he pushed past Shane and was gone.

"What the hell, Jake?" Violet pulled on a robe as she stood. "Why are you dressed like a cop? And who is this? And what are you doing here?"

"Your boss in tonight?"

"Jimmy? He's in and out like always. What is all this stuff? Carpeting?"

Shane dumped the canvasses on the floor.

"This is Shane," said Jake. "And I've been shot in the arm."

"Jesus. Sit down on the bed!"

Jake did one better. He pitched face-forward onto the bed, briefly losing consciousness.

"I need rubbing alcohol, tweezers, bandages and a lighter," said Shane.

"You think this is the emergency room? I've got tweezers

and a Zippo. And a bottle of scotch. We can tear up the pillow-case for bandages."

"Fine. Just get 'em." Shane rolled Jake over so his breathing passages faced upward, then tore the left sleeve off his brother's uniform shirt. It was soaked through with blood and stuck to the bullet's entry point. When Shane ripped it free, the blood began to flow again and Jake moaned.

"Okay, you're still alive. Good start."

Violet returned with the requested items. "What do you want me to do?"

"I guess you could suck his dick while I take care of his wound. Isn't that what you usually do?"

"Fuck you. I'm helping you out here. I don't have to do this."

"Just give me the scotch." She handed him the bottle. He pulled off the cap and took a long swig, then poured a generous double shot into Jake's wound. Jake moaned again. Shane set down the bottle. "Okay, now the tweezers."

Violet passed them over. Shane leaned in close to the wound and jammed the tweezers into the hole. Now Jake was wide awake. Shane's first clue was the screaming.

"We can't have that," said Shane. "We don't need to attract any attention here. Just pretend you're hiding from the Japs in the jungles of Oochie Boochie or whatever the fuck."

"Give me...something to...bite on."

"Sweetheart, hand me one of those pillowcases."

"I'm not your sweetheart." Violet passed him a pillowcase, which he folded several times until it resembled a serviceable gag.

"Open wide," he said. Jake did so and Shane shoved the pil-lowcase into his mouth. Jake bit down and Shane got back to work with the tweezers, poking and prodding his way through torn flesh until he heard the clink of metal on metal. "Found it," he said. He dug deeper. "Hold tight, I think I've got a grip. On three. One…two…" Shane yanked on the hunk of metal in Jake's arm, prying it loose along with another gush of blood. Jake stopped screaming, only because he'd passed out again. Shane took the pillowcase from his mouth and tied it around Jake's upper arm, turning the gag into a makeshift tourniquet.

"Whiskey!" said Shane. Violet handed him the bottle. He took another pull, then poured the rest of it over the ragged hole in Jake's arm and tossed the bottle aside. "Hand me the Zippo." She did so and Shane flipped it open. He took the tweezers by its bloodied pincer end and held the handle in the lighter's flame.

"What are you doing?"

"You'll see." Shane held the flame steady on the handle even as the pincers grew nearly too hot for him to hold. When the handle began to glow red, he snapped the lighter shut, tossed it aside, and pressed the handle to Jake's wound. A sizzling sound and the smell of burning flesh filled the air. Shane counted to five, then pulled the handle away, revealing a blackened patch of skin on Jake's arm. "There. The wound is cauterized, or partly cauterized anyway. Enough to stop him from bleeding to death. Now tear up that other pillowcase and use the strips as bandages. I gotta piss like a racehorse."

"Thanks for letting me know." While Shane tended to his business, Violet found a pair of scissors and cut the pillowcase into lengthwise strips. She carefully wrapped the strips around Jake's arm, tucking the edges inside the wrap to hold it in place. When she was done, she slapped his face. She didn't hold back.

Jake stirred awake. "Where's Shane?" Just as he asked, he heard the toilet flushing. "Oh."

"You mind telling me what's going on here? If Jimmy shows up, we're going to have a lot of explaining to do."

"You don't know the half of it."

"So tell me."

Shane returned from the bathroom. "Might as well tell her, Jake. We don't have any secrets left at this point."

"I'll tell her. But you gotta get out of here, Shane."

"What?"

"Like Violet said, if Dryden comes back here and finds us, the shit is gonna hit the fan. I mean even more than it already has. You don't need to stick around for that. Get out of here. Get rid of that uniform. Get home. I'll call you in the morning and we'll figure out our next move."

Shane hesitated. "So what, I just leave you here? With her? And the paintings?"

"Well, I doubt you'll get far tonight with a bunch of paintings tucked under your arms. The cops are already all over the museum. They've circulated our descriptions. The sooner you get out of here, the better."

Shane took a moment to gather his thoughts, then nodded. He walked to the door, put his hand on the knob, then looked back over his shoulder. "Be careful, Jake."

"I will. And I'll call you tomorrow. Don't worry."

"All right." With that, he was gone.

"Okay," said Violet. "First of all, you owe me three hundred bucks. Second, what the hell is going on here?"

He told her everything.

OCTOBER 20, 1986

The Red Sox had won the first two games of the World Series on the road and were coming home to Fenway. The Mets were in big trouble. So was I.

I met Shane Devlin at the Fallout Shelter on the travel day. "How 'bout them Sox?" he said, as if he hadn't half-strangled me to death the last time I saw him.

"Yeah. Pretty exciting."

"Why don't you buy me a Knickerbocker?"

"Yeah. Why don't I?" I did, and two for myself.

"So what's the good news?" he asked.

"Good news?"

"Yeah. I assume you've been working on our little project. Like we discussed."

"I've been working on it. I have a possible lead. Turns out there are these old stables in the basement of Charlesgate. There's a bunch of old shit stashed away down there, including, I'm told, some paintings."

"Fantastic. See that? Everything's going our way."

"Oh yeah. For sure."

"So let's go check them out."

"I don't think it's going to be that easy. I'm pretty sure they keep the stables under lock and key."

"So let's go look at it. I've picked a lock or two in my day, kid."

"No doubt. So we'll take a look. Can I finish my beer first?"

"Be my guest."

I finished off my first bottle and got started on the second.

Shane wandered over to the jukebox, eyed the selections for a minute or two, then made his way back.

"I don't know any of those fuckin' songs. There's one by Frank Sinatra, but I don't recognize it."

"They don't have music in prison?"

"Sure. There was a radio in the metal shop, the younger guys would play the rock and roll station, but it was all the same to me. Maybe I'd remember some of 'em if I heard 'em."

"The Beatles? You must know the Beatles."

"I know one of them got shot. We were watching *Monday Night Football* and Howard Cosell broke the news. Tell you the truth, though, I was never all that interested in music. Never had any records. Or whatever those new things are, the little silver coasters."

"Compact discs."

"I guess they sound better, huh?"

"That's what they say. Look, honestly, I'm really not all that interested in making small talk with you, considering what happened last time."

"What do you mean? What happened?"

"What happened? You grabbed me by the neck and slammed me against the elevator wall. There were threats. Not really the level of trust you want in a partner."

He laughed. "Kid, that was nothing. You need thicker skin, you're gonna get involved in this kind of work."

"What kind of work? All I wanted from you was a story for the paper."

"At first, sure. But you're just like anyone else. Dangle a little money in front of your nose and everything changes."

"Hey, if we find these things I'll be doing a public service to turn them in. Yeah, we might have to bend a rule or two along the way, but if it all works out, who's gonna care?"

"Oh yeah, you'll be a hero. But what if we have to do more than bend a rule or two?"

"What are you talking about?"

"I'm just saying it's never as easy as you think it's gonna be. I mean, yeah, there's a chance we just waltz in, pop the lock on these stables and find the paintings sitting there on top of a chest of drawers. I personally hope that's exactly what happens. But I'm not counting on it."

I drained the rest of my second Knick. "Well, let's find out, shall we?" I paid the bartender and we headed out the front door and up the steps to Marlborough Street. One block west and a right turn later, we were at the front entrance of Charlesgate. I signed "grandpa" in again, but this time, instead of taking the elevator up, we headed downstairs to the basement. There wasn't much to it: the laundry room, unoccupied, on the right, a door marked MAINTENANCE ONLY on the left, and one unmarked door at the end of the hall. It was locked, of course. And it was locked well. There were two deadbolts along with the doorknob lock. Shane tested the knob, then leaned his shoulder into the door and shoved hard once, twice, three times.

"You sure this is it?" he asked.

"I don't see where else it could be."

"Well, I don't think we're gonna force our way in there. We're gonna need the keys. So who has them?"

"The RD. The resident director."

"So you're gonna have to get the keys from him."

"And how am I going to do that?"

"We just talked about this, kid. What you're willing to do. You're gonna have to kill this guy."

I just stared at him. He held my gaze for a long, terrible moment. Then he started to laugh.

"I'm just fucking with you, kid. God, you're way too easy. What kind of asshole kills a guy just to get his keys? Look, just figure it out. Because otherwise I'm gonna figure it out for you. And you may not approve of my figuring."

"Fine. Let's get out of here before someone comes down to do their laundry and wonders why I'm showing grandpa the basement."

We went back upstairs and I signed Shane out. I walked him to the exit, then used the intercom phone to call up to my room. After two rings, Murtaugh answered.

"You're not there," I told him.

"Actually, I am here."

"Well, find somewhere else to be for the next hour, will ya?"

"Why? Are you about to get your dinky stinky?"

"Yeah. I'm about to get my dinky stinky. So clear out and make sure to lock the door behind you. I'll buy you a Knick later."

"You talked me into it."

I hung up, re-entered the building, and walked down the hall to the left of the front desk. I knocked on the door of the RD's office. No answer. I tried the door, which was unlocked, and pushed it open. Gerald Torres, the resident director, was sitting at his desk talking on the phone. He flashed me an irritated look and raised an index finger. I nodded apologetically, closed the door and took a seat outside his office. Uncle Sam glared down at me from the opposite wall, strongly suggesting I not wait for the draft.

Five minutes passed before Torres opened his door and beckoned me in.

"What can I do you for?"

"I hate to ask, and I know we only get two of these a semester, but I locked myself out of my room and I really need to get in like soon. My roommates aren't around and I have a paper due by five o'clock and my only copy…"

"Yeah, I get it. As long as you understand you only get one more for the semester. You lock yourself out after that, you can't come to me for help."

"Understood."

I watched as he fished a massive keyring out of his lower left desk drawer. This was it: the ring that held the key to every door in the building, including the stables. At least I hoped that was the case. He followed me up to the sixth floor and unlocked my door for me. I thanked him and he was on his way. Now I knew where he kept it—I just had to figure out how to get my hands on that keyring.

With his afternoon suddenly free, Coleman dropped by Jackie's office to invite her to lunch. He considered calling first, but decided he'd rather catch her off-guard. Even a suspended cop is still a cop at heart.

Hill-Robenalt occupied most of the 30th floor of the John Hancock building. The receptionist greeted him with an expectant smile. "Can I help you?"

"I'm here to see Jackie Osborne."

"Do you have an appointment?"

"No, I just thought I'd invite her to lunch."

The receptionist narrowed her eyes. "Your name?"

"Martin Coleman."

She exhaled with relief. "You're the cop."

"You've heard of me?"

"Jackie's mentioned you once or twice. I just wanted to make sure I don't have to *call* a cop."

"What does that mean?"

"You know, the restraining order. Jackie's stalker. Didn't you help her out with that?"

This was news to Coleman, but he didn't miss a beat. "Oh. Sure. Why, you thought I might be her stalker?"

"Well, I never actually saw him. I shouldn't have said anything, it's just office gossip."

"No worries. Could you let Jackie know I'm here?"

"Oh, duh. Sorry about that." She pushed an extension on her desk phone.

"This is Jackie."

"Jackie, Martin Coleman is here to see you."

There was a pause. Not an obvious one, but again, Coleman was a cop to the bone. He knew hesitation when he didn't hear it. "Oh, of course. Send him back."

The receptionist killed the call and flashed Coleman another smile. "Third door on the left, past the kitchen area."

"Thanks…"

"Kat."

"Thanks, Kat." Coleman nodded and set off in the direction indicated. When he reached the third door, he knocked.

"Come in!"

He did. Jackie sat at her desk, framed by an expensive view of the Back Bay. Coleman whistled.

"Nice digs," he said. "I can see your house from here, as Jesus once said."

"I didn't know you were coming. Did something happen?"

"Sort of. But really, I just came by to ask you to lunch."

"Oh, I wish you'd called. I'm having lunch with a client today. A rep from Fox in L.A. We're setting up this insane junket for the new *Planet of the Apes*."

"What's a junket?"

"It's where we treat the entertainment press to a lavish trip, put them in a room for some happy talk with the talent, show them the movie and hope we've treated them well enough to get some positive press. We're handling the whole East Coast for this one, which is kind of a coup."

"Best *Apes* movie was *Conquest*, 1972. Black Power allegory. Caesar's speech at the end—'and that day is upon you now!'—gives me chills every time."

"I've never seen any of them. Maybe we should switch jobs."

"Well, that wouldn't go so well for you since I don't have one at the moment."

"What? What are you talking about?"

"I'm suspended for a week. And I'm off the Charlesgate case."

"Why?"

"Because the Man doesn't approve of my love life."

"Wait—this is because of me?"

"Because of us. But you didn't do anything wrong. I did. And my partner ratted me out."

"That sucks!"

"Yeah, but on the bright side, I don't have to park ten blocks away and shinny up your fire escape every time I want to see you."

"Well, that's good. But still."

"Yeah. Anyway, you're right. I should have called first. I guess I'll catch up with you later?"

"For sure."

Coleman nodded and made for the door, then stopped and turned back. "I had a funny little exchange with your receptionist Kat."

"I'm sure you did. She's a character."

"I bet. But it took me by surprise. She seemed to think I had helped you arrange a restraining order."

Jackie rubbed her forehead. "Ugh. She's such a blabbermouth."

"So am I correct in guessing this restraining order was against Charles White? And you didn't tell me because…?"

"I didn't actually go through with it. I thought about it. I told you he was a little…"

"Handsy, you said. Stalker, Kat said."

"Kat exaggerates."

"Well, if he wasn't a stalker, why did you contemplate this restraining order?"

"Honestly, I was sort of joking about that. Kat took it too seriously. I wasn't really worried about this guy. He's a little twerp."

"He's a dead little twerp."

"What?"

"The Rhode Island State Police found his body right off the interstate a couple days after the Charlesgate murder. Took 'em this long to ID him. He was burned beyond recognition, two bullets in the back of his head."

"You can't be serious."

"Serious as two bullets in the head, and it's a good thing you never filed that restraining order. Otherwise I might have to bring you downtown for questioning. If I weren't suspended, I mean."

"What are you saying? You think I killed this guy?"

"Of course not. But it would sure as shit look like motive if you'd made this stalking thing official with the authorities."

"Oh my God."

"According to the Rhode Island staties, White has a history of this sort of thing. A student filed a restraining order against him when he was working at RISD in Providence. He was tried for rape."

"This is crazy. Look, there's no way I—what? Followed this guy to Rhode Island and shot him in the head? Then set him on fire? I mean, when did this happen? I'm sure I have an alibi, I mean…"

"Relax. Obviously I don't think you had anything to do with this, but it definitely complicates things. Our whole theory about why he might be our Charlesgate killer? Well, what if it had nothing to do with the Gardner paintings at all? What if he wanted the keys to your condo so he could be waiting there when you got home?"

She held a vacant expression for a long moment and then, all of a sudden, broke down sobbing. Coleman came around to her side of the desk and put a hand on her shoulder. She flinched away from him.

"Hey," he said. "I'm sorry. I'm not trying to upset you. But if you genuinely felt like you were in danger from this guy—"

"I told you, I didn't! He was a little creep. I was venting at drinks with the girls, and Kat, that fucking blabbermouth—"

"Don't be mad at her. I'm sure she's just concerned. Look, you obviously have nothing to worry about from this guy anymore. That's the good news."

She pulled a Kleenex from a box on her desk and dabbed at her cheeks. "Good news. Right. How do I know these Rhode Island cops aren't gonna come sniffing around?"

"Because we're in Massachusetts."

"So what, they coordinate with someone in your office? They call in the FBI?"

"Just settle down. For all we know, they'll have this thing solved by happy hour. It may be completely random, some kind of highway psycho."

Jackie's phone buzzed and she hit the intercom button. "Yes?"

"Your lunch appointment is here."

"*Thanks*, Kat." It would take a truly oblivious individual to miss the sarcasm, but from what Coleman had learned, Kat might just be that individual.

"You bet!"

Coleman kissed Jackie on the head. "Sorry about all this. Are you gonna be okay for this meeting?"

"Yeah. I'm fine. Work Jackie doesn't give a shit about Off-Duty Jackie's problems."

"That's a good way to be. Wish I could manage that myself."

She stood, straightened her skirt, and kissed him on the cheek. "See you later?"

"Hells yeah. I got nothing but time."

He watched her walk away.

JUNE 16, 1946

Jake paced outside the entrance to the Rusty Anchor in the early morning light. He'd know the right moment when it arrived.

Three hours earlier he'd been in Violet's room at the Charlesgate. His shoulder still hurt like a sonofabitch, but the bullet was out and the wound was clean and bandaged. He'd survive. Well, he'd survive the gunshot injury. Whether he'd survive the night was still in doubt.

"This is unbelievable," Violet said, when he'd finished regaling her.

"None of it was planned. Obviously."

"So what am I supposed to do with this junk?" She waved an arm toward the paintings on the floor.

"Hide them. You know this building better than I do. There's gotta be somewhere you can keep them safe. Temporary like."

She was about to make a smart remark when a pounding came at the door. "Violet! Open the fucking door!"

"Shit," she whispered. And then louder, "I'm with a customer!"

"The fuck you are. No customer I know about. If someone's in there with you, he's a dead man."

"Jesus, Jimmy! Give me a minute."

"I've got a key, you fuckin' lowlife bitch. You forget about that?"

Jake heard the key in the door. The knob began to turn. He scrambled to his feet and took a position to the right of the door just as it began to swing open. He head-butted Dryden as he entered and knocked him back into the hall.

"What the fuck?" Dryden struggled. He kneed Jake in the balls. Jake rolled onto his back, moaning. Dryden stood and kicked him in the head. "What the fuck is your problem?" He kicked again. Jake grabbed Dryden's foot, yanking him off-balance. He collapsed and Jake rolled on top of him. He hauled back and drove his good arm into Dryden's throat.

"My problem? I got no problem. Can't say the same for you."

Dryden clawed at his own throat. Jake stood. Behind him was Violet's open door. In front of him, a closed door leading who knew where. Dryden got to his hands and knees and drove his shoulder into the back of Jake's legs. Jake fell against the door in front of him, which crashed open to reveal the back staircase. He caught his balance on the bannister and looked straight down, six stories to the floor below.

Jake felt the bannister crack as Dryden's full weight hit him, but it didn't break. Dryden's hands went for Jake's throat. Jake's knee found Dryden's midsection. What breath Dryden had managed to catch left his lungs all at once. Jake shifted his weight, let Dryden's momentum carry him over the bannister, and watched him plummet six stories to his death.

Jake didn't stick around to perform the last rites. He back-pedaled across the hall and pushed a stunned Violet, who was standing in her doorway, back into her room. He quickly closed the door and pressed his ear to it. A few seconds passed. He heard a woman scream.

"Shit." He turned to Violet, who was sitting on the bed, staring ahead in a near-catatonic state. Jake slapped her hard and she jolted to life, swinging her fist at his head. He grabbed her wrist and twisted her arm.

"Oww!"

"Okay, so you're awake. Good. Because one of your co-workers is out there, or more likely, on the phone to the cops right now."

"Jesus. You killed Jimmy."

"It was self-defense. And he was a fucking degenerate pimp."

"He was my boss."

"Well, now you're in business for yourself. How do I get out of here?"

"I don't know! Take the fire escape down to the courtyard. You can get on the second-floor roof overlooking the alley from there."

"And then what?"

"I guess you'll have to jump. What do you want me to say?"

"Fine. Just—look. Stash these paintings in your closet. Once the cops have come and gone, find a safer place for them until I can get back here. I'll make it worth your while."

"Sure you will. You already owe me three hundred bucks."

"I'll double it. Hell, I'll ten-times it. Three grand when I get back. But I gotta go." He grabbed the oversized suit jacket Violet's client had left behind, shoved open the window over the radiator, and slipped out onto the fire escape. He didn't look back at Violet. If the rest of his night went badly, or maybe even if it didn't, he figured he'd never see her again.

When he ran out of fire escape, he dropped down into the courtyard on the second floor roof. Thirty years earlier it had probably been a hot spot for drinks, but now it was rat-infested and strewn with garbage. The alley below was cobblestone, about a twenty foot drop and nothing to soften his fall. But what was a little more pain at this point? He put on the whale's jacket, feeling like a twelve-year-old trying on daddy's suit. He lowered himself over the side, hanging onto the ledge until his legs were dangling. He dropped and rolled as he hit bottom, but it didn't help much. Pain shot up his calves and his knees began to throb immediately. As was becoming a regular occurrence that night, the sound of approaching sirens filled the air. Jake didn't hang around to greet them.

He stuck to the back alleys and darkened side streets, methodically making his way toward the harbor. His hope was to slip out of town as quickly and quietly as possible, find somewhere to lay low and heal up, and come back when the heat died down. He hoped Violet would still have the paintings. He hoped no one, not the cops, not the friends of Dave T, would come after Shane. But that was a lot of hope, a commodity Jake had never invested in too heavily.

When he reached the docks, he searched for the next ship out of port. He spotted a likely candidate in the *Tori Kay*. Longshoremen were loading it up with cargo, which meant the crew was likely boozing it up at the Rusty Anchor, an all-night social club for seafarers. Jake made his way over and sized up the patrons as he paced back and forth in front of the window. He couldn't get served without ID proving he was an active seaman, but he wasn't thirsty anyway. He just had to find a likely mark, and as the dawn broke over Boston Harbor, he spotted him. The tattoo on his bicep told all.

He entered the Rusty Anchor and walked straight up to the man with the tattoo, who was downing a shot of whiskey.

"Got a light, mate?" Jake asked.

The man looked up. "You don't have a cigarette."

"Well then, you got a cigarette *and* a light?"

"Beat it, fella."

"I see you were on the *Indianapolis*. I was in the neighborhood myself." Jake reached into his collar and pulled out his dogtags. "We both know a little something about floating around in the ocean waiting for sharks to eat our asses."

The man from the *USS Indianapolis* eyed his dogtags. "Is that right, swabbie?"

"Yeah. I spent seventeen days in the hold of the *Arisan Maru*. Got blown up by our own boys and watched some of my best mates drown while we waited to get rescued. And I gotta say, Uncle ain't as grateful as I'd hoped. Having a bit of trouble finding work."

"Yeah. Hard times all around, I hear."

"You hear right. But I thought maybe, one swabbie to another, maybe I could crew up with you. I mean, you could always use another able seaman, am I right? Especially a brother from the fleet."

The tattooed man gave him a long stare. "You in trouble? Being straight with me now."

Jake shrugged. "Getting out of town for a while wouldn't be the worst idea."

"That's what I thought. Well, we always got room for one more guy can tie a half-hitch, especially one from the fleet. If Uncle ain't gonna look out for us, we gotta look out for each other, right?"

"I can tie a half-hitch. I might have to tie it one-handed for a while." Jake pulled the whale's jacket aside to give his new friend a look at his injured arm. "Might have to visit sick bay once we're out of port."

The man from the *Indianapolis* nodded. "I think we can arrange that. One thing you can say about the crew of the *Tori Kay*, we ain't got much love for Boston's finest. We're shoving off within the hour. You better come aboard with me."

"I really appreciate this, seaman…"

"Donnelly. Art Donnelly."

They shook hands. Jake glanced to the window. "Red sky at morning…"

"Ladies take warning."

Jake laughed. It felt good.

OCTOBER 21, 1986

We were sick of the Fallout Shelter, so Murtaugh, Rodney and I decided to watch Game 3 at the Cask and Flagon, directly across Lansdowne Street from Fenway's famous green monster. We were packed in shoulder-to-shoulder and the air was thick with sweat and cigarette smoke. You could hear the cheers from the park a few seconds before the TV broadcast caught up, not that there was much to cheer about. The Mets scored four runs in the top of the first, en route to a 7–1 victory. The Sox still led the series two games to one, but it felt like we were already trailing.

Rodney and I stopped at Nuggets, Kenmore Square's dank, musty cave of a used record store, on the way back to Charlesgate. I thumbed through the rack of Dylan records, pondering yet again whether I should drop four bucks on a vinyl copy of *New Morning*. Most of my mind was elsewhere and Rodney took notice.

"What's a matter, chief? Pussy on the brain?"

"What?"

"Purple Debbie. That big scene she made at the Canteen. Chief, you gotta get on top of that."

"On top of what?"

"That pussy. Look, I know what you're thinking. You think you're in college and these are the golden years of ample pussy. Pussy running hot and cold from the faucets. You figure you can be choosy. You can pick and choose the pussy you get."

"Could you stop saying pussy? It's making me uncomfortable."

"What would make you more comfortable? Vagina? Should I say vagina instead?"

"Maybe not talk about female genitalia at all? Maybe let's not make that a topic?"

"Don't be a pussy, Donnelly."

"See—"

"Yeah, I said it again. Pussy pussy pussy pusssssss!"

"Good talk, Rodney." I decided to go with *Desire* instead of *New Morning*. Over the next few weeks, I would wear out the groove in "Isis." Rodney followed me to the register.

"See, I know what your problem is. You've got your eye on Jackie St. John. But the key to getting puss…getting with women is to stay in your lane."

"I see. So Purple Debbie is in my lane."

"Well, truthfully, she's in the breakdown lane. She's like an off-ramp to some boring suburb you never planned to visit. She's—"

"Yeah, enough with the highway metaphors."

"All I'm saying is, you will always regret the road not traveled. It doesn't have to be your final destination. Just a pit stop along the way. And with that, my highway metaphor is complete."

"Well, let me put a bow on it by noting that Purple Debbie is in my rearview mirror. Do you get that one?"

"I get it."

I paid the Samoan dude with the purple mohawk for *Desire* and headed back toward Charlesgate. The sight of the building filled me with dread. I had to figure out how to get the stable key out of the RD's office. I was meeting Shane Devlin the next day and he'd expect me to have it. I could have used some advice, and Rodney was actually shady enough that he'd have a pretty good idea how to proceed, but he was a blabbermouth. All my friends were blabbermouths. There was no such thing as a secret in our group if more than one of us knew it, so I had to keep my mouth shut. If I was going to get pulled down by Shane, I wasn't going to drag my friends down with me.

Again I considered going to the police, but what exactly would I tell them? What had Shane done wrong that I could prove? Besides, if I was going to be honest with myself, I was just as excited about the prospect of pulling off a caper as I was apprehensive. I was young and to some degree I still felt invincible. If I went through with this, there could be a book in it someday. A real true-crime bestseller.

So I stayed up late in the sixth-floor lounge, watching the Citgo sign blink on and off, and I came up with a plan. Not a great plan, but I thought it might work.

The next morning I took a Political Science quiz I'd totally forgotten about and met with Mighty Rob McKim to explain that the next installment of my Charlesgate series would be delayed due to "developing circumstances" about which I declined to elaborate. He wasn't happy with me, but it seemed like nobody was these days.

I got back to Charlesgate at quarter to noon, hoping Gerald Torres hadn't gone to lunch yet. I hung around by the mailboxes pretending to read a letter from home and keeping half an eye on his door. At ten past noon he popped out of his office, closing the door behind him. I'd hoped he wouldn't bother to lock it during business hours, and that proved to be the case.

"Heading out to BosDeli," he told Missy at the front desk. "You want anything?"

"No thanks. I'm still clogged with grease from breakfast this morning."

"All right. Back in a few." I watched until he was out the door, then waited until Missy was occupied with signing a visitor into the building. Glancing both ways down the hall, I slipped into the RD's office. The big keyring was right where I'd seen him put it the night before, in the bottom desk drawer. I grabbed it, peered out through a crack in the doorway until the coast was clear, then made my escape.

BosDeli was one block east on Beacon, maybe a six-to-eight-minute round-trip. With the lunchtime rush, I figured it would take Torres at least ten minutes to wait in line, give his order, and wait for the boss to make his sandwich. That meant I would have at least fifteen minutes before he got back. I decided to take no more than twelve, just in case everything went way too smoothly for him. Smart thinking, right? It would have been even smarter had I been wearing a watch.

I jogged downstairs and checked the laundry room, which was empty. I approached the stable door and started trying the keys, one after another, in the top deadbolt. I kept glancing over my shoulder and listening for footsteps on the stairs. One by one, the keys failed to unlock the door. At about the time it felt like ten minutes had passed, I realized to my horror that I had no way of checking the time. No watch, no clocks in the basement. Fuck it. I kept shoving keys into the top deadbolt.

Nothing.

Nada.

No good.

On what may have been the twenty-fifth try, I felt the tumblers turn as I twisted the key. I tried the second deadbolt. For a second it didn't budge and I thought I'd have to start all over again to find a different key, but I gave it another shove and felt the deadbolt give way. The doorknob lock gave easily—all three on the same key, a stroke of luck. I pushed on the door and it squeaked open. I could see nothing but darkness beyond. I pulled it shut and slid the key I needed off the ring. If my luck held out, Torres would have no cause to visit the stables over the next few days. Why should he?

I pocketed the key and sprinted back to the staircase and up to the lobby. Just as I arrived, I saw Torres coming in the front door carrying a BosDeli bag. I was fucked.

MAY 6, 2014

Jackie sat across from Charles White's replacement in the Emerson alumni records office, Wendy Tucker. Until a few days earlier, Wendy had been White's administrative assistant. Jackie had interacted with her briefly, coming and going. She seemed nice enough, but the promotion took Jackie by surprise.

"So are you the interim director or…?"

"No, it's official. Honestly, the promotion has been in the works for a while."

"Really? Was Charlie planning on leaving?"

Wendy laughed, then covered her mouth as if realizing that might not be the most appropriate reaction. "It was planned but it wasn't *his* plan."

"I see."

Wendy leaned across her desk. "Well, you dealt with him, right? You know how he was. So imagine me in my position." Wendy gestured to herself as if to say, "Obviously, I'm hot." Her confidence was not misplaced.

"So he was…inappropriate in the workplace?"

"To say the least. He was a sleazy little scumbag. Not that he deserved to die, but…"

"So have the cops talked to you?"

"I got a call from someone in Rhode Island. I didn't hold back."

"You mean…you told them he was harassing you?"

"Oh yeah. I gave 'em all the gruesome details."

"And you aren't worried…you know, that someone might think you have a motive…?"

Wendy's eyes went wide, as if the thought had never occurred to her. "Really? You think I'm a suspect?"

"I just mean...I mean I'm worried, too. A little. Anytime the police want to ask questions..."

"I don't have a gun. I've never even shot a gun. Heck, I've never even been to Rhode Island."

"I'm sure it's nothing to worry about. They're just doing their jobs."

"Yeah. They said it was just a formality, you know?"

"Sure."

"Anyway, let's not dwell on that. Your reunion, it's coming up, right?"

"Two weeks from Saturday."

"Wow. So how's it coming along? Anything I can do to smooth the waters for you?"

"Well, we've got the ballroom at the Charlesgate nailed down. But we're responsible for supplying the booze, the bar staff, the DJ, stuff like that. Charlie volunteered to cover all that even though it's really not his responsibility...but I guess we know why he did that. Anyway, he never got back to me with the final confirmations...obviously."

"Right. Well, he wanted the credit for it, but he didn't really do anything other than pass it on to Special Events. But it looks like you're covered. Our usual caterers are on board, they'll supply the booze and bartenders. For the DJ, it looks like Special Events booked Johnny Eighties."

"Johnny Eighties. Great."

"Yeah, right? I mean, not to knock your generation's music, it's great. Just a little overplayed, am I right?"

"You are so right."

"Anyway, Johnny Eighties also has his own karaoke setup, for after the drinks get flowing."

"Because who wouldn't want to hear a 46-year-old development executive crooning 'Everybody Wants to Rule the World' after six or seven Long Island iced teas?"

Wendy laughed. "Well, it's your party."

"No, that's cool. I'm sure it will be fun, I'm just…nervous about this whole thing. There's going to be a lot of people here I haven't seen in a long time."

"I can imagine. Oh, that reminds me! We got that video transfer back from the A/V lab."

"Video transfer?"

"Yeah. A bunch of VHS camcorder stuff Charlie had submitted to be digitized. I've got a thumb drive here somewhere…" Wendy rooted around in her desk for a moment before emerging with a flash drive. She handed it to Jackie.

"Oh, right," said Jackie. "I didn't think he would have gotten around to this. Our friend Brooks checked a camera out of the TV depot one weekend and spent the whole time chasing us around the dorm asking us what we were going to do with our lives. Should be some funny stuff on here. And some scary hairstyles."

"Aww, I bet you had to beat the boys off with a stick."

"No, I had my daddy's shotgun." No sooner were the words out of her mouth than Jackie realized it was probably a dumb thing to say given what had just happened to their mutual acquaintance, but Wendy didn't seem to notice. "Anyway, about the billing for all this…"

"Oh, don't worry. Everything's taken care of."

"How's that?"

"Well, as I'm sure Charlie mentioned, Alumni Relations has a reunion budget that cover the in-house stuff—the catering, the booze, up to five thousand dollars. Stuff like that. An anonymous donation from one of your classmates takes care of the rest, including the ballroom rental and an open bar all night. Of course, everyone's still responsible for their own travel and lodging, but other than that…"

"Really? One of my classmates? Who?"

"Well, it's anonymous."

"Oh, I know but…right. Well, that's great, I guess. I hope whoever it is lets me know…I dunno. I suppose it doesn't really matter. But I'm nosy."

"Honestly, I don't know who it is either. It was all arranged before I took over here."

"Well. One less thing to worry about, huh?"

"Absolutely."

"All right, well…if you happen to get the urge to sing Blondie songs with Johnny Eighties, feel free to drop by on the 24th."

"Maybe! I've always wanted to check out that building, the Charlesgate. I heard some freaky stories about that place. Gina Gershon on *Celebrity Ghost Stories*?"

"Yeah, I saw that one. Okay, Wendy. Take care."

"You too."

Jackie pocketed the flash drive and left the office. Her meeting with Wendy Tucker had cleared up little. In fact, it had only raised more questions. She vaguely remembered Charles White saying he'd sent out a general email to her class asking for vintage videos and photos, but had heard no more about it. And an anonymous donor? It was true that her class had spawned a few success stories, including the producer of two of the most popular (and mindless) sitcoms on television. She had heard back from none of them. Could it be Tommy? Maybe he'd decided against attending the reunion and had sent a fat check instead. There was also the matter of Wendy Tucker and how woefully underqualified she seemed to be for her new job. Had there been a settlement of some sort with the administration following a threatened harassment suit? Given White's history at RISD, it wasn't outside the realm of possibility.

As she headed out of the building, she nearly ran smack into a man on his way in. He reached out and grabbed her by the shoulders, holding her in place, then quickly removed his hands as if realizing he'd overstepped his bounds.

"Sorry. Thought you were gonna plow right into me." He smiled, but there was no warmth behind it. He was heavily muscled and heavily tattooed, with a prominent scar across the bridge of his nose, and his general demeanor suggested he was responding to a casting call for a prison film.

"No problem," said Jackie, forcing a cold smile of her own. "Lost in thought, I guess."

"Never happens to me. My advice: don't think. That's a joke."

"I get it."

The man narrowed his eyes. "Hey, I know you from someplace?"

"No. I think I would remember."

"You sure? Because I've definitely seen your face before. I wouldn't forget it."

"I'm positive. You have a good day."

She nodded and quickly made her way down to the street. She glanced back when she reached the corner and saw the man waiting in the open doorway, still looking in her direction. She hurried across the intersection and did not look back again.

When Jackie got home she poured a glass of merlot and sat down at her laptop—her new personal laptop, the claim for which was now on file with her rental insurance agency. She fired it up, took a sip of wine, and inserted the flash drive. She clicked on it, opening a folder with a list of Quicktime files: Charlesgate-1, Charlesgate-2, and so on. She clicked on Charlesgate-1. A decidedly non-HD video image filled her screen. A crackle of static followed by a shaky shot of a familiar hallway. It was the hall right outside her condo, as it had been in the mid-to-late-'80s. It looked narrower and dingier than she remembered it. The blue carpeting was stained and faded. A garbage can in the corner overflowed with refuse. The dorm room doors visible in the frame were decorated with pictures cut out of magazines and vinyl message boards covered with chicken-scratch handwriting. Jackie watched herself come around the far corner, digging through her bag for her keys. Her dyed candy-apple-red hair was piled high on her head. She was dressed in layers: at least two oversized t-shirts and a sweatshirt over a jean skirt. She looked up, saw the camera facing her and shook her head disdainfully.

"Jackie St. John, everybody!" It was Brooks' unmistakably high, sing-song voice.

"What are you doing, Brooks? Come on, I haven't had a shower."

"Isn't she lovely, folks? Tell me, Jackie St. John: What are you going to do with your life?"

"I'm going to take a shower. No cameras."

"I mean big picture. After you graduate. What are you going to do with your life?"

"I don't know. I'm going to be a famous, high-powered producer."

"Oh, you're going to be famous too, huh?"

"Why?"

"I keep asking that question and everyone keeps telling me they're going to be famous."

"We're an optimistic bunch. What is this for?"

"I'm making a documentary!"

"Our life here isn't anywhere near exciting enough that it would make for any sort of interesting documentary."

"You're missing the point. This is a slice of life. A nostalgia piece. We will look back on this someday and feel all wistful and shit."

"Well, to all you people watching this twenty years from now, I no longer look like this."

"Are you married? Do you have children?"

"I am married to my third husband."

"What happened to the first two?"

"They disappeared under mysterious circumstances. They were never seen again."

"Maybe they ran off together."

"Maybe they did. Okay, run along, Brooks."

"Thanks, Jackie!"

The video went to snow. Jackie clicked it off. "I'm going to need more wine," she muttered. She went to the kitchen and poured another glass, quickly downed it, then poured another and returned to her desk. She scrolled through the videos. There were eight files in all. Randomly she clicked on Charlesgate-4. She saw Tommy, Murtaugh and the Rev sitting in their back room. She shivered to realize it was the same room she was sitting in now. A few inches away in space, an eternity in time. It appeared to be very late at night judging from their slurred speech patterns. They were engaged in a spirited debate about the relative contributions of David Gilmour and Roger Waters to the Pink Floyd sound. She smiled and clicked it off. She chose another file at random.

Charlesgate-6 opened with a tracking shot through the Charlesgate basement. The camera turned to the right to reveal the empty laundry room.

"Dude, let's get out of here," said a voice she didn't recognize.

"Shut up, man. I'm telling you, it was open last night. Try the door."

"I dunno…"

"Come on!"

The camera focused on the knob of an unmarked door. A hand reached into frame and turned it. The door opened inward.

"I told you, man."

"Dude, it's fucking dark in there."

"Wait, there's a light on this thing." The image twisted and went out of focus while someone fiddled with the camera. A spotlight appeared on the far wall. "I got it. Okay, let's go."

"You first. You've got the camera."

"Fine."

The camera pushed in through the doorway. The spotlight picked up a box on the floor loaded with vintage lighting fixtures. It shifted to focus on a stack of chairs leaning against one wall. The camera moved further into what looked like a tunnel.

"Dude, that's enough. Let's get out of here. It's fucking creepy down here."

"Chill out, man! There's nothing down here but a bunch of old junk and probably some rats."

"Yeah, but you know Paul Seitz from the third floor? He was down here one time and out of nowhere he sees this burning kid, I mean like this little boy on fire, come running straight at him. Scared the living fuck out of him."

"That's bullshit, man. He musta been high."

The light drifted along a wall, then whipped down to the floor and over to the opposite wall. The image was grainy and indistinct. The light whipped the other way.

A hooded figure cast a shadow on the wall.

"Oh, shit!"

The image went black.

JUNE 16, 1946

Violet waited for the cops to come question her. The paintings were stashed in the closet, but not well hidden. If the law had any cause to search the room, they'd be found in five minutes. But the cops never showed. She heard one of them downstairs, talking to Dorothy, the dumb bitch who'd called them in the first place. From what Violet could make out, the cop had no patience for her story about hearing an argument between two men before Jimmy Dryden met his maker. As far as he was concerned this was an accident pure and simple, and he had no interest in pursuing the matter toward any other possible conclusion.

Violet waited until she saw the cop's cruiser pulling away toward Kenmore before going out to the hall and banging on Dorothy's door.

"What the fuck is wrong with you?" she asked when Dorothy answered.

"Wh-what do you mean?"

"You call the cops down here? To our place of business?"

"But Jimmy—"

"Is dead and that's that. As far as I'm concerned, it was an accident."

"But I heard—"

"Did you hear *me*? Did you hear what I just said?"

"Yes, but—"

"But nothing. It's over. It doesn't matter one way or another how he died, just that he's dead. We don't work for him anymore. And you don't work for anybody. You have two minutes to get your shit together and get out of here. And don't ever come back."

"But—"

"But but but but nothing! Two minutes! Go sell your ass down in Scollay Square." Violet watched Dorothy run back into her room sobbing. For her part, Violet had no tears. Dorothy was nineteen and fresh-faced and wouldn't last ten minutes in the Square before another Jimmy Dryden scooped her up and made her his star attraction. Young pussy never went out of style. Pushing thirty, Violet had only a few good years left. Jimmy's untimely demise might be an opportunity in disguise. She could run the sixth floor of Charlesgate as well as he ever had.

She lit a cigarette and sat by the window, watching and waiting. Nearly ninety minutes passed before an ambulance pulled up in front of the building. Busy night in Boston. Two attendants stepped out of the vehicle and entered the building. Five minutes later they exited, carrying a black plastic bag between them. Violet gave Dryden a farewell salute as they loaded his gift-wrapped corpse into the back of the ambulance. She watched it pull away.

What would happen now? The cops hadn't asked any questions, but by morning Dryden's friends would know he was dead. And they might not be as quick to accept that his demise had been an accident. These guys all had enemies. And they might come around asking questions. And they were far more dangerous than the cops.

It might be best to get out of town for a few days. She could always stay with her sister down in Lakeville. Sally's husband would bitch about it, but not too loudly. One night he'd slip out of their bedroom and come down looking for free samples. She'd offer some up and he'd keep his complaints to a dull roar. It had happened before. She could probably get away with staying there a week or so while the heat died down. Then maybe she'd come back to the Charlesgate, acting all innocent. Oh, Jimmy's dead? That's terrible! So you need somebody to run things around here?

It might all work out, but there was still the matter of the paintings Jake had left in her custody. If his crazy story had any truth in it, they were worth a lot of money. And if she hid them well enough, she'd have leverage if and when he came back for them. He already owed her $300 and said he'd pay ten times that amount if she held onto them for him. So what were they *really* worth? A hundred times that much? A thousand?

It was worth finding out. She pulled the paintings out of her closet and, one by one, unrolled them and looked them over. They all looked pretty good to her, but one in particular caught her eye. A man with his back to the artist. Two women, one on either side of him, the one on the left playing a piano or some other keyboard instrument. Two pictures on the wall: paintings within a painting. As she stared at this image, she began to tell herself a story about the three people in it. But the story never quite came together; there was a mystery here that could never be solved. She liked this painting very much. She thought it would look good hanging over the fireplace in the house she'd own someday once she was running things at the Charlesgate. And what a great story she'd have to tell about it.

But she had to hide it first, along with the others, and she knew just where to do it. She couldn't handle them all at once so she gathered a half-dozen paintings and drawings in her arms and made her way out into the hall.

"What is all that?"

Violet turned to see Dorothy standing in front of her room clutching a shopping bag stuffed with clothes. "I gave you two minutes."

"I'm sorry but I needed to pull myself together!"

"Never mind that. Set your stuff down and help me with this, and maybe I'll think about letting you stay."

"Really? Oh, thank you, Vi! I'm sorry I called the cops, I just panicked and—"

"Just shut up, put your stuff down and get the rest of these paintings from my room."

Dorothy did what she was told. Once she'd collected the rest of the art they shuffled over to the elevator and Violet shoved the handle to direct the cab down to the basement.

"What is this stuff? Where did it come from?"

"I'll explain it all in a minute. I just really need your help first."

"Okay. Sorry. I know I talk too—I'm sorry."

She was quiet the rest of the way down, although it clearly took every ounce of effort she could muster. When the elevator reached the basement, Violet slid aside the gate and gathered up her half of the paintings. "This way."

Dorothy followed her down the hall to a door at the end. Violet set down her armful and pushed on the door. It gave easily.

"What is this?"

"These are the stables. Back when this place was really swinging, the hoity-toity would put their horses down here."

"Wow. You mean back before cars?"

"You got it. There's a tunnel at the end that leads up to the surface a couple blocks away. Once in a while I have to sneak a high-roller out this way. Now just carry that stuff in there and I'll show you where to put it."

"It's really dark in there. Are you sure—?"

"It's okay. I've got my Zippo." Violet pulled her lighter out of her pocket and flicked on the flame. She gestured for Dorothy to enter the stables. Dorothy shrugged and stepped into the darkness. Violet followed. She lowered the Zippo until its flickering light picked up a box stuffed with artifacts from Charlesgate's glory days, one of which was a heavy marble gargoyle she'd admired last time she'd been in the stables. Dorothy stopped and turned.

"Where do you want me to put these?"

"You can drop them right there."

Violet waited until Dorothy had set down the paintings before bringing the gargoyle down on her head. Dorothy dropped to the floor and Violet brought the gargoyle down again. And again. After a half-dozen blows, there wasn't much left of Dorothy's head. Certainly not a face that could be identified. Violet dragged her deeper into the stables and dumped her in the last stall on the right. The body would be found eventually, but Violet doubted it would be anytime soon.

She flicked her Zippo again. She slowly made her way back toward the door into the basement until she spotted what she was looking for. A long-discarded Persian rug, rolled up and stuffed in a refrigerator box. She dragged out the rug and unrolled it. She then placed all but one of the stolen paintings inside the rug, rolled it back up and stuck it back in the box.

That left only the painting she truly admired, the one she planned to keep for herself. Reading the paper the next day she would learn it was called *The Concert* and had been painted by someone named Vermeer. She had a special hiding place in mind for this one. And before she left the Charlesgate for what turned out to be the last time, she hid it there.

OCTOBER 21, 1986

I nearly plowed into Torres on his way through the door with his BosDeli sandwich. I could hear his massive keyring jingling in my pocket. To me it sounded like the bells of Big Ben.

"Donnelly," he said. "Don't tell me you locked yourself out again. Because as I explained—"

"No, I know. I've got my keys. All the keys I could ever need."

He looked at me like I was an idiot, which was appropriate since I felt like an idiot. Somehow I had to get the keyring back into his desk before he went into his office. I didn't think I could count on Jackie St. John running through the lobby naked, but short of divine intervention I had nary a clue how I was going to pull this off. Lucky for me, divine intervention was in the cards this time, in the form of my old friend the fire alarm.

"Oh crap," said Torres. "Never fails. All right, everybody out!" He took off for the staircase. It was his job to check every floor and make sure all the stoners and slackers complied, even though the alarm went off at least once a week. I watched him go, then broke into a dead run down the hallway to his office. I dumped the keys off in his desk, then melted in with the rest of the crowd heading out of the building.

Standing in the park across the street, I felt someone tugging on my sleeve. I turned and saw Shane Devlin standing over my shoulder. "What the fuck?"

"I think you mean 'thank you.' I just saved your ass, kid."

"What the hell are you talking about?"

"I pulled the fire alarm."

"You—how did you—?"

"Look, kid. I may have spent forty years in the can, but I still know how to create a diversion when I need to."

"How were you even—were you in the building?"

"Fuck yes, I was in the building. I sweet-talked Missy there at the front desk, which wasn't hard because I think she's already got a crush on your sweet ol' grandpa."

"And why were you even there in the first place?"

"Kid, you really think I'm going to leave anything to chance at this point? You told me you were gonna try to get the keys at lunchtime today. Missy signed me in at 11:30. 'Oh, I was supposed to meet my grandson, he must be a little late, we're so proud of him and by the way, I really gotta use the toilet, yah yah yah.' I parked my ass by the men's room and watched you the whole way. So the only question I have now is did you find the key?"

"Yeah, yeah, I've got it."

"Way to go, kiddo. So as soon as they let us back in the building, what do you say we get started?"

"Maybe we should wait for the excitement to die down a little bit."

"Kid, you may not be in much of a hurry, but I'm sixty-three years old. I got health issues. I say no time like the present."

"Yeah, but—fine. Whatever. Might as well get it over with."

"Sounds like you don't expect this to amount to much."

"Honestly, no. I have to admit I'd be more than a little surprised if we waltzed into the stables and found the most priceless collection of stolen art in history sitting there waiting for us to scoop it up. Maybe that's just me."

"You ever bought a lottery ticket, kid?"

"Uh…yeah, sure. Once in a while I'll buy a ticket for the Megabucks."

"Well, what I heard once? You got about as much chance of

picking the winning number as you do of guessing one specific inch of highway on a road trip from Bangor, Maine to Amarillo, Texas. Not too good, right?"

"So?"

"So think how much better our odds are of finding those priceless paintings in the basement across the street."

"Yeah...that doesn't really add up for me."

"Well, that's your problem, not mine. We're getting to work as soon as—"

"Attention! Attention!" Torres and a fire marshal were standing on the top step of the Charlesgate entryway. Torres was waving his arms. I wondered if he'd found time to eat his sandwich. "It's all clear! You are free to re-enter the building!"

Shane nudged me. "See, kid? It's time to get to work."

It took a while to get back inside, as students slowly shuffled two-by-two through the front entrance, trading stories about how drunk they were the last time a fire alarm went off. No one even bothered trying the elevator, so the line for the staircase extended out into the lobby. The line to go upstairs, that is. There was no line, no waiting, to go down to the basement, which is where gramps and I now headed. If anyone had asked, I'd have told them I'd been doing laundry when the alarm went off, but nobody asked.

Once we reached the stable door, I realized I didn't have a flashlight with me. I was about to mention this when Shane reached into his jacket pocket and pulled out a penlight. "You just think of everything, don't you?" I said.

"I'm a professional."

"Yeah. A professional mop-pusher."

I glanced back over my shoulder, then pushed open the door. Shane flicked on his penlight. We stepped into the stables and I closed the door behind us. Shane's light provided limited visibility. I could see about six feet in front of us before every-thing went dim. Boxes were piled on either side of us, stacked against the walls.

"Might as well start right here," Shane said. "Why don't you pull down the top box from that stack and I'll hold the light while you dig through it."

"I see I've been assigned the more labor-intensive portion of this task. I know, I know, you're 108 years old and you're going to drop dead any minute."

I reached up and tugged on one corner of the top box, about a foot above my head. It didn't budge. "This thing is fucking heavy."

"Well, put some elbow grease into it. I swear, you kids today are all pampered fairies."

It took a while. I'd shove the box a couple inches one way, then a couple inches the other way. My rudimentary under-standing of physics suggested there was only one way for this to end, but it's not like paintings are fragile objects, right?

Sure enough, I felt the box giving way and stepped aside. It crashed to the floor and I heard something shatter inside.

"Nice, kid. You're a regular cat burglar. Subtle as a fucking earthquake."

"What can I tell you? If you can't help me move these things, maybe we need another accomplice."

"Fuck that. Open it up and see what's inside."

The box was roughly the size of my illegal dorm fridge. I popped open the top and removed part of the lamp that had broken on impact. "Isn't this box a little small to be holding those paintings?'

"They ain't all big. There's a few drawings by Degas that would fit in there easily. Finding those might not be quite as good as finding the Rembrandt or the Vermeer, but it would definitely be worth our while."

"You sound like quite the art expert."

"I've had a lot of time to study up on these things."

"Yeah. Forty years. You said."

"You're a real fucking smartass, kid. Didn't your father ever smack you around when you ran that mouth of yours?"

"I'm sure he wanted to, but my mother wasn't having it. She said this smart mouth of mine would make me a lot of money someday."

"Well, the jury's still out on that one."

"Look, there's nothing in here but junk. I mean, for all I know these ashtrays date back to the Ming dynasty and are worth a fortune, but there's definitely no art in here."

"Next box."

And so it went. We made our way through six boxes on the left and six boxes on the right. Maybe an hour and a half, maybe two hours had passed. The beam from Shane's light began to flicker and he slapped the penlight against his thigh a couple times.

"Your batteries are running out," I said. "I think that means it's time to call it a day."

He reluctantly agreed. I opened the door half an inch and peered into the hallway. The coast was clear. We stepped back into the basement and I locked the doorknob behind me, leaving the deadbolts alone.

"I think maybe I should hang onto the key," said Shane.

"And why is that?"

"Well, I wouldn't want you coming down here and looking without me. What with you living here and me…not living here."

"How about if we make a copy of the key? Each have one."

"That doesn't change the scenario I just outlined to you, does it? Doesn't alleviate my concerns."

"I guess not." Honestly, I couldn't fault his logic. I probably *would* have looked without him if I'd had the key. So I handed it to him and he pocketed it.

"Thanks, kid. Now let's go up and say goodnight to Missy. You know, I think I got a shot with her."

"You've got a sense of humor. I'll give you that."

"You wanna put money on it?"

"I sure don't."

MAY 7, 2014

Coleman picked up a bleacher seat from a scalper outside Remy's restaurant and took in the getaway day game between the Red Sox and the Cincinnati Reds. It was a Wednesday afternoon and he had nothing better to do, even though it was a fucking interleague game, which he hated on principle. In a few days he'd be back on the job, on desk duty, trying to dig his way out of the doghouse. But here and now it was a warm, sunny day at Fenway Park and the beer was cold and the World Champs were winning.

Exiting onto Lansdowne Street to the victorious strains of "Dirty Water," Coleman checked his phone and saw he'd missed a call from the Rhode Island cop, Childs. He hit Redial and ducked into the souvenir shop across the street.

"Childs."

"Hey there, Sergeant. It's Detective Coleman up in Boston."

"How's it going up there?"

"Just walked out of Fenway after a Sox win, so it doesn't get much better."

"Nice. It's been way too long since I got to a game."

"My treat, next time you get up this way. I saw you called me earlier?"

"Yeah, you asked me to keep you posted on the Charles White investigation."

"For sure."

"Well, the bad news is I'm not gonna be able to do that much longer. J. Edgar is taking this thing over so this is my last day on the case."

"The Feds, huh? What do they want with this?"

"They weren't interested in sharing that information with me, if you can believe that."

"Will wonders never cease."

"Anyway, they're gonna search this guy White's apartment up there in Boston. I figured I'd let you know in case you want to get in on it."

"Hey, I appreciate it."

"No problem. Just tell me I can still give you a ring for those Sox tickets whenever I get up there."

"You best believe it."

"Oh, I almost forgot. Before the FBI took this thing over, we put in a request for White's phone data, like I told you. It hasn't come through yet, but I'm expecting it this afternoon. If you want, I'll keep you in the loop on that."

"That would be great. Was his phone on him when he was found? Melted or whatever?"

"Nope. We sifted through the ashes in that dumpster and no such luck."

"So if someone still has it and they use it now…"

"We'd definitely get a hit on that."

"Oh, one more thing, as Columbo used to say. No security cameras in the alley?"

"Nah. We checked the ones from the parking lot and inside Dunkin's, but if they pulled in the back and left the same way, we wouldn't see shit anyway."

"That sucks."

"Yep. Anyway, if that phone data comes in, I'll shoot you a call. Probably a couple hours or so."

"That'll work." Coleman hit End Call and pocketed his phone. He felt a little bad for not telling Childs he was no longer on the case, but not too bad. He figured he'd do more with the information than Carny ever would.

Coleman milled through the postgame scrum down to Kenmore Square. He popped into Nuggets, the used record store that remained virtually unchanged through all the upheaval the square had seen over the decades. Everything surrounding it was shiny and upscale, but Nuggets was still the cramped little dungeon it had always been. Coleman didn't even own a turntable anymore, but he enjoyed browsing through old album covers, particularly in the jazz section. They evoked a smoky, mysterious night world he'd always wanted to inhabit but never managed to locate.

After an hour or so, he wandered down to the Corner Tavern and drank a Harpoon Ale at the bar. He didn't know it, but twenty-five years earlier the Corner Tavern's location had been occupied by a much seedier bar called the Fallout Shelter. It was a Cold War era joke that expired in the early '90s, along with the original version of the bar. But the contours of its interior were not all that different. It smelled better and the beer was more expensive. That was about it.

When he finished his beer, Coleman checked his phone. It was quarter past five. Jackie should be home soon. He scrolled through his contacts, found the number for Woodward, the art detective, and hit Send. The call went to voicemail. "Mr. Woodward, Martin Coleman here. Sorry I haven't been in touch in a couple days, but...I've run into a bit of a snag. workwise. Give me a call when you get a chance and we can compare notes." He ended the call. Maybe Woodward had given up and gone back to England.

Coleman paid for his beer and walked the block back to Charlesgate East. He stood, hidden by the corner of the building, and watched. Twenty minutes later, Jackie crossed the street at Beacon and headed into the building. He gave her a five-minute head start, then walked over to the entrance and buzzed her intercom number.

"Hello?"

"Boston police."

"Are you downstairs?"

"Guilty."

"Are you stalking me? You know I don't react well to that sort of thing."

"Yeah, but I also know you won't file a restraining order, so what the hell."

She let him dangle for fifteen seconds, then buzzed him in. He rode the elevator up to the sixth floor and knocked on her door. The door opened. A roll of toilet paper bounced off his nose.

"You're a dick," she said.

"Still guilty," he replied as she opened the door wider and let him in. "I sure do love this fucking condo."

"I know. I'm starting to think you're going to marry me and then kill me so you can inherit it."

"Can we arrange that? Can we rework your will right now? I can call my lawyer."

"Eat shit. Can I offer you a glass of wine?"

"Sure. Can we drink it on my soon-to-be patio?"

"So you can push me six stories to my death? How can I resist?" She fetched a bottle of merlot and two glasses and they sat on the rooftop deck, watching a car attempting to navigate around a row of garbage cans in the alley below.

"So I talked to Charles White's replacement at the Emerson alumni office today," Jackie said.

"Oh yeah?"

"Cute girl. He harassed the shit out of her, too."

"Sounds like a real loss for humanity."

"She says she didn't kill him."

"Good enough for me. Although, funny little footnote. Turns out the Feds are interested in this thing."

"Really?"

"Yeah, they're taking over the investigation."

She sipped from her glass. "Are you watching me for a reaction?"

"What do you mean?"

"Are you expecting me to break down sobbing and say 'I confess! I killed him!' I mean, I don't want to disappoint you."

"Jesus. Of course not."

"Really? Because I can't seem to shake the feeling that you think I killed this guy. Or at least had something to do with it."

"I'm a cop. We always seem suspicious. Seriously. I don't think any such thing."

"Why not?"

He set his wine on the table, leaned in and kissed her. She didn't try to stop him and he didn't stop for a long time. Finally he came up for air. "Does that answer your question?"

"Not really," she said. "I think you'd want to kiss me even if you thought I was a murderer. Do you deny it?"

"You're paranoid. But no, I don't deny it."

"Okay, so eliminate me as a suspect. You're the cop. Tell me why I couldn't have done it."

"I can't do that. You *could* have done it. Based on the limited information I have at this point, anyone could have done it. I just don't think you did."

The opening chords of "Dirty Water" emerged from Coleman's pocket. He pulled out his phone, checked the number and answered it. "Coleman."

"It's Childs again. I have an update."

"Shoot."

"We got the records request back from Verizon. I'm texting you the phone numbers for the last five calls he made. Or at least, the last five that were made from his phone."

"Excellent."

"I've got to send the data on to J. Edgar, but there's also a photo taken a few hours before we found his body. Means nothing to me, but maybe it would to you. I'm texting it to you now."

"You're a prince, Childs. I'm gonna get you home plate seats for the fucking World Series."

"I won't forget you said that. I gotta go."

"Later."

Coleman ended the call and checked his text messages. A photo message appeared at the very top. He tapped it and the photo filled his phone screen. It showed an upscale condominium Coleman recognized immediately, because he happened to be sitting in it at that very moment. A framed movie poster was smashed on the floor, glass scattered all around.

Coleman checked the next text. A list of phone numbers and call times popped onto the screen. At the top of the list—the last number called from White's phone—was Jackie's cell.

JUNE 23, 1946

As Violet had predicted, a week passed before her sister announced it was time for Violet to make her way back to Boston or wherever the hell else she wanted to go as long as it wasn't Sally's house. Also as predicted, Sally's husband Norm had collected rent for her visit in the form of a 3 A.M. blowjob on the couch. What she hadn't guessed was that the latter event would instigate the former, as Norm's sounds of ecstasy had been loud enough to wake up Sally, prompting her to discover her husband's dick in her sister's mouth. Violet couldn't blame her for making it very clear that she wouldn't be invited back for Thanksgiving dinner.

That didn't matter anymore. By now the heat would have died down at the Charlesgate. She could slip back in, make sure the paintings were still in their hiding place, then track down whoever was now running things in the building and try to cut a deal. She'd been following the story in the papers and rumor had it the Gardner planned to offer a reward for the safe return of the stolen art, possibly up to $50,000. She figured she could leverage her inside information into a management role on the sixth floor, maybe split the reward fifty/fifty with the house. Jake would be pissed off if he ever came back, but that was his hard luck. He hadn't offered her anywhere near that much, and she didn't owe him a thing. Quite the opposite. Besides, possession was nine-tenths of the law, right?

She caught the first bus to South Station in the morning, then rode the T to Kenmore. As soon as the Charlesgate was in sight, she could tell something was wrong. When she got closer, it became clear that her plan had hit an unexpected snag. Two cops were standing in front of the main entrance, which was bolted shut with chains and padlocks. She took a deep breath and walked up to the slightly nicer-looking cop.

"What happened here?"

"Who wants to know?"

"I live here."

"No, you don't live here. Nobody lives here no more."

"How's that?"

"This building has been seized by the Boston Police Department. The people who used to live here and work here, they don't no more."

"Why not?"

"I'm sure you wouldn't know anything about this, ma'am, but turns out there was a great deal of illegal activity taking place here. In the course of a criminal investigation, it was discovered that the owners of this building, on paper anyway, had not paid any property taxes in quite some time. Consequently the building has been completely evacuated and is set to go on the auction block. Rumor has it that some these big colleges around here have interest in using it as dormitory space."

Violet's heart sped up; she could feel it beating in her neck. The cops had always turned a blind eye because they'd always been paid off. Now, on the same night, the two men with the biggest interest in keeping the police at bay—Dave T and Jimmy Dryden—had both met an untimely demise. If no one else had stepped in to fill the void, the cops would no longer have an incentive to ignore the illegal goings-on at the Charlesgate. On the contrary, they could bust the place and sell it to the press as a big win. Which was apparently what had happened.

"Anything else I can help you with, lady?"

"No…thanks. I was just curious." Violet smiled and turned back toward Kenmore Square, weighing her options. She could come back later and try to break into the building. She might find an open window or maybe sneak in through the stables. But she expected the stables would be locked up tight, and there might even be night watchmen stationed inside the building. A smarter move would be to talk to someone in a position to get the Charlesgate reopened for business. Someone with whom she could cut a deal. Dave T and Dryden may have run things at the Charlesgate, but they didn't run organized crime in Boston. She remembered Jimmy bitching a few times about having to pay ten percent to a man in the North End who would cause big trouble if he didn't get his cut. And surely this man wouldn't be happy that his cut would no longer be forthcoming. If she could reason with him, maybe he could settle things with the cops and get the Charlesgate up and running again. Maybe they could partner up, split the reward for the paintings and the take from the sixth floor. Maybe even find someone to take over Dave T's poker game. She knew this man would miss that game if it wasn't around anymore. So it was settled. She would have to go see Marko.

He would recognize her. The boss of the Boston mafia had stopped in to see her a few times after finishing up with poker night, at least until he'd traded in for a younger model when Dorothy came around. He'd always had very specific, unusual requests. He liked her to bite his nipples until she drew blood, and he liked to bite hers, too. He liked her to squeeze his balls until he screamed. One time he asked her to wear a dildo in a harness and mount him from behind, but he'd chickened out as soon as the rubber tip touched his anus.

She wouldn't try to blackmail him with this information, of course. Maybe she'd hint at things he wouldn't want revealed, hint at things they might pursue further once they were partnered up. She would have to play it just right. The Italians weren't exactly in the business of partnering up with women, but she thought she could sell it. And it wouldn't be any trouble finding him. He'd be holding court at the back table of the Prince Street Social Club. Getting to that back table might pose a challenge, however.

She jumped back on the T at Kenmore and rode down to the Haymarket stop. She crossed at the light and walked a block up to Hanover Street. To her, it was always like stepping back in time. The walkways grew narrower, with three-story brownstones crowding in close on either side of the cobblestone streets. The cafes spilled out onto the sidewalks, where men sat at tiny tables sipping wine and speaking Italian. A few of them made catcalls as she passed, with one particularly excitable older gentleman yelling out what might have been either a marriage proposal or a death threat.

She turned left on Prince Street and walked one block toward North Square. Paul Revere's house was behind her as she approached two enormous gentlemen standing outside the doorway to One Prince Street.

"Sorry," said the slightly larger of the two. "This ain't ladies' night."

"I'm here to see Mr. Marko."

"That's funny. He didn't tell us to expect no company."

"He'll want to talk to me. Tell him it's Violet from the Charlesgate. Tell him I've got a business proposition. Tell him… tell him if he won't talk to me, I'll have no choice but to talk to you."

The two giants exchanged a puzzled glance, then the larger one tilted his head slightly toward the door. The other one nodded and stepped inside.

"Nice evening, huh?" said Violet.

"Oh yeah. Real temperate. I was thinking of going for a swim."

She lit a cigarette and offered him one. He declined. A moment later, the slightly smaller giant emerged from the doorway. "Boss says he'll see her."

"How about that? Life hasn't lost its power to surprise. Head on in, miss."

And so Violet went where few women had gone before: inside the Prince Street Social Club. It basically looked like an indoor version of the street cafes she'd passed along the way. Men crowded around small candlelit tables, drinking wine and speaking Italian. But at each table, all conversation stopped as she walked by. It took an eternity to cross the room, but finally she was standing in front of Marko's table. He was easily the smallest man in the room: whippet-thin and no taller than five-foot-eight, although his slick helmet of hair added at least two inches to his height. He smiled and gestured to the seat opposite him.

"Miss Violet. An unexpected pleasure. Please sit. Can I offer you some calamari?"

She sat. "I don't know what that is."

"It's fried squid."

"Oh. I don't think so, thanks."

He laughed. "Well, it's not for everyone. I have to say I'm surprised to see you here. And I was *very* surprised to hear what you told my boys outside. It sounded like, I don't know, a threat." He smiled again.

"No, of course not. They must have misunderstood."

"I figured that was the case. Let me pour you a glass of wine and you can tell me why you're here." He did so.

"Well…I guess you must have heard about what happened over at the Charlesgate."

"I heard Jimmy took a header off the sixth-floor staircase. Tragic. And the same night Dave T turned up dead at the museum. That was a real shame. I am really going to miss that poker game."

"That's what I thought."

"Tell me, how is that girl I've been seeing over there lately? Dorothy? How is she holding up?"

"Oh, I…think I heard she took a bus back home."

"Back home. Where was she from?"

"I think somewhere in New Hampshire."

"New Hampshire? I would have guessed Kansas. You know, Dorothy, Kansas? No, I'm joking. I know you girls don't use your real names."

"No, we don't." She sipped her wine.

"So this is why you came down here? To tell me something I already know about that piece of shit Jimmy Dryden? No offense."

"No, none taken. But no, that's not all I wanted to tell you. See, the cops have shut down the Charlesgate. I figure because Jimmy and Dave T were paying them off and now that's not happening anymore."

"So what do you want me to do about it?"

"Well, no reason to let a viable business opportunity go to waste, am I right? I thought maybe you and I could partner up to get things up and running again. Who knows, maybe we could even coax Dorothy to come back."

"Interesting idea. No offense, again, but I don't see myself partnering up with a cocksucking whore. Just not the way I do business. You understand."

"I understand it's unusual. But I think I can sweeten the deal for you."

"How's that?"

"You know that thing Dave T was up to the night he was killed? I'm guessing he didn't clear that with you."

"He did not. And I would be very angry with him were it not for the fact he's gone on to his just reward."

"The cops don't know who killed him. But I do. It was Jimmy. He killed Dave T and that driver they found dead in the car. The three of them were in it together. They planned it together and then Jimmy took them out."

"No shit. And you know this how?"

"Jimmy came back to the Charlesgate in a panic. He hadn't planned to kill them but things went bad in a hurry. But he had the paintings. He wanted me to help him hide them."

"But then he had an unfortunate accident."

"Yeah. Well, maybe it wasn't an accident like they said. Maybe an ambitious woman saw a chance to advance her station in life."

Marko raised his glass. "Salud." He finished off his wine and set down the glass, grinning from ear to ear. "That is some story, Miss Violet."

"It's all true. Only one person on earth knows where those paintings are now. And you can be the second. You can fence them, turn them in for a reward, whatever you want to do. I only ask two things. One, a ten percent finder's fee. And two, a fifty/fifty partnership on reopening the Charlesgate."

"Very fair terms. Except let's forget the Charlesgate. We're done with that place. From what I hear, Boston University has the inside track on buying it and turning it into student housing. But so what? It's only real estate and we've got plenty of that all over town. We can open a bigger and better whorehouse any-where we choose. Fifty/fifty like you said. But I can't just take your word for this. I gotta see this art for myself."

"I'll tell you where it is if you tell me we have a deal."

Marko grinned and extended his hand. She shook it. "It's a deal. So spill." She told him about the stables and the rug rolled up in the second stall on the right. She didn't mention the secret hiding place where her favorite painting was stashed.

"Tell you what," said Marko. "I'll go over and check it out myself tonight. If it's as you say, and I'm sure it will be, we're in business. But I'm gonna have to ask you to wait here until I get back. I'll have one of my boys keep you company. Now like I said, I'm pretty sure it's going to check out. But it's only fair to tell you. We got a nice, shiny new sausage grinder in the kitchen there. And if, for some reason, it *doesn't* check out, I'm going to come back here and personally feed you into that sausage grinder. Feet first."

Marko smiled again, stood and whistled. The front door opened and the two enormous men stepped inside. "Joey, you're gonna stay here and keep an eye on Miss Violet. Paulie, we're gonna go see a man about a rug."

Shane Devlin was in a particularly foul mood as we got started on our second day of searching the stables. The Red Sox had lost the fourth game of the World Series the night before, their second loss in a row at home. The series was all tied up and home field advantage now reverted to the Mets. Shane had seen it all before and he wasn't happy.

"Always the same with these cocksuckers. In '46 I was listening to the series on the radio while my trial was going on. I could barely give a shit whether or not I got the death penalty because Ted Williams hurt his elbow in a fucking practice game and wasn't worth a shit. I got my sentence on the day Pesky held the ball and Enos Slaughter scored the winning run for the Cardinals. I couldn't tell you which hurt me worse."

"I'd say you need a serious dose of perspective," I said, digging through yet another box of worthless knickknacks. "Sure, you spent forty years in the can, but we're going on sixty-eight years without a championship here."

"I'm not laughing."

"You should be. That was funny."

What happened next wasn't funny. Shane whacked his penlight across my nose. Blood gushed from my face and I howled like a kicked dog as I dropped to my knees, clutching my nose. "Why the fuck did you do that?" I finally managed.

"Kid, I'm sick and tired of you running down my time in stir like it's a fucking joke. I spent ten years in Charlestown and another thirty in Walpole. Two of the most dangerous, disgusting hellholes on this planet. I used to wake up at three in the morning with rats running across my face. In Charlestown

my cell didn't even have a window, just a cheap piece of ply-
wood that didn't begin to keep out the cold in the middle of
fucking February. The men I lived with in Walpole were the
scum of the fucking earth. They all said they were innocent,
but I was the only one who really was. Oh, it wasn't all bad. We
had movie night. We could listen to the Sox on the radio, and
when TV came along, we could watch the games. We had a
creepy inmate selling ice cream in the prison yard. One time I
got in an argument with him because I asked for a creamsicle
and he insisted I'd asked for a fudgicle. I broke his fucking nose
in three places. His name was Al DeSalvo. You know who that is?
The fucking Boston Strangler. So if I broke the Boston Strangler's
nose, what the fuck do you think I'll do to you?"

I didn't have a reply to that because I was too busy trying to
stop the bleeding from my own nose.

"Oh, no smartass remarks? Well, let me tell you one more
thing. I've got the key to this place. I've got Missy upstairs
practically licking my balls. So what the fuck do I need you for
anyway? And don't say I need you to move these boxes. I'm just
making you do that so I don't have to do shit. But believe you
me, I could move 'em if I had to."

I rummaged through the box and found a fancy linen napkin.
I leaned my head back and pressed it to my nose. It was more
than a bit musty but I didn't care at this point.

"There you go, kid. Hey, I just want you to know where you
stand. I've been a good sport. But I'm done with your com-
ments. You smart off to me one more time, they're gonna find
pieces of you in all these boxes someday. Are we crystal clear?"

I nodded as best I could with my head tilted back and bloody
cloth jammed up my nose. For the first time he really seemed
to take note of my condition.

"All right, maybe it's time we called it a day," he said. "Get
that fixed up and meet me here same time tomorrow."

✿

Ten minutes later in room 629, Murtaugh was asking me what the fuck happened to my face.

"I tripped running down the stairs because I was late for class."

"Yeah, that doesn't sound like you. You should go to the emergency room."

I did. I spent almost two hours in the waiting room trying not to stare at the guy spitting blood into a Styrofoam cup before a doctor would see me. He determined that my nose wasn't broken but that the cut would need stitches, which he administered. As I walked back to Charlesgate feeling like Jack Nicholson in *Chinatown*, I pondered my options. It was a little before 10 P.M. I had to meet Shane at three o'clock the following afternoon. That meant I had to pull an all-nighter to accomplish what I had in mind.

I retrieved my Buick from its prime parking spot with the broken meter and aimed it north. I caught the last two innings of Game 5 on the radio and managed to distract myself from my own problems as the Red Sox withstood a late charge by the Mets to hold on for a 4–2 win. I stopped once for gas, No-Doz and a 64-ounce Coke. At 3:30 A.M. I pulled into the driveway of my parents' house on the coast of downeast Maine. Normal people were sound asleep. My father was loading lobster traps into his pickup truck.

"Hey, Dad."

"Tommy. Didn't expect to see you on a school night."

"I'm not staying long. I need to ask you a favor."

"Ayuh. Whatcha need?"

"I need to borrow a gun."

MAY 7, 2014

Coleman pocketed his phone.

"Bad news?" Jackie asked.

"Not sure. You got a pen and paper I can use?"

"Uh…sure. Hang on a minute."

She scrounged up a pen and a yellow legal pad and handed them to him. "What are you doing?"

"I'm making a timeline." Coleman leaned over the pad and started jotting down notes, consulting his phone several times along the way. When he was done he stared at the pad, tapping the pen against his teeth.

"Well? Are you going to share?"

"We might have a problem."

"How so?"

"Did White call your cell at 3:55 A.M. on the 25th?"

"I dunno. Did he? I mean, he called me a few times after our last meeting, but I always let it go to voicemail."

"It was a trick question."

"How so?"

"At 3:55 A.M. on the 25th White had already been dead for anywhere from twelve to twenty-four hours. But somebody called your number from his phone."

"Well, like I said, I didn't answer any calls from his number. I programmed my phone so they'd go straight through to voice-mail. And he never left a message. You can check it and I'm sure you will."

"I believe you but it's out of my hands now. The FBI has taken over this investigation. But the good news is I'm gonna walk into my LT's office tomorrow and get my job back."

"How is that?"

"Because I was right about our Charlesgate murder. My new pal Hayden Childs down in Rhode Island just texted me this photo from White's phone."

Coleman held up his phone. Jackie's eyes widened as she recognized the image.

"It was him. White broke into my condo…"

"Looks that way. But the timestamp on the photo indicates it was taken on the night of the 24th, which is the day after we found Rachel O'Brien's body."

"So what does that mean?"

"Could mean he killed O'Brien and came back later. Maybe something spooked him. Remember, he had the keys and it took a few days for the building management to change all the locks. Or maybe—"

"He was hiding out in here for two days, waiting for me to come home."

"Yeah. Maybe. Either way, the FBI has his phone data now, which means they have that photo and your phone number. You're gonna be hearing from them. And when they figure out the connection, they're gonna call my boss to tell him they're taking over the Charlesgate case and folding it into their overall White investigation. They're gonna hope both murders tie into something bigger—serial killer, international drug trafficking, terrorism…"

"Unsolved art museum robbery?"

"I don't know if they'll make any connection with the Gardner thing. But they'll be looking for a big win, especially in the Boston branch of the bureau. Ever since Whitey Bulger's been back in the news, it's dredged up all the bad publicity from the corruption that ran rampant in the Boston FBI back in Whitey's heyday. So they'll dig around. They'll turn White's apartment upside down. And they'll be coming after you. Hard."

"Are you trying to scare me?"

"I'm trying to prepare you. Because when they find out the last call made from his phone was to you, they're going to question you. At length. They're going to get their claws in your life and they're going to dig deep."

"I've got nothing to hide."

"I know. But they're not just gonna take your word for it. Look, I've got a friend in the Boston bureau owes me a favor. I don't know that he's going to be assigned to this case, of course, but I can pick his brain at least."

"I don't understand any of this. If White killed Rachel O'Brien and then broke in here a day later and stole my laptop...who killed White?"

"Who knows? He sounds like a guy who made a lot of enemies. Whoever it is, they still may still have his phone. They definitely called you from the phone after White was already dead."

"Called me why?"

"A guess? They saw your number come up frequently in his call log. They figure you're someone he knows well. They called the number with the intent of establishing that he was still alive at 3:55 A.M. and that you were the last one he talked to. They hoped White would never be identified—that's why they burned the body—but if he *was* identified, the police would definitely check his phone records. They picked you as a red herring."

"Wow. You really do think like a cop. But I have another question."

"Shoot."

"If the FBI ends up taking over the Charlesgate case, what makes you think you'll be getting your job back?"

"Because I get to walk into my LT's office and say 'I told you so.' We could have had a nice easy win for the department if he'd left me on the case. Instead, J. Edgar takes it away and gets the credit."

"Does your boss usually respond well to 'I told you so'?"

"I might be a little more subtle about it."

"One more question."

"Okay."

"Do *you* still think all this ties in with the Gardner robbery?"

"Maybe. Maybe White found something out. Maybe he did kill that girl to get those keys, not to stalk you but to get into some other part of the building. Because he believed those paintings were still here. Maybe he was using your condo as his home base, knowing you were out of town. Maybe he had partners. Maybe he was holding out on them and they found out. Maybe they killed him."

"That's a lot of maybes."

"That's what my job usually is. A whole lot of maybes."

"You're good at your job, aren't you?"

"Only when they let me do it."

They ordered in from Bertucci's and Coleman spent a couple hours coaching Jackie for her inevitable grilling at the hands of the FBI. They watched an episode of *Game of Thrones* until Jackie grew tired of his relentless questions about who was who and what was going on, then retired to the bedroom for what Coleman would later remember as the single greatest night of sex in his entire life. He slept so soundly afterward, he didn't even stir when Jackie left for work. He didn't wake up until the Standells blared from his phone at 10:30 in the morning.

"Coleman," he mumbled.

"This is Detective Coleman?"

"Like I said."

"This is Bernie Hahn from Robertson Renovation and Remodel."

"Well, I don't need any remodeling done and I'm on the no-call list for solicitations, so…"

"No, you called me. I had a message waiting when I got back

from vacation. Something about the Charlesgate renovations a few years back?"

Coleman sat up and rubbed his eyes. "Oh. Right. Thanks for getting back to me."

"What did you want to know?"

"You were involved with turning the Charlesgate into condos?"

"I was. I oversaw the whole remodel. We tore that place down to the timbers inside."

"There must have been a lot of junk in there, piled up over the years."

"You better believe it. Total nightmare."

"Anything valuable? You know, stuff dating back to the building's days as a luxury hotel?"

"Sure. Stuff from every era. It was like a goddam archeological dig."

"And what happens to all that stuff? Does it just get taken to the dump, or…?"

"Depends. If it's just crap, sure, we haul it off. If it looks like it might be worth something, it gets set aside and a rep from the auction house goes through it. If he thinks it's junk, we dump it. If not, he catalogues it and warehouses it. When we're done with the building, they auction all the good stuff off."

"And that's what happened in this case?"

"Sure. It would have all been auctioned off a few years ago."

"So this auction house would have a list of every valuable recovered from the Charlesgate?"

"Yep. You can probably still find it on the web. I'll text you their info."

"Great. Anything stand out in your memory? For instance, do you remember coming across any paintings?"

"Sure, there were paintings. All kinds of decorations and little artsy doodads. They'll all be on that list."

"Understood. One more thing. You say you tore Charlesgate down to the rafters. Is there anywhere in the building where something might still be hidden? You know, from before the renovations?"

"I don't see how. Then again, that was a pretty weird place. You'd tear down a wall and find a whole corridor you didn't know was there. Guys were getting lost in there all the time. We heard all kinds of stories about the place being haunted, and some of my guys actually believed it. But once we got it all torn down in there...no, I can't think of any way something could still be hidden in there."

"And that includes downstairs in the stables or whatever?"

"Oh yeah. That was a project, but we converted those into living units and storage space. There was a tunnel leading out of there back in the day, but it's all sealed off now. And everything was cleaned out of there, just like everywhere else in the building."

"Makes sense. Okay, I'll check out that auction house. I appreciate your time, Mr. Hahn."

"You got it."

Coleman ended the call, then scrolled through his contacts to his wife's cell number. He hit Send and listened to it ring three times and go to voicemail as usual.

"It's me," he said after the beep. "We're still playing phone tag, probably because neither one of us really wants to talk to the other. But I need to see Alicia. I ain't gonna be no absentee father and she ain't gonna grow up thinking my punk-ass cousin is her dad. So call me back."

He slammed his thumb down on the red bar and dragged his ass out of Jackie's bed. He wandered out to the kitchen, where he found half a pot of coffee waiting for him and a key on the counter. A note under the key read: "Lock up when you go. xoxo Jackie." He filled a coffee cup, sat down and checked for the text from Hahn. It was there, along with the link to the auction house website. He clicked it and searched the site, but didn't have any luck finding lists from previous auctions. Not that it mattered; it's not as if he expected to find Rembrandt's *Storm on the Sea of Galilee* listed for bidding. Obviously if some reputable auction house had recovered the stolen Gardner art, it would be back in the museum now.

The whole Gardner thing was starting to feel like a wild goose chase anyway. He had enough on his plate without trying to track down some longshot lottery ticket. Woodward, the art detective, had never called him back the day before. He decided to place a courtesy call just to let Woodward know he was dropping out of their little treasure hunt. He found the number in his contacts and hit Send. It rang twice and then:

"Hello?"

"Mr. Woodward? It's Detective Coleman."

"How ya doing, Coltrane?"

Coleman winced. "Carny? Shit, I must have dialed you by mistake."

"No mistake. You called your friend Woodward all right."

"What? Why the fuck are you answering his phone?"

"Because I was standing here looking down at his dead body when his phone started to ring. Being the seasoned murder police I am, I decided to answer it and see who was on the other end. Imagine my surprise to hear your voice!"

"Shit. Woodward's been murdered?"

"Yeah, I'm guessing that's how he got these two bullet holes in the back of his head."

JUNE 23, 1946

Marko watched the Public Garden drift past the window of his Bentley. He sat in the back seat. Paulie, the slightly larger of his two bodyguards, was driving.

"You sure this is a good idea, boss?"

"Sure, why not?"

"I thought we were laying low is all. This whole thing with the Mullens."

"The day I worry about the Mullens is the day I find a new line of work. The Mullens worry about *me*."

"Of course. It's just, you know, you need me to pick up a rug, I'll go pick up a rug. I'm capable of such a task without adult supervision."

"That's not in question. But this is a very special rug if what Miss Violet tells me is true. Now, it may not be true, but I'd like to see for myself. Because if it's *not* true, I'm going to enjoy demonstrating to Miss Violet what happens when you tell stories to the wrong people."

"Understood."

"Just pull up across the street here and let's take a look."

Paulie turned right off Commonwealth Avenue onto Charlesgate East. He pulled up next to the park across the street from the building. "Looks like we got one cop standing out front. The doors are chained and bolted."

"Got bolt cutters in the trunk?"

"Of course."

"We may not need them. Let's just have a talk with this guy first. You recognize him?"

"Seen him around, I guess. I don't think we've had drinks together at the Parker House."

"Well, he looks like a reasonable fellow. Let's go have a chat."

Paulie shut down the engine. Marko felt the Bentley's suspension sigh with relief as Paulie squeezed out of the car. He came around to the passenger door and opened it for Marko, who stepped out, smoothing his jacket with both hands. The cop eyed them with uneasy suspicion as they crossed the street.

"Evening, officer," said Marko.

"What do you want?"

"Hey," said Paulie. "No need to take that tone. Do you know who this is?"

"Easy, Paulie," said Marko. "Officer, I apologize for my friend. He's worked for me a long time and as such he's used to seeing me treated with respect. But it's a big city and I'm sure you have concerns of your own."

"I know who you are," said the cop.

"That's good, Officer…?"

"Pinkham. And I'll ask you again. What can I do for you?"

"See that, Paulie? Officer Pinkham phrased it a little nicer. That's really all we can ask. Here's the situation, Officer Pinkham. I left a piece of my personal property here at the Charlesgate last week. I've been meaning to come by and pick it up but this is the first chance I've had. And lo and behold, it looks like you've got it locked up tighter than a nun's asshole."

"This building has been seized by the Boston PD. Any property you may have left inside is likewise now Boston PD property."

"Ooh, that's not the answer we were looking for, is it, Paulie?"

"Not even close, boss."

"Perhaps we should clarify the matter for Officer Pinkham. We understand our request may pose an inconvenience for you while you're standing out here protecting and serving the good people of our fair city. But we're more than willing to compensate you for said inconvenience. Paulie?"

"Yeah, boss?"

"Compensate the man."

Paulie pulled a thick roll of bills from his pocket and began peeling them off one by one.

"Mr. Marko, it appears to me that you're attempting to bribe an officer of the law. If I'm wrong, I'm wrong. But if I'm right, I have to tell you that's not a very smart idea."

"Peel off a few more, Paulie."

Paulie peeled off a few more.

"Gentlemen, I'm going to have to ask you to return to your vehicle and vacate the area. That's not a legal parking spot."

"Oh, my mistake, Officer Pinkham. I didn't realize you were a meter maid." Marko took a step closer. "I think you might want to reconsider."

"Hey, fellas! Mind if I join the party?"

Marko glanced over his shoulder to the source of this last interjection. He saw another beat cop approaching, holding a steaming cup of coffee in each hand. The cop jogged up the steps and handed one of the cups to Pinkham, shooting him a hot look as he did.

"The more the merrier, Officer...?"

"McCullough. I don't mean to interrupt your conversation, but it looked to be getting a bit heated and I thought maybe I could help smooth things over."

"That would be very helpful," said Marko. "As I was telling Officer Pinkham here, I left a piece of my personal property here last week and I'm simply asking for the opportunity to reclaim it. I realize the building has been seized by the police, but I don't see any reason I should lose an item very dear to me just because the owners here failed to pay their taxes."

"I understand, Mr. Marko. But out front here...it's maybe a

little too public. Prying eyes and all. Tell you what, why don't you and your friend pull your car into the alley around back and we can take care of this there."

"But, Danny—" Pinkham sputtered.

"Pipe down. Mr. Marko is a respected businessman in this town and if he has a piece of his personal property in here, the least we can do is accommodate him."

Officer Pinkham had no response, but it was clear he didn't approve of this development. Marko didn't care.

"That's a great idea, Officer McCullough."

"Good. Pull around and I'll meet you there, let you in the back way."

Marko winked at Pinkham and followed Paulie back to the car. He watched with delight as McCullough chewed out Pinkham on the front steps of the Charlesgate. Paulie backed up and drove around the block, down Marlboro to Mass Ave, where he took a left. He drove half a block and threw it into reverse, backing the Bentley all the way down the alley and rear-ending at the Charlesgate.

"Remember that guy's name, Pinkham. He don't seem to want to be friends."

"I'll remember."

McCullough came around the corner just as Paulie and Marko stepped out of the car.

"Paulie," said Marko. "Remember what we were trying to give Officer Pinkham back there? Give that to Officer McCullough with a couple hundred more on top."

Paulie counted off ten bills, folded them and passed them to McCullough, who smiled and pocketed them. "This way, gentlemen." Paulie and Marko followed him to a rear entrance. "The front door, the chains and all that, it's mostly for show. The news photographers eat that shit up. This one, I just need to find the right key…"

McCullough tried four or five keys before hitting on the right one. The door swung inward, revealing a service entrance leading to the grand ballroom, unused since the Depression.

"I assume you gentlemen can find your way from here?"

"We can. Thank you very much, Officer McCullough."

"You're welcome. I'll give you a couple hours before I come back to lock up."

"That should be plenty of time."

"Oh, and you better take my flashlight. The electricity has already been turned off." McCullough unclipped the flashlight from his belt and handed it to Paulie. He watched them enter the building and close the door behind them, then walked back to the phone booth at the corner of Marlboro and Mass Ave to make a call.

Inside the Charlesgate, Paulie flicked on the flashlight. "Where we going, boss?"

"Downstairs. Let's go through the ballroom here, see if we can't find the lobby. I'll know my way from there."

It took a bit of trial and error and some backtracking, but eventually they found their way to the lobby. Marko directed Paulie to the stairs leading to the basement. Once down there, they again wandered a bit before finding the door to the stables. Marko tried the knob. It was locked.

"Knock it down," he told Paulie.

Paulie got a lumbering start and slammed his shoulder against the doorjamb. The door cracked and splintered but didn't quite give. He repeated the process. On the third try the door gave way, nearly causing Paulie to pitch face-first into darkness. He caught himself in time and Marko followed him into the stables.

"Jesus," said Paulie. "It fucking reeks in here."

"Second stall on the right she said."

Paulie walked ahead and flicked his light at the aforementioned stall. "There's a rug here all right."

"Good news. Let me take a look." Marko kneeled and rolled the rug open. "Move that light closer." Paulie did so. The image of a ship tossed in a storm came into focus. "Bingo. This is it."

"Jesus. You smell that?"

"Yeah. It stinks. Help me with this."

"One second." The stall went dark as the beam from Paulie's flashlight swept across the opposite wall.

"Come on, Paulie, quit fucking around."

"Holy shit. Boss, take a look."

Marko stood, cracked his knuckles, and followed the beam of light to a stall deeper in the stables. "Jesus Christ." He bent down to examine the dead body Paulie had found. It was a woman. Her face was unrecognizable but Marko was pretty sure he knew who she was. He leaned in and unbuttoned her shirt. He pulled it open, exposing her breasts.

"Ah...whatcha doin', boss?"

"Bring that light closer."

Paulie did so. Marko fingered the dead girl's left nipple. He saw scars surrounding it. Scars from bite marks. His bite marks.

"Dorothy Gale," he muttered.

"What's that, boss?"

"I said I can't wait to get back home and thank Miss Violet for all her help. Let's get that rug and get the fuck out of here."

They dragged the rug back up the stairs, through the ballroom and out the service entrance to the alley. Maybe forty-five minutes had passed since they'd entered the building. They loaded the rug into the back seat of the Bentley. Marko climbed into the passenger seat and Paulie got behind the wheel, the suspension once again groaning beneath his weight. He started the engine, slipped it into gear and headed for Mass Ave. He never got there. Headlights flashed ahead. A black Mercury Eight was parked at the end of the alley, blocking his way.

"What the fuck is this?" Paulie leaned on the horn. The Mercury didn't budge.

"Oh shit." Marko ducked below the dashboard. He fumbled in his jacket for his pistol as a cacophony of gunfire, breaking glass, and the big man's dying screams filled his ears. He looked up to see Paulie torn to shreds in the driver's seat and realized he had curled himself in the fetal position on the baseboard. Unacceptable. No way were they going to find him like that. He sat up and peered over the top of the dashboard. Two men were walking toward him, each holding a bottle in one hand. The bottles were stuffed with flaming rags.

Marko raised his gun above the dashboard and emptied the chamber, hitting nothing. The Mullens tossed their Molotov cocktails through the shattered windshield. The car, the Mob boss, his dead henchman, and a priceless collection of stolen art were engulfed in a hellish fireball. It would have made quite a show for anyone with a window view on the east side of the Charlesgate, but there was no one left to see it.

OCTOBER 24, 1986

My father didn't miss a beat as he loaded another newly repaired trap into the scuffed and muddied flatbed of his beat-up Ford pickup. "Didn't realize college was so dangerous you'd need a gun."

"Actually you tried to get me to take one when I first went down there. Said you wouldn't live in a city like Boston without at least one good firearm."

"I wouldn't live there at all."

"I realize that."

"Can't set foot out your door without worrying about getting mugged every night."

"That's me. Getting mugged every night in the big city."

"Well, you show up here at 3:30 in the morning with a broken nose asking me for a gun, I don't imagine it's for show and tell."

"It's not broken."

"Hardly the point."

"I know. But it looks worse than it is. This is just for protection. I don't expect I'll have to use it."

"You're talking like we've already agreed to this."

"Dad, I know where you keep your guns. I could have just waited for you to go out to haul and taken one."

"Why didn't you? You want me to talk you out of it?"

"No. I just didn't see any reason to sneak around. I figured if I told you I needed a gun, there'd be no more to say about it."

He nodded. "Ayuh. I'll let you have my .22. It won't take down a water buffalo, but I doubt that's why you're asking. At least you know how to use it."

Once he'd realized he wasn't going to turn me into a fisherman, our father/son bonding had mostly consisted of listening to Red Sox games on the radio and plinking down at the quarry. On a Saturday afternoon we'd drive out where the streets had no name, set up bottles, cans, milk jugs and whatever else my dad could find bouncing around in his flatbed, and shoot at them. There wasn't a whole lot of conversation beyond "a little low" and "hold your elbow steady," but that was all right. It beat filling bait bags in ten-degree weather in the middle of Frenchman's Bay.

My father rooted around under the driver's seat of his pickup for a minute, finally emerging with his .22 pistol. He came back and handed it to me butt-first.

"Nothing fancy," he said. "I traded a flatlander a bucket of shedders for it. It's unregistered, so whatever you plan to do with it, it won't come back on me. You're on your own."

"You sure about this? What if you get carjacked on your way to the Winter Harbor pier?"

"Oh, I got one of them Ginsu knives strapped to my sun visor. I'll be all right." We both laughed. Some annoyed critter in the darkness across the street expressed its displeasure. "That goddam fool across the way. Ever since his wife passed, he's lost his mind. He's got chickens, ducks, goats, a horse, a pig, and he had a peacock until a fox got in the dooryard and ate it. And he's got a room in the back there he calls his roost. Leaves the windows open, he's got birds flying in and out of there all hours of the day and night. But he brings us fresh eggs once a week so your mother says I have to put up with his foolishness."

"That sounds like her."

"What are you up to, son? Are you mixed up in something? I have friends, you know."

I knew. Downeast lobstermen were a tight-knit clan. They could be vindictive and merciless, and they'd take on the whole

Boston Mob if my father asked. "It's nothing like that, Dad. Just a little misunderstanding. I'm sure I can clear it up."

"Use your words, son. That's what you're good at. But if you do have to use that thing, you'd best remember what I taught you."

"I will."

"All right then. I gotta get out to haul."

"Yeah. I gotta get back. Give Mom my love."

"Can't do it."

"Why not?"

"Because you were never here."

"Right. Well…I'll see you at Thanksgiving."

"Ayuh. Go Sox."

"Go Sox." I climbed back in my Buick and waved as I pulled away. It was another five hours back to Boston. I popped a couple more No-Doz and cranked up WZON, the Bangor rock station owned by Stephen King. "Who Made Who?" AC/DC inquired. I had no answers. At some point along the way I lost the signal, but I barely remember that. It was 9 A.M. by the time I pulled back into my secret parking space, still miraculously unoccupied. I staggered into Charlesgate and managed to get all the way to my bed before passing out.

My dreams were chaotic but vivid. I was on my father's lobster boat alone. A much larger ship loomed over me as the waves tossed me from bow to stern. I could barely struggle to my feet. I noticed a terrible taste in my mouth, which filled with a gritty, sandy substance I could not choke down. I spit it into my hand, which filled with my own teeth. I could barely spit them out fast enough to avoid suffocating. A shadow fell over me as the other ship closed in. I looked up. It was the Charlesgate. And now I was inside it and I heard familiar voices and I felt my bed fall away beneath me and…

✿

I was awake. I blinked. The Rev was passing a joint to someone. They both giggled. Shane took a hit off the joint. Was I really awake? I was.

"What the fuck?" I managed.

"Hey, Tommy. Your grandpa here wanted to try some weed, so I figured why not?"

Shane handed the joint back to the Rev, held the smoke in his lungs for a beat, then exhaled.

"Morning, sleepyhead!" he said. He and the Rev broke down giggling again. I looked at my clock radio. It was 3:30 in the afternoon.

"I overslept," I said.

"It's okay," said Shane. "I always wanted to try this stuff. One great thing about being an old man, no one can tell you what to do."

"And how do you like it, *grandpa*?"

He giggled again. It freaked me out. I drove all night to get a gun because I was afraid of *this* guy? All at once the past twenty-four hours felt like part of one long dream. Had I really seen my dad at my childhood home the night before? I was pretty sure I had, but I couldn't prove it because I'd been so exhausted when I got back to Boston, I forgot all about the pistol stashed under the driver's seat of my Buick.

I sat up and ran my fingers through my hair. "Sorry, did we have plans today, grandpa?"

"We sure did. And you are now half an hour late."

"Think you can give me another half-hour? To shower and whatnot? Seems like you might want to sit still a while and stare at your hands or something. Rev, you mind hanging with my grandfather for a few?"

"Not at all, chief."

Normally Shane might have snapped at me, but for some strange reason he was in an unusually mellow mood. "Do what you gotta do, Tommy. You know we're all proud of you."

I nodded and made a show of gathering my toiletries. I was pretty sure Shane didn't notice when I slipped my car keys into my bathrobe pocket. The Rev was busy showing him the cover of *Wish You Were Here*.

Out in the hallway in my bathrobe, the first person I encountered was Rodney. For once fate was on my side.

"Good morning, sunshine."

"Hey, Rodney. Listen, I need a favor and you're the only man for the job."

He made a show of eyeing me up and down in my terrycloth robe. "Sorry, chief, but if you need someone to scrub your back, I think Brooks is your man."

"No." I tossed him my keys. "There's a .22 pistol under the front seat of my car."

He wrinkled his nose. "A .22? What, are you going squirrel hunting?"

"Just get it for me, will you? I'll be in the shower across the hall. This is my towel. Slip the .22 inside it and don't ask any questions."

"I warn you. I am going to use that towel to wipe my fingerprints. So if you're planning to frame me for something, it's not going to work."

"Duly noted. Thanks, chief."

"Anytime."

Rodney was true to his word. When I got out of the shower and checked my towel, the .22 was nestled inside. I went back to my room to find that Shane had settled back into his usual irritable form. "You leave any hot water for the rest of the people who live here?"

"Sorry. I had to shank a guy who was trying to play *Who Dropped the Soap*?"

His eyes flashed with anger. "Get dressed. We're fucking late."

The Rev, who had been noodling on his bass, set it down. "Think I'll see what's on offer at the Canteen."

"You can stay," I said, grabbing my jeans and some clean underwear and heading into the back room, towel still in hand. "We'll be out of here in a jif." I closed the door behind me and unwrapped the gun. Once I was no longer pantless, I jammed the pistol into my waistband. I added a WBCN Rock 'n Roll Rumble t-shirt and a Members Only jacket to my ensemble and checked myself in the mirror to make sure the bulge of the gun wasn't visible. Running the towel through my hair, I opened the door and stepped back down into the front room.

"Okay, grandpa," I said. "Ready to go."

We rode the elevator down to the basement and went through the usual security protocols (basically looking left and right) before Shane keyed us into the stables. We'd gone through all the boxes stacked in the first few stalls, and the stables had grown increasingly disorganized as we neared the back wall. Items too large to be packed away neatly were piled on top of each other: chairs with cracked legs, precariously perched mirrors, an upside-down grandfather clock. It looked like someone had ransacked an antiques shop in search of hidden treasure, which wasn't far from the truth.

"It doesn't look good," I said.

"Let's just get this over with."

For once he was willing to help me move some of the heavier items, but as we got closer and closer to the end of our task, his mood darkened even beyond his usual pissy demeanor. His jolly afternoon interlude with the Rev was now long forgotten.

It was nearly nine o'clock when he tossed aside the last stick of broken furniture. Our search had been fruitless. The paintings weren't there.

"Fuck!" he shouted, slamming his fist into the side of a heavy oak armoire.

"Take it easy," I said. "We tried. It was always going to be a long shot, right?"

He turned his hot, live-wire fury on me. "A long shot? That doesn't work for me, kid. You know that nice job I had mopping the floor at McDonald's? Well, I don't have it no more. See, my manager, this smug little shit half my age, he was giving me crap this morning about how the floor didn't have that welcoming McDonald's gleam. Not up to the company standards. Do it over. Well, maybe he was right. I've seen cleaner floors. But I'll tell you what, I'm all done with smug little shits like him telling me what to do. I took that mop handle and I knocked his teeth out onto that floor. Whole lotta blood, too. That welcoming McDonald's gleam, right? Anyway, I walked out of there, I came straight here. I can't go back to that halfway house. My parole officer will be waiting for me. And he's a smug little shit, too. Just like you."

I felt the handle of my dad's .22 pistol snug against my gut. We were in the danger zone now, as far back in the stables as we could be and with no help to be found. For the first time, it seemed entirely possible that only one of us was walking out alive.

"So here's how it's gonna be," he continued. "We can't find those paintings? That's too bad for you. Because I still need the money, and if I need to get it another way, you're gonna help me."

"What do you mean?"

"I need to get gone, which means I need at least five grand to clear town and hole up somewhere until things cool down."

"I don't have five grand!"

"But you can get it. Someone's paying for this college, putting you up in this building. Your parents, your grandmother. They have money."

"I'm on scholarships. I have student loans. My family doesn't have that kind of cash on hand, and if they did, they wouldn't just hand it over to me."

"Well then, we'll have to get it another way. Tomorrow night. Game 6. A chance for the Red Sox to win their first World Series of my lifetime. That bar you like is gonna be hopping. Lotta cash changing hands. We hit it right when they close."

"We...*hit* it? Meaning rob it? Are you crazy?"

He leaned in close. I felt his hot breath on my neck. "What do you think, kid?"

I touched the handle of the .22 through my jacket. I could pull it and put three bullets in his belly and end it right here. He seemed determined to meet that kind of end anyway. I'd have to explain it away somehow. Killing a defenseless old man? That wouldn't look too good on my college transcript. But I couldn't keep going along with his crazy plans. He was going to lead me into a shitstorm that might end with my own death, or at least a long stretch in prison. Still, I couldn't bring myself to pull the gun. It was a line I was unwilling to cross.

Use your words, my father had said. It seemed my words were all used up. But maybe I had one more bluff left.

"Sure, we could do that," I said. "But we're not done looking for the paintings yet."

"What are you talking about, kid?"

"There's still someone who might know where they are. She's lived here a long time and she's seen it all. We need to talk to Mrs. Coolidge."

Coleman flashed his badge and the uniform nodded, lifting the crime scene tape so he could pass underneath. He'd elbowed past three camera crews on his way to the scene, and now reporters were shouting "Detective! Detective!" at him as if he could tell them a damn thing about what had happened.

Actually, the media crush did tell him two things: The vic's identity had already leaked, and someone had pieced together his profession and the location where the body had been found. The Gardner heist was about to be back in the news in a big way.

Coleman spotted Carny and Lt. Weir huddled near the museum entrance. This wasn't the original entrance, the one Shane and Jake Devlin had approached dressed as cops nearly seven decades earlier. The Gardner had built a brand-new wing that had opened two years earlier, and now a couple of crime scene techs were combing the entryway for evidence, bagging and tagging everything bigger than a flea's eyelash. The guest of honor, however, had already been removed from the premises.

"There he is," said Carny. "Man of the hour."

"I gotta hand it to you, Coltrane," said Weir. "When you step in it, you don't stop until you're neck-deep in the shit."

"Woodward on his way to the morgue?" Coleman asked.

"Yeah, you just missed him," said Carny. "Sorry you didn't get a chance to say goodbye, but maybe you'd like to tell us about the last time you saw him? Or maybe you could back up a little bit and tell us how the fuck you know this guy in the first place."

"I only met him a couple times. Last time I saw him was

Monday night at Grendel's in Harvard Square. He was poking into the Gardner heist and thought maybe we could combine our efforts."

"You having nothing better to do."

"It's not like that."

"Well, what's it like, Trane? Cause I gotta tell you, it's not looking too good right now. And it's gonna look even worse when the ME pulls those two slugs out of Woodward's skull and they end up matching the two your friends down in Rhode Island found in your Charlesgate suspect. I figure we've got until maybe noon before the FBI swoops in and folds this mess into their ever-expanding investigation. Which is fine for us, less for us to worry about. But I were you, I'd spend that time looking for a good lawyer."

"What exactly do you think I've done? You think I killed this guy and the other one down Pawtucket?"

"I really don't know what to think about you anymore," said Weir. "What exactly was your plan? You and this Woodward were gonna crack the Gardner case together? Split the money? Only something went bad between the two of you, is that it? Maybe that witness you've been fucking got in your ear. Hey, it's really not my problem anymore, like I said. You are now indefinitely suspended. And honestly, Carny here has been agitating for a new partner for a while now."

"Oh, is that right?" Coleman flipped his partner the bird. Carny responded in kind. "So no one's interested in hearing my side of this?"

"I told you. The FBI will probably be delighted to hear your side of it."

"And I told you I barely knew this guy. Yeah, I should have mentioned the Gardner connection, but it seemed so far-fetched. Part of me was just humoring this nice old guy."

"But most of you was greedy. See, Carny here read through your file on the Charlesgate. You know, once you'd been removed from the case. Ain't that right, Carny?"

"Yeah. Seeing as how you never shared it with me when we were working the case together."

"Like you gave a shit. You never showed the slightest interest in that case. I pulled an all-nighter copying those articles at the Emerson library while you were getting shitfaced at the Tap with Sully and the boys."

"Congratulations. Let us know where to send your Medal of Valor. Anyway, right there on top, with lots of words circled in red pen, was a 1986 article from the Emerson newspaper. This crazy story about how the missing Gardner paintings were stashed in the Charlesgate in 1946. Fascinating stuff."

"Yeah, but the cops looked into it at the time and said it was bullshit."

"Which didn't stop you from pursuing it."

"We had no motive for the Charlesgate murder except the dead girl's keys went missing. I figured if there was even a remote chance the killer was looking for the Gardner art, it was worth investigating."

"Well, it makes me wonder. This woman who happens to live in the Charlesgate, this woman you happen to be fucking, it makes me wonder when all that started. This woman whose condo was supposedly robbed. Or maybe that was just a piece of misdirection on your part. Maybe you and this woman cooked it up ahead of time."

"Wow. It's a great feeling, knowing you guys have had my back all along."

"Don't keep turning this around on us. You went off the reservation. You were conducting your own private investigation. Not to solve our case but to line your pockets."

"I was trying to solve the case. I didn't see the harm in looking into the Gardner thing while I was at it. If I found the paintings, it would be a win all around, right? The department looks good. This place gets their art back."

"And you get rich."

"Well, you don't have to worry about that. The paintings aren't there. I talked to the contractor who remodeled the place a few years back and there's no way—"

"Hey. Trane. We don't care. Okay? We've had enough of your bullshit to last a lifetime. Now if you'll hand me your badge and your weapon, you can be on your way. Men are working here."

Coleman shook his head but complied.

"Melendez!" Weir called. One of the crime scene techs jogged over. Weir handed him Coleman's sidearm. "Send this to the lab. Have 'em run ballistics against the slugs they pull out of Woodward's head. And tell 'em to be prepared to hand it over to J. Edgar by this afternoon."

"You can't be serious," said Coleman.

"You still here? This is a crime scene, citizen. Now fuck off."

Coleman stared for a long moment but words wouldn't come. He settled for a dismissive wave and ducked back under the crime scene tape. As he left the Gardner and headed down Fenway, he grabbed his phone from his pocket and scrolled through his contacts. He was about to select Jackie's name when his cop brain kicked in and he thought better of it. Instead he took a right on Brookline and walked four blocks to the Cask 'n Flagon. A twentysomething dude-bro in a tank top and backwards Red Sox cap was taking chairs down from the tables.

"Not open yet, buddy," he said.

"Oh, that's okay. I was just—is there a phone in here I could use?"

"You ain't got a phone?"

"Well, yeah. But my wife checks it and I've got this hot piece of ass on the side…"

The dude-bro laughed and tossed his iPhone to Coleman. "Call's on me, man."

"Hey, I appreciate it."

Coleman punched in Jackie's number. She answered on the second ring. "Hello?"

"It's Coleman."

"Oh. I didn't recognize the number."

"I'm not using my phone. I'm already in enough trouble. We both are."

"How's that?"

"Woodward's dead. Shot twice in the back of the head, just like White."

"Wait, refresh my memory. Woodward is…the art detective?"

"That's right. The art detective I was working with. Who until this morning, as far as I know, only two people knew I was working with. Me and you."

"Meaning what?"

"I was hoping you could tell me."

"Are we going to do this again? I tell you I had nothing to do with this and you say you believe me?"

"I'm a cop, Jackie. 'I believe you' is just what we tell people when we want to keep them talking."

"I see. So all the times you said 'I believe you,' I shouldn't have believed you."

"Well, I *wanted* to believe you. Still do. All I know for sure is there's another guy dead and I didn't do it. But maybe I'm being set up to look like I did."

"Meaning I set you up."

"Not necessarily. But if the ballistics show my gun fired the bullets that killed Woodward, then I'm gonna be out of options."

"So in this scenario, what? You sleep over at my place. I sneak out at night with your gun, kill this Woodward, sneak back in and put your gun back, then go on about my day because…why?"

"I don't know, Jackie. I know both you and Woodward met with White. Maybe White was working both you and Woodward for leads on the Gardner stash. Maybe you were working with White and something went bad between you. But I'm not a prosecutor. I don't care about motive, only means. Now maybe the ballistics come back and there's no match and I just blew up what could have been a good thing between you and me for no fucking reason. But if they *do* match, I know two things for sure: I didn't kill Woodward, and you and only you had the means to make it look like I did. So if you have anything you want to tell me, now would be a good time."

"As a matter of fact, detective, I do have something to tell you." Jackie sounded on the verge of tears.

"I'm listening."

"Go fuck yourself."

JUNE 24, 1946

"What is it about this place?"

Sergeant Higgins' gaze drifted from the rear of the Charlesgate back to the smoking husk of the Bentley and finally to McCullough, the patrolman who'd called in what appeared to be a gangland slaying. The fire department had finally cleared the scene, leaving Higgins with the prospect of sifting through the ruins.

"Not sure what you mean, Sergeant."

"I was just here a week or two ago. That pimp who slipped on a banana peel and cracked his melon. Open and shut, an accident. Except the old man got a stick up his ass on account of this supposed witness heard the departed jawing with another individual. Won't rubber stamp it for me. Says to hunt her down and bring her in for further questioning. Well, of course this twist never shows her face again. No one's seen her since that night. My guess, upon realizing she could no longer ply her trade here, she skipped town. All I had is an alias anyway. Dorothy Gale, like in that Munchkin movie."

"There's no place like home," said McCullough.

"What's that?"

"You know, from that movie. That's what Dorothy says."

"Well, there you go. This Dorothy probably decided there's no place like home. Meanwhile, I get stuck with an open case file when it should have been put to bed right away. Well, the old man's always had it in for me. And now this."

"Yeah. A real mess, huh?"

"I guess I've seen worse but I'd have to think about it. So you and your partner there…"

"Pinkham." McCullough spared a glance at his partner, who

declined to make eye contact. He looked like it was taking every ounce of effort he possessed not to explode.

"Right. You were around front of the building when Antonio Marconi—excuse me, Tony Marko—and one of those fat fucks he pays to watch his ass pulled up in front and asked to access the building."

"That is correct."

"A request you and Officer Pinkham declined."

"Of course. He said he'd left a piece of personal property inside. We told him to take it on the arches in not so polite terms."

"And how did he respond to that request?"

"Not well. Mr. Marko informed me that he had friends in high places who would see to it that I spend the rest of my law enforcement career handing out parking tickets."

"Unfortunately, some truth to that."

"I figured as much. But I didn't become a cop to do the bidding of gangsters. If the people in charge don't like it, well, I guess I'm in the wrong line of work."

"We need more with that attitude, McCullough." Higgins glanced over at Pinkham, whose hands were clenched into tight, reddening fists. "So after making these statements, did Mr. Marko and his goon take their leave?"

"We thought so. But clearly they pulled around the block, entered through the alley, and proceeded to gain forced entry through this back door." McCullough indicated the service entrance, which stood partway open. The lock assembly hung loosely from the splintered doorjamb. The door had been forced by a crowbar. McCullough knew this because he'd forced it himself after the Mullens blew up the Bentley but before the firefighters arrived on the scene.

"Right," said Higgins. "So we can assume Mr. Marko and his associate gained entry, either did or did not retrieve the piece of personal property—given what's left of the car, we'll probably never know—and got back into the vehicle. But they never made it out of the alley."

"All I know, Pinkham and I are standing out front drinking our coffee, counting the minutes until this guard-the-henhouse detail wraps, you don't mind my saying, and all the sudden we hear this enormous explosion. We run around back here and there's an inferno like you wouldn't believe—hell on earth. Ain't that right, Pink?"

Pinkham offered a tight nod and gritted teeth.

"It's odd," said Higgins. "I mean, first thing that comes to mind, this is a Mullen job. They've had a beef with Marko, and Guinness bottle bombs are their specialty. We may never prove it and personally I could give two shits if the micks and mooks want to blow each other up, long as no innocent bystanders get hurt. But it does puzzle me a little bit."

"How's that?"

"Well, let's say it was the Mullens. How did they happen to know Marko was going to pick tonight to retrieve his personal property? It's almost like they were tipped." Higgins sneaked another look at Pinkham, who was studiously examining his shoes.

"I dunno," said McCullough. "Maybe Marko was set up. Maybe the Mullens sent someone to let him know he better get whatever needed getting out of this here building tonight. Like it might not be here tomorrow."

"It's possible. Actually, that's a pretty good guess. I tell you what, Officer McCullough, you may have a mind for this kind of work. I don't see you guarding this empty building for much longer. Bigger and better things in your future."

McCullough smiled. Pinkham did not.

✲

By morning, word was out. The bodies would never be posi-
tively identified—there wasn't enough left to identify—but the
circumstantial evidence could hardly be refuted. Marko was
dead. And that was bad news for Violet, who had spent the
entire night in the office at the Prince Street Social Club waiting
for the boss to return and make her rich. By the time she saw
the first rays of dawn through the office window, she was pretty
sure that wasn't going to happen. Something had gone wrong.

The way Joey saw it, it was simple. Whore shows up at the
social club, tells the boss something that gets him up off his ass
for the first time in weeks. Boss never comes back. Boss was set
up by whore. Whore has to die.

The sausage grinder threat had been a hollow one. Who
would want to contaminate a perfectly good sausage grinder
with the body of a lowlife whore? No, Joey had other ideas.
Shortly after 7 A.M., he entered the office.

Violet stood. "Finally. I've been here all night, no one has
talked to me—"

"Easy, lady. You hungry? Want some breakfast? Coffee?"

"No, I just…where is Mr. Marko? We made a deal."

"Yeah, about that. See, I think that deal is off the table. Mr.
Marko, he never came back from where you sent him. Matter
of fact, way it looks to me, he was set up to never come back.
Would you know anything about that?"

Violet's heart caught in her throat. "Of course not. Why?
What happened?"

"You don't need to worry about that. Your worries are over."

"Whatever this is, I swear, I didn't have anything to do with
it. You can ask…" She trailed off.

"I can ask who?"

Violet had no answer for that.

"That's what I thought. Now, I don't know if you pulled this stunt to get in good with the Mullens, or you were with them all along, but it really doesn't matter. Whatever they may have promised you, you're never going to get it."

"No! I don't know the Mullens! This has nothing to do—"

"Save it for St. Peter, if that's the way you go. You'll know pretty soon. Let me explain exactly what's going to happen. I have a very sharp knife I use only on special occasions. It was a gift from a butcher down on Salem Street. I love this knife. I'm gonna take this knife and I'm gonna start cutting things off you. Fingers. Toes. Ears. There's gonna be a lot of screaming—from you, not from me—so we're gonna do this down in the cellar. I've already got plastic laid out because it's going to be messy. When I'm done, when there's nothing left of you bigger than a ribeye from Rossi's, I'm gonna keep a souvenir. You have nice eyes, so I'm thinking an eyeball."

Violet wanted to scream but nothing would come. That didn't last. Joey did exactly what he said he'd do. When he was done, there was no one left on earth who knew where Vermeer's *The Concert* could be found.

He kept the eyeball for about a week. One night while having drinks with Frankie Pot Roast at the social club, Joey slipped it into his friend's glass. "Oh! Frankie! There's an eyeball in your highball!" They both had a good laugh over that one.

OCTOBER 24, 1986

I was about to knock on the door to #311 when I decided it might be a good idea to prepare Shane for what was about to happen.

"I should tell you, Mrs. Coolidge is a little out there."

"Meaning what?"

"She's kind of mixed up. Like she thinks the CIA is after her, you know. She might be schizophrenic or something. But she's been here a long time, she knows a lot about the building, she's seen 'em come and go. If we can keep her focused, there's a chance she could help us out."

"I dunno, kid. Sounds kinda like a waste of my time, and I don't have time to waste."

"I understand that, but we've come this far, put in all this time and effort. We shouldn't give up on the paintings until we've exhausted every resource."

"Fine. Let's talk to your crazy friend."

I nodded and knocked on the door. As before, a long moment passed before the door opened a few inches and suspicious eyes peered at me from behind the chain lock.

"Hi, Mrs. Coolidge. It's Tommy Donnelly."

"I can see that."

"I brought a friend with me, he'd love to meet you."

"Is he a sex maniac?"

"Not at all."

"That's too bad." She closed the door. I could hear her unlatching the chain.

"I think she was joking," I said.

"I picked up on that, kid. Thanks."

The door opened and she motioned us in. Shane's demeanor perked up at the sight of the boxes forming a narrow path from her doorway to her cramped living quarters.

"Whatcha got in all these boxes?" he asked.

"Why would I share such personal information when we haven't even been introduced?"

"This is Shane Devlin," I said. "Do you recognize the name?"

"Some reason I should?" She gestured to her threadbare orange couch. I stepped aside and let Shane deal with the springs digging into his rear end.

"No reason," he said. "I used to hang around here some, but it was before your time."

"You don't look like a cop to me."

"I'm not a cop. Where'd you get that idea?"

"You look like you just escaped from prison."

"You're not far off, lady."

"Mrs. Coolidge."

"Mrs. Coolidge. So now that we're introduced, you feel like telling me what's in all these boxes?"

"Books. All full of books and I've read them all."

"Just books, huh? Nothing else?"

"Why? You think I keep my sexy underwear in there?"

"That doesn't really interest me. I'm interested in something I left behind in this building. About forty years back."

"A dead body? They cleared them all out a long time ago."

"What else did they clear out of here?"

"Evidence. The secret files. The film cans."

"Evidence of what?"

"The conspiracy, of course. See, it all started when this place was built in—"

"Mrs. Coolidge!" I shouted louder than I'd planned, but I

had little interest in letting her get sidetracked on one of her wild tangents. "That's not what we're looking for."

"Well, what are you looking for? King Tut's tomb?"

"Close," said Shane. "Some nice paintings I had to leave here back when I had to go away from a while. Did you ever hear anything about those?"

"Oh, sure. They came for those a long time ago, too."

"Who came for them?"

"That's classified."

Shane rolled his eyes. Clearly he wasn't planning to spend a lot more time humoring Mrs. Coolidge.

"It's okay, Mrs. C," I said. "He's got clearance. I checked him out myself."

She eyed him skeptically. "That true?"

"Yeah, of course," he said. "I've got all the clearances."

"I'd ask you the password but they change it every day."

"Yeah. It's a real pain in the ass. So tell me: Who came for the paintings?"

"The Kennedys, of course. That's what it was all about. The Mob stole the paintings. The Kennedys got 'em back. They blew up the Mafia don right back here." She hooked a thumb over her shoulder toward the Pit and the alley beyond. "You can look it up. Oswald was a patsy. Sirhan Sirhan, too. It was Mob retaliation. The paintings are still hanging in the White House, but only five people know where to find them. The second Richard Nixon tried to burn them but he got caught. That's why he had to resign. Watergate was a distraction."

Shane smiled and leaned forward. "That's all very interesting, Mrs. Coolidge. I wonder if you can think of one reason I shouldn't take one of these useless couch cushions and smother you to death with it?"

"Excuse me?"

I managed a nervous laugh. "He's just joking, Mrs. C."

"I've heard worse threats from better men."

"I think we should be going. Shane?"

He stood, looming over Mrs. Coolidge, smiling with no mirth. "Yeah. I think we should."

I shrugged apologetically at Mrs. Coolidge as Shane stepped past her, back into her self-made corridor of boxes. I followed him to the door and out into the hallway.

"You trying to make a jerk of me, kid?"

"No, of course not. Listen, I warned you—"

"Then why did you waste my time?"

"I—I genuinely thought she might have some real information. I knew there would be some gibberish, but I thought there might be some truth, too."

"Oh, there was some truth. There was a Mafia don got his ass blown up in that alley."

"What? You didn't tell me that."

"Why would I have?"

"Well, what happened? Did he know about the paintings?"

"No way of knowing. But it was big news at the time. This Mrs. Coolidge would have seen it. Mixed it up in her head with all that Kennedy shit. It means nothing."

"These paintings. One of them was a Vermeer, right?"

"That's right."

I thought about a hazy night spent with an occult expert in the Bay Village. A sketch I'd drawn of the Rev as a skeleton. A sketch I'd signed "Vermeer" for reasons I could no longer recall.

"There's one more guy we should talk to," I said.

"Kid, you are on thin ice right now."

"I understand, but—"

"Who is he?"

"His name is Sprague. He's a...uh, he's an expert in the occult."

"The occult. Witches and shit."

"I know how it sounds. Just let me call him. If it doesn't pan out, we'll go to Plan B."

"Plan B."

"Like you said. Game 6 of the World Series. Packed house at the Fallout Shelter. Lotta cash for the taking."

I hoped I sounded convincing, but the truth was I would never let that happen. I'd tip off the cops and have them waiting as we came through the door in ski masks or whatever Shane had in mind. But I sure didn't want it coming to that.

After spending a long moment lost in thought, Shane finally responded. "Okay, kid. Call him. But two things."

"All right."

"One, if this is another blind alley, that's the end of it. No more bullshit, you and me take down that bar tomorrow night."

"And two?"

"Like I said, I can't go back to the halfway house tonight. And I don't have money for a hotel room. So I'm staying here with you."

"I don't know as my roommates are going to be too thrilled with that."

"What makes you think I give a shit?"

MAY 9, 2014

The FBI agents had agreed to meet Jackie in a conference room at her lawyer's office—not that she actually had a lawyer aside from Block & Mairs, the firm that had handled her divorce. But Gary Mairs had recommended a criminal attorney, Merle Bertrand, and it was in his conference room, with Bertrand at her side, that Jackie now faced off with Agents Hoff and Afshar.

"Thank you for agreeing to meet with us today, Mrs. Osborne," said Hoff. "I'm sure your lawyer here advised you otherwise."

"I have nothing to hide and I just want to get this over with."

"And yet your lawyer is present," said Afshar.

"As is my right."

"Of course. Just noting it for the record."

"That's good," said Bertrand. "I'd like my client's cooperative attitude on the record."

"And so it is. Mrs. Osborne—"

"Could you not call me that? I'm divorced and I plan to go by my maiden name from now on."

"Very well, Ms....St. John. Can you tell us how you know Charles White?"

"He was the director of alumni records at Emerson College. I met him when I started planning my upcoming class reunion. I just wanted to put together a mailing list of everyone in my class but Mr. White thought he could be a lot more help to me."

"Nice guy, then."

"He seemed that way at first. But it soon became clear that his helpfulness was just a cover for...well, trying to get close to me."

"In a sexual way."

"It seemed to me."

"How many times did you meet with him?"

"Four times at his office. He would try to get me to meet him out for coffee, but I wanted the…protection, I guess, of the workplace environment. But even that didn't work, because the last time I met with him, he kept leaning in, touching my arm. Nothing you could really pin down until I was leaving, he grabbed my arm really…inappropriately. Like a vise grip so I couldn't get away until I agreed to have dinner with him."

"Did you?"

"I agreed, but I never had dinner with him. I programmed my phone so all his calls would go straight to voicemail."

"But you never reported his actions to anyone. The police or a college authority."

"No. I thought about it, but on reflection it all seemed a little thin. I figured avoidance was the best strategy."

"Did Mr. White express a particular interest in any of your other classmates?"

"Not that I recall."

"So he never expressed any interest in Thomas Donnelly? Or an article he wrote for the *Berkeley Beacon* back in 1986?"

"Agent Hoff," said Bertrand. "This line of questioning doesn't strictly line up with what we had discussed prior to agreeing to meet with you."

"Some new information has come to light."

"In that case, I'm going to have to advise Ms. St. John not to cooperate further."

"It's okay," said Jackie. "I don't have a problem with the question. Yes, as a matter of fact, he was very curious about Tommy and whether he'd be attending the reunion."

"And this article," said Afshar. "About the Gardner museum

heist and the rumors that the paintings might be hidden in the Charlesgate. He asked you about that?"

"Yes. And I told him what I know, which was that the police investigated after the article ran and found no evidence that the rumor was true."

"And when you discussed this matter, was anyone else present?"

"Was anyone else…I don't follow."

"It's pretty simple. Where were you when you and Mr. White discussed this matter?"

"In his office, like I told you. I only ever met him there."

"And could anyone overhear your discussion?"

"Well… I guess his assistant could have. Her desk was maybe ten or twelve feet away in the outer office, and I don't think he had his office door closed. In fact, I'm sure he didn't because I insisted on keeping it open."

Afshar reached into a manila folder, pulled out an 8x10 photo, and slid it across the table to Jackie. "This assistant, is this her?"

Jackie examined the photo. "Yeah. Wendy Tucker."

"When is the last time you saw Ms. Tucker?"

"Well, she took over Charlie's job after…well, *after*. So I met with her on…Tuesday."

Afshar pulled another photo from the file and slid it across the table. "Do you recognize this gentleman?"

Jackie eyed the photo. It appeared to be a mug shot of a man in his early thirties: shaved head, goatee, a hard stare. "No. I don't…wait a minute." Jackie noticed a scar running across the bridge of the man's nose and a memory clicked into place. "Yes. Last time I met with Wendy, on my way out of the building, I almost ran smack into this guy. He was on his way up the stairs and he was…intense."

Afshar nodded to Hoff.

"All right, Ms. St. John," said Hoff. "That's all we have for you today."

Jackie and Bertrand exchanged a puzzled glance. "That's it?" she said.

"That's it," said Afshar. "We have your contact information if we need to pursue this further, but for now we're done here."

Afshar collected the photos and slipped them back into his folder. He and Hoff stood, nodded and walked out of the conference room.

"What the hell was that?" said Jackie.

"I don't have a clue," said Bertrand. "I have to say, Ms. St. John, I was not expecting this session to go well for you. Maybe you have a guardian angel looking out for you."

"I seriously doubt it."

AUGUST 9, 1947

Over a year passed before Jake returned to Boston. He'd left town the morning of June 16, 1946 aboard the *Tori Kay* bound for Morocco. Jake essentially began his time aboard the ship as a stowaway. His new friend Art Donnelly walked him aboard just before dawn, telling the seaman standing watch that Jake had an urgent message for the captain from the harbormaster. The seaman showed little interest as he waved them aboard.

Donnelly brought Jake to his quarters and told him to stay put until told otherwise. He tracked down the three other seamen with whom he shared the cabin and notified them that a brother from the fleet would be staying with them and that there was no need to inform the bosun's mate until the Fort Point Channel had disappeared over the horizon. None of them had a problem with that.

Between shifts Donnelly brought Jake to the sick bay. There wasn't actually a doctor aboard the ship, just a deckhand with some first aid training, and the sick bay wasn't much more than a medicine cabinet and a cot, but Jake was able to get his wound cleaned and redressed sufficiently to ward off any infection.

Jake spent his first two days aboard the ship doped up on antibiotics and painkillers, drifting in and out of consciousness, barely eating the scraps Donnelly brought back from the mess. By day three he was ready to start earning his keep. Donnelly presented him with a new able seaman's license, forged by a Swede who worked miracles as the ship's cook. Jake's new name was Louis Albertson and he hailed from San Diego, where Jake had done his basic training.

The bosun's mate was suitably pissed off when Donnelly introduced him to his new deckhand Louie, but before long they were swapping stories of their time in the Pacific theater. In the end, it was easier just to add Albertson to the crew's registry than to make a big deal about it. The captain would never even notice.

On the morning of his sixth day at sea, Jake stood in the aft second deck, a raw wind cutting through his borrowed denim shirt, and tossed his dogtags into the Atlantic. He was Louis Albertson from then on, or at least that was the plan.

By the time the *Tori Kay* pulled into the port of Tangier five days later, Louie was one of the guys. An exotic haven for postwar expatriates, the city offered countless diversions for sailors far from home. It was also a hotbed of espionage and criminal activity, as Jake learned when an ex-swabbie who ran a bar near the waterfront directed him to a forger who could provide him with a passport for a price. Donnelly advanced him the money, and by the time the *Tori Kay* pulled out of port forty-eight hours later, Jake's Louis Albertson identity was airtight.

He remained in the employ of the *Tori Kay* as the ship unloaded and reloaded in Southampton, Antwerp, Rotterdam, and a half-dozen other ports of call. He stood the engine room watch, washed and painted the deck, chipped rust, repaired lines, handled tow lines in and out of port, and generally did whatever the bosun's mate asked. While in port, he availed himself of every amenity the local red-light district had on offer. His old life receded behind him like the evening tide. That night at the Gardner museum faded like a half-remembered dream.

Boston news was hard to come by in any case. One night in Galway, he happened upon a news item about the Gardner heist in the *Irish Independent*. The FBI agent assigned to the case gave only the sketchiest of details, but it was clear that there were no real leads. A sidebar noted an uptick of violent crime in Boston in the days surrounding the heist, including a double murder and the presumed gangland slaying of Mob boss Anthony Marko. A suspect named Shane Devlin was awaiting trial in the former case while another, his brother Jacob, was being sought. Jake got so drunk that night in Galway his shipmates had to carry him back to his bunk.

After three months at sea, the *Tori Kay* was ready to return to its home port, but Jake was not. He shook hands with Donnelly, thanked him for all his help and promised he'd make it up to him someday. But Donnelly never saw him again. He continued to work the *Tori Kay* for another four years until he'd earned enough to buy his own boat—one equipped for lobster fishing. He and his wife Maddie and their eight-year-old son moved to a small town on the coast of Maine, where Donnelly lived out the rest of his days, eventually passing the family business on to his son. He lived long enough to meet his grandson, Thomas Arthur Donnelly, born in 1967, but a lifetime of hard work, hard drinking and heavy smoking put him in the ground by the time the 1970s rolled around.

As for Jake, he took his leave of the *Tori Kay* and signed on aboard the *Chanticleer*, a freighter out of Amsterdam. He was Louis Albertson now and nobody could say any different. Louis was tightlipped about his past, but that was common among his peers. It turned out a lot of people went to sea to escape who they were and become somebody else. He didn't stand out at all.

One night in Liverpool he got drunk with a chief engineer from Fall River and let his cover slip. After a beer or twelve, he was anxious for news from home.

"It's been about a year," Jake said. "I missed the World Series, but I guess I didn't miss much."

"It was an exciting series. Just the wrong ending."

"You know what was in the news around the time I left, was that museum robbery. You know, up there not far from Fenway."

"The Gardner, yeah. They're still scratching their heads over that one."

"Really? Those paintings never turned up?"

"Not last I heard. My guess, whoever took 'em got 'em out of the country in a hurry. Left two dead guys behind. Nice haul from what I understand. You'd think they could have split it four ways and been happy about it."

"Yeah, who knew art thieves could be so cutthroat?"

"Crazy, huh?" He motioned to the barman. "Hey, two more pints of bitter down here."

"It was also around that time, that double murder. The cop-killing. You hear anything about that?"

"Oh, them poor bastards they found in the trunk up to South Station?"

"Yeah, yeah. I heard they caught one guy but not the other."

"Right. The one they caught, that sonofabitch is gonna fry. His trial lasted about five minutes, but that's how it goes in these cop killings. The other guy is his brother and he ain't shown his face since. Can you believe that? He's gonna let his little brother take the rap while he's probably sunning himself on the beach in Acapulco or somewhere."

"Yeah. Sounds like a real piece of shit."

Jake said good night, then waited outside for the chief engineer from Fall River, whose face was barely recognizable when a couple of his fellow engineers found him in the morning and helped him back to their ship.

It was time to go home. Jake worked his way back the way he'd come, hooking on with a transatlantic freighter in Tangier where his new life had begun. One sweltering August morning in 1947, he set foot in the city of Boston for the first time in fourteen months. He wasn't too worried about being recognized from his picture hanging in the post office. He'd grown a bristly beard, shed nearly twenty-five pounds, and his skin was baked a ruddy brown. He bore little resemblance to the pasty, clean-shaven fugitive who'd fled town with his arm hanging useless at his side.

He checked the newspaper and saw the Sox were in town and scheduled to play the Yankees at one o'clock. He walked all the way, up State Street to the Common and the Public Garden, then Beacon Street to Charlesgate East. He leaned on a parking meter and watched the Charlesgate entrance for fifteen or twenty minutes. A steady succession of young women, late teens, early twenties, streamed in and out of the building. They looked nothing like the young women who used to frequent the Charlesgate. It was clear that these were students. Even before he'd left town, rumors had circulated that Boston University was interested in buying the building for use as student housing and that was evidently what had happened.

He continued on Beacon to Kenmore Square, hooked a left up Brookline Ave and grinned as the left-field wall came into view. He paid two dollars at the gate and took his seat ten rows behind first base, hot dog and beer in hand. The Yankees took a 3-2 lead into the sixth, but the Red Sox scored two in the bottom of the inning and ended up winning 6-4.

After the game ended and most of the crowd had filed out, Jake remained, staring out at the lush green field. His return home had been everything he could have dreamed. But now it was time to go see Shane. And after that, nothing would be the same.

OCTOBER 24, 1986

I searched through my wallet for the phone number of the "occult expert" Sprague, but I couldn't find it. "Hey, Rev," I said. We were all sitting in the Love Room drinking beer: me, Murtaugh, the Rev, Rodney, Brooks, and "grandpa." A regular guys' night in.

"Whuzzat?"

"You know that guy Sprague in the Bay Village? The one with the killer hash?"

"Oh, hell yeah."

"You didn't happen to get his number, did you?"

"Of course. Anyone who can get shit like that Turkish delight, I'm gonna need his number."

I tossed the phone to the Rev. He dialed the number and handed me the receiver. After a few rings, the answering machine picked up. "There are things known and things unknown," said Sprague's recorded voice. "Either way, I'm not at home. Leave a message." Beep.

"Oh, hey there. This is Tommy Donnelly, we met a week or two back and you said you'd be really interested in checking out the Charlesgate sometime. Well, this is a good time if you're up for it. Just punch in 629 on the intercom downstairs and we'll come get you. Later."

I tossed the receiver back to the Rev and he hung it up.

"Well?" said Shane.

"That was an answering machine, grandpa. Some fancy '80s technology you wouldn't understand."

"Hey, don't be mean to your grandfather!" said Brooks, who was busy painting his fingernails black.

"Thanks, lady," said Shane. Brooks turned beet red while the rest of us tried to stifle laughter.

"Brooks is a guy, grandpa."

"Oh. Sorry, Brooks."

"It's okay, Mr. Donnelly."

"Let me ask you, Brooks," said Shane. "Are you a queer?"

"*Excuse* me?"

"Grandpa, come on. This isn't 1952."

"Hey, no offense. If he likes boys, he likes boys. He wouldn't be the first I ever met."

"I don't like boys," said Brooks. "This is what girls like nowadays, Mr. Donnelly. You should let me take you clubbing. You'll be painting your nails black in no time."

"I think I'll pass, Bruce."

"*Brooks*."

"Right."

There was an awkward moment of silence, during which Rodney struggled to hide how much he'd enjoyed the entire exchange. Finally Shane drained his beer and stood. "You got a towel, Tommy?"

"A towel? Uh…sure. What for?"

"Whaddaya think for? I need a shower if you haven't noticed."

"Oh. Sure." I went to the closet and found what appeared to be a reasonably clean towel. I tossed it to Shane, along with my bathrobe. The image of him wandering the halls of Charlesgate with only a towel wrapped around his waist was too horrifying to contemplate. He set the towel and bathrobe on his chair and began to unbuckle his pants.

"Hey, grandpa? Maybe do that in the other room?"

"I got nothin' you boys haven't seen before."

"I'd rather not take that chance."

Shane shrugged, picked up the bathrobe and towel, and went into the outer room. I stood at the door and listened until I heard the door to the hallway slam shut. I opened the door a crack to make sure he was gone, then slumped back into my chair.

"Chief," said Brooks. "Your grandpa's kind of an asshole."

"He's not my grandpa. He's a psycho on parole. He spent forty years in prison for killing two men, including a cop. And if he has his way, I'll either be dead or in jail tomorrow night."

Another awkward moment of silence followed. Finally Murtaugh, the only one who'd already known Shane wasn't my grandfather, spoke up. "So what can we do to make that not happen?"

And with that one question, I felt like a fifty-ton weight had been lifted from my chest. At the same time I felt like an idiot. I had friends. Friends who maybe could help me out of my predicament. I'd been so worried about confiding in them for fear of getting them in trouble, I'd almost forgotten they might be willing and able to keep me from getting killed.

So I told them everything and we came up with a plan. If it worked it would keep me out of jail without killing Shane, which we all agreed was the ideal scenario. When Shane got back from the shower, wearing my bathrobe and running my towel over his head, we put it in motion.

"Hey, Tommy," said Rodney. "You oughtta ask your grandpa to join us."

"Oh, I dunno," I said. "I think we have other plans."

"Join you for what?" Shane asked.

"Game 6 tomorrow night. There's going to be a big viewing party down in the ballroom."

"Sounds like fun," said Shane. "But I think we're watching that somewhere else. Right, Tommy?"

"That's right."

"Oh, you're not gonna want to miss this," said Rodney. "Alpha Pi Theta, you know, the fraternity I'm in? We're setting the whole thing up. Cash bar for those over twenty-one, or at least those with ID that says they're over twenty-one. They're gonna have a half-dozen TVs with the ballgame on, and some games of chance, too. Roulette wheel, blackjack, shit like that."

"Is that legal?" Shane asked.

"Well, it's all for charity. The Jimmy Fund. We planned it weeks ago and, lucky us, it happens to coincide with Game 6. It's gonna be quite an event. Students, faculty, staff…maybe a couple hundred people altogether. We should be able to raise a shitload of money for those poor cancer kids."

Shane caught my eye. I raised a "whaddya think?" eyebrow.

"That does sound like fun," said Shane. "You think I'd be welcome at this shindig?"

"Of course! Like I said, it's for charity. The more, the merrier. We're gonna test the fire codes in this old rat trap, that's for sure."

"All right," said Shane. "Count us in."

I shrugged. "Fine. Anything for a good cause."

And the rat trap was set.

Jackie thought about going back to the office, but she'd already requested the whole afternoon off and didn't think she'd be able to concentrate on setting up press screenings for the new *X-Men* movie. So she jumped on the green line to Kenmore and walked home, where she was not terribly surprised to find Coleman waiting for her on the Charlesgate stoop.

"Hey, Jackie."

"I guess 'go fuck yourself' was too ambiguous for you?"

"No. I got it. I deserved it. But you deserve to know what I found out today."

"So tell me."

"Can we go inside?"

"No, you can tell me right here."

"Jackie…"

"Just tell me, *detective*."

Coleman slumped against the entryway. "Okay. Well, I think I told you about my friend in the Bureau. I called him today to see if he knew anything about their investigation into the White murder and…all the rest of this. He said you were being questioned downtown but it was only a formality. They already had everything they needed—a confession, video evidence, the whole nine."

"What are you talking about?"

"White had an assistant. Wendy Tucker."

"I know."

"And Wendy Tucker has a boyfriend. William Ambrico. Slick Willy as he's known on the street. A real piece of shit three-time loser. In and out of juvie, eighteen months in MCI Concord for aggravated assault, questioned and released in a bank job down on the Cape. His family tree reads like a history of organized crime in Massachusetts. His great-uncle Francis, known as Frankie Pot Roast, ran the North End Mob in the '50s until the Feds ran him in for tax evasion and he got shivved in the shower at Walpole in '63."

Jackie swallowed hard. She had no doubt that this William Ambrico was the man she'd encountered on the steps outside the Emerson alumni office, but saw no reason to share that information with Coleman. "And so what?"

"And so one day after you met with White, White gets to talking with Wendy about you and how he's helping you and how he thinks he's got a shot with you."

"Oh, for chrissakes."

"You know, trying to make her jealous, like she better jump aboard the Charles White Express before it leaves the station. She's overheard part of your conversation with White, so she asks him about it, acting like she's all impressed with him. And now he's telling her about your friend Tommy and his article about how these valuable paintings might be hidden in the Charlesgate, and wouldn't it be cool to sneak in there and try to find them? And she thinks, yeah, that would be cool, but not with you, asshole. So she goes home, tells Slick Willy all about it. He's intrigued, of course. Sets up an appointment under a fake name, Charles Finley, to tour an open unit at the Charlesgate. The plan is just to look around, get a feel for the place. But Willy, he's got no stealth mode. He sees this big keyring the realtor has and he decides, spur of the moment, he'll just have to kill her to get it. He chokes her out on the spot. Spends a couple hours sneaking around the building, trying the keys on any door that looks like it might have some kind of storage area behind it. I dunno, offices, conference rooms, janitorial closets, whatever. Short attention span, though, he gives up and goes home."

"Did he tell Wendy what he did? That he killed Rachel O'Brien?"

"No, he claimed he picked her pocket for the keys. That's how dumb this guy is, because the next night the murder is all over the news. Wendy sees it. And White also sees it. And knowing Slick Willy's reputation, he puts two and two together, figures he's been cut out of the loop. He heads over to Wendy's place, which is also Willy's place. He tries to blackmail them. He knows Willy killed the woman and he'll go to the cops if they don't cut him in. He's saying this to a guy *he knows* just killed someone like he was tying his shoes. And he says they need him, because he knows you have information on your laptop that will help them find the paintings."

"What?"

"Yeah. Like we speculated before, he must have thought you had Donnelly's email address and if they had your laptop, they could get ahold of him by posing as you. And White knows you're out of town on business. You made sure he knew that."

"Well, congratulations, detective. You got one thing right."

"Come on. Put yourself in my shoes."

"Okay, fine. I'll play detective. This Slick Willy kills Charlie White. Shoots him twice in the head."

"With a gun the Feds now have in evidence."

"So now they gotta get rid of the body. Slick Willy, being such an ace criminal, decides to dump him over the state line. Takes his wallet and phone, drives him to Rhode Island and dumps him."

"Yep. He's got White wrapped up in a length of carpeting. Douses it with gasoline, tosses it in the dumpster behind Dunkin's and drops in a match. But before he does all that—"

"He goes to the Charlesgate. He's still got the keys. They haven't changed the locks yet. He lets himself into the building and into my apartment. Takes the laptop. Smashes my framed *Annie Hall* poster, either because he thinks Woody Allen is a creep or he thinks I've hidden the paintings behind it."

"Shit, I hadn't even thought of that."

"Explains why you find yourself out of work. He takes a picture of the scene, using White's phone, which he's already taken off the body. Calls my number from this same phone, a few times, even after he's dumped White's body, hoping to make me look suspicious in the event the body is ever identified."

"You got it."

"Worked like a charm on you."

"And I'll always regret it."

"So what about your friend Woodward? The art detective?"

"He'd been calling for White at the Emerson office. Bonus for Wendy out of all this, she now has the job of the man her boyfriend murdered. On Tuesday, Woodward calls one more time before heading back to England. He gets talking to Wendy, explains he's an art detective investigating the Gardner museum robbery and he'd been discussing a lead with White. She takes down his contact info, calls Slick Willy, tells him this guy has a lead on the paintings. Which is not exactly what he said, but whatever. Slick Willy calls Woodward, says he's a friend of White, sets up a meet outside the Gardner after hours. At this point Woodward should have called me, but he decides to handle it on his own. Well, why should he be the first one to make a good decision in this whole mess? Anyway, Woodward shows up for the meet, Willy tells him to spill the beans or else, but Woodward's got no beans to spill. Woodward says something about calling the police and that's all Willy has to hear."

"Two shots in the head."

"Right, but security at the Gardner has improved since 1946, and this time the cameras catch it all. Feds identify him pretty quick because Wendy was already on their radar. Along with you, she was one of the last people called from White's phone, and she mentioned her relationship with Ambrico when they questioned her. Feds show up at their apartment with a warrant. They find the murder weapon matching the bullets from both White and Woodward, they find White's phone, they find your laptop, the whole shooting match. Wendy flips on Slick Willy, gives him up for the first two murders, cuts a deal that puts her in for six years. Slick Willy's looking at a full boat with no parole once he's convicted, which won't be a problem."

"So that's it?" said Jackie. "Case closed?"

"That's it. Unfortunately you won't get your laptop back until after the trial."

"I've already replaced it anyway. I do have one more question, though."

"Shoot."

"Did you ever, even for a minute, think I was innocent?"

"Of course, Jackie. I never really thought you were involved, it's just…"

"Yeah. The cop in you. So does this mean you're off the hook with the BPD?"

"Not exactly. I'll keep my rank and pay grade but they're gonna bury me in a deep, dark hole."

"Somewhere you can work on your dollhouse furniture."

"What?"

"Didn't you ever watch *The Wire*?"

"Nah. I can't stand cop shows."

"Well, you really missed out." She smiled tightly and unlocked the front door. "You really missed out, Martin."

She stepped inside and closed the door behind her.

"No shit," said Coleman.

Shane Devlin sat on his bunk in his eight-by-twelve cell on Death Row, thumbing through a dog-eared paperback copy of Raymond Chandler's *The Big Sleep*. He'd never been a big reader but there wasn't much else for him to do between now and his date with Ol' Smokey. He certainly never had any visitors, which made it that much more surprising when the screw from Chelmsford told him someone was waiting to see him.

"Who?" Shane asked.

"Guy named Louis Albertson. Says he's doing some work on your appeal."

Shane set down his book and stood while the guard unlocked his cell and slapped the cuffs on him. To date his court-appointed lawyer had shown exactly zero interest in his appeal so it was quite a surprise to hear that someone he'd never heard of was waiting to discuss the matter.

Shane followed the screw from Chelmsford down to the visitor's center. A dozen or so convicts were chatting with their wives or lawyers. One man sat alone at a table near the door. He was sinewy and sunbaked, with a scraggly beard. For nearly a full second, Shane didn't recognize his own brother.

He took a seat at the table, his cuffed hands in his lap.

"Hi, Shane," said Jake.

"Fuck are you doing here? Are you crazy?"

"No one knows who I am but you. I've got a fake passport, everything."

"You're still taking a hell of a chance."

"Had to. I did you wrong, brother."

"You did the smart thing. I was dumb. I went home and fell

asleep. They had our fingerprints all over your car, our clothes from the South Station garbage. I had no alibi. Dave T was no fool. Until he was."

"Yeah. But you never should have had to take this rap alone."

Shane shrugged. "If it wasn't this, it would've been something else. I'm no angel. Never was."

"But you don't deserve to die."

"And I don't want to. But there's nothing to be done about it now."

"I'm not so sure about that."

Shane lowered his voice. "What, Jake? You gonna bust me out? Where have you been for the past year anyways?"

"I been all around the world. Working cargo ships. My name is Louis Albertson now, officially anyway."

"Well, that's a good thing. You go right on being Louis Albertson. You should have never taken the risk of coming here."

"I can't live with this, Shane."

"Shut the fuck up. Of course you can. I'm the one who can't live with this. The state of Massachusetts says so. That's the difference between you and me. I know exactly when I'm gonna die, right down to the minute."

"Maybe not."

"Come on. My appeal? That's going nowhere. When did you get back to town, anyway?"

"Two days ago."

"And have you been to the Charlesgate?"

"I went by the other day. It's a women's dorm now."

"I know that. But that doesn't mean those paintings aren't still there."

"Shane, forget about those paintings. Marko probably had them in his car when his ass got blown to kingdom come. What the hell else would he have gone to the Charlesgate for?"

"But you don't *know* that."

"No. I don't know that. But I've had plenty of time to think, all my time at sea. I've thought a lot about that poker game at the Charlesgate. What an impulsive decision that was to take it down. And it worked to a point. But I look at everything it set in motion. Pat dead. You on death row. And this whole thing with the paintings. We would have never been involved, it would have gone a whole different way. Maybe Dave T uses the Casey cousins instead. They get away with it, fence the paintings, no harm no foul. I mean, except for the art lovers. But that whole chain of events, we set it off with that poker game. And who knows? Maybe it's just getting started. As far as anyone knows, those paintings are still out there somewhere. There's no telling what we set in motion."

"Who gives a shit? I mean, by all rights you should have drowned in the Pacific Ocean three years ago. But here you are."

"And it ain't right. I was ready to die for my country. I sure as hell better be ready to die for my brother."

"What the fuck are you talking about?"

"Cutting a deal. Turn myself in for the cop killing, let 'em give me the chair on condition they commute your sentence to life with the possibility of parole. Like you said, I've been on borrowed time the last three years anyway. You know how I've been since I got back from the war. It's like I never really came back, like I died over there and everything since is just... waiting around. For nothing. Face it, I'm dead already. No reason you should go too, for a crime neither of us committed."

"Come on, Jake. The dice have been rolled. You're there and I'm here. There's gotta be a reason. You're off the hook. Take your good fortune and run with it. I've made my peace with this."

"It doesn't matter. It's too late. I already made the deal, Shane. They know who I am. I asked to see you one more time as part of it."

"What the fuck?"

"It's true. They're gonna take me straight to your cell on death row from here. You'll be put in gen-pop. It's all worked out. I found a lawyer yesterday and we sorted it all out."

"You've gotta be outta your mind."

"Maybe. But here's the thing, Shane. I never looked out for you the way I should have. This is my chance. So, what the fuck, maybe you could be a little gracious about it."

Shane ran his hand over his eyes. "Parole, huh? You think that will ever happen?"

"I dunno. No time soon, that's for sure. But if you ever do get out of here, I want you to make me a promise."

"Anything. Of course."

"Don't go after those paintings. If they haven't been found by the time you get out, don't go after them. They'll bring you nothing but trouble."

Shane wiped a tear away. "Sure, brother. You got it. I love you, Jaybird."

"I love you, too. Now quit bawling, will ya?"

Shane nodded. "It's funny, you know. I been thinking lately about my last meal. What it was gonna be. And I remembered we already had a last meal. You remember? At the Union Oyster House? The night of the heist."

"I remember. Lobster Newberg. Maybe that's what I'll have. Would be appropriate."

"Those cherrystones? They made me sick. I puked my guts out that night. Never again."

Jake smiled. "You're gonna be okay, kid. You're gonna walk out of here one day. Don't fuck it up."

OCTOBER 25, 1986

As first pitch approached, Shane insisted on going over the details one more time. I grabbed the sketch Rodney had drawn and explained it again.

"There's going to be two cash bars, here and here. Beer and soda only, so it's not like there's gonna be trained mixologists on duty or anything like that. Sodas are a buck, beers are two. Cash only. Over here they have three blackjack tables. Roulette wheels here and here, and a poker table here for the big donors. That's how it works. They're not really gambling for money. They make a donation to the Jimmy Fund and they get a stack of chips. End of the night, the winners get a donated prize. Gift certificate for Legal Seafood, autographed Dewey Evans jersey, shit like that. What's funny?"

"I was just thinking. This whole thing started with me taking down a poker game in this building. And that's how it's gonna end, too."

"Yeah. Poetic. Anyway, the cash donations are collected at the door. The way Rodney explained it, they periodically take the cash into the Blue Room, which is sort of the command center for this whole thing. They tally it up, write it down on a deposit slip, throw it in one of those zippered bank bags. But it all stays in the Blue Room until the end of the night, when the last of the cash is collected from the bars."

"And that's when we hit it."

"Yep. Rodney will be our inside man for ten percent of the take, as we discussed."

"I woulda gone to twenty, but don't tell him that."

"Our secret. So Rodney and his frat brothers are supposed to lock the door to the Blue Room when they go in and out, but he's gonna accidentally forget. When he gives us the high sign, it's go time. We walk in, grab the bank deposit bags, make our getaway through the window overlooking the alley, which he'll leave open a crack."

"And what if there's trouble? What if there's someone else in there, or someone comes in while we're in the middle of it?"

"Rodney's supposed to keep them occupied."

"But what if? You gotta ask 'what if' in this business, kid."

"First of all, I'm not in this business. This is one and done for me. Second, if someone comes in, we take care of them. There's no security guards *per se*. Just some members of the college administration, Rodney's frat brothers, like that. You don't think we can handle it?"

"Oh, I'm sure I can. Especially since I found this in your dresser drawer." He raised his shirt. The butt of my father's .22 pistol was sticking out of his waistband.

"My father gave me that," I said. "For protection."

"And that's exactly how we're gonna use it. So hey, father knows best."

For once I was speechless.

An hour later, with Game 6 underway and the ballroom starting to fill up, I told Shane I was grabbing a couple of sodas for us. I tracked Rodney down near the poker table.

"Please tell me you made the call," I said.

"I made it. Called BPD, told 'em I knew where a parole violator would be tonight. They had a lot of questions. And they definitely want to have a word with you when this is all over."

"I understand that. So what's the plan?"

"They've got four plainclothes officers in here. Or on their

way, I dunno. They're not exactly planning to introduce themselves to me. Don't send cop-looking guys, I said. Send guys
who look like speech and theater instructors. It's none of your
fucking concern who we send, they said."

"Great."

"I think I talked them into waiting until the game is over to
nab him. Told 'em we're having a charity event and want to
raise as much money as we can before they make a big scene.
The Jimmy Fund name rings out with these guys, which
helped. But they also agreed to wait because they want to
catch this guy with his hand in the cookie jar. Imagine the
headlines? BPD bust cop-killer robbing from cancer kids?
These guys will never have to buy a drink again and they
know it."

"Good. But there's a complication."

"Fuck, yeah! Dewey! One-nothing Sox!"

"Huh?" I whipped my head around and got a look at the
replay. With everything else going on, I'd almost forgotten that
the Red Sox were on the verge of winning their first World
Series in sixty-eight years.

"So what's the complication?"

"Oh, uh…that .22 pistol you got from my car yesterday?
Shane has that."

"He has a gun? On him now?"

"Yep."

"Chief, I don't know who the cops are in here. I have no way
to tell them."

"Right. Well, as long as he thinks there's nothing to worry
about, maybe he'll keep it in his pocket."

"And on that happy note…"

"On that happy note, I need to grab a couple sodas and get
back to him."

✿

If you were alive and aware in New England that night in 1986, you have your own memories of Game 6. Sox fans hung on every pitch, praying for deliverance. But not me. I'd been waiting my whole life for this moment and I could barely concentrate on the game. Shane was the same way. During a commercial break in the fifth inning, he nudged me and pointed to a couple of Rodney's frat brothers, who were carrying bundles of cash into the Blue Room. He may have been enjoying the game, but he still had his eye on the prize.

The Mets tied it up in the bottom of the fifth, leading to a chorus of groans and a few scattered cheers. I saw a girl in a Mets cap stand on her chair and pump her fist. It took me a second to realize it was Jackie St. John.

"You know that girl?" Shane asked me.

"Yeah, Jackie. She's from New Jersey but I don't hold it against her."

"I bet you'd like to hold your dick against her."

"Richly detailed observation there, gramps."

"There's still time for me to knock every single tooth out of your head, kid. Something tells me I'd really enjoy it."

The Red Sox retook the lead in the top of the seventh on a ground out by Dwight Evans and the crowd went crazy. The Mets tied it up in the bottom of the eighth and Jackie and a dozen or so others whooped and hollered.

"Helluva game, kid."

"I'm having a hard time enjoying it."

"Why?"

"Why? Because of what we're planning to do when the game is over."

"That's for later, kid. This is now. That's a lesson I learned on death row. Living in the moment."

"You never did tell me why they didn't execute you."

"Wish they had, huh?"

"I didn't say that."

"I had a guardian angel looking out for me. Turned out to be my brother. He took the fall for me. I watched him die. March 22, 1948. They asked if I wanted to be a witness. My right as his only immediate family. I thought if I could be there for him in his final moments, if I could remind him he was doing this for me, it might be a comfort for him. It wasn't. When he saw me in the gallery, he started to squirm and scream. Yelling he didn't want me to see this. But it was too late. They put the hood over his head and pulled the switch. I watched my brother die." He took another swallow of soda. "You know he made me promise him something, the last time we spoke."

"What was that?"

"He made me promise not to look for those paintings if I ever got out. I guess he figured they were bad luck or some silly shit like that."

"Maybe he was right."

"I'm not superstitious, kid. Never was. Promise died when he did."

The game went to extra innings. The Red Sox scored two in the top of the tenth. And suddenly what Shane had said about living in the moment made sense. The room around me melted away. My anxiety about what was to come faded. There was only this night in Shea Stadium and a burden that had weighed on a city for nearly seven decades, about to be swept away by a tide of euphoria.

"Calvin Schiraldi, trying to finish off the Mets and the 1986 baseball season," said announcer Vin Scully. Wally Backman led off the bottom of the tenth for the Mets. "Little poke-job to left, Rice coming over. One away." Keith Hernandez was next. "And that's hit to dead center. Henderson gonna run it down. And the Mets are down to their last out."

Shane nudged me. "Let's get in position."

"Get in position? The game is about to be over. What happened to living in the moment? Let's enjoy this."

"We will enjoy it. From right there." Shane pointed to a spot near the Blue Room door. We started making our way over as Gary Carter came to the plate.

"Lined into left field," said Vin Scully. "Base hit for Carter and the Mets are still alive."

"Dammit, we shouldn't have moved," I said.

"Why not?"

"We disturbed the mojo."

"You're nuts."

"It's bad luck, is all. You don't tamper with the baseball gods."

Kevin Mitchell pinch-hit for Rick Aguilera. "Curveball! And that's gonna be hit to center, base hit. And now suddenly with two out in the tenth inning, the tying runs are aboard and Ray Knight will be the batter."

"See that?" I said. "If we lose this, it's your fault."

"I told you, kid. I'm not superstitious. If they lose, which is not gonna happen, it's their own fuckin' fault."

We'd reached the spot about ten feet from the Blue Room. I scanned the ballroom. So far everyone was still in celebration mode, albeit a bit more muted now. I caught sight of Jackie, seated nearby on the aisle of the third row. She had the rally cap going. Ray Knight swung and connected.

"And that's gonna be hit into center field, base hit! Here comes Carter to score and the tying run is at third in Kevin Mitchell. And the Mets refuse to go quietly."

"Goddammit," I said. The room grew quiet except for the handful of Mets fans. Jackie was standing now. I glanced at Shane, who was starting to look worried.

"Just get this last fuckin' out," he said. "We don't need more extra innings."

McNamara strode to the mound, signaling to the bullpen. Schiraldi walked off, head hung low, and Stanley came jogging in.

"Something ain't right," said Shane.

"No shit."

"I mean in this room. Something ain't right."

Again I scanned the ballroom. If the cops had made themselves conspicuous, I couldn't tell. I figured they were as wrapped up in the game as everyone else. After all, they didn't know Shane was armed. So what did they have to worry about?

A deafening roar of anguish echoed through the ballroom and my head snapped back to the nearest TV in time to see another Met cross home plate.

"What the fuck happened?"

"Kid, I'm telling you. There's something wrong here."

"The fucking Mets just tied the game! The winning run is in scoring position!"

Shane nodded toward the nearest beer stand, where two men in their mid-thirties stood, arms folded, staring at the screen. "Those guys are cops."

"Come on. That guy in the blue shirt is my Ethics professor."

"If you fucked me, kid…"

"Little roller up along first," said Vin Scully. "Behind the bag! It gets through Buckner! Here comes Knight and the Mets win it!"

Pandemonium in the ballroom. I heard the sound of breaking glass. Someone's beer whizzed past my ear. The two guys who'd been standing by the bar weren't standing there anymore. Neither was Shane. Somehow over the rest of the noise I heard a woman scream. I turned to see where it was coming from. I saw Jackie with Shane's arm around her neck. In his other hand my father's .22 pistol, pointed at her head. Within fifteen seconds my life had become a waking nightmare.

"Listen up! Listen up!" Shane dragged Jackie to the front of the room, blocking the biggest TV screen so everyone would take notice. The tenor of the room turned on a dime, from despair to terror. The noise died down.

"Nobody panic," said Shane. "First of all, this thing ain't over. There's another game tomorrow night. Second thing, I'm gonna need all the cash from that back room or else I'm gonna have to put a hole in this nice young Mets fan's head."

I'd love to tell you I did something heroic to save Jackie's life. I did no such thing. I kept searching the room for the guys Shane had pegged as cops, but I couldn't see them anywhere. I made brief eye contact with Murtaugh, who shook his head in disbelief.

"Here's what's gonna happen," Shane said. "My accomplice right there, Tommy Donnelly, he's gonna go in that back room and come out with all that money in a big sack. Aren't you, Tommy?"

"Shane," I heard myself saying. "Just put the gun down. It's over."

"I already told you. Like Yogi Berra said. It ain't over 'til it's over. Now granted, he was a fuckin' Yankee, but you gotta admit the man had some wisdom."

"Come on, Shane. How do you see this playing out? You're right. The cops are here. If you pull that trigger, it's gonna be all over for you."

"Actually, kid, it's all over for you."

What happened next unfolded in some order I couldn't process in real time. I saw the gun in Shane's hand move away from Jackie's head. Logically, that must have happened first. I heard gunshots, I don't know how many. I saw a body slump to the floor, heard a sickening splat. I saw Jackie, drenched in blood like Carrie at the prom, her hands trembling beside her head, her mouth wide. Something heavy knocked me to the ground.

Things came into focus. One of the cops was on top of me. The other was kneeling beside Shane's lifeless body. Jackie hadn't moved. She appeared to have gone into shock. Someone cuffed my hands behind me and pulled me to my feet.

"Are you hit?" said the cop.

"What?"

"Are you hit? Did he shoot you? Are you bleeding?"

"Uh…no. I don't think so. What happened?"

"Your friend there just tried to kill you. My partner shot him in the head. You'll get a chance to thank him because we're gonna be talking all night long."

And we did. The two cops, Beckstead and Jenkins, drove me downtown, put me in an interrogation room and sweated me past dawn. How did I know Shane? How long had I known he was an ex-con on parole? How long had we been plotting to take down the charity event? How many years in prison did I think I was looking at?

In the end, they let me go. I told them the truth, with one notable exception. I knew my Dad had never registered the .22—a tourist had traded him the gun for a bucket of lobsters—so I played dumb about that. They couldn't think of a crime to charge me with aside from harboring a fugitive, but since Rodney had called in Shane's location on my say-so, and since that call led to the BPD foiling the attempted robbery of a charity event by a convicted cop-killer, they declined to pursue the matter. Inadvertently or not, I had helped make them look good.

I told them everything about our search for the Gardner paintings in the Charlesgate stables, too. The next day the BPD, in conjunction with the FBI, entered the building and searched it from top to bottom. They combed over every inch of the stables Shane and I had already covered. They turned up nothing.

I may have gotten off the hook with the police, but the Emerson administration was another matter. After some deliberation they decided not to expel me. But my time living in Charlesgate had come to an end. I'd signed Shane into the building multiple times under false pretenses. I'd stolen a key from the Resident Director. I'd endangered the entire student population through my actions. I had to go. It was just a formality for Torres to tell me so.

I sat outside his door on the afternoon of October 27, waiting for him to invite me into his office so he could tell me to find off-campus housing post-haste. The World Series had ended the night before in anticlimactic fashion. Even though the Red Sox took an early 3–0 lead, the Mets came back to win the game and the 1986 championship. I didn't watch the game. In fact, I never saw it until many years later. Only after the Red Sox won it all in 2004 did I get around to watching Game 7 on DVD. I was finally ready to see it.

As I sat outside Torres' office, I once again locked eyes with Uncle Sam, staring back at me from the framed vintage poster across the hall. Once again I thought about how out of place it looked. A relic from Charlesgate's past. It was as if Uncle Sam was trying to tell me something.

And suddenly I knew what it was.

The Berkeley Beacon

OCTOBER 31, 1986

Charlesgate Confidential, Part III: A Confession

TOMMY DONNELLY, BERKELEY *Beacon* STAFF

Welcome to the third and final installment of *Charlesgate Confidential*. This feature comes to an end under rather embarrassing circumstances. I never intended to emulate Hunter S. Thompson, but somehow I've become a central figure in my own story. If you've read the front page of this issue, you already know many of the details in this latest sordid chapter of Charlesgate's checkered history. Shane Devlin, recently paroled from prison after serving 40 years for two murders, was killed by Boston police in the Charlesgate ballroom immediately following Game 6 of the World Series.

The news story speaks for itself. All I can do is relate the events as I experienced them. I have to own up to my share of the blame for what happened on Saturday night. As a journalist, I'm still a work in progress. I made mistakes in my pursuit of a story. I won't make them again.

It started on October 10, when I met a man named Shane Devlin at Pizza Pad in Kenmore Square. It was lunch hour and the place was crowded, so I wasn't that surprised when he took a seat in the booth across from me. I *was* surprised when he told me he'd just been released from MCI Cedar Junction, and I was *very* surprised when he told me he had a juicy story about the Charlesgate.

His story was incredible—literally, in the sense that it was not credible. He told me he was not responsible for the crime of which he'd been convicted because he'd been robbing the Gardner Museum at the time. What I didn't know then was that the Isabella Stewart Gardner Museum heist was one of the legendary unsolved crimes in Boston's history. Many have been suspected, many have taken credit, but no one has ever been charged and the thirteen stolen works of art have never been recovered. Had I known all of this, I would have laughed off Devlin's story on the spot. Instead I was intrigued, and as readers of this series know, I'm always up for a good Charlesgate story. Shane Devlin had a doozy.

Devlin claimed that he and his brother Jacob, along with their cousin Patrick Egan, had robbed a poker game on the eighth floor of the Charlesgate a week prior to the Gardner heist. There is no way to verify this. The men at the poker game were professional criminals, according to Devlin, and they weren't about to go to the police to report that their illegal game had been robbed. They were more inclined to mete out justice in their own fashion.

The man who ran the poker game was known as Dave T, but his real name, unknown to any of his associates at the time, was Maurice Levine. This much is easily confirmed because Levine was found dead on the scene of the Gardner heist. According to Devlin, Levine coerced him and his brother to participate in the museum robbery after arranging to have their cousin executed. After the heist, during which Jacob killed both Levine and the getaway driver, Joseph Cahill, the Devlin brothers took the stolen paintings to the Charlesgate.

It's a matter of public record that Shane Devlin was arrested on June 16, 1946, the day after the Gardner heist, but not for that crime. Instead he was tried and convicted of the murder of two men whose bodies were found in the trunk of a car registered to his brother Jacob. One of the victims was Devlin's cousin Patrick Egan. The other was a Metropolitan Transit Authority police officer named Edward Gould. Shane was sentenced to die in the electric chair and his brother was not seen again in Boston until more than a year after the Gardner robbery. Shane Devlin was saved from death when his brother resurfaced and confessed to the murders. Shane's sentence was commuted to life and Jacob Devlin died in the electric chair at the Charlestown State Prison on March 22, 1948. By that time the Charlesgate, the last place either Jacob or Shane Devlin had seen the stolen Gardner paintings, had been sold to Boston University for use as a women's dormitory.

Shane Devlin believed the paintings were still somewhere in Charlesgate when he was released from prison earlier this year. I agreed to aid his search for them willingly at first, hoping the long shot would pay off with an incredible exclusive for the *Berkeley Beacon*. I soon came to distrust Shane Devlin, who increasingly resorted to intimidation and threats of violence to keep me in line. I never truly believed the stolen art was still in the building (if it had ever been there), but

I did believe one of two things: either Shane Devlin's story was true or he had convinced himself it was true.

More than one Monday morning psychiatrist has theorized that the Devlins' participation in the Gardner heist was a delusion brought on by Shane's survivor's guilt following his brother's execution. I couldn't say. The events of Saturday night have been capably reported by *Beacon* editor Robert McKim in the front page story. I can only add that the Boston police, in conjunction with the FBI, have conducted a thorough search of Charlesgate in recent days. As far as they are concerned, the Gardner heist remains an unsolved mystery.

MAY 24, 2014

Even twenty-five years later, I still dreamed about Charlesgate. In accordance with dream logic, it was never the same place twice. Sometimes it was still a dorm, and due to a clerical error I was forced to return and resume my academic career, living among students half my age. Sometimes it was a crumbling ruin I'd rediscovered in some post-apocalyptic landscape. At least once it was a decaying space station, drifting into a dying sun in some remote corner of the galaxy. Almost always I found new hallways, hidden passages, staircases without end. Charlesgate may not have been haunted, but it has always haunted me.

And now it loomed before me, big as life, in broad daylight on a Saturday afternoon in May 2014. From the outside, nothing had changed. I was suspended in time. I was living inside a dream. Beyond the front door, nothing would be the same. I took a deep breath, walked up the stairs, opened the front door and went inside.

A temporary desk was set up in the lobby, with security guards standing on either side. A kid in a tie who looked about fourteen years old sat behind the desk, blinking at me expectantly.

"Uh, hi," I said. "Thomas Donnelly?"

"Oh my God. They said you weren't coming!"

"Well, I guess I didn't RSVP. Is that okay?"

"Of course! Do you want a nametag?"

"I don't think so."

"Right. Why bother? Anyway, it's right down the hall here to your left, first hallway on your right. It's the Gold Room, the big ballroom, you can't miss it."

"I sure can't."

Everything I'd done in the past twenty-five years, all my accomplishments and accolades, all melted away as I made the long walk toward my rendezvous with destiny. As I approached, I heard music wafting into the hall: "Ship of Fools," by World Party. My past was about to consume me whole.

I stepped into the ballroom for the first time since that long-ago night the ball went between Buckner's legs and Shane Devlin's brains splattered all over Jackie St. John's Keith Hernandez jersey.

> *We're setting sail*
> *For a place on the map*
> *From which no one has ever returned*

Tables, maybe twenty altogether. Eight to a table. Laughter, conversation. People standing, milling about, getting each other drinks. A couple approached me, the woman wide-eyed and laughing.

"Tommy! You're here!"

"I am."

"Oh my God, you don't recognize me!"

It took a second. "Purple Debbie?"

She laughed again and swatted her date on the arm. "I told you! I told you they called me Purple Debbie!"

"I believed you!" Her date, a bespectacled Asian man with an easy grin, offered his hand. "George Wu. I'm Debbie's husband."

I shook his hand. "Great to meet you, George."

"George is your biggest fan! He's read all your books!"

George reddened. "Well, I don't know about that. I mean, I have read them all, but I think Debbie might be your biggest fan. When we were first dating she would always go on and on about how she and Tommy Donnelly were such great friends in college."

"Yeah," I said. "It's true. We had a great group of friends."

I smiled at Debbie. She gave me a big hug. It was as if she had no recollection of how our friendship had come crashing down a quarter-century earlier. Why should she? She had George now, he seemed to be a nice guy, and whatever had happened between us was just something she'd packed away in an old suitcase of college experiences. This was probably the exact right attitude to have.

"Well, great to see you again. Nice to meet you, George." I shook his hand once more.

"You too! Let's get a photo later."

"Of course."

I waved goodbye to Debbie and made my way toward the bar. "It's the End of the World as We Know It" blared from the sound system.

"Can I get a beer?" I asked the bartender.

"We've got Bombshell Blonde, Armadillo Amber and Charlesgate IPA."

"Really? Charlesgate IPA? Sounds like a winner."

He poured my beer and I dropped a five in the tip jar. I scanned the room. I smiled when I spotted them. A balding Murtaugh and a woman who must have been his wife. A graying Brooks next to a man I didn't recognize. The Rev, whose dreadlocks had evolved into massive tentacles running far down his back. Jules, a little heavier but seemingly not a day older. An empty seat. And Jackie St. John. I sipped my beer and weaved my way through the tables, past classmates long forgotten, stopping behind Murtaugh's seat.

"Who brought the Ouija board?" I said.

My heart was in my throat. An eternity passed before they looked up, acknowledged my existence and started laughing.

"Donnelly, you cocksucker!" said Murtaugh.

"Hey!" said Brooks, shooting Murtaugh the stinkeye.

"Sorry. I meant: Donnelly, you sack of shit! You flew all the way from Australia?"

"Yep, twenty-two hours. Finally got the chance to watch the last season of *Lost*."

"My condolences."

I felt my legs disintegrate beneath me. "Jesus. Am I happy to see you guys."

"Yeah?" said Jules. "Is that why you're so good at keeping in touch?"

"I'm a dick," I said. "You knew that, right?"

"Hell, yeah," said the Rev. "How you like that beer?"

"It's pretty fucking good."

"Glad to hear it. I made it."

"Of course you did." I caught Jackie's eye and gestured to the empty seat next to her. "Where's your date?"

"Back with his wife from what I hear."

"Oh. Sorry to hear that."

"Don't be. Have a seat, Tommy."

I sat down next to Jackie St. John. The DJ played "Don't You Forget About Me."

"This guy really wants to make us feel ancient, huh?"

"It's Johnny Eighties," said Jackie. "That's his job."

"Great." I glanced around the ballroom. "No Rodney?"

"Our invitation apparently couldn't pierce his tinfoil helmet."

"That's too bad." I locked eyes with Jules. "I didn't expect to see you here. You were a year behind us, no?"

"I only had a semester's worth of credits to finish after junior year, so they let me pick my graduating class. I chose you guys!"

"Excellent choice. Man, this is freaky. I was just thinking how I haven't set foot in this room since the ball went through Buckner's legs."

"Really?" said Jackie. "*That's* what you remember about that night?"

"Oh my God. You must hate my guts."

"I did. I'm not gonna lie. I was such a wreck after that. I felt like they should have given me all A's for the semester, you know, like they do when your roommate commits suicide."

"I think that was an urban legend."

"Whatever. The point is, my grades went in the crapper that semester. But I got over it. And you know, every baseball fan of a certain age has a story about where they were that night. But I have the best one. The most exciting, at least."

"I guess that's true. I still can't ever apologize to you enough."

"We all came up with the plan together," said Murtaugh. "We all share some blame for what happened."

"Not me," said Jules. "I didn't even know anything about it until the next day. I hate sports."

"Anyway," said Jackie. "We've been over this. It's ancient history."

"Yeah, let's get to current events," I said, punching Murtaugh in the shoulder. "So, chief, you gonna introduce me to your wife anytime soon?"

He gestured to the woman sitting next to him. "Who, her? I've never met this woman in my life."

She rolled her eyes and extended her hand, which I shook. "I'm Genevieve. Nice to finally meet you. David has all of your books but has never read any of them."

"I went to Emerson," he said. "I'm functionally illiterate. I did see that miniseries of *Deadsville* on the Murder Channel."

"Hey, I just cashed the check."

"One of my clients was in that," said Brooks. "She was Dismembered Girl in Van #3."

"Oh yeah," I said. "She was great. Can I have her number?"

"Not a chance."

"So Brooks, you brought a friend?"

"This is my husband Greg."

"Your—husband? You mean you're *gay*?"

"Ha ha ha."

"Sorry, Greg," I said. "He always took great pains to assure us he liked girls."

"I caught him with his dick in his hand one night," said Murtaugh. "I didn't care he was jerking off, I just wondered why he was watching *Monday Night Football*."

Greg laughed. "Hey, I took a girl to the junior prom. Ditched her for the backup quarterback and blew him behind the gym while they were dancing to Night Ranger inside."

"Motorin'! You've got a keeper here, Brooks."

We laughed. We drank. We danced. We watched a video montage of vintage camcorder clips from our college days, scored to "Young Americans." Johnny Eighties cranked up the karaoke machine and after six or seven of the Rev's Charlesgate IPAs, I took the mic for a stirring rendition of Men at Work's "Down Under." No time had passed. No grudges were held. No one wanted it to ever end.

But end it did. The clock struck midnight and Johnny Eighties packed up his gear and I hugged Murtaugh and Jules and Brooks and the Rev and we exchanged phone numbers and assured each other we'd stay in touch and get together again soon. And then it was just me and Jackie, sitting alone in the ballroom where I'd managed to put her life in danger all those years ago.

"I need to show you something," she said. "A video I found."

"Two girls, one cup? I've seen it."

She swatted my arm, got up and walked over to the podium where a laptop was rigged to an overhead projector. "That Charlesgate video montage we watched earlier? I left something out. It freaked me the fuck out. Maybe you can explain it."

She cued up a clip and an image filled the projection screen:

a tracking shot of the Charlesgate basement as it had been in its dormitory days. Two male voices whispered on the soundtrack. A hand turned the knob of the stable door, which opened. A flashlight illuminated the familiar-looking junk piled inside. The camera spun to find a hooded figure standing in the stables. The image went to black, by which point I realized what I'd been watching.

"What are you laughing at?" Jackie asked. "This is some *Blair Witch* shit!"

"Yes and no."

"You've seen this before?"

I nodded. "My first published piece in the *Beacon*. End of freshman year, before I was on staff, I reviewed the Emerson short film festival. This was my pick to click. Remember Paul Seitz, he was two years ahead of us? This was his short, or part of it, anyway. It was all shot on VHS, and the conceit was that the tape had been found in an empty Charlesgate dorm after classes ended for the summer. So you're right to mention *Blair Witch*. Paul Seitz beat 'em to it—this is like the first found-footage horror movie."

"Well, it fooled me."

"I'd forgotten all about it. I didn't realize they'd filmed in the stables. This was months before Shane and I went down there."

"Huh." Jackie sat back down at the table. "Just another Charlesgate hoax." She picked up a bottle of Cabernet and tried to refill her glass, but the bottle was empty.

"Well," I said. "I better get going. I'm driving up to Maine in the morning to see my parents."

"It's been a long time, huh?"

"Yeah, they visited me in Sydney…jeez, eight years ago? I mean, we Skype and all that, but it's been way too long."

"Sure you don't want to come up for a nightcap?"

"Up where?"

"Upstairs. I live here."

"You've gotta be shitting me."

"I shit you not. I live on the sixth floor."

"Seriously? Well…of course. How could I say no?"

And as if in one of my recurring dreams, I was riding the elevator to the sixth floor and walking down the hall and into Jackie's condo. I went to the nearest window and looked down at what used to be the Pit and realized I was standing right where the head of my bed used to be. Same space, another time.

She led me out to her rooftop deck and handed me a glass of wine.

"I was out here once before," I said. "The Rev and I decided to have a beer on the roof. We made it almost thirty seconds before an RA on the fourth floor yelled across the Pit at us to get the fuck back inside."

We sat and clinked glasses.

"I have to say, I really didn't think you'd show."

"That makes two of us. I didn't think I'd ever come back here. For one thing, as I may have mentioned, it's a long fucking flight from Australia."

"Come on. First class. Good drugs. No problem for you."

"Yeah. Well, to tell you the truth, I was on the fence. But about a week ago I saw something online…well, I'm egotistical enough to have a Google Alert for my name. And it popped when this couple was arrested for murder. Three murders, one in this building. And one of the victims was Nicholas Woodward. You know, I tried to talk to him back in '86 when I was researching that piece for the *Beacon*. He'd moved back to England, though, and I couldn't afford an international call. And putting two and two together. I figured this had to be about the Gardner heist and my article and…that's why I had to come back."

"I don't follow you."

"I'm responsible. In some way I am. All these years later, those psychos wind up reading my article, they think those paintings might still be here somewhere. They kill Woodward and the girl here and that other guy from the alumni office…"

"You're not responsible. No more than I am," Jackie said.

"What are you talking about?"

And she told me the whole story about Coleman and White and Wendy Tucker and…well, you already read it here.

"That's crazy," I said when she'd finished.

"What's crazy is the fact that those paintings were probably never here in the first place."

"They *were* here," I said. "That's why I came back."

"What?"

"After all that happened, Game 6, Shane holding that gun to your head—"

"Forget it. I told you."

"No, this is what I'm trying to tell you. I knew they were gonna kick me out of here. That was a no-brainer. So I'm sitting outside the RD's office waiting for the axe to fall. And I'm looking at this framed poster of Uncle Sam on the wall. You remember that?"

"Oh yeah. It was kind of creepy."

"It was. And it always seemed out of place to me. Like it was something left over from an earlier era. Like someone found it in the basement, thought it was cool and hung it on the wall."

"Sure."

"So it occurs to me that just because Shane and I had gone through everything in the stables didn't mean we'd gone through everything that had *ever* been in the stables. Right? So anyway, Torres calls me into his office and reads me the riot act. He tells me I've got forty-eight hours to find a new place to live. Late that night, two or three in the morning, I sneak back down. Take the poster down off the wall. It's got an old-fashioned frame with a wooden backing held on by a couple of screws. I unscrew the backing and take it off. And there behind the poster is this sheet of canvas. I peel it back as carefully as I can. It's been there a long time, and crumbs of paint are sticking to the back of the Uncle Sam poster, but there's no mistaking what it is. *The Concert* by Vermeer."

"Holy fucking shit."

"Yeah. So I roll it up, tuck it under my arm, put the poster frame back together and hang Uncle Sam back on the wall. I take the painting upstairs and stick it in a duffel bag. I take it with me when I move off-campus."

"Where did you end up going?"

"This guy Sprague, an 'occult expert' I'd interviewed about the Charlesgate. He lived in the Bay Village. I'd called him when I was desperately trying to get Shane off my back, and he returned the call while I was packing. I happened to mention I was looking for a place to live, he had a spare room he wasn't using, so I ended up finishing out that semester and the next living there. Aside from the occasional noisy séance, it was fine."

"So what did you do with the painting?"

"I wasn't sure what to do. I definitely wanted to leverage it into something positive, career-wise. I mean here I'd done it: I'd cracked the case the FBI and the BPD never could. I'd proved that Shane's story was true. I thought, this is my ace in the hole. As long as I'm the only one who knows about it, I'm the only one who can tell the story."

"But why not just turn it in for the reward? Five million bucks, you could write your own ticket for whatever kind of career you wanted."

"Believe me, I thought about it. A lot. For one thing, I'd only found one of the paintings. A dozen others were still missing. So I wasn't even sure if the reward would apply. Also, the whole story of me and Shane and the…incident in the ballroom, all that had all just been in the news. The cops were already not too happy with me and if I suddenly turn up with this stolen painting…who knows, maybe they file charges against me."

"So what did you do?"

"I went to the Gardner museum. I went to the gift shop and bought a poster of *The Concert*. A full-size reproduction. And a frame. I slipped the real thing into the frame, right behind the poster, and I hung it on the wall."

"Cheeky."

"Cocky. Disrespectful. Tempting fate. But what the fuck, still kind of funny, right? I didn't think it would be there long. Just until I figured out how to use it to my advantage. But I never figured it out. During my senior year I got an internship with the *Post-Gazette*, this little weekly newspaper in the North End. At first I was just helping set the type, running errands, but then they started giving me little writing assignments. Covering community meetings, stuff like that. I met some interesting characters, let's put it that way, and some of them liked to talk. One night I'm covering one of those meetings, and when I come out, my car is gone. I'm all bent out of shape, I mention it to one of my new friends, he says he's going to make a call. Twenty minutes later a tow truck pulls up and sets my car down. A guy gets out and hands me an envelope with a thousand dollars in cash in it. 'Sorry, kid. My mistake.' A couple drinks later, my new friend is telling me all about this scam a couple local guys—non-connected guys—are running out of the Boston parking enforcement division. They tow your car. You call about it, they have no record in the system. You report it stolen. A few months later you get a letter in the mail telling you your car has been crushed into a cube because you never claimed it from the tow yard. And they're charging you for the crushing fee. You call and read them the riot act—'you told me you had no record of my car, yada, yada'—they deny it, they don't care. They never crushed it. They've got their own chop shop, they ran your car through it months ago and it's gone without a trace, sold for parts."

"Nice."

"So armed with this information, I talked to a couple of other new friends who confirmed the story. No one goes on the record, but I've got three sources naming names, so I'm ready to run with it. The *Post–Gazette* wants nothing to do with it. The *Herald*, though, they're all over it. I broke the story and got the byline, the Feds investigated, and a bunch of crooks went to jail. Trust me, no one has ever been so happy to have their car towed."

"Unbelievable."

"Right? Anyway, you don't need me to rehash my whole career for you. Suffice it to say that I was never in a position where I absolutely had to make a decision about *The Concert*. A couple years later I'm working the police beat in Hermosa Beach, California. I befriend this one cop who decides he wants me to tell his story about infiltrating this criminal surfer gang. That became *Zuma Nine*, my first book. Then I did *Army of Angels* and that hit the best-seller list. Somewhere in there I was married for about five minutes to a woman who deserved better. In fact, that's the only thing we ever agreed on. A couple books later I'm in Australia, researching the Outback Ripper for *Deadsville*. And I just…never came back."

"Until now."

"Yeah. Until I saw that report about Woodward being murdered. Here we are in 2014 and people are still killing each other over these paintings stolen almost seventy years ago. I feel responsible. Like if I'd turned *The Concert* in back then, none of this would have ever happened."

"I disagree. In fact, I'd say it's exactly the opposite."

"How do you figure?"

"Say you returned the painting, the story hits the news. Now everyone knows there are at least a dozen Gardner paintings still out there. Every crazy in town would have descended on this building, believing they were in here somewhere. Imagine this place with a hundred Shanes running around. Someone would have definitely gotten hurt. We all would have had to move out."

"Wow. You've got this whole alternate universe mapped out."

"I'm just telling you. If one of those paintings turns up after so many years, it's going to set off a frenzy."

"Well, maybe. But it doesn't matter. The painting isn't mine. It belongs back in the Gardner. In fact, the gears are already turning. I've got a lawyer negotiating with the Gardner and the FBI as we speak."

"Negotiating what? Your share of the reward?"

I laughed. "No. I don't need the reward, I don't want it, and I don't think I'm entitled to it. I just want to make sure there are no legal repercussions. They get *The Concert* back free and clear as long as I have complete immunity from any charge they can dream up. I mean, I didn't steal the thing, but I was in possession of stolen property for more than twenty-five years. It's just a precaution against the cops or the feds ever finding out I'm the one returning the painting. Right now only two people know: you and my lawyer."

"Well, I appreciate your trust. But are you seriously not going to take credit for this? Write a book about it?"

"Oh, I'll write a book. To be published posthumously. I don't want to be the center of a story like this while I'm alive. I get enough attention as it is."

"Poor baby."

"Hey, I'm grateful. I've lived a charmed life in a lot of ways. The marriage didn't work out so well, but these things happen."

"Indeed they do."

"So this cop you were seeing. Any chance of patching that up?"

"Absolutely no chance."

"Sorry to hear it."

"Don't be. It's better this way. He's got a kid and he should be in her life. That was never my goal."

"Cheers to that. Keeping our carbon footprint to the bare minimum."

"Exactly. Hey, Tommy, I'm gonna ask you a question and I want you to be honest."

"At this point, what choice do I have? Shoot."

"You had the hots for me in college, didn't you?"

"You're goddam right I did."

She smiled. "I could tell."

"I never had a shot, did I?"

"Not a snowball's chance in hell."

We both laughed. "I didn't think so."

"Things change, though."

"Yeah? I wonder about that. Sometimes I'm not sure anything has changed. Downstairs with you guys earlier, it was like no time had passed at all."

"I know what you mean. But we're both different people now, aren't we?"

"I guess we are." I checked my phone. "Christ, it's 2:30 in the morning. I better go. It's a five-hour drive to the ancestral manse tomorrow."

"The T stopped running hours ago."

"I better call a cab."

"I've got plenty of room. You're welcome to stay."

"Really?"

"I should warn you, I strangle people in my sleep."

"I figured as much."

"So how about one more glass of wine?"

"How about?"

She poured off the rest of the bottle. I heard a far-off siren. Across the Pit on the fourth floor, a light went out.

"So when do you fly back to Oz?"

"That's an open question. But I've been thinking."

"Yessss?"

"The murder condo down the hall. Has that been sold?"

"Not as far as I know. What with it being the murder condo and all. Why?"

"I was thinking. If I'm going to write this book, the posthumous one, what better place to do it than right here?"

"Are you serious?"

"Absolutely. I'll call the realtor tomorrow. That is, if you don't mind having an old friend for a neighbor."

"I'd love it. Now we just have to convince Murtaugh, Brooks, the Rev…"

"And Purple Debbie!"

She laughed. "And Purple Debbie to move in. Then we can all live in the past."

"Yeah. But honestly, I don't want to live in the past anymore. I feel like I've been doing that all along. Hanging onto something I should have let go a long time ago."

"In that case, I'm not sure this is the place for you. A lot of ghosts in Charlesgate. I don't know if you've heard."

"Oh, I've heard. But I never did believe in ghosts."

"Well then you better not sleep on the couch. My poltergeist friend tends to rattle around in the wee hours."

"That's too bad. I'm kind of a light sleeper."

She stood and gestured inside. "Well, I'm going to bed. It's the first door on the left as you go inside. I believe you boys used to call it the Love Room."

"No ghosts in the Love Room?"

"No ghosts at all. Whenever you're ready."

She left me alone on the roof deck. I thought back to a long ago night standing in the park across the street, Jackie holding my arm above her head, announcing to anyone who would listen that I was the guy who saved Charlesgate. I never was that. But maybe it wasn't too late. Maybe all those dreams over the years weren't a haunting from the past but a premonition of the future. Charlesgate and I were reunited at last, and maybe our best days were still ahead of us.

I finished my wine and tossed the empty glass into the Pit. I heard it shatter in the dark distance. A light went on across the way.

AFTERWORD

On March 18, 1990, thirteen works of art, including Vermeer's *The Concert*, were stolen from the Isabella Stewart Gardner Museum in Boston by two men dressed as police officers and wearing fake mustaches. This really happened, although obviously it did not happen on June 16, 1946 as it did in these pages. My version of the Gardner heist is a highly fictionalized variation on the real event. I could have made up a fake museum and some phony priceless artwork, but what would be the point? Call it creative license, but for the record let me make it clear that Jake and Shane Devlin, Joey Cahill, and Dave T are all completely fictional characters who definitely did *not* rob the Gardner. (As of this writing, the case remains unsolved, but on May 22, 2014, the FBI announced that credible sources had confirmed sightings of the stolen artwork.)

The Charlesgate is a real building in Boston's Back Bay, and its history roughly conforms to the outlines described in these pages. It opened in 1891 as a luxury hotel in the Hub of the Universe. The Depression hit it hard and it was allegedly taken over by the Mob. From 1947 to 1973 it was a women's dormitory for Boston University. For the rest of the 1970s it was a tenement populated by drug addicts and devil worshippers. Emerson College purchased it in 1981. I lived there from 1985 to 1988. Not a week goes by that I don't dream about it. Many of my friends claimed they'd seen ghosts within its walls. I never did. In fact, I never did any of the things depicted in this novel. I certainly never purchased a fake Maine driver's license from a classmate for the purpose of illegally purchasing alcoholic beverages. Who would believe such a thing?

The Jimmy Fund, the charity for which Rodney and his frat brothers held a casino night on October 25, 1986, is a real organization supporting Boston's Dana-Farber Cancer Institute, raising funds for adult and pediatric cancer care. Check them out at http://www.jimmyfund.org.

I'd like to thank Philip Freeman, Andrew Osborne, and Stephen Lewis for reading an early draft of this novel and offering invaluable feedback. Special thanks to my editor Charles Ardai, whose boundless enthusiasm for this project is matched only by his sharp critical eye for detail. Last but not least, I'd like to thank the Boston Red Sox for breaking the curse in 2004 and winning it all again in 2007 and 2013.

Today the Charlesgate is, in fact, a high-end, very expensive residential condominium. I can't afford to live there. Please tell all your friends to buy this book.